Stephen King
AND AMERICAN POLITICS

HORROR STUDIES

Series Editor
Xavier Aldana Reyes, Manchester Metropolitan University

Editorial Board
Stacey Abbott, Roehampton University
Linnie Blake, Manchester Metropolitan University
Harry M. Benshoff, University of North Texas
Fred Botting, Kingston University
Steven Bruhm, Western University
Steffen Hantke, Sogang University
Joan Hawkins, Indiana University
Agnieszka Soltysik Monnet, University of Lausanne
Bernice M. Murphy, Trinity College Dublin
Johnny Walker, Northumbria University

Preface

Horror Studies is the first book series exclusively dedicated to the study of the genre in its various manifestations – from fiction to cinema and television, magazines to comics, and extending to other forms of narrative texts such as video games and music. Horror Studies aims to raise the profile of Horror and to further its academic institutionalisation by providing a publishing home for cutting-edge research. As an exciting new venture within the established Cultural Studies and Literary Criticism programme, Horror Studies will expand the field in innovative and student-friendly ways.

Stephen King
AND AMERICAN POLITICS

MICHAEL J. BLOUIN

UNIVERSITY OF WALES PRESS
2021

© Michael J. Blouin, 2021

All rights reserved. No part of this book may be reproduced in any material form (including photocopying or storing it in any medium by electronic means and whether or not transiently or incidentally to some other use of this publication) without the written permission of the copyright owner except in accordance with the provisions of the Copyright, Designs and Patents Act. Applications for the copyright owner's written permission to reproduce any part of this publication should be addressed to the University of Wales Press, University Registry, King Edward VII Avenue, Cardiff, CF10 3NS.

www.uwp.co.uk

British Library Cataloguing-in-Publication Data

A catalogue record for this book is available from the British Library.

ISBN   978-1-78683-646-5
eISBN 978-1-78683-647-2

The right of Michael J. Blouin to be identified as author of this work has been asserted in accordance with sections 77 and 79 of the Copyright, Designs and Patents Act 1988.

Typeset by Chris Bell, cbdesign

Printed by CPI Antony Rowe, Melksham

Dedicated to Willow

Contents

	Acknowledgements	ix
1.	**Prelude:** The (Im)possible Politics of Stephen King's Fiction	1
2.	**The Bachman Books and America's Death Drive**	33
3.	**King's Cars and the Grinding Gears of Post-Fordism**	53
4.	*Firestarter*; or, the Smelting of a Neo-liberal Subject	71
5.	*IT*, Individualism, and the Idea of Community	89
6.	**Interlude:** *The Langoliers* and the Political Event	109
7.	Human Capital in *Rose Madder*	121
8.	*Under the Dome* and the Deteriorating Demos	139
9.	*The Outsider* and the Shifting Shapes of Trumpism	161
10.	**Postlude:** Revolutions of *The Stand*	179
	Notes	189
	Bibliography	207
	Index	225

Acknowledgements

WHEN I DECIDED to return to Stephen King's fiction, it felt like coming home. I spent a good deal of my time in college locating countless treasures in the dark and dismal corners of his works – an endeavour that eventually nudged me into a career in academia. Most fortunately, I met my future partner Kate in a course dedicated to this subject. Our shared appreciation of King's writing helped to spark our love. I decided to chart my own path in the years that followed by gaining greater insight into critical theory as well as popular culture (specifically, in conversation with neo-liberalism). But the road has led me back to King. One day, I found myself quite unexpectedly sitting down to think through his fiction with fresh eyes. What ensued was the profoundly joyful experience of writing this book.

Kate gave me the time and space to write this book, and she inspired me on a daily basis to be a better person. Her generous spirit reminds me that things can, in fact, always be otherwise. My daughters Emerson and Willow distracted me, in the best possible way, and filled my heart with light when the nature of the research weighed me down. My mother Melissa provided me with confidence when doubts crept to the surface. I am extremely fortunate to have these people in my life.

I also owe a great deal to my most formative professors, Tony Magistrale and Gary Hoppenstand, both highly respected experts on King's fiction. Once upon a time, they taught me to take King seriously and to reflect upon unlooked-for aspects of his corpus. As a collaborator on a recent project, Tony continued to model how to be an innovative reader of King, and for his years of mentorship, I remain eternally grateful.

A huge thanks to Collin Hawley, my graduate research assistant, who spent hours tracking down obscure sources. He did a phenomenal job. Colleagues and friends that supported me unconditionally include Lee Blackburn, Heather Hoover, Tim Dillon, Amy Edmonds and Joseph Baker. I am also grateful to the Buckham Fund for providing me with the means to come and speak at the University of Vermont on the topic of all things Stephen King.

Finally, I must extend my gratitude to the thoughtful readers that have offered me vital criticism as well as healthy doses of encouragement: the tireless reviewers at the University of Wales Press, Todd McGowan, Scott Michaelsen, John Sears, Simon Brown, Patrick McAleer and Steven Bruhm. Without their keen insights, this book would not exist. Of course, the errors and missteps that remain are solely my own.

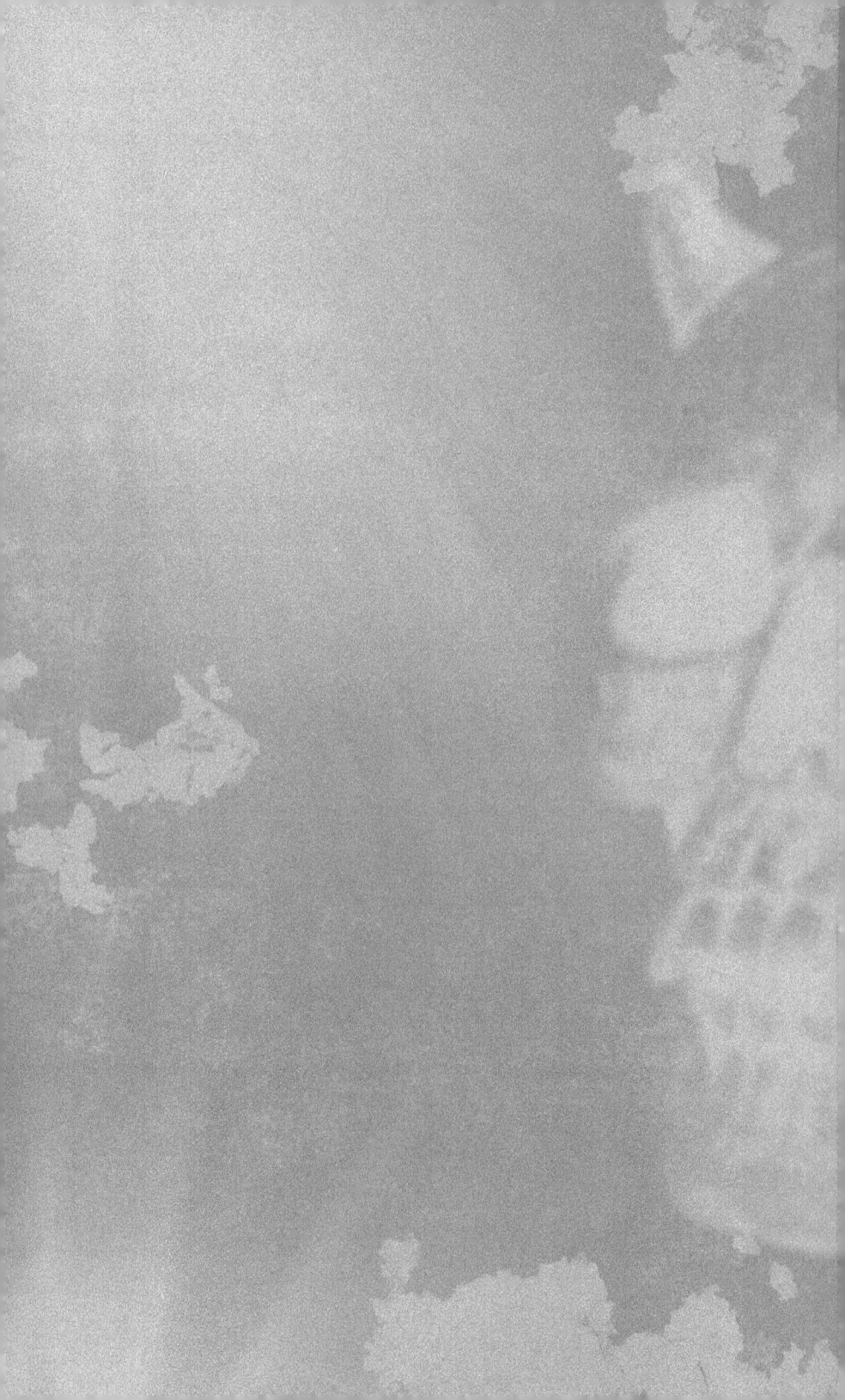

1

Prelude

The (Im)possible Politics of Stephen King's Fiction

FROM *CARRIE* (1974) to *The Institute* (2019), Stephen King's fiction reflects dramatic political upheavals of the past fifty years, including disillusionment in foreign wars, disenchantment with the welfare state and a drift towards theocracy. For nearly every major concern of the era, readers will find a corresponding work.[1] To address this correspondence, the book adopts several aims. First, it takes stock of the dominant political themes in King's universe to understand better the relationship between his writings and the contexts in which they emerge. Secondly, it expounds upon moments of cohesion as well as conjuncture (at times, his texts involve a consistent set of commitments; at other times, his texts suggest tension or uncertainty). Finally, it politicises King scholarship because many of his critics too readily accept the claim, trumpeted by King himself, that his fiction remains 'anti-political'.[2] In contrast to the analyses of cultural politics in King's corpus undertaken by a wide range of critics, I concentrate in the pages that follow upon how his texts engage with politics proper, which is to say, the never-ending (re)formation of groups with shared interests. This book examines how King's narratives reflect as well as challenge the role of politics as a passionate struggle that has been steadily displaced over the last fifty years by America's all-consuming focus upon economics. If we minimise this aspect of King's fiction, we undervalue an incredibly rich vein of interpretive possibility.

Rather than attend to the cardinal function of politics as a persistent wrangling, scholars of King's work sometimes put forward a thin conceptualisation by exposing evidence of social decay, or commenting upon a broad middle-class habitus in a manner that treats politics as a secondary – not constitutional – attribute of being human. This approach perhaps seems reasonable enough when, for instance, we consider the intentionally massive scale of King's 1977 novel, *The Shining*: '[The Overlook] forms an index of the whole post-World War II American character' (King, *Shining* 281). But we might worry, alongside Douglas Cowan, that scholarship on this subject tends to be satisfied with relatively 'parochial understandings' of complex terms. The general use of the term 'politics' in certain analyses serves as 'a superficial abstraction, [an] empty placeholder' that means too much and too little. Consequently, it becomes commonplace to map 'easily recognizable' ideas of the 'sociopolitical' onto King's narratives in a manner that downplays the complicated part that politics actually plays (Cowan 13–15). Although King and many of his critics frequently present the politics of his fiction as external to everyday life (an ill-fitting adornment, or a bad habit foisted upon a bedrock called society), I wish to survey how politics comprises King's multiverse at its most primary level.

Of course, to say that critics have not given the political aspects of King's fiction their due is not to argue that critics have produced no valuable commentary on the subject. Tony Magistrale, for example, opens his landmark study of King's fiction with the observation that his stories are 'politically focused' (*Landscape* 25). Craig Ian Mann posits, 'King has always been a political writer' (199). And Douglas W. Texter adds, 'King's work in general is much more political than critics . . . want to admit' (45). Built upon a foundation laid by these insightful readers, the following book charts how political concepts weave their way into the pages of King's fiction.

We might sympathise with critics that produce more anaemic accounts of the politics in King's fiction because of the prominent method for reading that is bundled together with his prose. Specifically, King endorses a method of reading that adamantly refuses to 'get political'. Although his non-fiction treatise *Danse Macabre* (1981) admits the influence of the Cold War and the Kennedy assassination on his creative process, it relegates these connections to his unconscious, as he doubts that horror writers ever intend to 'wear a political hat'. *Danse Macabre* opens with an outright denial that his texts harbour any 'disguised' political commentary (*Danse* 6, 131).³ His fiction similarly disinvites readers from politicised interpretation. The novella *Apt Pupil* (1983) treats politics as window dressing for barbaric human behaviour, insisting that 'politics is just so much tired bullspit to cover up the gooshy stuff' (130).⁴ Likewise, a character from *11/22/63* (2011) argues that nothing is ever truly about politics anyway: 'At the bottom it's always a woman' (540). And Bill from *IT* (1986) succeeds as a popular novelist as a result of his withholding of political engagement: 'If fiction and politics ever really do become interchangeable', he notes, 'I'm going to kill myself' (122).

By disinviting the political, King's fiction reflects a cultural shift into neo-liberal rationality: 'the insistence that there are only rational market actors in every sphere of human existence' (Brown, *Undoing* 99). Sociologists Pierre Dardot and Christian Laval define the shift as

> The dilution of public law in favor of private law; configuration of public activity to the criteria of profitability and productivity; symbolic devaluation of law as the specific act of the legislature; strengthening of the executive; prioritization of procedure; a tendency for police powers to break free of any judicial control; promotion of the 'citizen-consumer' responsible for arbitrating between competing 'political offers.' (303)

Over the last fifty years, this unique rationality spread as the United States curtailed *homo politicus* and idealised *homo economicus*.⁵ In theory, to be political means to engage in moral deliberation, to sustain a capacity to generate associations with fellow subjects and to invest in public goods. To champion *homo politicus* is to recognise what German philosopher Immanuel Kant posits nearly two centuries earlier – that dignity is not synonymous with price, and so we must confess 'an irreducibility of the political and moral to the economic' (303). Indeed, the designation of the political signifies a field of open conflict, an interminable sense that when it comes to communal governance things could always be otherwise. As a result, we cannot reduce the political to a citizen-consumer's relationship with what is normative in their society (a tendency that has been taken up elsewhere in the study of King's politics). After all, King's stories routinely separate ethical behaviour from the political imagination, as when the school-age protagonist of *Doctor Sleep* (2013) skips an assigned chapter in her textbook on 'How Our Government Works' that she finds to be 'majorly boresome' – and a mere twenty pages in length – to read the apparently more important chapter, 'Your Responsibilities as A Citizen' (205). Counter to King's thoroughly private portrait of an ethical life, real-life politics requires public demonstration, institution-building, as well as the messy work of passing legislation. Whereas *homo economicus* understands her relationship with social norms as a personal matter to be navigated with economic tools, *homo politicus* can choose to eschew financial motivation and stir up alternative associations. I will develop this definition of the political further in the next section.[6]

Importantly, though, the following chapters do not 'isolate politics from everything else' (Wiley 12). To politicise King's fiction, we need not ignore or conflate other facets of American life, as tomorrow's singular focus upon *homo politicus* would be no more palatable than today's exclusive focus upon *homo economicus*. Moreover, Adam Kotsko denies that a clear border between the two ever exists, insisting that their relationship is continually being reconfigured. I do not denounce King's fiction (or many of its critics) for being anti-political in order to substitute my own hierarchy of interests – to pick a side, for example, in the debate between neoliberalism and a more radical democracy. In truth, the repression of the political as well as its return are at times equally terrifying, and of even greater consequence, they are always-already intertwined. We must examine the tumultuous intersection of the political and economic features of King's works by addressing a tendency among his interpreters to overstate the 'sociopolitical' character of his corpus (when economic factors are more forcibly in play), at the same time that we call attention to a tendency among these interpreters to under-appreciate the political aspects of King's stories (in places where politics remains exceedingly influential).

The remainder of the text inspects how, on the one hand, King's brand of anti-politics affirms the status quo of a growing demo-phobia in the post-1960s United States alongside a hyper-inflated emphasis upon economic growth. On the other hand, there is a spectre haunting Stephen King's America, and that spectre is the concept of the political. King's stories repress this concept, but it eternally returns. Consequently, as we track the ways in which the political has been repressed in his page-turners, we consider how this repression serves as a necessity in efforts to release America's stifled political energies. Precisely because of its ardent anti-politics, King's fiction preserves the political as a fantastic force as horrifying as it is hopeful.

The repression (and return) of American politics

The repression and return of American politics in King's fiction occur during an era in which citizens gradually lose faith in electoral processes that they are told to deem as too slow and inefficient (at least, the logic goes, when compared with corporate governance). Justifying the fears of Carl Schmitt, managerialism replaces democratic sparring as American citizens start to understand 'politics only as a shadow of economic reality' (*Crisis* 20). In turn, when the corporate approach of elites fails to produce satisfactory results for a majority of the populace – a failure perhaps most glaringly exposed by the financial crash of 2008 – voters look to peculiar, even outright gothic, sources for alternative answers.[7]

To establish a broader context, it may suffice to remark briefly upon how, following the departure of the US from the Bretton Woods agreement in 1971–72 and the subsequent shift into floating exchange rates, influential capitalists are less and less held in check by the demands of democratic constituencies. What emerges in the wake of this departure is a 'virtual senate' of investors and lenders that 'exercise "veto power" over government decisions by threat of capital flight' (Chomsky 219). Corporations are held less accountable because the forces behind globalisation grant them extraterritoriality and allow them, in the process, to mute the voice of 'the people'. As examples of this depoliticisation, we might consider the (in)famous Public Act 4 in Michigan, otherwise known as the 'local government and school district fiscal accountability act' (2011), in which economic managers can be appointed to make executive decisions for a community should that community's financial matters fall into a state of disrepair. Or Tennessee legislation (HB 1632) that constrains locally elected officials from mandating affordable housing in their municipality (2016). Or recent efforts to pass the BDS Act – an act that condones state-imposed penalties against citizens wishing to boycott or divest from enterprises affiliated with Israel (2018). Or bill SB96 in Utah, a 2019 bill designed to restrict Medicaid expansion after voters approved the expansion at the ballot box. These examples are only a handful of the recent manifestations of depoliticisation in the United States. The list goes on. As we will see shortly, King's fiction shares a number of goals with these initiatives: to critique the so-called nanny state; to laud leadership by managers such as police officers, entrepreneurs or rogue actors; and to spark fear of the masses by treating 'the people' as gullible, unreasonable and prone to zealotry. Whether he intends to do so or not, King helps to sustain America's widespread de-democratisation via his popular paperbacks.

To understand how King's texts reflect this phenomenon, we must flesh out our definition of the political. To be political means preserving the potential to forge new alliances, overturn the establishment and express dissatisfaction with the current state of affairs. The concept of the political evokes core antagonisms within any social order: a tremendously unstable and disruptive plurality that can, at any given moment, exceed organisational limits. Thanks to the interminable nature of the political, one cannot imagine a government that could satisfy every demand made by every taxpayer, and so groups must wrestle with one another to align (and realign) in perpetuity. Claude Lefort describes the political as 'principles that generate society or, more accurately, different forms of society', forms that 'appear and then disappear' (*Democracy* 217, 54). According to theorists like Ernesto Laclau and Chantal Mouffe, the 'stable articulatory structures' of government could never bring closure to the 'surplus of meaning of "the social"'; instead, the concept of the political denotes the (im)possibility of articulating a permanent social arrangement (Laclau and Mouffe 82). In a word, this signature of the (im)possible – with its internal brackets – conveys a dual movement in which we pursue a fully satisfied society and actively recall the futility behind such a premise.

To visualise how King's fiction reflects a restless political impulse in tension with the confines of institutional politics, let us turn for a moment to King's *The Tommyknockers* (1987), a novel that represents American politics along these lines. The town constable of Haven, Maine likes to think of her job as community service, not 'politics', because she believes that government toil inevitably devolves into a 'drive . . . to dominate'. Meanwhile, unaware of his own drive to dominate, the protagonist seeks to overthrow 'the establishment' due to its reckless obsession with nuclear weapons. His activism, however, proves to be barbaric. At one protest, the police arrest him for wielding a gun; later, during a heated argument on the subject of nuclear weapons, he murders a colleague. King's *Hearts of Atlantis* (1999) upholds this fear of activism when Carol accidentally kills an innocent bystander during a heated protest. In this way, *The Tommyknockers* exposes the radioactive side of political engagement in a manner that defuses the appeal of antagonism for his readers. The story suggests that, in the game of politics, participants find 'devils on every side' (213, 396, 314). Although the 'good guys' of *The Tommyknockers* think of themselves as benevolent voices of reason, their political idealism marks them as intrinsically power-hungry.

In *The Tommyknockers*, to be political means to desire utopia while being driven, unaware, by the vanity behind such a proposition. Crucially, the narrative condemns political strife as well as the illusion of its end. Theodor Adorno and Ernst Bloch discuss how the concept of the political depends upon the (im)possibility of its final articulation. Adorno anticipates the main sentiment of *The Tommyknockers* when he recognises that utopia is far too monolithic to be truly attainable: 'There is nothing like a single, fixable utopian content.' The potency of the political will forever endure because members of heterogeneous populations can imagine a vast array of different utopias. At the same time, Bloch responds, these members persist in presupposing 'the conception of, and longing for, a possible perfection' (Bloch 7, 16). Indeed, the protagonist of *The Tommyknockers* reveals the self-sabotage behind his desire for a perfect society when, on an unconscious level, he admits that he does not genuinely want to complete the struggle: 'If your politics never get the chance to be tried out', his unconscious whispers, 'You never have to worry about finding out that the new boss is the same as the old boss.' Said another way, while many of the novel's characters persist in reaching for flawless community – a true Haven to be distinguished from the deeply flawed town of the same name – the novel proclaims an ultimate 'ANSWER TO EVERYTHING' to be unattainable (except, it warrants pointing out, in dreams). Correspondingly, King's novel closes with two children entering into a peaceful slumber: 'Ninety-three million miles from the sun and a hundred parsecs from the axis pole of the galaxy, [the children] slept in each other's arms.' Despite its anti-political tenor, *The Tommyknockers* preserves the political as a powerful (im)possibility. Even when Americans appear to desire static institutions, they are still driven to hunt for better arrangements. King's text stresses this point by referencing Mohammedan rug-makers that 'always include a deliberate error in their work' to maintain their status as 'fallen creatures' (159–61, 558, 213). According to *The Tommyknockers*, then, a functional society unsuspectingly retains 'deliberate errors' to carry on the all-important ritual of political contest.

Along the same lines, Laclau and Mouffe describe organisational politics as 'an "order" that exists only as a partial limiting of disorder'. Positions of dominance can only ever be placeholders, or 'sutures', because society is a never-ending sequence of formations, 'none of which could aspire to be *the* truth of society'. For a community to endure, its mythic totality – its Edenic 'original absence' – must be forever deferred (Laclau and Mouffe 177, xxiii, 37; author's emphasis).

[The construction of social objectivity and political identity as a closed, self-contained structure] is ultimately impossible but, nevertheless, necessary (we are necessarily engaged all the time in identity construction exactly because it is impossible to construct a full identity) . . . It is in the moment of this prevention which is simultaneously generating – or causing – new attempts to construct this impossible object – society – that the moment of the political is surfacing and resurfacing again and again. (Stavrakakis 4)

The Tommyknockers illustrates how the spectre of the political in King's fiction preserves an ongoing, vital friction between a fantasy of permanent control and the unconscious admission that control remains indispensably up for grabs.

According to a number of contemporary political philosophers, this notion of a perpetually restless political is best upheld under democratic regimes: 'Democracy is the regime that, in welcoming conflict, social and political debate, makes room for the possible, for the new' (Lefort, *Writing* 262). Democracy widens the field of political contest to all takers, regardless of their prescribed status, and so 'welcomes and preserves indeterminacy' (*Democracy* 16–17). And yet, in the United States over the last fifty years, democratic channels have been aggressively closed in favour of economic competition between market actors. Prominent intellectuals as well as politicians 'establish limits to popular sovereignty in the name of liberty' (Mouffe, *Democratic* 4). In particular, proponents of 'patterns and procedures' react to the egalitarian 'outbursts' of the 1960s by tamping down democratic excess and assigning the perceived glut of the political back to its 'proper place' (Rancière, *Dissensus* 47, 53). The role of democracy dissipates.

Tormented by the so-called spirit of the 1960s, King's corpus outwardly prefers social hierarchy to the initiatives proposed by the likes of Laclau, Mouffe or Jacques Rancière.[8] Naysayers disqualify the hyper-political 1960s – a decade that saw the rise of groups like the Students for a Democratic Society (SDS) – by claiming that activists from the era 'didn't seem to know what they were for', or that they were 'mindless, nihilistic, and destructive' (Flacks 24). Following the revolutionary fervour of 1968, the tide turned decisively against the decade's political rancour as moderates and conservatives petitioned for naive aspirations to be cast into the dustbin of history. In their more reactionary moments, King's texts also project the long-lost 1960s outward in order to resist the 'anarchic foundation of the political'. For instance, whenever citizens in his fictional towns rally together, the result is a petrifying expression of 'populist backwardness' (Rancière, *Hatred* 62, 70). King's 'people' instigate retreats from democracy: into the arms of militants (*From a Buick 8*); into the embrace of experts (*Under the Dome*); or into the euphoria of pure negation (the Bachman books). By disavowing the political, and employing in its place the folksy, blue-collar 'common sense' of citizen-consumers, King's prose proudly declares itself to be elementary, unplanned and unpolished (and therefore, readers are led to assume, anti-political). Of course, simplicity is never really anti-political; it is a deliberate political strategy.[9] Fredric Jameson comments, 'The call for a "plain style," for clarity and simplicity . . . is an ideology in its own right' ('On Jargon' 118). Nonetheless, the majority of King's heroes are considered heroic because they rebuff the call to political action and subsequently remain disconnected from 'the people' that they rescue. King's fiction thus represses the political by abjuring antagonism in the name of cynical detachment or commonsensical competence. By drastically narrowing the ambition of the protagonist, these texts focus upon preserving the family unit instead of redeeming the demos.

King's fictional universe highlights technocratic adroitness while downplaying the role of shared governance. Although his narratives do evoke invisible communal connections (as in the 1996 novel *The Green Mile*), these connections are always limited to a handful of elite individuals that alone possess the capacity to promote community. Since political bodies like the city of Derry are inevitably corrupt, smaller platoons – to borrow Senator Daniel Patrick Moynihan's (in)famous phrase – are the best that these texts can devise: 'King believes that the most politically viable unit is one small enough to hear and respond to individual opinions' (Casebeer 48). In the novella *The Mist* (1980), residents in a small Maine town retreat from Lovecraftian terrors into the Federal market. The name of the market (Federal) underlines the novella's preoccupation with what does or does not hold together a body politic. Once the titular mist arrives, citizens devolve into a state of violent combat: 'out-of-towners' versus natives; 'your people' versus 'my people'. Con artists engorge themselves on the promise of politics as they rise up to seize control of the store, until the Federal becomes a 'loony bin' populated by residents that are so frightened they will 'turn to anyone' for guidance (98–9, 142, 127). At the story's close, the protagonist forms a small platoon to drive away from the Federal. Because the only hope for 'the people' is to follow the lead of this rogue manager, King's novella presents managerialism 'not as a particular set of interests and political interventions, but as a kind of nonpolitics – a way of being reasonable' (Duggan 10). That is, *The Mist* rejects the competing factions in the Federal by taking what it mistakenly presumes to be a non-political path: after the collapse of the Federal, the commonsensical manager abandons the demos to focus exclusively upon the preservation of his close-knit crew.

During the transformative period of the previous fifty years, popular discourse in the United States becomes similarly saturated with managerial jargon. American society is no longer imagined to be a web of interdependence, as the government turns away from egalitarian projects like the New Deal and the Great Society in favour of pro-business strategies to empower the powerful few by increasing the reach of their corporations into untapped areas like prisons or once-conserved public lands. More and more individuals, James Kwak argues, invoke Economics 101 'to explain all social phenomena', in effect reducing human activity 'to economic first principles that dictate simple solutions'. We subject 'the entire sphere of social interaction' to black-and-white algorithms (8, 11). This appeal to economics as a method for achieving absolute consensus, or a cure-all for social ills, greatly diminishes the role of public debate (after all, who can argue with mathematics?). It is worth noting that this sort of economism influences King's fiction in subtle ways. His works do not blatantly champion the free market. Initially, in fact, the Federal offers an unpleasant commercial rat maze, a 'Skinner box – modern marketing techniques turn all customers into white rats' (King, *Mist* 50). In this way, King's texts appear to be vaguely anti-capitalist, and so they cannot be offhandedly mistaken for the balm prescribed by strident neo-liberals. However, as his readers discover time and again, King's works do neo-liberal work by stripping democracy of its core antagonisms to espouse in their place a purportedly reasonable non-politics. Resigning readers to a world driven by the innovation of citizen-consumers rather than the 'power of the people', King's narratives repress political aspiration in the name of 'being sensible'. Schmitt critiques the illusion of such a post-political world: 'A domination of men based upon pure economics', he states, 'must appear a terrible deception if, by remaining non-political, it thereby evades political responsibility and visibility' (*Concept* 77–8). During the period under review, the United States privileges the juridical field to resolve conflicts, free-market ideologues seek an aggregative model in which the electoral arena closely resembles a marketplace, and figures like John Rawls and Jürgen Habermas conceptualise a consensus model to replace vibrant clashes with predictable algorithms. King's works reflect this nearly ubiquitous chase of a 'pain-free politics' (Mouffe, *Democratic* 112–20).

In spite of this characterisation, King's fiction remains hard to place on the partisan spectrum. On the one hand, the Republican Party ostensibly drives depoliticisation when, according to its dissenters, it tamps down democratic expectations in favour of strengthened security. Leaders on the right deride protestors by painting them as an unwieldy 'mob': for example, in the run-up to the 2020 presidential election, the GOP tested the slogan 'jobs, not mobs', while insisting that left-wing activists were 'paid to protest'.[10] In these instances, the right delegitimises 'the people' as ungrateful, untrustworthy and (ironically enough, given its neo-liberal ethos) predominantly propelled by financial incentives. But King's fiction may be more fruitfully placed in conversation with the Democratic Party because it mimics how the Clinton and Obama administrations celebrate a professional-managerial class populated by elite outsiders that are sent to save 'backwards' rural residents. As I argue in the chapters that follow, although King's characters defy academia by hurling insults at the intelligentsia (in particular, his fiction incessantly maligns English professors), the blue-collar veneer of his texts belies a broader distrust of the public. His heroic technocrats safeguard 'the people' with neither sanction by, nor accountability to, the demos, thus performing an 'ersatz politics' that diverts readers from a 'sincere discussion of policies'. In this fashion, King's works inhibit the meaningful address of America's most pressing political issues (Frank, *Listen* 228–9).

The failings of democratic man

Needful Things (1991) exemplifies King's anti-political message. When a strange salesman arrives to sell to its citizen-consumers whatever their hearts' desire, the town of Castle Rock quickly unravels. Caught in a hedonistic whirlwind, the townspeople slide into madness, while the level-headed sheriff races to preserve some semblance of order. Rancière argues that, for detractors of democracy, the basic (yet ever slippery) notion of 'the people' triggers a sense of the ungovernable, calling to mind a citizenry's 'irresistible growth of demands' (*Hatred* 7). Disparagers like James

Buchanan from the Virginia Public Choice School decry 'democratic man' as immature, prone to unreasonable consumerism and bound to follow blindly zealots of all stripes.[11] These disparagers declare that 'democratic energies . . . engorge the political' and, to combat an engorged democracy in which a 'mob' ceaselessly re-articulates what its society should provide to it, they espouse rigid law-and-order models (Brown, *Ruins* 62). King's narratives likewise feature unflattering portrayals of democratic man that serve to check a perceived excess of legislative demands. On this front, Castle Rock is one of many similar towns that dot the map of his fiction. The citizen-consumers of Chester's Mill in *Under the Dome* (the subject of chapter 8) vote against their best interests, acquiesce to religious extremists and lack the disposition to survive when confronted by a shortage of consumable goods. Elsewhere, the residents of *'Salem's Lot* (1975) – set in a town appropriately named after a pig – are described as 'aggressively' gluttonous, 'not bright', petty, abusive, as well as 'apelike'. The town residents are perverted, desensitised and quite pleased, by the end of their tale, to become the walking dead that they have always-already been (235, 34, 49). And in *Revival* (2014), the townspeople are 'rubes' with 'maxed-out credit cards' that 'don't deserve the truth . . . they have set aside what brains they have' (228, 270). Examples abound. We cannot overstate the extent to which King's fiction degrades 'the people'.

But because these texts tend to be cloaked in relatively superficial leftist garb, their de-democratisation can be difficult for readers to spot. *Needful Things* offers an appraisal of consumerism run amuck when it theatrically gestures at the Gulf War as well as America's obscene thirst for oil. In a manner typical of King's stories, the novel underscores how capitalism offers false satisfaction by depicting citizen-consumers that numb the pain of their existence with the purchase of useless goods. The text's main purveyor of this soul-sucking squandering, Leland Gaunt, embodies the free-market frenzy of the 1980s as he waxes poetical that free trade is what 'made this country great' and he creates needs in his consumers through a kind of hypnosis that he embellishes with slogans that read like a litany of buzzwords from the decade: 'Selfish people are happy people', or 'everything is for sale' (132, 503, 461). For critics of a perceived surfeit of democracy in the 1960s, Rancière writes, 'democracy (is) nothing but the reign of the narcissistic consumer'. *Needful Thing*s in turn discourages political involvement by lingering upon the citizen-consumer's 'voracious appetites'. King's democratic man remains too irrational to govern himself – a hypothesis advanced when the carnal impulses of Castle Rock's lumpen horde come to the fore due to 'sexual liberation and the reign of mass consumerism' (Rancière, *Hatred* 23, 70, 66). Through the orgasmic response of Gaunt's intractable female customers, *Needful Things* represents 'the people' as hormonal, irresponsible and harbouring unrealistic demands that lead to unadulterated chaos.

Yet *Needful Things* also provokes its readers with an approach that can at times feel quite political. For instance, when the novel critiques individuals with 'cash registers for hearts', King's reader is seemingly invited to attack the underpinnings of a neo-liberal state. Upon greater scrutiny, however, the text's pillorying of consumerism might be more aptly identified with Mark Fisher's 'gestural anti-capitalism'.[12] *Needful Things* actually forecloses any political response to what ails Castle Rock by rendering such answers untenable. The sheriff presents himself as a 'tough sell', unthreatened by blind consumerism thanks to his procedural proclivities, his insistence upon 'doing his job', as well as the protective barrier of 'police language'. He separates himself from the rest of the town by believing in neither commercial scams (peddled by Gaunt) nor governmental delusions (peddled by the town's grotesque Selectman). 'Politics only stretches so far' for this officer of the law as he upholds a commonsensical order, dictated by the worthy few (101, 184, 135, 113).

Needful Things is hardly an isolated case in the King corpus. *The Eyes of the Dragon* (1987) affirms the extensive role of depoliticisation in his fiction.[13] Although it is true that the fantasy genre habitually celebrates a 'good king', when we place *The Eyes of the Dragon* in conversation with the rest of King's body of work (specifically, with works like *Needful Things*), we begin to see his fable in an entirely new light.[14] Randall Flagg – a character to whom I return in the Postlude – threatens to politicise a kingdom's affairs by fomenting insurrection. An embodiment of the (im)possible political, he sews seeds of mischief to destroy the monarchy through 'bloody revolt . . . a thousand years of darkness and anarchy'. In response, the protagonist extols the 'goodness of the law' used to police dumb masses that invariably succumb to Flagg's charisma: 'Above all else, the kingdom must endure – there must be no revolt.' By the close, King's novel posits a 'rightful king' against 'rebels and usurpers', thereby casting the potency of the political back into the shadows where it will remain for centuries, awaiting the opportunity to return (51, 204, 312). Like *Needful Things* – indeed, like so much of King's fiction – *The Eyes of the Dragon* privileges neo-feudalism.

Many of King's texts conjure a political glut in order to police it. This foundational paradox sheds light upon the dual impulses at work throughout King's fiction. After a team of outsiders liberate 'the people' from aristocratic manipulation in *'Salem's Lot*, the novel doubts its so-called liberation: 'I was just following orders. The people elected me. But who elected the people?' (305). 'The people' must be free; 'the people' must be kept in check.[15] The sheriff of *Needful Things* magnifies this paradox when he aspires to reach a place where politics could come to an end: 'Voters elect me . . . to preserve and uphold the law' (112). Although he gestures at a 'good democracy' in which there must be legitimate elections (like the one that led to his ascent into the position of sheriff), the very same election that elevates him to power initiates a forfeiture of legislative options for the masses. As the sheriff polices the status quo, he tamps down upon ecstasies of a 'bad democracy' – that which must be limited; that which can only 'stretch so far'. For the sheriff of Castle Rock, 'the scary stuff' is a citizenry that must be protected from its own worst impulses. Even as the text pans across the faces of townspeople to evoke 'sheep who have lost their shepherd', which is to say, a democracy desperately in search of a proper course, the pastoral sheriff cannot stop the town's self-destruction: 'It was my town. But not anymore' (543, 638, 798). *Needful Things* therefore oscillates between the hopefulness of democracy and its contemporary corpse.

This anti-democratic undercurrent resurfaces again in his screenplay for the television movie *Storm of the Century* (1999), a piece that retells *Needful Things* in a slightly different register. Once more, an ominous outsider visits a small town to create chaos and then sell a unique brand of relief. The story exposes the citizens of Little Tall Island off the coast of Maine to be gullible buyers as they purchase an array of useless goods in anticipation of an impending winter storm (a correlation that again confuses empty-headed consumerism with political engagement – the scarlet letter of the designation 'citizen-consumer'). 'It doesn't take much to amuse island people', reads a particularly derisive stage direction. During the storm, residents rapidly mutate into a 'crowd of lookie-loos' that must be controlled by 'whip and chair' (132, 193, 18). Echoing *'Salem's Lot*, residents of the island resemble a 'herd of pigs that [run] into the ocean and drowned themselves' – a blank-eyed horde that is easily manipulated and eminently corruptible. In the penultimate act of the screenplay, King's outsider forces the demos to forfeit one of its children or face utter destruction. What follows is a troubling display that undermines the essential premise of democracy: invoking John Stuart Mill's 'tyranny of the majority', the 'mob' of Little Tall Island sacrifices an innocent child in the name of an assumed greater good. When the constable (a carbon copy of the sheriff in *Needful Things*, indeed, a carbon copy of all of the technocrats and would-be militants that comprise King's America) interjects to stop what he understands to be a barbarous overreaction, a crowd member reminds him of a painful truth: 'This is still a democracy!' Singularly focused upon their own self-preservation, the residents of Little Tall Island prefer to violate the rights of the minority (in this case, an innocent child) than to die in the name of an abstract principle. Put differently, King's fiction upholds a *liberal* value – private rights – only by undercutting a *democratic* one – free and fair elections. In the end, the town constable, who, like the sheriff, at first considers himself to be a shepherd that tends to a flock of naive sheep, realises that the conceit of democracy is fatally flawed (255, 306, 247). He never outright abandons democracy (I am, he proudly declares, 'the man you elected'), but he repeatedly insists to the 'mob' that his managerial role cannot be usurped (he remains dutybound 'to enforce your laws'). 'Help me do my job', he implores the horde, ostensibly asking it to promote greater democratic engagement, before promptly stifling its participation with the command: 'Grab your stuff and go home.' When the town at last enacts its will and sacrifices a vulnerable child to expedite its return to normalcy, the constable abandons his forsaken island, following the sheriff from *Needful Things* into the proverbial sunset: 'I'm done here' (332, 96, 364). Simply stated, King's *Storm of the Century* disinvites political wrangling in favour of elitist supervision.

I do not wish to suggest here, or in the remainder of this book, that King's fiction provides only a monolithic account of American politics. In reality, King's works are infused with a diverse array of political sentiments. Indeed, from an alternative vantage point, we could read the retreat into atomism in *Needful Things* as evidence not of an invasive neo-liberal mindset, but as a reminder of the inherently fragile nature of citizenship. The citizen-consumers of Castle Rock – or Little Tall Island, or any number of haunted hamlets in King's multiverse – share their pain with one another to lessen personal agony and, as a result, they eventually heed 'the cries of the badly wounded' instead of chasing 'ephemeral' pleasure, thus redefining citizenship through renewed attention to personal limits, weakness and interdependence (*Needful Things* 272). *Needful Things* could be interpreted as encouraging readers to imagine a neo-Keynesian government that caters to an imperfect human condition. This interpretation resists the premature closure offered by a citizenry that rejects political recourse by accepting the blame for its own mistreatment (e.g. at the close, it is revealed that the residents of Castle Rock apparently 'knew what they were doing' all along). In their acutely political moments, King's stories imply that things could always be otherwise (372).

However, while *Needful Things* does partially disenchant its reader of bald economism, and King's readers cannot overlook how the villainous Gaunt boils everything down to 'a question of supply and demand', the novel nevertheless lionises professional-managers.[16] The sheriff's pretence of neutrality barely obscures his exclusionary worldview, and so his anti-political posture remains categorically political. When an individual denounces an adversary by calling them 'political', and assumes a 'non-political' position of superiority, the individual engages in an antagonism intrinsic to politics (Schmitt, *Concept* 32). Therefore, *Needful Things* rehearses a sleight-of-hand that will be quite familiar to contemporary readers by promoting anti-political solutionism to achieve its specific political ends.

Economized identity politics in *Gerald's Game*

King's texts maintain the dominant ideology of their era by attacking caricatures of cultural conservatism without seriously addressing the structural economic changes that are taking hold. Certain critics might interject that King's fiction – specifically, his output from the 1990s – engages with identity politics. We must remember, though, that in the late twentieth century, the concept of identity starts to resemble (in some cases, but certainly not all) a commodity as well as a tool for self-marketing. Identity is routinely reduced to 'a thing to be possessed and displayed' by the citizen-consumer (Gilroy, *Against* 103). King's narratives frequently treat identity as a set of commercial choices made by autonomous actors.[17] They concern themselves with issues of race and gender by following marginalised characters that seize the capacity to tell their personal story.[18] A later chapter concerning *Rose Madder* (1995) explores how the protagonist composes her identity to achieve a sort of 'liberation' that may strike the reader as quite political but which actually relies heavily upon the framework of financialisation. *Rose Madder* neither necessitates solidarity between members of a group nor tracks new groups that foster more egalitarian arrangements. Another chapter analyses how *Firestarter*

(1980) portrays identity as a private matter wholly divorced from communal input.[19] Judith Butler argues that the revised category of 'woman' put forth by texts like *Rose Madder* or *Firestarter* is predominantly 'produced and restrained by the very structures of power through which emancipation is sought' (4). When it leaves untouched the problems of an economised identity politics, scholarship on King can appear more political than the corresponding texts prove to be.

The problems with economised identity politics are numerous. For one, subjects during this period – in particular, women – experience an intensified 'conflation of the political and the psychological', as their society markets to them self-help techniques with which they are supposed to grapple with shrinking government aid. Janice Peck examines how women are told that societal problems stem from their 'faulty attitudes' and so they bear sole responsibility for adjusting themselves to social change without demanding political reform. 'It is entirely possible to feel more positively about oneself', Peck writes, 'without challenging the existing system . . . [to] define empowerment primarily in terms of individual transformation' (32, 38). King's female protagonists subscribe to this premise by 'taking self-healing to a new level' (King, *Lisey* 556). A significant influence upon King's publications in the 1990s, these self-help tracts propose rehabilitation that burns away traces of political strife in deference to consumerist nostrums.

In *Gerald's Game* (1992), protagonist Jessie wrestles with her demons to escape from the patriarchy. Whereas King's *Misery* (1987) at least attempts to depict a heated confrontation between the sexes, *Gerald's Game* reduces this sense of antagonism to a private consideration of social norms.[20] For much of the novel, Jessie exploits her inner resources and displays the 'tireless adaptability' required to survive in a neo-liberal state (238). The final section of the novel adopts first-person narration in a move that purportedly allows her to construct her own narrative and, the logic goes, to seize complete control over her identity. And yet, because *Gerald's Game* remains rooted in a larger Cult of Self, it does not intentionally present self-help as a political enterprise. Quite the opposite: 'Individuation is fundamentally – and deliberately – depoliticizing' (Dean, *Crowds* 84). Jessie tells herself to cease 'bitching and moaning and get down to business' because pity is worth less than a 'pisshole in the snow', as she realises that she must rely upon herself if she ever wants to stand on 'her own two feet'. She eventually takes charge of her own therapy by writing and selling her tale to others: 'I have to do it myself' (306, 377, 328, 433).

By the novel's end, *Gerald's Game* equates feminism with gritty self-reliance, presenting the 'woman problem' as self-sabotage rather than a sign of systemic inequality.

Although *Gerald's Game* moves to purge itself of what it decries as noxious politics, the novel maintains a political residue through the voice of Jessie's college friend, Ruth (a stereotypical child of the 1960s that once attended rallies as well as avant-garde plays). Ruth's prior mode of resistance resonates with Jessie's current attempt to break free from her physical and mental prisons. At first, the text represses Ruth for what it describes as legitimate reasons; like the sheriff in *Needful Things*, Jessie appears determined to thwart her friend's unruliness: 'Rather than heterogeneous, conflictual, temporary, unbounded, and in need of support from objects and figures that exceed it', Jodi Dean expounds, 'the subject as individual is impossibly, fantastically independent and enduring. The crowd becomes unconscious again in the continued operation of enclosure effected by the individual form' (*Crowds* 113). To a hyper-individuated Jessie, Ruth seems vengeful as well as violent, bubbling to the surface in times of desperation when Jessie feels particularly 'primitive' or 'savage'. Embodying the 'feverish' decade of the 1960s that was 'too bright to be real', Ruth 'freeloads' in Jessie's head (41–5, 55, 94, 107). *Gerald's Game* subsequently subdues Ruth's antagonism by locking her inside of Jessie's unconscious. At the same time, King's novel – like its protagonist – quashes the political by drawing it incessantly to the surface, with a double movement akin to French philosopher Michel Foucault's 'repressive hypothesis' in which Victorians summon sexuality by constantly repressing it. In a word, Jessie cannot 'unhappen' Ruth (137). By repeatedly remembering Ruth's drive to 'bring down the hammer', *Gerald's Game* evokes the political as a more potent force due to its association with the unconscious. The unconscious and the political share the trait of being fundamentally ungovernable. Ruth and her crowd cannot be suppressed forever and so the feminist gatherings of Jessie's adolescence continue to haunt her – heterogeneous; conflictual; a support system that transcends her limited capacities – and remind King's reader that Jessie's managerial self-cure has not entirely erased her political profile. King's fiction frequently attends to a 'crowd' that has been relegated to the unconscious – be this 'crowd' positive ('the shining' that unifies strangers), negative (the homogeneity of the cretinous rabble) or both at once. Eliciting the cacophony of the unconscious, *Gerald's Game* unwittingly spurs a political re-birth because, even as the text augments a presumably anti-political foundation by tasking Jessie with her own rehabilitation, it ultimately divulges its political underpinnings (that is, the hegemonic and counter-hegemonic blocs that comprise Jessie's fractured interior world).

While previous studies of King's cultural politics have engaged with Jessie's resistance to patriarchal norms, the chapters that follow delve into the broader political constitution of King's multiverse. The careful reader will note that *Gerald's Game* closes with a missive addressed to Jessie's hyper-politicised friend: 'How much we are moved by others, even when we are priding ourselves on our control and self-reliance' (444). In actuality, Jessie does not need Ruth as fodder, or as a mere fungible for self-improvement; she sends a dispatch to the flesh-and-blood Ruth, a feminist with whom she shares much in common (and from whom she still has much to learn). The political thus returns from repression within King's America on at least two fronts: first, as a 'dead zone' evoked by what a managerial society denies (the strife of the 1960s, embodied by Ruth); and secondly, as a collaboration with 'crowds' that cry out from dreams.

Breaking Bachman

If the political can never be fully excised from King's America, what are we to do with its vestiges? What are we to make of 'the mob' in Castle Rock, the hippie Ruth or the myriad ghosts from the 1960s that spook his multiverse? In the second chapter, I investigate how this deferment manifests through King's highly publicised division from his alter ego, Richard Bachman. This deferment is so crucial to what follows that I must underscore it from the start. King's 'fraternal twin' functions as a repository of political angst, a 'rainy-day sort of guy' that King declares to be a 'state of mind'. In his prefaces to the Bachman novels, King conducts his Constant Reader to consider these texts as evidence of curbed parts of his psyche (King 'Importance'). Critic Stephen P. Brown plays along with the premise, chronicling Bachman as 'King in a minor key' (Brown 'Stephen'). King continuously ruminates upon his relationship with his nom de plume: in *The Dark Half* (1989), he works out 'his relationship to his pen name'; in 1996, he traverses the same plot twice to tease out the consequences of the Bachman/King split: *Desperation* as King and *The Regulators* as Bachman (Russell 81). While readers might be compelled to categorise the King persona as anti-political and the Bachman persona as political – after all, King downplays the role of politics in fiction written under his name while he overtly politicises Bachman-as-Other by classifying him as 'a superannuated hippie-type' – the actual demarcation is never quite so clean (quoted in Wood 148).

In truth, King's personas depend upon one another for their coherence. Expressing the restlessness of a disenfranchised child of the 1960s depressed by his generation's failure to generate lasting change, Bachman's stories understand that absolute fulfilment through organisational politics remains an (im)possibility. The Bachman books respond to this futility by suspending the political and treating it as a spectral presence. Even though they are tasked with remembering what is missing – the articulation of a utopian society that could please everyone – Bachman's protagonists refuse to stay silent, destroying themselves in spectacular fashion. We might question the efficacy of their self-immolation (the second chapter interrogates this idea at length), but we cannot deny that the brazen political energy of these tales disrupts the ennui of the 1970s. In short, Bachman's fiction memorialises the longing for a flawless society as an aching wound that will not heal, and the King persona responds to this death drive by dismissing Bachman as too macabre as well as plastering over his antagonism with a cadre of elite managers.[22]

The magnitude of this foundational split becomes clear in King's under-analysed novel *Insomnia* (1994), a text that reveals the extent to which King's persona diverges from the Bachman facade (without, in the process, expunging it). Scrutinising a gory fight between pro-life and pro-choice factions in Derry, Maine, *Insomnia* implies that 'bad democracy' leads unfailingly to horrific violence. The novel wonders aloud how protagonist Ralph, self-described 'Peacemaker Number One', might resolve the conflict and reach a satisfactory consensus (King recycles the name Ralph to describe an equally banal peacemaker in his 2018 novel, *The Outsider*, analysed in chapter 9). Unwilling to take a side, Ralph dismisses the war over reproductive rights as 'poison', a form of 'madness' that appears to be catching among a swarm of untrustworthy 'spear-carriers' (316–19, 202, 215). In this way, *Insomnia* degrades politics as a bunch of marching and counter-marching, 'name-calling and fist-shaking', an unpleasant disruption of the 'normal' flow of events. A neighbourhood police officer elevates impartial management over the passionate conviction of protestors when he ranks activists according to their 'ass-ache quotient'. Ralph echoes this sentiment when he argues that it would be better if everyone wasn't so 'shrill' (a not-so-subtle jab at the text's demonstrators: 'She is woman, hear her roar . . . and if we're lucky, the whole thing will quiet down with no one dead'). To quell the uprisings in Derry, he proposes that the two sides go and get drunk to bury the hatchet or handle things – as they do in the 'real world' – through quid pro quo arrangements. His proposals dismiss political organisation and legislative petitions by obscuring the fact that the values championed by the camps are deeply held (174, 269–72). And yet, despite the anti-political solutionism common to King's persona, *Insomnia* retains a Bachman-esque undercurrent.

Insomnia articulates a constitutive need for disagreement within a healthy democracy: an acknowledgement that, because every society involves sundry interests, absolute consensus will always prove to be (im)possible. This recognition not only challenges the utopian ambitions of Derry's doe-eyed demonstrators, it also reveals dissatisfaction to be the *sine qua non* of American politics. As Ralph's dead wife repeatedly reminds her husband, 'It's a long way back to Eden.' In Bachman's universe, politicians are not delusional because they continue to fight for their cause; they are delusional because they believe that their fight could ever be fully resolved. *Insomnia* stresses that for naive protestors 'it's about being *right* . . . [wanting] the argument to *end*' (400, 270; author's emphasis). The Bachman persona returns to expose how unsophisticated it would be for the citizens of Derry to imagine a world without political wrangling; at the same time, when the novel employs strong anti-political rhetoric (as it routinely does), the King persona represses this wrangling with the fantasy of an 'end'. Suffering under 'the strain of living on the edge of confrontation', citizen-consumers in Derry cannot disentangle the talking points of the city's managers from their accompanying drive to dissension (400, 270, 567). The King/Bachman twins cannot be cleaved. (King habitually plays with this fundamental schism in the years to follow; for example, Blind Willie from *Hearts of Atlantis* remains internally divided between his apolitical, bourgeois self and the politically infused side of himself that only manifests after dark.)

Even as King's persona persists, and his alter ego supposedly dies from 'cancer of the pseudonym', the idea of Bachman lives on (indeed, I argue that his voice becomes all the more powerful when he starts to 'speak from beyond the grave'). As a 'state of mind' to be restrained but never abolished, Bachman's spectre inspires us to buck the widely preferred hermeneutic and politicise King's fiction. Moreover, to re-read his works with this split in mind is to locate a core tension in contemporary American politics: namely, its utopian kernel alongside its compulsory dissatisfaction. Stalked by Bachman, King's fiction reflects the de-democratisation of the past fifty years while, at the same time, suggesting the sanguine prospects of a more radically democratic future.

Dispatches from dreams and dead zones

In sum, the political plays a pivotal role as a remnant in King's multiverse. Before addressing this repression and re-emergence, though, we must unpack the relationship that his fiction forges between the unconscious and American politics. In the exemplary case of *Dreamcatcher* (2001), King portrays a rigid, bureaucratic military at odds with a dormant democratic spirit. The raw force of the political resurfaces to upset the novel's fascists when, in a concentration camp at the aptly named Jefferson Tract, inmates form a spontaneous 'mob' of 'kamikaze deer-hunters' that propels itself into a 'no-guts-no-glory banzai charge'. 'Infected' individuals long to join forces due to their shared interests; they 'link up' with one another to achieve a 'fuller' vision of society. One of King's characters hears 'a crowd of opposing voices' within his unconscious – recalling the feminist group of *Gerald's Game* – and learns to find pleasure in 'the wrangle' (587–9, 617, 765). At the periphery of the text's many camp fences linger unforeseen alliances and countless opportunities for unexpected connection as the novel juxtaposes poetic as well as political cross-fertilisation with authoritarian restraint.

Despite the romance behind the novel's resistance, *Dreamcatcher*'s eruptions grow grotesque as the invisible psychic bind of the body politic reveals itself to be as oppressive as the hyper-patriotism peddled by the text's tyrants. Momentarily taming the wrangle, King's hunters psychically weld themselves into a mystical Oneness in order to combat hostile invaders. But, as Alain Badiou argues, by cajoling the hunters into a delusional (and destructive) Oneness, this transcendental bond pushes King's small platoon to mirror its militant wardens. The story's 'thesis of an essence behind the relations within the polity' reveals itself to be hazardous when, after the hunters jointly dream of killing a childhood bully, they are horrified to watch their shared dream come to fruition. The group's act of dreaming as One proves to be unsustainable – and, *Dreamcatcher* suggests, mercifully so. The shift by the hunters into organisational politics, which is to say, into a psychic consensus that empowers them to commit horrible atrocities, is never a cause for much celebration.[23] When their altercations resolve into telepathic unity, and the once heterogeneous 'crowd' congeals via a singular 'American Dream', something fundamental is lost. In response to this coercive Oneness, King's text undermines 'politics as a communitarian bond' (I return to this tension in chapter 5 with my reading of King's *IT*). Traces of this unconscious strife allow the hunters to reject the dreamcatcher of the US military, and thereby to protect dreams that manage to slip through the cracks: dreams that are poetically as well as politically charged because, unlike the narrow-minded dogma espoused by commanders that simply 'follow orders', these dreams still generate random associations (Badiou, *Can Politics* 32–3, 36). In *Dreamcatcher*, the vitalism of the American Dream depends upon a tacit assumption that it cannot be caught or scrutinised in the light of day. Whereas institutional politics involves making Two into One, the political enjoins us to break the One back into Two.

The promise of political resistance endures in *Dreamcatcher* because it cannot be made normative. In his review of King's work, Adrian Daub comments, '[The story] doesn't have to be an allegory for "socio-anything," because the politics . . . bubble up in the novel' (Daub). This 'bubbling up' confirms how King's *Dreamcatcher* connects emancipatory politics with the mechanisms of the unconscious. To expand upon this connection, let us turn to one of King's novels that has received renewed interest of late due its jarring parallels with the election of Donald Trump, *The Dead Zone* (1979).[24] A populist politician named Greg Stillson – a figure that foreshadows Trump with startling clarity – feeds upon conspiracy theories, hides his 'weird' financial disclosures, resembles a 'carnival pitchman' and allows disenfranchised citizens to 'thumb their noses at a political establishment' (326, 289, 291).[25] To expose a crucial fissure between institutional politics and the restless political, between oppressive dreamcatchers and pluralist dreams, *The Dead Zone* references Washington Irving's 'Rip Van Winkle' (1819). In Irving's nineteenth-century tale, at the time of Rip Van Winkle's disappearance into the Catskill Mountains, the local tavern is named King George's Tavern; when he returns to the village after his lengthy slumber – having missed, in the interim, the entire American Revolution – the tavern sign is now dedicated to a different George (George Washington). Before he leaves, townsfolk idly debate politics; upon his return, townsfolk idly debate politics. From Peter Stuyvescent and the Dutch control of New York, to British rule, to self-rule, Irving's story charts a troubling continuity: the empty-headed masses continue to submit to authority figures and take seriously the pointless posturing of political pundits.

Yet due to Irving's invisible punctuation mark (a gap between pre- and post-revolutionary societies; a gap that divides the possible from the impossible), the genuine transformation occurs in Rip Van Winkle's dream-state: 'There was something strange and incomprehensible about the unknown, that inspired awe and checked familiarity' (775). That is, Irving's reader discerns a breakage between the insufferable reality of establishment politics and the embryonic fantasy of a political uprising that reoccurs, over and over again, when we least expect it. The germ of the revolution happens not when we are awake, but when we at last allow ourselves to sleep. Regularly harkening back to Irving's fable, *The Dead Zone* chastens individuals who harbour political ambition. 'College boys', for one, are deluded by academics into 'reaching conclusions', while Johnny's psychic abilities are kept in check by occasional reminders that he can neither know the mind of God nor manipulate the Wheel of Destiny. When he realises that his knowledge has dead zones, Johnny (wisely, it would seem) longs to fade into 'utter obscurity' (310, 172, 258). The modern equivalent of Rip Van Winkle's hibernation, Johnny's dead zones offer a remedy for the stagnant state of American politics by opening up a politics of the blind spot. This politics of the blind spot deflates utopian delusions by conserving the *potenza* of dreams that have not been imposed from a singular source (like the US military), but 'bubble up' freely from an unruly unconscious. Only a blind spot can keep citizens receptive to sudden undoings of the social order (I discuss King's rendition of the political event at length in the Interlude). 'Every thing's changed', Irving's hero exclaims upon waking. 'And I'm changed – and I can't tell what's my name, or who I am!' (781).

Initially unable to grasp a politics driven by blind spots, King's protagonists tend to 'overswing', applying their energy to fruitless social engineering. Consequently, Johnny's plan to assassinate Stillson does not work as he intended it to work. It works because Stillson reveals his true colours when he shields himself from gun fire with a child, thus accidentally baring his sordid character to the world. In a word, Johnny's plan succeeds by failing (273). The political, like the unconscious, manifests precisely (and, in fact, only) when King's protagonist does not demand to master it. When caught in the dreamcatcher, the political/unconscious forfeits its essence – and so it must return once more from repression. On and on goes the macabre dance. Institutions, government schemes, forced consensus: in these ways, and a range of others, King's fiction gestures at the political indirectly by dwelling upon its antithesis. Admittedly, when the hunters forgo the gift of a shared dream, and when Johnny forfeits his gift of prognostication, the (im)possibility of *Dreamcatcher* and *The Dead Zone* may strike the reader as something like surrender. While the line between unattainability and resignation is indeed a thin one, the (im)possibility at the heart of King's fiction upholds a pivotal aspect of American politics: even when it appears to be forgotten, the agitation of the political can never be stilled. 'Nothing is ever lost', Johnny learns (402). And thankfully so, because if the open-endedness of the political were somehow to be replaced by consensus, what would become of the Sisyphean American Dream?

A profusion of political potential runs through King's work like an electrical current. Set in the year 1970, the unsettled inklings of the 1960s are gone before the first pages of *The Dead Zone*, and yet they press in upon every word that follows, like 'trace memories' or 'voices from another room'. King's fiction preserves the 1960s as a dream that is best left formless, revealing how, in the aftermath of this (hopelessly) idealistic decade, the political is deferred instead of denied. The idea of the 1960s serves as a dead zone in the American psyche that, by its very definition, can never be brought completely into consciousness. King's works understand the political to be a lost object when they liken idyllic visions of the hyper-politicised 1960s to 'God's jewel box'. The futile pursuit of an end to antagonism drives Johnny onward, as he is moved, unaware, by a compulsion to keep his struggle going: 'Some things are better lost than found' (111, 70, 401, 124). By the conclusion, he acknowledges that he can do much more for his society as a ghost than as an assassin.

The phantom of the 1960s signifies an enshrouded credence that things could always be otherwise (the sentiment that King's fiction evokes rather than announces aloud, in what Henry James would describe as a vulgar fashion): 'The truth inside the lie, an illusion that magnifies the truth' (King, 'Five' 75). Specifically, King's fiction aligns the 1960s with inaccessible Truth by relating the decade to the lost city of Atlantis. This lacuna signals the all-but-vanished strife of the 1960s, preserving 'a promise that has to be kept even though – and precisely because – it can never be fulfilled. It is a democracy that can never "reach itself," catch up with itself, because it involves an infinite openness to that which comes' (Rancière, *Dissensus* 59). *The Dead Zone* presents the ballyhooed 1960s as *the* missing object of American politics when Johnny goes into his coma and his love interest Sarah decides to marry a Republican politician. After he miraculously wakes from his slumber, Sarah unwittingly throws her wedding ring into the toilet – an act that readers are meant to interpret as conveying her barely veiled urge to return to a time (the 1960s) before she resigned herself to the status quo. Her ritual of throwing away and retrieving the ring recalls Freud's *fort-da* game: Sarah, driven to scratch at the scab of unsatisfied desires from the 1960s, revives her constitutive lack. Her pleasure stems from the repetitive loss of her imaginary wholeness, her 'perfect life' with the genial Republican. She desires Johnny and the 1960s not in spite of but because of the fact that they are absent. In King's multiverse, then, the 1960s is a wound to be endlessly reopened – a wound that brings pain as well as pleasure because tarrying with it (but never seizing it outright) stimulates us into chasing once again a plurality of (im)possible dreams. As a yawning hole in King's America, the idea of the 1960s keeps us moving. Consequently, readers of *The Dead Zone* discover that democracy thrives upon agitation instead of tranquillity and, without this continuous agitation, the nation's modus operandi would simply disappear.

King's fiction further stresses this point by presenting Johnny's final epistle as a wound that must be perpetually re-opened by readers. In anticipation of his own death, Johnny writes a missive 'from the dead zone', effectively transforming himself into a voice from another room that wishes to be forgotten (but can never be lost). He goads readers to keep fighting while, at the same time, telling them that he does not want them to 'feel the pressure to recite back' to him his own actions (268). Another King novel concerned with ghostly inscriptions of the 1960s, *11/22/63* (2011), posits that political change does not require a plot advanced by either protestors or politicians. When an aspiring writer travels back in time to prevent the assassination of John F. Kennedy but ends up triggering unforeseen terrors, he decides that no person should attempt to customise politics based upon his or her personal preferences. Like Johnny, the writer composes a missive addressed to the future (the manuscript of *11/22/63*) which functions incidentally: not by dictating outcomes, but by encouraging the reader to dream unimpeded and to tarry with her own dead zones. If King's writers alter the political landscape, it is because they are gone, or because people like them could never have really existed in the first place. The formative dissatisfaction of American politics is not merely thematic in King's corpus; it remains woven into the fabric of the texts themselves.

In King's fiction, the political arrives as a dispatch, which is to say, it arrives as a text. Like the missing object – a City on the Hill; a discarded wedding ring that acts as the engine of American politics – the written word eternally gestures elsewhere. After all, the meaning of any given word could always be otherwise. King's recent retrospective on his college years contrasts his latent creativity with the fixity of his initial forays into writing. On the one hand, he admits that fiction served as a catalyst for his youthful activism. 'Fiction', he admits, 'has the power to change lives.' On the other hand, he recognises that political impulses coursing through his veins in college followed the doomed path of his early artistic ambitions. His stirrings took a form (aesthetic as well as legislative) that now strikes King as inauthentic, artificial and pretentious – in King's way of thinking, it seems all too political. The message to his readers is clear: King's political and writerly desires have proven to be fruitful when they – of necessity – miss their mark. He illustrates this deferral by juxtaposing his 'ostentatious' attempts at writing with what he perceives to be the deficient contrivances of his fellow students in their protest against the war in Vietnam. King argues that his classmates erred the moment that they stopped antagonising the American government and constructed a coherent movement to replace it. As *The Tommyknockers* taught us, the new boss is never very different from the old one. Happily, according to King, the 'bad writing' of organisational politics maintains an intimate connection to the furtive and fertile political – a promise of 'good writing' that pulsates just below the surface of correspondences that have been too carefully cultivated. Said another way, King liken the political to a poetic spirit that ought to be 'fleetingly expressed' instead of baldly declared (King, 'Five' 40, 75). His body of work argues that only by never arriving at its destination, by staying forever in circulation, can the political retain its potency.[26]

The Institute and the political shadows of King's America

To close out this Prelude, let us briefly turn to King's latest novel, *The Institute*, a work that recapitulates many of the themes that the following chapters address. In this text, King returns to the tried-and-true formula of a shadowy government organisation that sets out to destroy the nation's children in the name of self-preservation (the anti-democratic premise of *Storm of the Century*, but on a grander scale). The political elements that surface throughout his fiction are all present: a tyrannical government; youths with untapped potential that rebel against authoritarian captors; the valour of a rogue individual (a 'runaway') in tension with the transcendental bonds that unify, for better or worse, a body politic. Most importantly, *The Institute* debases the role of American politics in everyday life, in particular, its tendency to institutionalise or drift into bureaucracy, while sustaining a spectre of dissatisfaction that might yet inspire change. Unable to balance upon this fault line for very long, King's fiction frequently falls into one of two major categories: the citizen-consumer's fantasy of absolute escape from antagonism (*Needful Things*), or tales of unresolvable dissatisfaction (*The Dead Zone*). There are yarns spun by the restless ghost of Bachman, and then there are accounts by the anti-political King. Like most of King's texts, *The Institute* wavers between each category.

On the one hand, as a tale of political dissatisfaction, *The Institute* undercuts the utopian agenda of a government that wants to harness children with precognitive abilities to engineer the future. Like *Dreamcatcher* and *The Dead Zone*, this text denounces any brand of politics unwilling to acknowledge its blind spots. The novel accentuates this message by drawing attention to the government's barbaric efforts to achieve control. As a writer who narrowly avoided being drafted into the Vietnam War, King shows himself to be a by-product of the 1970s: a dyed-in-the-wool opponent of the bloated Cold War apparatus.[27] Once more, the political arrives in King's fiction indirectly – in dreams, in as-yet-invisible psychic alignments with individuals from across the globe, or in the unconscious potential of a singular subject. The political erupts by accident, before quickly receding back into the recesses of the unforeseeable. At the close of the novel, an official informs the team of rebel rousers that when they overthrew the Institute they made a terrible mistake because the Institute's 'proactive measures' are actually vital to the preservation of world peace. Nevertheless, the 'proactive measures' of the Institute are met with general disdain by King's young rebels. If politics means planning for tomorrow, *The Institute* preaches that we should focus on what is absent, on that which politics could never hope to deliver: an arrangement that could satisfy every unique subject. In contrast to the gluttony of the Institute, an entity that fattens children up by offering them alcohol, candy and tokens, and thus makes them co-dependent, the text closes with a call for greater dissatisfaction: 'It might be better to wait. Better to save some for later' (557). As we have already seen, the concept of the political at its foundation demands that we always save something for later. It recycles the rug-maker's mistake from *The Tommyknockers*: an imperfection that leaves open (in perpetuity) unexpected opportunities for communal betterment. This necessary surplus eludes the 'rationalists' of the Institute that wish to put a punctuation mark at the end of the sentence of American politics. Interestingly enough, the novel's youthful protagonist Luke collects campaign buttons for *losing* presidential candidates, stashing them away inside his Little League trophy. Through this unusual hobby, he undermines his own premature sense of victory or resolution with talismans that conserve the yearning for a better world. As signifiers of absence that trigger political hunger, these campaign buttons remind Luke that, yes, things could still always be otherwise. King's novel implies that today's politicos cannot adequately handle the reality that political life must remain 'circumstantial and transitory' (Oakeshott 7). Michael Oakeshott laments that hyper-rationalised politicos advocate a fool-hardy sort of precognition. Although the visiting official from the Institute claims that he can forecast the future with clinical precision via a set of complex algorithms, neither he nor his fallen colleagues can truly account for the unmanageable possibilities of the children in their custody. Government officials discover the hard way that the political cannot be reduced to bald economism. Raw potential hums loudly just beyond the next set of doors, building steadily to a crescendo.

On the other hand, as we can extrapolate from this ready-made alignment of the novel's moral with Oakeshott's thesis (Oakeshott served a significant intellectual within the early neo-liberal movement), *The Institute* slips into a neo-liberal mould. Because the novel stands out as one of the King books that aims to transcend antagonism rather than sustain it, readers may struggle to separate the text's emancipatory politics (described in the previous paragraph) – in which gaps in the master's knowledge expose escape routes for the slave – from the text's tacit support of free-market fundamentalism – in which individuals forfeit their autonomy to a magical marketplace that intentionally produces gaps in their knowledge. It is important to remember that a politics of the blind spot can look eerily similar to an economics of the blind spot. In *The Institute*, highly individuated subjects exist in a state of near constant (re)networking as they mine their own internal resources. Luke, for example, is lauded for his ability to be 'global', to remain amenable to different interests and to exemplify how human bodies become 'an investment. A stock with good growth potential.' The novel heightens the value of an extreme self-reliance, that old chestnut in the King's corpus: 'What you did for yourself was what gave you the power' (50, 390). *The Institute* pines for a world with less government oversight, a deeper appreciation for volatility and a more prominent role for the police instead of politics.[28] For instance, one of the text's rogue heroes, police officer Tim, operates from a state of exception in which he must break the rules to save the world from itself. After shooting a (white) suspect that proves to be innocent, Tim is redeemed, or more accurately, it turns out that readers should never have doubted him in the first place. When the narrative begs its reader to trust Tim's impulses, even though they are not foolproof, it neutralises political wrangling in favour of a precarious alternative. So what will it be for King's America – dissatisfaction or consensus?

The Institute glimpses the inherently dynamic nature of American politics. Jacques Lacan claims, 'Repression and the return of the repressed are the same thing' (Lacan, *Seminars* 191). Haunted by Bachman, King's canon paints a comprehensive portrait of the mechanisms that drive the political nature of human beings, and therefore we cannot reduce King's output to mere naive anti-political sentiment.[29] His texts promote chaos and neo-liberal management; they demand democracy and they extol the virtue of technocrats. This book analyses how King's fiction, often counter to its stated intentions, endlessly provokes the political. Even within the mirthless landscape of *The Mist*, the power of the political periodically returns, as citizens enter into a New England town meeting to espouse 'the grim necessity of people chewing over the same information, trying to see it from every possible point of view' (88). Through their occasional discernment of this grim necessity, King's narratives refuse managerial consensus as a complete cure for what ails them. Furthermore, the endurance of this grim necessity in King's thrillers reveals why critics continue to find these works so helpful in attending to the ascent of Trump. Without a robust outlet for antagonism (one unhindered by economic disparities), politics materialises in its gothic guise – an impending threat that these fables never fully forget. Equal parts relentless despair and unflagging optimism, King's fiction tracks America's repression of the political in tandem with its unsettling return.

2

The Bachman Books and America's Death Drive

THE BOOKS ATTRIBUTED to his pseudonym Richard Bachman remain some of Stephen King's most politically charged works to date. In particular, *The Long Walk* (written in the 1960s, published in 1979), *Roadwork* (1981) and *The Running Man* (1982) each underscore the brokenness of the American political establishment by following a discontented generation of young people as it is transformed, in the aftermath of the 1960s, into a ticking time bomb at the hands of heartless bureaucrats. While these novels forecast a dystopian future – indeed, they can be read as partially complicit in laying its foundation – Bachman's works also suggest a psychoanalytically inflected politics by juxtaposing America's yearning for wealth, oil and imperial power with the nation's hidden drive for self-destruction – what I will refer to as the death drive of American politics. David Punter writes of King's fiction, 'The desire for disappointment is a very strong one . . . [King offers a] prolonged work of surrogate mourning which occurs before the fact' (136). In just this way, Bachman's works force us to ask what kind of changes, if any, might rehabilitate a society caught in a state of self-sabotage. These texts thus establish a trend that persists throughout King's fiction:

at the very moment that these books resign themselves to the tenets of neo-liberalism – specifically, the rejection of politics as an appropriate answer to community ills – they (unconsciously) conjure radical alternatives.

To interpret the politics of Bachman's texts, readers face a number of hurdles. For one, it is quite easy to take King-as-Bachman at his word: 'King has asserted, both non-fictionally and fictionally, that politics, or other message-type proselytizing, should never be the driving force of fiction.' If political themes do crop up in the King/Bachman universe, it must be by osmosis, that is, it can only be because the author obliquely 'tapped into cultural fears', and never because his works harbour a distinctive agenda (Giannini 232–4). Nonetheless, the Bachman texts do cultivate a unique political position: their will-to-destruction marks an explosive shift away from the military-industrial apparatus, away from Fordist-Keynesian calibrations and away from the idealism of the postwar era: '[These texts display] a deep disenchantment with the arrogant assumptions of the accepted order' (Newhouse 268–9). As a consequence of the suffering that protagonists experience at the hands of a state-corporate nexus that does not adequately address the rehabilitative needs of citizens, Bachman's books articulate a politics of pure negation (a modality that plays a vital role in the decades to come) by tracking 'protagonists who are sociologically so tightly determined and whose free will is so limited that they find violence and self-destruction as their only means to take a stand' (Strengell 218). Bachman's protagonists do not construct surrogate worldviews, but are instead content to destroy the established order and maintain a cynical bent that actually augments, rather than refutes, the era's dominant ideology.[1] Said another way, Bachman's books spark a form of self-immolation that is less about sacrifice in the name of the greater good than it is about laughing maniacally at any attempt to plan a better future. Moreover, because suffering, depicted in Bachman's fiction as a natural part of human existence, cannot be remedied by government strategy, these novels dim the political voltage of the 1960s and thereby promote the fatalistic view that all policies for communal betterment are fundamentally unworkable. In their depiction of suffering as above and beyond 'mere politics', these books normalise pillars that prove crucial in the rise of neo-liberalism.[2]

Composed for an audience nursing fresh psychic wounds from the conflict in Vietnam, high-profile political assassinations and incessant stagflation, Bachman's books depict a political body psychologically driven to its own demise. Whereas previous Fordist-Keynesian arrangements acknowledge the infantilism of citizens, the inherent vulnerabilities that accompany citizenship and the horror that individuals are always at risk of becoming 'losers' in a hyper-competitive economy – traumas, they claim, that must be anticipated as well as mitigated – Bachman's books, like emerging critics of this arrangement that argue it is Fordism-Keynesianism (not neo-liberalism) that infantilises citizens, transpose this sense of vulnerability into calls for greater self-governance. At the same time, his stories arrive always at self-destruction: at the close of each text, after treatment of the demoralised subject reveals itself to be futile, an existential void remains. Through its destruction of utopian hope as well as its demolishment of authority, Bachman's texts foster a spirit that can appear (at best) complicit in an increasingly fashionable drive to deregulate, disaggregate and dismantle.

Yet for readers today Bachman's futility needs not inspire widespread de-politicisation. Although his texts undermine the idea of utopia by insisting upon the basic imperfection of the human condition, they simultaneously make the case that to achieve a perfect consensus, in which all interests align and everyone could be fully satisfied, would be to paralyse the potency of the political itself. When cast in a more propitious light, even though the pursuit of utopia may be inherently self-defeating, Bachman's brand of self-defeat is necessary in order to sustain the restlessness of American politics and its never-ending chase of that 'more perfect union'. His storyworld frames the unconscious drive to fail as that which keeps citizens hunting for something other than authoritarian numbness. In spite of its resignation to a politics of pure negation, then, Bachman's characters at least acquire enough insight to resist singular visions espoused by encroaching fascists. Readers may have surmised by this point that Lacanian analysis and Bachman's fiction have much to say to one another. Although we might initially register Lacan and Bachman as 'anti-political', because their texts focus upon characters that covet dissolution over collective organisation, their works remain profoundly political by signifying for readers the (im)possibility of a perfect society.[3] Given his refusal of consensus and cure in the name of sustained dissatisfaction, Bachman *avec* Lacan encourages us to strive, to undermine hegemony and to persist as primarily political creatures.

The desire to win at all costs

The Bachman books reconsider the hyper-competitive ethos that grips the United States in the 1970s, described by Franco 'Bifo' Berardi as a 'necro-economy: moral prescriptions and legal regulations have been annulled by the all-encompassing law of competition' (136). In *The Long Walk*, teenager Ray Garraty enters a competition of young men that must walk for as long as they can in an attempt to win a grand prize; the state then summarily executes the losers. In *Roadwork*, Bart Dawes – a name that evokes the Dawes Act of 1887, in which Native American lands were confiscated by the American government – must compete to preserve his house from being demolished by the local government. And in *The Running Man*, Ben Richard competes in a televised gameshow in which he must evade assassins to claim a sizable prize to save his infant daughter's life. A line from King's novel *'Salem's Lot* (1975) effectively sums up the Bachman ethos: 'Nobody beat the system or won the game' (152). Bachman's texts focus upon rigged contests as symptoms of America's late twentieth-century necro-economy.

When we consider how the US government's ever-increasing demand for violent war games immediately precedes the publication of the Bachman books, we can safely read the competitive ethos on display in Bachman's universe as a by-product of the nation's bloated military-industrial complex. Specifically calling upon images of the conflict in Vietnam, Bachman's state pits young men against one another in contests that they could never hope to win. A grim reality materialises during the 1970s in which the apparent ideals of the Great Society, like well-calibrated progress for all, stability or predictable growth, clash with the harsh conditions of a stagnating economy, a depressing turn that 'consigns the majority of people, places, businesses and institutions to the status of "losers"'. William Davies contends, 'A culture which valorizes "winning" and "competitiveness" above all else provides few sources of security or comfort' (xvi–xvii).[4] To survive the deflation of the post-war bubble, the dominant narrative goes, American culture must venerate competition above all other aspects of communal life. In turn, Americans remake competition, previously a means to an end, into an end-in-itself. Bachman's demented federal government likewise inflates the importance of rivalry when in *The Long Walk*, for instance, The Major (a 'society-supported sociopath') orchestrates the Walk with a clear purpose, a purpose that he summarises in his speech that begins 'with Competition, progressed to Patriotism, and finished with something called the Gross National Product' (12, 23). As minor parts of the imperial machinery, Walkers like Garraty are meant to compete because competition, the Major soliloquises, is inexorably good for the United States, that is, competition and patriotism are practically synonymous. The heavy-handed state in *Roadwork* similarly forces its citizens to jockey with one another without any real hope of winning, a futility underlined by the government's pointless gamesmanship: 'The city's Gestapo agents' busily work to build 'new roads for energy-sucking behemoths while kids in this city are starving' (234). Government bureaucracy demands intense wrangling to increase Gross Domestic Product through energy-producing exercises that co-opt citizens as well as their property for no more dignified reason than to keep everyone competing.

Bachman conflates the strife required by the state with the strife demanded by corporations as his state-corporate nexus forces individuals to produce and consume while harbouring delusions of advancement. The ominous Network in *The Running Man* exists as a hybrid construct, a government run like a sinister business, with countless gameshows that offer a 'crooked table' at which citizens must gamble away their very lives. Meanwhile, 'the fiction of upward mobility' keeps them jockeying with one another in a bleak cycle. Bachman's state-corporate nexus therefore elevates particular values over others: efficiency over egalitarianism, expertise over fairness and meritocracy over cooperation. Most prominently, his politicians operate the government like a ruthless contest by ejecting 'losers' in order to accumulate 'fresh new talent' (44, 200). This concept of a compulsory gameshow reveals how, over the course of an increasingly mirthless 1970s, economic motivations are made to trump other cultural concerns – a shift made evident in the multitude of perverse tools with which televised contests entice contestants to give up everything in the pursuit of 'the stuff of dreams, the bread of life'. In Bachman's multiverse, the all-important profit motive alters perceptions of heroism by no longer associating heroism with improvement of the lives of others, but with competition-for-competition's-sake. As a representative from the Network tells contestants: 'I find you to be a courageous, resourceful group, refusing to live on the public dole . . . true heroes of our time' (5, 30).

In its critique of the era's hypercompetitive ethos, Bachman's novels forecast what some critics have seen as the function of reality television within a neo-liberal state. Laurie Ouellette underscores the role of reality programmes such as 'The Walk' and 'The Running Man' in forging neo-liberal subjects through a certain kind of spectacle. Garraty and

Richards compete for crowds and, through their performance, spectators are habituated to disdain 'state authority and intervention, [and accept] a heightened form of personal responsibility and self-discipline' (Ouellette 248). Garraty and Richards are not the only ones tasked with cultivating survival skills for the cut-throat world of tomorrow. The sensorium of the crowd is vicariously conditioned. This monolithic focus upon competition translates into a broader cultural disorientation when, lamenting that his company used to be run by people that care, Bart mourns: 'Now we're part of a corporation with two dozen other irons in the fire – fast food, Ponderosa golf, those three eyesore discount department stores.' The Bachman books routinely allude to a 'grotesque' Monopoly game to underscore how unbridled competition overwhelms all of American life: 'Those guys downtown . . . It's just dollars and cents to them' (*Roadwork* 38, 148, 171). In short, Bachman's protagonists desire fulfilment within a system that will never pay out, a system in which they could never hope to win. Bart decries his former corporate employer for stringing along young workers with no intention of rewarding them. Reward is an illusion, he claims, because even if you happen to 'win', by allowing yourself to be subsumed within meaningless machinery, you have already lost. Indeed, the 'triumph' of Richards at the close of *The Running Man* only perpetuates the system that he despises by inspiring participation in a vicious cycle without end. One of Garraty's fellow Walkers realises, too late, that 'everyone loses' (*Long* 138). Desire in these texts is constantly created even as fulfilment is frequently furloughed.

Importantly, Bachman's protagonists respond to this fatalistic situation by claiming 'victory' not through the pursuit of a better life for themselves or others, but by beating the state-corporate nexus to the punch, which is to say, by destroying themselves before they can be destroyed. Simply put, they respond to the hollowness of the military-industrial machine by annihilating themselves without any commitment to improving the lives of future generations. Tony Magistrale describes Bachman's 'predominant theme of negativism', a negativism, I would hasten to add, that resonates strongly in the decades that follow the publication of these books (Magistrale, *Landscape* 96).[5] If Bachman's books are 'political' at all, it would seem to be a 'politics' driven exclusively by disruption as well as disintegration. Subsequently, it can be argued that Bachman's novels 'exaggerate the state's negative role in society', and they go 'too far in the evacuation of the form of the state'. In their full assault upon the state-corporate nexus, these texts manifest the dream of dismantlement as every attempt at detonation of 'the establishment' eventually circles back upon itself, thus 'reinforcing what had become a kind of anti-political orthodoxy' (Dean and Villadsen 1–2, 19). A prime example of the era's anti-political orthodoxy, the ruinous impulse of Bachman's books – the devastation caused by their death drive – helps us to understand how anti-Vietnam sentiments as well as other counter-cultural refusals of the 1960s have been gradually re-entrenched within the neo-liberal psyche.

Colin Crouch defines this politics of negation by delineating between positive rights – which stress democratic participation and greater access to resources – and negative rights – which stress individual rights (such as property ownership) against the state-corporate nexus. Negative rights, Crouch argues, serve as the sole focus of politics today. Consider, for example, Bart's refusal to allow the state to reclaim his house, or Richards's refusal to be coerced by the Network. These characters hold tightly to their negative rights until, in the end, they cherish only the right to demolish their own bodies. In place of a utopian dream, cue the wrecking ball. Running parallel with the late Carter administration (in particular, its deregulation of the airline industry) as well as the early Reagan administration, Bachman's books feature radically disembedded subjects that forever seek to blow up a corrupt central government. Of course, this encompassing 'atmosphere of cynicism about politics and politicians, low expectation of their achievements, and close control of their scope and power . . . suits the agenda of those wishing to rein back the active state' (Crouch 13, 23). From this perspective, Bachman's destructive vision coheres a bit too neatly with the emerging demands of late capitalism, dovetailing with a contemporary politics of negation that remains unable 'to provide good reasons to support collective approaches to political, social, and economic problems'. From this perspective, Bachman's wrecking ball offers what Jodi Dean calls 'little more than the denunciation of all possibility of knowledge and truth' (*Democracy* 4, 9). His suffering protagonists extract themselves from their rigged competition by flipping the table on their way out, leaving future competitors with nothing to which they could cling. If the outcome of Bachman's fiction is a 'win', it looks an awful lot like losing.

Indeed, Bachman's books pair futility with absurdity. Although he technically 'wins' the Walk, Garraty keeps running, choosing death over capitulation; Bart detonates his home (and himself) rather than vacate the premises with cash in hand; Richards flies a plane into the Network building instead of accepting a prominent role in its administration. Crucially, these figures do not aim to strengthen the demos; they aim only to weaken America's military-industrial complex. 'If you're protesting something', Bart comments, 'It's because you think something else would be better . . . I don't know.' At the close, Bachman's characters decide that there is 'no good place to make your stand in the world' (*Roadwork* 137–8, 305). Because Bart's self-destruction is devoid of sacrificial quality, it disinvites readers from conceptualising his final act as a form of protest, and invites them instead to deride any and all activists of a political stripe. Bachman's texts highlight maniacal laughter, as when Garraty laughs 'long and hysterically', or when Richards laughs the kind of laugh that 'comes freely and helplessly from the deepest root of the stomach' (*Long* 134; *Running* 185). In his introduction to a collection of essays from his time at the University of Maine in the 1960s, King says of his student cohort: 'We couldn't stop laughing' (80). Rather than be earnest about their struggle or foster new political commitments, Bachman's protagonists simply laugh, forfeiting their own desire because their desire (or so the logic goes) remains invariably tied to the incentives of a congenitally flawed system. These 'heroes' represent what Lacan calls *les non-dupes errent*. By depicting futility as part and parcel of the human condition, Bachman's texts remain tautological: their claim that life is inherently absurd triggers ever more absurdity as the appropriate response to whatever ails them. In brief, Bachman's books presuppose that the correct answer to any request for social betterment is to revise the upbeat political mantra of 1968 – 'Demand the Impossible!' – into the more concise and morose cry, 'Impossible!' (a biting response that normalises the utterances of an up-and-coming cadre of neo-liberals).

The drive to lose

As the preceding section suggests, the desire to 'win' in Bachman's fiction, as well as the implicit critique of this desire, is never quite what it appears to be. Specifically, in these works the struggle to find fulfilment remains an indispensable delusion, and only when his protagonists accept loss – that is to say, only when they admit that they are constituted by loss – do they seem to experience genuine enjoyment. The closing explosions trigger ecstasy (a kind of jouissance) as the protagonists are released from the spells cast by consumerism and militant American politics. More than King's later works, Bachman's novels depend upon Lacan's psychoanalytical formulas.[6] Todd McGowan expounds upon this foundation in his examination of the psychic structure undergirding capitalism (a structure, I might add, that appears to encompass the political economy as a whole). According to McGowan, capitalism functions because it acknowledges, and then draws upon, a drive for dissatisfaction: 'Capitalism has the effect of sustaining subjects in a constant state of desire. As subjects of capitalism, we are constantly on the edge of having our desire realized, but never reach the point of realization' (*Capitalism* 11). For example, a consumer wants to purchase the latest Apple product. The act of waiting for its arrival stokes their desire, and so – because they are still actively desiring – they remain at their most 'satisfied' when the new product has not yet arrived. When the consumer eventually attains the item, they are disappointed to some extent because the item could never live up to the idealised vision that they maintained prior to its arrival. This 'failure' illustrates how the capitalist game succeeds not in spite of but as a result of its inherent (im)possibility. In short, capitalism contains a Lacanian secret: its endlessly deferred gratification reveals how we are most satisfied when we are not yet satisfied. Lacan's *objet a* – the lost object; the yet-to-arrived Apple product – keeps subjects in a constant state of trying to win the competition in order to receive the ultimate prize. 'Winning is only a detour on the way to losing', McGowan claims. 'Failure is the subject's mode of success' (31). Put differently, capitalism depends upon a Lacanian logic that can be readily applied to the hyper-partisanship of American politics in which every 'win' over one's opponent, such as 'owning libs' or 'torching right wingers', is actually an imperative loss. After all, if the subject refuses to stand down from her competitive posture, she ensures future antagonism (instead of consensus) as well as sustained imperfection (instead of cure), and therefore she preserves the life-giving continuation of her own desire.

The Long Walk stresses this psychic repetition of loss in its opening gambit: no one really knows why they participate in the Walk. What is absent from the lives of these young men that they willingly drag themselves through this traumatic experience? Is it glory? Fame? A fellow Walker advises, 'Plumb the unplumbed depths.' In response, *The Long Walk* interrogates the lacunae at the root of all human contests: 'The whole Walk seemed nothing but one looming question mark. He told himself that a thing like this must have some deep meaning.' When he passionately fondles a young woman in the crowd, and observes his resultant arousal, Garraty discovers that the answer has been from the beginning linked to sex (194, 54, 79). But what is it exactly about the woeful Walk that spurs his sexual fervour? If, as critics like Thomas Horan claim, dystopian fiction tends to 'find ethics in eroticism', and so it invests in 'the revolutionary potential inherent in sexual desire', Bachman's fiction problematises the correlation between satisfaction and revolution by presenting us with revolutionaries driven by dissatisfaction rather than fulfilment (19, 22). In other words, against a prominent tendency in dystopian fiction to couple erotic urges with moral regeneration, Bachman's young men are driven to disaffection. The missing object lures Walkers into disaffection by adopting myriad forms: Garraty recalls seeing his mother naked, 'hairy and cut open'; his closest friend nurses a scar, received from a woman refusing his advances, that provides a signal of his lover's absence: 'His hand had gone to the scar and was rubbing, rubbing, rubbing' (84, 106). Although they consciously pursue the Major's 'ultimate prize', the Walkers unconsciously maintain a void that cannot be filled because if they were to reclaim the missing object, they would cease walking and to cease walking, literally as well as figuratively, would be to cease living. Paradoxically, then, the boys must maintain their sense of loss in order to avoid losing.

To return to the missing object in a different guise, the boys later contemplate the Lacanian desire of the Other (another fundamental loss that orients their Walk). As Lacan posits that there is no desire that is not the desire of the Other, a central impetus for the Walk is a veiled call to find behind one's own desire the desire of the Other. For instance, the Walkers desire to win the game because the Crowd as well as the Major desire them to pine for this outcome. At the same time, upon seeing his mother and his girlfriend in the masses, Garraty realises that he is not their *objet a* and that they actually desire to win through him (and so his desire to win has actually been their desire all along). Slavoj Žižek condenses the conundrum: 'One should always bear in mind that the desire 'realized' (staged) in fantasy is not the subject's own but the *other's* desire' (*Plague* 9, author's emphasis). When Garraty comes to grips with his condition, he feels 'disappointment, the sense of loss', and he suddenly hates his girlfriend as well as his mother because their desire has kept him playing the Major's dreadful game (Bachman, *Long* 374, 343–6). The Crowd; the Major; the object of one's affection – satisfaction always exists somewhere else. This unceasing deferral trudges the boys along in their grotesque quest.

In its final tally, *The Long Walk* refers to the missing object – indeed, the death drive itself – quite directly: 'We want to die, that's why we're doing it' (179). Again, the novel ends with Garraty 'winning' the Walk, but as he crosses the threshold, he is not satisfied. Because there is no purpose in his existence without the Walk (or some alternative social structure that might facilitate his unfulfillable desires), he must keep walking. 'The subject does not want to be cured', McGowan posits, 'because it associates healing with the loss of its foundational loss, a prospect much more horrifying than the pain of the neurosis' (*Capitalism* 32). To experience genuine enjoyment, competitors in the political economy of the United States must admit that they are being driven to neither consensus nor cure. Similarly, *Roadwork* tracks a protagonist that like Garraty discovers a gaping hole at the core of his existence. He confronts his manager with a demand to know what it is that the manager wants out of his career, a question to which his manager enigmatically replies: 'I want what everyone wants' (105). The manager's answer reveals a key truth through omission: he provides a non-answer, a deferred resolution, an absence. For much of the novel, Bart wrings his hands at the futility of it all as it seems that he has been driven to sabotage his own happiness.

This unconscious drive manifests in Bart's interactions with two of the most complicated resources in the public imagination of the 1970s – oil and money. For context, in the 1970s, oil shortages and rampant financialisation intensify a central lack upon which the American Dream has been premised, thus highlighting the Lacanian undercurrent of America's political economy: an outward thirst for success (more petroleum! more wealth!) that veils a yearning for merciful failure (given the not-so-secret reality that gas is a rapidly fading resource and the prospect of wealth is flat-lining). In literal as well as symbolic ways, oil consumers continue to be driven by what is already gone. Bart becomes 'intimate' with oil when he decides to use it to blow up the roadwork; as he siphons the oil, he feels it, tastes it and gets truly acquainted with it for the first time, even though he has used it 'almost every day of his adult life'. Real as well as imagined barriers to energy consumption – including government restrictions on its use, amplified by the Carter administration's public service announcements – make Bart's hunger for oil ever more intense. When an official tells the American public to conserve energy, he responds by running his blender all night long. Bachman's book violently connects America's lack of oil to Bart's existential lack when, in the novel's finale, he quite literally merges with the absence that constitutes his psychic structure via his own combustion, delivered by tanks of gas that he rigs to explode.

Following the decision to remove the United States from the Bretton Woods agreement (1971–2), Bart similarly encounters money in a more intimate manner. He continues on his self-destructive course by going to the bank to withdraw a large sum of (physical) cash, even though 'a bank was a place where money was supposed to be like God, unseen and reverentially regarded' (175, 258). Much like oil, in the 1970s paper money, once 'sanctified and totemized', starts to grow increasingly invisible to the public eye: 'Money no longer has any foundations; it has literally represented nothing ever since the speculative economy . . . became brutally divorced from the "real economy"' (Dufour 163). Said another way, the floating currencies of the 1970s reveal their status as a missing object (that they always-already were), a missing object that propels the subject to labour and speculate with ever greater intensity. When Bart finally feels the money in his hand, he feels disappointed because he knows, even before entering the bank, that this missing object would have been better kept unseen. By familiarising himself with paper money at the dawn of the financial age, he enacts a sort of self-sabotage.

When he connects with the twin missing objects that increasingly fuel modern society through their privation (oil and paper money), Bart encounters a gap between his conscious desire and his unconscious drive. His experience helps Bachman's reader to acknowledge that contemporary notions of wealth and gas are structured in the collective imagination upon a fundamental lack, which is to say, they exist to be exchanged for something else, something that is not already there (like other commodities or physical propulsion). In a word, they are driven to be made absent again in perpetuity. And Bart's search for his life's purpose follows a similar circuit: to preserve the forward-motion of his own desires, he must evade satisfaction by stalking material totems that could only ever expose him to the futility of his endeavour, until he admits at last that his psychic investment in 'some destructive impulse . . . had been part of him all along'.[7] He realises that he initiated the loss of his job, his wife, even his beloved television set: 'In his dreams he committed suicide over and over.' He relives this traumatic loss at his core on an endless loop, by novel's end associating his death drive with the loss of his son, who was born 'with a built-in self-destruct' in the form of a brain tumour. Bart's climactic explosion is described like a tumour that metastasises: 'Life seemed only a preparation for hell' (138, 189, 113, 215). Deep within his psyche, Bachman's antihero seems programmed for recurring loss.

In sum, *Roadwork* evokes the *objet a* through numerous analogues – from oil to money to a deceased son to a demolished home. Furthermore, Bart encounters profound political losses (such as victims of the Kent State shooting, Robert Kennedy and Martin Luther King, Jr.) during his inquiry into what everyone truly wants. The text's answer: to lose a piece of oneself, again and again and again. Like America, a nation built upon an apparatus that requires an abiding lack (capitalism as well as democracy), Bart can only discover a degree of enjoyment by admitting the imperfect character of his own political economy. In one of his last acts, he contemplates a song by The Rolling Stones, 'You Can't Always Get What You Want'. He understands from hearing the song that he cannot get his son back any more than he can satisfy his urge for other missing objects but he also admits that this impossibility does not 'stop you from wanting it'. Once he accepts the constitutive division between his desire and his drive, he experiences a 'joyous delirium' (305, 296). McGowan observes, 'The recognition that we are not really pursuing pleasure frees us' (*Capitalism* 50). In Bachman's storyworld, the potency of a character's release from the pleasure principle proves to be tremendous: Bart's explosion, for instance, looks 'like a Saturn rocket . . . like a magic carpet' (Bachman, *Roadwork* 307). His eruptive last act defies description and words fail as the narrative metastasises into a string of insufficient metaphors – the explosion is *like* a rocket; the explosion is *like* a magic carpet. These fantastic referents (rockets, magic carpets) refuse stable definition, thereby launching the reader's imagination outward into the realm of the unknown. If he seeks a resolution to these burning desires through cure or consensus, Bachman's reader achieves only more loss, whereas – if the logic of the novel holds – Bart's spectacular disappearance should please the reader more than a conventional restoration of the character's quotidian life because it refuses to foresee any false return to contentment. *The Running Man* ends in equally spectacular fashion as Richards flies his escape plane into the Network's headquarters: 'The explosion was tremendous, lighting up the night like the wrath of God' (219). With each of Bachman's negative spectacles, another open-ended metaphor accompanies another loss during heightened moments in which the reader might typically expect some kind of reconciliation. At the close of his texts, Bachman's protagonists shed even their corporeal existence in the name of aligning themselves with their symptom, or more to the point, with their abiding lack.[8] By identifying with the absence that defines them, these characters immunise themselves to America's satisfaction/dissatisfaction matrix and, in the process, avoid being reduced at last to 'mainstream lunacy', or to a 'safe headline' in the local newspaper (*Roadwork* 294). Richards remarks, 'Say your name over two hundred times and discover you are no one' (*Running* 204). By identifying with the existential void, Bachman's characters become inseparable from the grand absence that constitutes their being.

To an extent, then, Bachman's misanthropes undermine a common perception that the self-destructive character of American politics can be attributed to malevolent authoritarians or the ignorant masses. Like McGowan, Mladen Dolar examines how self-sabotage occurs in the spheres of psychoanalysis as well as politics due to the fact that neither enterprise actually aims to achieve its advertised ends. According to Dolar, practitioners in these arenas unconsciously avoid total cure (analysts) as well as definitive consensus (politicians). Even if it was possible to achieve utopian results, such an achievement in psychoanalysis or politics would destroy their *raison d'être*, and therefore 'antagonism is the air' that practitioners must breathe. 'It is not unification and union . . . that is the basis of a political (or psychoanalytic) precept, but precisely its crack, its fissure, its impossibility, its untying that presents an opening for the political (or the psychoanalytical)' (19, 22). The unsatisfying conditions that ostensibly depoliticise Bachman's books – and, following all of the unpleasantness in these stories, who among us would continue to place their trust in organisations driven by self-sabotage? – in truth preserve a requisite sense of dissatisfaction that perpetuates political engagement. At this juncture, let us pause to recapitulate the thesis of the book: Bachman's death drive articulates the repression as well as the return of the political. While readers might respond by rejecting politics as doomed to fail, it is the (im)possibility of politics, in fact, that re-designates human beings as *zoon politikon* and empowers them to avoid becoming pawns to fascists. Still, Bachman's mode of winning-via-losing raises important concerns to be considered in what remains of the chapter. What is the reader to make of the uneasy alignment in Bachman's books between an unsavoury politics of pure negation, outlined in the first section, and the more redemptive Lacanian principles that I have outlined in this section? Should his reader embrace a merciful sense of failure? Refuse all political agendas? And, if trauma is an inevitable part of the human experience, what kind of politics (if any) could rehabilitate such a dispirited world?

Resignation or rehabilitation?

From one vantage point, many of the ideas covered in the previous sections on Bachman's Lacanian dissatisfaction align a bit too comfortably with neo-liberalism. We could indeed argue that Bachman's case for the death drive of American culture in the 1970s does precious little to resolve systemic crises and, at its worst, even disincentivises the activism that marginalised peoples desperately need. If we are not seeking a 'good society', and if we enjoy a lack of progress more than its achievement, is American politics just another woeful 'hang-up'? McGowan admits, 'Psychoanalytic theory never preaches, and it cannot help us to construct a better society' (*Enjoying* 285). If this is true, readers discover in psychoanalytic theory merely an affirmation of the cynicism that swells at the dawn of the twenty-first century, as Bachman *avec* Lacan conjoins with other insidious efforts to resign us to the notion that political action is futile and political subjects eternally impotent. Andrew Collier writes, 'Lacan's theory serves to normalize capitalist damage . . . this alienation is made so deep that nothing we can do by way of transforming human societies could alter it' (41). And yet, while Bachman's fiction stresses the complicity of Lacanian analysis in a broader movement to devalue the political, and while Bachman's texts do at times suggest submission to a world with 'less politics', Bachman *avec* Lacan ultimately preserves the potency of the political since, as we shall see, this pairing disenchants the subject of her dogged pursuit of cure or consensus and allows her, in turn, to realise the radical heart of democracy. In short, when read through Lacanian precepts, Bachman's books enable readers to reject the stasis of utopia as well as the neutrality of neo-liberalism in the name of prolonged unrest – the lifeblood of any democratic regime.

Yet we cannot proceed without unpacking the potential complacency of Bachman's books in the ascent of neo-liberal thought in America. Although, as McGowan claims, our daily acts of consumption appear to depend upon delusions of satisfaction accompanied by unconscious self-sabotage, the same may not be so readily said of the abstract 'spirit of capitalism' that has been present in public debates since the 1970s. The prevailing attitude towards capitalism is increasingly one of resignation, in which capitalists no longer promise (even superficially) to satisfy all of the individual's desires. Many capitalists now openly admit that their choice is merely the best of bad options. Recycling Fredric Jameson's well-known dictum, Mark Fisher describes 'the widespread sense that not only is capitalism the only viable political and economic system, but also that it is now impossible even to *imagine* a coherent alternative' (*Capitalist* 2, author's emphasis). According to Fisher, neo-liberal thought sours the rose-tinted view of capitalism from the mid-twentieth century by shifting the goalposts from a relentless need to win to a basic struggle to survive. Bachman's prototypical subjects as a result 'feel like nothing: negated, denied, disenfranchised'. Optimism no longer plays even a token role in their psychic processes: 'The abandonment of the burdens of history and of truth, a self-abandonment, is intoxicating in the way one drowns one's sorrows. Cynicism liberates the modern individual from the burdens of taking responsibility for transforming society' (J. D. Taylor 14, 104). Bachman's labourers are apparently 'well-adjusted' to the neo-liberal mould because, if 'real enjoyment is in the barrier to progress', they might as well embrace 'collective fatalism and a sigh' (106). These sighs of release, which will sound to some ears like a kind of forfeiture, prompt readers to ask why they should not give up activism, organisation or any commitment to the bettering of society and simply enjoy their lack. Fewer social safety nets; greater vulnerability; less relational baggage due to a decrease in solidarity – under neo-liberalism, the subject can finally cast aside her inconsequential quest for social improvement and erase residual fixations from the failed experiments of the 1960s. For certain readers, Bachman's Lacanian sensibility lionises a familiar brand of anti-politics in which we assume the end of 'grandiose political projects' (Stavrakakis 99). Correspondingly, it remains difficult to find much breathing room between Lacanian disenchantment and capitalist realism (a genre that reflects an extensive loss of optimism in the capacity of capitalism to improve living conditions). Thoroughly chastened, Bachman's characters strip 'the world of sentimental illusions and (see) it for "what it really is"' (Fisher, *Capitalist* 11). His novels track characters as they come to terms with capitalist dissatisfaction as their default mode of being.

From this standpoint, the American death drive that manifests in Bachman's narratives promotes acquiescence to the harsh actualities of the current situation: 'The hope that . . . suffering could be eliminated easily [is] painted as naïve Utopianism' (Fisher, *Capitalist* 16). Bachman's disenfranchised individuals learn how promises made by politicians invariably fall short of healing their existential imperfection. When Garraty encounters the unavoidable rift between his desires and the American death drive, for example, he reaches out for 'an end to the agony of the movement', exclaiming in the process: 'To hell with having my every heart's desire' (Bachman, *Long* 220, 362). Elsewhere, Richards rejects a comfortable place in the upper echelon by accepting in its place a fundamental lack at the centre of the national psyche: 'Middle and upper-middle class citizens . . . looked oddly incomplete, like [. . .] a jigsaw puzzle with a minor piece missing' (*Running* 152). None of Bachman's anti-heroes do much to protest British Prime Minister Margaret Thatcher's proclamation that There is No Alternative to the status quo (with the salient exception, of course, of their own self-destruction).

Bachman's novels suggest that the cure for a condition in which winning remains unimaginable is neither enhanced equality nor alternative rules for the game; instead, these fatalists (or, if we prefer, realists) respond to the folly of cure/consensus by turning back upon the self. Patrick McAleer comments, 'The suggested social necessity [of] self-interest and resilience in King's fiction prompts citizens to abandon any endeavor that reaches beyond the individual' (1222). Borrowing again from the neo-liberal playbook, Bachman's social order does not necessitate improved institutional structures, instead demanding innovative coping strategies from the individual. If political systems cannot satisfy everyone, the impetus must be placed squarely upon the subject's shoulders to adjust himself. This inflated individualism suggests that one's trauma must be contained – and capitalised upon – through nascent strategies of self-discipline. Anna McCarthy interrogates how 'the ineffable, self-annihilating experience of trauma' is, in these ways, transposed by neo-liberals into self-governance (21). Because the imagined cure is not activism on behalf of the group but myopic self-improvement, and because it ignores the broader community as well as future generations by focusing intently upon the self, we might read Bachman *avec* Lacan as codifying dissatisfaction for disadvantaged peoples. This forfeiture reflects a relative indifference to lived material disparities by critics that remain comfortable in their anti-political torpor. Although theoretically consistent, their willingness to 'subtract the illusion of the good' may be too bloodless to be tolerated by any audience invested in the achievable advance of social justice initiatives.

Yet Lacanian readers might interject that Bachman's books do not merely reveal a tendency towards resignation; their contrasting outlook, in fact, engenders a form of rehabilitation. One of the pressing concerns of our contemporary political moment is the question of how, if lack is truly stitched into the fabric of our lives, American society might be rearranged to minimise distress. According to Dominiek Hoens, Lacanian analysis (and, by proxy, Bachman's fiction) renews the potency of political engagement in three important ways. First, it deflates utopian illusions that are peddled by politicians acting in bad faith and accentuates the alienation demanded of any healthy democracy (consider, for example, the inevitable distance between representative and represented that cannot be overcome by magical thinking). Secondly, Bachman *avec* Lacan reminds citizens that power is finite, and that the 'place of power' remains eternally up for grabs. Finally, because subjects with divergent interests will never stop disrupting hegemony via novel forms of resistance, Bachman's work exposes the fallacy of terminal Truth and, as such, opens social arrangements to constant re-negotiation. In the endmost score, Bachman's protagonists must be interpreted as political by nature.

According to Yannis Stavrakakis, Lacanian analysis also inspires the return to a more salubrious version of democracy because democracy is based 'on the fact that no symbolic social construct can ever claim to master the impossible real'. That is, democracy endures against any singular common good by drawing upon vital divisions, upholding an impulse to fracture and securing the balm of imperfection against the threat of totalitarian enclosure (120, 132). We can read Bachman's universe not as promoting a callous indifference but as preaching an 'ethics of disharmony', endlessly re-politicising itself and actively juxtaposing what seems possible with what has been (erroneously) foreclosed as inconceivable. In his more Lacanian moments, Fisher argues that 'one strategy against capitalist realism could involve invoking the Real[s] underlying the reality that capitalism presents to us' (*Capitalist* 18). In other words, beneath illusory claims of hyper-competition advanced in the United States, we start to glimpse an underlying lacuna. This crucial recognition empowers us to debunk the many fallacies that bombard us on a daily basis. Through exposure to the aching wounds of Bachman's characters, his reader might be reminded of an infantilism inherent to all citizens: 'Actually existing citizenship . . . is an experience marked by the untidiness of irresolvable pain, the unspeakable position of helplessness and abjection' (McCarthy 37). Although Bachman's protagonists always appear to 'lose', readers need not respond by wondering how the subject could learn to 'win'; rather, they might do as his books suggest and re-define the misleading binary of 'winning' and 'losing'.

Once we acknowledge the American death drive, we need not rush to repress this new-found knowledge by 'rehabilitating' ourselves through Spartan self-governance. Quite the opposite: Bachman's novels provide an opportunity, if we are willing to take it, to imagine rehabilitative strategies that are less destructive, less distracted and less delusional, arrangements that might genuinely rehabilitate Garraty, Bart or Richards (not in the sense of cure or consensus, but in the sense of equipping citizens to come to terms with the hardships that many of us will assuredly continue to face). And so, while these texts unveil how the psychic distress of the 1970s has been obsessively exploited in the name of re-enforcing a politics of pure negation that benefits only the most powerful individuals in society, Bachman *avec* Lacan encourages us to re-democratise American life because 'the aim of psychoanalysis – to be able to deal with castration as a lack of being that gets located and operative . . . coincides with the kind of political subject democracy needs' (Hoens 107). As we shall see in the chapters to follow, how King's later novels adjust – or fail to adjust – to the death drive in Bachman's books reveals a great deal about the politics of King's fiction as a whole.

3

King's Cars and the Grinding Gears of Post-Fordism

STEPHEN KING HAS written several stories to date that feature possessed automobiles.[1] In *Christine* (1983), a car destroys Arnie Cunningham by convincing him to stay in his hometown rather than attend college; in *From a Buick 8* (2002), a car opens a gateway to an unknown dimension and instigates catharsis for Ned Wilcox in the wake of his father's death. Few scholars have discussed in detail how King sets both of these books in the twilight of the 1970s, a moment in American history that he portrays as blighted with corrosive (but inevitable) economic disturbances. In a word, *Christine* and *From a Buick 8* affirms British Prime Minister Margaret Thatcher's infamous mantra that There Is No Alternative to late capitalism by representing this larger cultural shift – although never wholly laudable due to its radical disruption of the lives of protagonists – as a regrettable necessity.[2] That is, the horrors associated with these possessed vehicles stem from an inability to age, to evolve, to 'keep up with the times' and so these novels expose how King's supposed criticism of the political economy actually supports several of its central tenets (a self-sabotage that renders quite literal the death drive of the Bachman books considered in the previous chapter). While the nightmares experienced by Arnie and Ned scream out for deceleration, King's car fables unwittingly accelerate the upheaval.

This chapter traverses a period commonly read through the lens of post-Fordism. Particularly relevant to the chapter's analysis due to its automotive connotations, this transitional era involves a pivot away from mass production that David Harvey describes as 'a shift from Fordism to . . . a "flexible" regime of accumulation' (*Condition* 124). Stuart Hall fleshes out a definition for us:

> A shift to the new 'information technologies'; more flexible, decentralized forms of labour process and work organization; decline in the old manufacturing base . . . the hiving-off or contracting-out of functions and services . . . a decline in the proportion of the skilled, male, manual working class, the rise of the service and white-collar classes and the 'feminization' of the workforce. ('Brave' 24)

Following 1979, previous modes of managerialism must adapt to keep up with competition on a global scale, as the demand for service workers and the explosion of the financial sector together displace the heady coordination between Fordist corporations and Keynesian governments.[3] The importance of the American car in this larger transmutation – its production, its reception, its gestures at mobility (in every sense of the term) – cannot be overstated: 'Motor cars, from which the age of Fordism derived its name, with its multiple variations on every model and market specialization . . . [are] at the leading edge of post-Fordism' (Hall, 'Brave' 24). King's eerie cars represent the departure of a manufacturing base from Arnie's hometown of Libertyville and the abject poverty left in its wake.[4] This chapter explores how the compulsions of financial capitalism surge through these haunted vehicles and decouple them from their Fordist origins.

At the same time, King's texts evoke a bygone era. Characters move quietly among shuttered monuments while a wind blows through Christine's frame 'like a factory whistle'. In contrast to the magical capriciousness of the cars themselves, the abject stasis of the labour force weaves in and out of King's narratives: a sign of what has been lost that eventually proves itself to be better left buried in the graveyard of history. For instance, the former owner of Christine, Roland LeBay (a card-carrying member of the lumpen proletariat), articulates the indignation of a working class forgotten amidst the reveries of financialisation when, in one bitter aside, he recalls how Dwight Eisenhower predicted 'a future of labor and management marching harmoniously into the future together' (King, *Christine* 253, 262). Relics of rapidly fading industries, the antithesis of Eisenhower's maudlin vision, plague *Christine*: 'The spectral economy continues to be haunted by the real economy, which hides but does not vanish' (M. Taylor 180). In a related vein, King's novels stress America's troubling dependency upon foreign oil, a dark underside to the nation's petroculture.[5] Following the Iranian revolution of 1979 and the numerous embargoes of the preceding decade, King's mysterious Buick materialises at a dying gas station that will soon be destroyed by OPEC. Before vanishing, the shadowy owner of the Buick declares: 'Oil's fine' (a refrain repeated throughout the novel). Of course, the oil is definitively not fine, as its shortage fuels a number of ongoing international crises. The bookends of *From a Buick 8* (1979–2001) highlight a specific window between the oil embargoes of the 1970s and the attacks of 9/11, a period that witnesses constant struggle over oil in the United States: how to increase access, how to control cost, and so forth. King's car stories exorcise images of an unpalatable post-industrial wasteland – the decay of America's odious petroculture; the ghostly shadows of a decimated workforce – to lubricate the reader's gradual shift into acceptance of (or resignation to) the imminent condition of post-Fordism.

To enact this uneven relay, King's accounts of haunted automobiles vocally reject what they consider to be outmoded political attitudes. They depict old-school liberals of the Fordist-Keynesian variety as hyperpossessive. Set in the ironically named Libertyville, where the intelligentsia has laid its poisonous roots, *Christine* presents Arnie's 'progressive' mother as a shrew that castrates her family, another one of the 'academic pseudo-liberals, the kind that Stephen King seems to despise' (Reino 86).[6] She is 'cold, semi-aristocratic' and 'for all [her] liberal thinking . . . [she] pretty much manage[s] Arnie'.[7] By replicating this maternal management in its monstrous machine, *Christine* denigrates the legacy of Fordism/Keynesianism as antiquated (at best). At the same time, as these novels lampoon 'liberals' like Arnie's parents, they stereotype 'conservatives' as cartoon characters that stifle the vital element of uncertainty that is simultaneously being romanticised by an increasingly influential financial sector. *Christine* treats Republican bankers as analogous to foolish teenagers that 'talk about change constantly and believe in [their] heart that it never really happens' (18–19, 132). Much like his narrow-minded liberals, King's conservatives cling to a Fordist-Keynesian capacity to dictate economic outcomes when, for example, a character stands against the radical change of these cars and then remarks that her obstinacy makes her 'feel like a Republican' (*From a Buick* 309). These narratives challenge the categories of Right and Left by presenting them to be as hopelessly nostalgic as King's outdated cars. At one point, *Christine* mentions a storm that knocks a tree down into the tax assessor's office ('a good place for it, many said'), and a politician shows up at the police station in *From a Buick 8* for a photo op, only to be mocked for his excessive showmanship (*Christine* 336). King's offensive against politicians of all stripes reveals the thesis of his car stories, indeed, of his fiction as a whole: although financialisation may be a bumpy ride, public officials should not be trusted behind the wheel.

To compensate for disruptions in the so-called normal order of things, King's works personalise, which is to say, de-politicise the ongoing process of financialisation. *Christine*'s Dennis accepts his loss of control as a part of 'growing up', while *From a Buick 8*'s Ned embraces heightened unpredictability as a method with which to deal with the untimely death of his father. In this way, *Christine* and *From a Buick 8* understand what has been called the New Economy as a sort of fait accompli. As they accelerate the devastation to reach a tragic endpoint, King's narratives become (unconsciously) complicit within a pattern of cultural dismantlement orchestrated by the conductors of high finance. Steven Shaviro writes of the subject living in this era: 'There is nothing that he can do except "[give] himself up to the snarl of the engine" . . . transgression is the actual motor of capitalism expansion today: the way that it renews itself in orgies of "creative destruction"' (24, 32). In form as well as content, then, *Christine* and *From a Buick 8* release us from the near constant application of the brakes being applied by Fordist-Keynesian supervisors. Although King's texts flirt with a political critique of post-Fordism – a critique with which readers might respond to the disturbing loss of social stability in places like Libertyville – King's stories nonetheless merge into the turbulent highways of capitalism, and (in a related sense) into what they posit to be the undisputable plot of human development. Said another way, King's car novels comprehend the metamorphosis of the American economy in the late 1970s and early 1980s as 'natural' by tracking autonomous vehicles alongside the bodily transformations of their pubescent protagonists. Gesturing at a shallow form of resistance to post-Fordism, King's portrayal of the economy's fantastic features falls flat in interrelated ways: 1) by evoking disaggregation in a manner that actually sustains the tenets of financialisation, and 2) by normalising post-Fordism as if it was a customary aspect of human maturation.

Accelerating profits

King's protean automobiles aim to ease the transformation of the physical as well as psychical presence of the all-American car. Once more, these stories arrive at the intersection of cataclysmic forces that converge in the year 1979: a year in which Lee Iacocca takes over Chrysler (a power grab that would fundamentally alter the trajectory of the car industry) and the Federal Reserve raises interest rates to set the stage for supply-side economics.[8] Consequently, capital migrates as General Motors and Chrysler divert their attention from tinkering with the assembly line to expanding dramatically the reach of consumer financing.[9] 'General Motors is not so much in the Fordist business of producing cars anymore; rather, GM is in the post-Fordist business of servicing cars (which is to say, financing and insuring them)' (Nealon, *Foucault* 60). Symptomatic of this altered agenda, King's vehicles exceed the conceptual forms that first fostered their mass production.[10] The most American of icons becomes an ageing reference point against which King's readers are asked to imagine something far less tangible. Capital unnervingly outpaces one of its primary fetishes.[11]

According to Paul Gilroy, the history of the American automobile doubles as a history of the pandemonium that accompanies the turn into late capitalism: '[Cars] are the ur commodity . . . [they] help to periodize our encounters with capitalism as it moves into and leaves its industrial phase' ('Driving' 89). The fate of the American automobile signals an increasingly credit-driven economy. Specifically, in the second half of the twentieth century, practitioners of Sloanism, named after the former president of General Motors (Alfred Sloan), start to believe that the primary object of the corporation is 'to make money, not just to make motor cars' (Sloan 64). Because Sloanism preaches flexible production under a decentralised management schema, GM abandons the practice of putting engineers or manufacturers in leadership positions in favour of appointing people with financial expertise – and little to no knowledge about automobiles. 'The automotive industry . . . functions entirely upon credit mechanisms (installments, leasing, etc.), so that the problems of General Motors have just as much to do with the production of cars as, if not above all . . . its branch specializing in consumer credit' (Marazzi 27). As a result, predatory lenders target vulnerable individuals in search of a vehicle to profit on late payment penalties, using title loans to attract desperate clientele that do not have the luxury of questioning usurious interest rates.[12] Simply put, following the seismic quakes of 1979, major car companies start to appear uncanny: familiar to American audiences, yet increasingly difficult for the layperson to wrap their mind around. As behemoth companies like Ford struggle to survive in a hostile world of price wars and takeovers, their destination is no longer the production of better machines, but short-range maximisation in the stock market. 'Industrial companies were adapting to the norms being set by . . . the darlings of the Street' (Halberstam 234). In King's hands, the American car, an avatar for financialisation mired in outdated Fordist iconography, serves as a floating signifier that thinly veils gaping absences in American life – capital flight; the illusory nature of mobility; the disconnected quality of capital unshackled from national obligations.[13] As a result, the all-American car becomes a totem of – what? Exactly where does its value now reside?

Christine only starts to suggest the bewildering spectres of high finance. At the dawn of Reagan administration – New Year's Eve, to be precise, at the doorway between 1979 and 1980 – Dennis takes a disorienting ride with Arnie that resembles Charles Dickens's *Christmas Carol* on speed: 'If there was a logical progression of events, it is lost to me now . . . a mad funhouse world' (390–1). Foreshadowing the mercurial Buick to come, Christine generates radically heightened feelings as change becomes an end in itself. Nevertheless, in *Christine* a scrap of genuine mobility endures because its titular vehicle can still move effectively in the material world: it can pass between gentrified and poverty-stricken neighbourhoods and it can accelerate as well as decelerate, depending on the circumstances. King's titular vehicle is upsetting, certainly, but it remains more solidly grounded in the iconography of a massive industry that, as of 1983, continued to loom large in the American imagination. Published in 2002, *From a Buick 8* quite literally arrives from a different dimension. Less of an automobile in the traditional sense, the Buick much more closely resembles a computer as it sits stationary in the police barracks, shifting the reader's attention with little friction between completely distant universes. A post-Fordist monstrosity, the Buick births a string of eccentricities from its trunk, but offers no concrete answers as to what exactly it will manufacture next. Whereas *Christine* gestures at struggles between social groups (even, albeit feebly, between classes), *From a Buick 8* focuses exclusively upon transportation of the most intense variety, upon the dizziness of something like a digital highway, and so the novel lacks any sign of the real-world crisis in Libertyville. Rather, it engenders an immobile storyworld fogged in by delusions of spectacular change.[14]

Birthed alongside financial inventions like derivative markets, King's Buick thus intensifies the eerie abstractions of *Christine*. By the time of *From a Buick 8*, capital evokes weirder sensations, summoning oddities from thin air and forcing readers to ask difficult questions about the very notion of value itself.[15] Mark C. Taylor writes, 'Playing with such phantoms and specters, traders in the 1980s and 1990s turn the art of finance into the magic of creation *ex nihilo* . . . to achieve the even more ancient dream of creation *ex nihilo* by making something (money, capital) out of nothing' (163). Ramping up the dread of Christine, King's Buick not only gestures at an impending loss of referentiality, it fabricates things out of nothing and, of equal significance, nothing out of things. That is, *From a Buick 8* concerns itself with a once-recognisable referent shorn of earlier associations as it explodes into a dizzying spectacle. In real-world terms, this transposition into pure pageantry parallels nascent pressures upon car corporations to pay 'much greater attention to quick-changing fashions and the mobilization of all the artifices of need inducement and cultural transformation that this implies . . . the ferment, instability, and fleeting qualities of a postmodern aesthetic that celebrates difference, ephemerality, spectacle' (Harvey, *Condition* 156). With neither clear beginning nor identifiable end, the machinations of the Buick's bizarre assembly line, and the political economy for which it acts as a metaphor, remain an utter mystery. It hurries forth Marx's night terror of 'an infinitely productive self-reflexive loop operating like a perpetual motion machine' (M. Taylor 259).

In short, King's possessed vehicle points to an accelerating economy with less definitive causes and effects. The Buick lacks the essential components to run: its controls are all 'stage-dressing'; its exhaust system is made entirely of glass. When the owner of the car appears to wash up on the shore of the nearby river, even his body turns out to be a garbage can, mere plastic regurgitated by late capitalist machinery (*From a Buick* 35–41, 59, 100). If under Fordism the American automobile marked the strength of technocracy, thanks to its plodding progression from producer to product to possession, King's Buick disassociates itself from traditional circuits of meaning-making. These car stories – each more acute than the last – rely upon the empty signifiers of an emerging information economy in which consumers are put to work assembling the *idea* of the automobile (a task accompanied by fewer hands-on manufacturing jobs for American workers). This dramatic restructuring weaves its way through popular perceptions of the car in part due to the rise of tie-in opportunities that alter the consumer's understanding of automotive iconography. In effect, automotive corporations wheel themselves from production company to marketing firm (Cray 353, 479–80). Given the rapid expansion of image-based industries, motor cars today are far more visibly assembled by customers labouring over media representations than by human beings working on a line.

In this brave new world, according to Mark Fisher, 'Capitalism [reveals itself to be] very much like The Thing in John Carpenter's film of the same name: a monstrous, infinitely plastic entity, capable of metabolizing and absorbing anything' (*Capitalist* 6). When profit is no longer to be found on factory floors, corporate America extracts it through predatory loans. In place of Fordist schematics, King's car stories likewise elicit supernatural debt/credit. The naive owners of King's cars invest everything in the upkeep of their most prized possessions: *From a Buick 8* implies that Ned's father loses his life due to his excessive protection of the car; *Christine*'s Archie sacrifices his soul to restore his beloved vehicle. These haunted automobiles therefore offer a deranged line of debt/credit that encourages young men to invest without an adequate source of income and, by so doing, slowly ruin their over-extended owners (or, more accurately, renters).

Churning out change with dreadful regularity, King's car stories evoke repressed aspects of post-Fordism that can best be described with the word weird. In *Christine* and *From a Buick 8*, a schism between the Fordist artefact (the car) and the unimaginable post-Fordist energies at work (capital on the move) leaves a distinctly weird impression. According to Fisher, weirdness appears at the edge of the familiar: 'An egress between this world and others . . . an *interplay*, an exchange, a confrontation' (*Weird* 19, author's emphasis). King's automotive horrors illustrate the utter weirdness of late capitalism by depicting vehicles that exist at an interstice of fading orders and worlds-yet-to-come: 'We glimpse that place where our familiar universe stops and the real blackness begins.' For example, in *From a Buick 8* an alien creature is thrust into Ned's sphere and a police officer is sent into the alien's realm, a dismal exchange that forces the troop to imagine what it would be like to enter a completely foreign environment. In the aftermath, an officer feels as though the troop stands at the precipice of 'some vast change' (73, 285). *Pace* Fisher, King's car stories portray an accelerated economy on the verge of transforming American culture into something else entirely.

Auto-deconstruct

Precisely because these stories appear to do the invaluable work of indexing contemporary mutations in the American economy, it is important for readers to pump the brakes and note that, in their rush to undermine stagnant social conventions and promote ever greater fluidity, King's texts unwittingly uphold some of the tenets of financialisation that are eating away at their fictional worlds. In truth, King's cars as well as their chronicles are less a sign of ironic distance than the (unconscious) acceleration of financial capitalism. If the previous section seems to suggest that the political critique of post-Fordism is alive and well, we must now take a detour because, in fact, the excesses of King's automotive terrors are less counter-cultural than they may initially appear. The ways in which these novels break down America's decaying petroculture as well as its festering industrial narratives do not push readers to imagine a different system; rather, they complement the alterations being made by Wall Street to preserve, and then extend, an ongoing imbalance of power.[16] Although it may feel redemptive for readers to track the form of zombie economics that replaces the ghouls of Fordism, an underlying monstrosity persists. The faux transgressions of King's cars – their persistent negation of an established order – wind up funnelling fuel into the snarling engines of post-Fordist America.

To illustrate this oversight, King's car stories may be considered alongside the accelerationist movement that took shape during this time: a loose assemblage of artists and philosophers including Gilles Deleuze, Nick Land and the Italian Autonomists (most notably, Michael Hardt and Antonio Negri). Accelerationists contend that we cannot hope to stop capitalism, or reverse its trajectory, and we must instead accelerate its demise. 'The only way out is through', Shaviro observes. 'In fully expressing the potentialities of capitalism, we will be able to exhaust it' (2–3). By exacerbating the drift into financialisation, *Christine* and *From a Buick 8* might aid us in imagining the impending collapse of late capitalism. These novels habituate a widespread disavowal of social structures, a disavowal made popular in the years following 1979, by dousing the intelligentsia with vitriolic insults – lame psychologists cannot imagine 'a language that's not their language'; scientists are repudiated for flying too close to the sun, a mistake that resulted in the atomic bomb (King, *From a Buick* 244, 167, 304). Of note, King's automotive narratives disassemble even the frameworks required for storytelling:

'If there's a formula . . . I don't see it.' Ned's nearly fatal flaw remains his demand that the 'authentic' tale of his father's death be told because he obsesses over the secret of the Buick. But when the unknown does adopt a form, due to the fact that 'we had to see it as *something*', this form offers a mere placeholder (198, 150; author's emphasis). Whereas Fordism advocates diligent calibration in the name of social betterment, King's post-Fordist stories deconstruct all efforts to impose a plot. When read in this fashion, we can begin to spot the tentacles of neo-liberalism crawling through King's storyworlds.

In parallel with the accelerationists, King's car novels defy Fordist-Keynesian mastery by promoting auto-deconstruction (a critical mode of reading that ceaselessly challenges textual authority): 'The Buick wasn't about what you know but what you didn't.' To underscore the anti-mastery that King's stories promote, Ned works as a dispatcher that must read between the lines to make meaning out of ideas that are not communicated directly. In addition, *From a Buick 8* closes with a discussion of obituaries in which an entire person's life is suggested by an assortment of words, a dissatisfying arrangement that prompts Ned to live without a sense of control over everything that happens to him: 'The lesson was . . . in the letting go . . . The world rarely finishes its conversations' (94, 307–13). Upon realising that no narrative could ever fulfil his demand to possess the whole Truth, he radically revises his outlook, and so King's tale adopts many 'surface elements familiar from American postmodernist fiction' (Sears 29). Most visibly, King's auto-deconstruction complicates nostalgic treatments of the 1950s, like when Frank Sinatra's hit song 'My Way' plays on the radio and listeners are dismayed by its insipid lyrics because they cannot make sense of Sinatra's over-confidence. When King's fiction makes hay by stressing elusiveness at odds with fixed meaning, it inadvertently complies with the voguish cultural demands of financialisation. In response, it is rather easy for readers to confuse gaps in the master's knowledge that open escape routes for the slave with gaps in knowledge required by a turbulent financial marketplace that wishes to remain unregulated. To accept King's car stories as an unproblematic critique of toxic nostalgia is to miss their culpability in promoting the era's economic remodel.[17]

King's accelerationist fiction maintains a complicated relationship with the economic machinations of the late twentieth century as these automotive tales reveal a crucial overlap between postmodern aesthetics and the ascent of supply side economics. Christopher Norris writes, 'It would be idle to pretend that deconstruction has not been put to . . . ideologically complicitous uses' (167).[18] The open-endedness of King's automobiles – their 'non-beginnings'; their 'ghostly inscriptions' – can thus be read as supplements of the speculative flights of high finance (Sears 10, 16).[19] Despite posturing to the contrary, King's post-Fordist texts promote an interpretive model that remains very much a part of the cultural apparatus under scrutiny.[20] On this point, I quote Jeffrey Nealon at length:

> It's becoming increasingly unhelpful to replay the drama that posits a repressive, normative 'stasis or essentialism' that can be outflanked only by some form of more or less liberating, socially constructed 'fluid openness'. At this point, we'd have to admit that privatized finance capital has all but obliterated the usefulness of this distinction: to insist on the hybridity and fluidity of X or Y *is* the mantra of transnational capital – whose normative state is the constant reconstitution of 'value' – so it can hardly function unproblematically as a bulwark against that logic. (*Post-Postmodernism*, 20–1, author's emphasis)

In a word, by inviting readers to opt for creative chaos over nostalgia, King's car stories cater to the very sensibilities against which they might otherwise serve as a bulwark.[21] To achieve greater unguardedness to the unknown, an outlook required for patient participants in the mercurial marketplace these novels (unconsciously) affirm the principles of financial capital. Thanks to their willingness to re-fashion everything, King's texts inject a shot of literary nitrous into the underlying spread of financialisation.

In response, critics of accelerationism help us to spot the trap into which King's car stories, and many other fictions from the period, tend to fall. 'We cannot hope to *negate* capitalism', these critics remind us, 'because capitalism itself already mobilizes a far greater negativity than anything we could possibly mount against it' (Shaviro 45, author's emphasis). King's readers experience acceleration within the cultural sphere in parallel with their experience of the period's economic mayhem and so, dizzying though they may be, *Christine* and *From a Buick 8* screech to a halt at the same dead-end: a world that lacks any fixed sense of value. By embracing a trendy propulsion to dismantle all regulative structures (be they material or immaterial), King's car stories conform to the demands of their particular time and place.[22]

Decelerating politics

In sum, *Christine* and *From a Buick 8* normalise the ongoing volatility of post-Fordism by perpetuating a denial of mastery (a denial inspired, to a not insignificant degree, by the rhetoric of prominent financiers). To make all of this acceleration less nausea-inducing, King's automotive tales utilise the stationary reference point of a boy's coming-of-age that is doubtless 'fast' for the likes of Arnie's mother but otherwise pedestrian. These works develop a biological analogy that treats the deconstructive impulses of post-Fordism as a *natural* extension of human development. Unlike the reactive LeBay, the precariat ('precarious proletariat') in King's fiction must come to accept that Fordist-Keynesian days are long gone. To facilitate this acceptance, King's car novels dwell upon detectives in pursuit of answers to unanswerable questions as they learn to let go of their ambition to dictate outcomes: 'I unfocused my eyes and let my mind drift away', says one chastened character; another character reports that innocence always dies and so he should be able to 'deal with' uncertainty (*From a Buick* 23, 350; *Christine* 470). The over-arching process of 'letting go' transcodes economic imperatives of the era into cultural expression. 'To function effectively as a component of just-in-time production', Fisher argues, 'You must develop a capacity to respond to unforeseen events' (*Capitalist* 34). Meanwhile, in contrast, LeBay refuses to prepare for these ever-fluctuating circumstances, and he will neither release his hold over Christine nor go quietly into that good night. Although the novel decries the information workers that replace manufacturers in Libertyville (such as Archie's 'egg head' parents), exiled workers like LeBay are demonstrably the novel's more devastating source of evil. The villain of *Christine* is not economic change in-and-of itself, then, but figures like LeBay that stifle industrial change by refusing to get out of the way and attempting to reverse the nation's odometer. Paul Virilio captures the argument: 'Stasis is death, the general law of the world' (89).

King's car novels cast dispersions on dispossessed caricatures like LeBay by depicting the transformation of places like Libertyville as an unavoidable phenomenon and then assuming any subsequent political resistance to be 'unnatural'. *From A Buick 8* neatly sheathes the Buick into a comprehensive plot when a character sports a prominent bumper sticker: 'My Karma Ran Over My Dogma.' The novel uses the idea of karma to synthesise post-Fordist cultural and spiritual mutability into an immovable force that supersedes human interference. In effect, the text smooths out the unpredictable ruptures of post-Fordism into 'variations on the same theme' (303, 298). *Christine*, too, displays the karmic connection between Arnie and his car when, in a vivid nightmare, the young man starts to resemble a Buddha (127). With its sweeping gestures at Buddhism, King's tales of haunted vehicles imagine economic variability to be part and parcel of a coherent metaphysical whole. In support of this broad theme of anti-mastery, which offers a tacit endorsement of the era's economic volatility, these texts also repeatedly reference Prince Hamlet as an existential constant: Ned enters 'Hamlet age', while Dennis starts 'to feel like Prince Hamlet, delaying' (*From a Buick* 15, *Christine* 408). Like the Buddha, Shakespeare's prototype provides these car stories with a template to contain the trauma associated with coming-of-age – a template that, in this case, fits parts of the possessed vehicles into a ready-made Oedipal chassis.

This Oedipal chassis lends support to a post-Fordist restructuring in which the American automotive industry moves from manufacturing motor cars to manufacturing drivers. In particular, *Christine* and *From a Buick 8* follow a relay from under the hood of the car to under the hood of the human: 'In post-Fordism . . . capital follows you when you dream . . . as production and distribution are restructured, so are nervous systems' (Fisher, *Capitalist* 34). That is, when money can no longer be derived from the hands of the worker, the system must yield its profits from the worker's body. The metamorphosis of King's automobiles expands steadily into the corporeal form of its renters (a phenomenon known as 'biocapitalism' that King takes up again in novels like *Firestarter* [1980] and the 1996 release, *Rose Madder*, considered at length in later chapters). Consequently, King's reader spends more time attending to the 'emotional work' of Arnic and Ned, to the management of their teenage angst, than to the manual labour that these characters conduct upon their cars (Phipps 9–11). If the status of the American automobile once offered a barometer for the state of the national economy, the car owner's body now has a similar function as we witness a significant reversal: '[Arnie] serves the car's needs instead of the opposite' (Egan 152). In this brave new world, a disparate 'body shop' emerges.

With eyes firmly trained on 'evolving' teenage bodies, King's novels obsess over psychoanalytical and anatomical foundations to social problems instead of attending to economic realities. When it comes to cars, King's focus has arguably been there from the beginning: 'Cars were less about transformation in the public imagination than they were about pure pleasure, excitement, and sex' (DeWitt 38). *Christine* presents the vehicle as a fetish to compensate for losses experienced by a pubescent Arnie, including his ongoing separation from his mother.[23] In an accelerationist fashion, the car stories inscribe the tumult of post-Fordism into physical and psychical DNA, thus rendering post-Fordist fluidity synonymous with a teenager's hormonal imbalance: 'The mind is a powerful and often unreliable machine' (*From a Buick* 61). The characters in *From a Buick 8* – a text that focuses extensively upon the psychology of grief – struggle to piece their lives back together by transitioning from what is lost (a lacuna that marks where Ned's father used to be) to what is found (a tale that they are trying to tell about their grief). The son must cope with 'growing pains' that are unsavoury but necessary parts of any successful life. By filtering economic and technological mutations through an imaginary teenage physique/psyche, King's car novels chalk the shift away from Fordism up to inevitable human maturation. This concession decelerates the emotional overdrive felt by displaced labourers like LeBay and, in turn, depoliticises potential responses to the mayhem that ensues.

From a Buick 8 employs another stationary reference point to calm the reader's acute motion sickness: the militarised state. To resign oneself to the sickening acceleration of post-Fordism, the text posits that readers should respect managers of a different ilk than the Libertyville intelligentsia. King's car stories borrow a page from the playbook of policymakers during this era by ostensibly refusing mastery, in part (as we discussed in the previous section) by exploiting the counter-cultural strains of postmodern fiction, and also by stripping the state down to its barest martial functions. Because its officers veto democratic engagement, the police unit seems to be the only logical choice to monitor the mysterious Buick: 'No cross-talk, no jostling for position . . . [no] gumming things up with a lot of stupid questions' (114). The troop that guards the Buick handles unrest with a carefully cultivated 'disinvitation to deliberate' (Brown, 'American' 708–9). Unsurprisingly for readers familiar with King's corpus, the characters in *From a Buick 8* respond to the turbulence of post-Fordism in an illiberal fashion by ceding management to elite rogues. The novel therefore quells the weirdness of its titular car with an authority that it advances 'as a kind of palliative magic' the text 'resolves' its crisis via police procedure instead of political intervention (Sears 220). As another illustration, the soundtrack of *From a Buick 8* involves a cacophony of 'flat and colorless' police voices: 'How quickly their senses dulled, rendering the marvelous mundane'. Commanding officers speak at a volume 'as calm as an Audobon guide', using a 'weirdly matter-of-fact tone' (239, 194, 133–4). The text declares militancy to be the best of bad options by starkly contrasting the rigid stratagem of the police with the partially glimpsed horrors emanating from the Buick. In the end, *From a Buick 8* smuggles in a revised managerialism that the novel appears to elevate above the Fordist-Keynesian model it has been mowing down since the first page (in chapter 8, I examine how King's 2009 novel *Under the Dome* similarly refuses democratic involvement in favour of a cadre of powerbrokers).

At this juncture, a pressing problem with King's car stories becomes clear to us: one of the sole modes of critique available in his multiverse appears to be an accelerationist one – a mode of critique that ultimately does not break/brake with late capitalism's general 'aims of production'. To reject the methods of re-containment advanced by King's novels – be they hormonal, Oedipal or martial – involves being tempted into *ever more intensive negation*. It is precisely for this reason that critics accuse accelerationists like Deleuze of inadvertently acting as purveyors of post-Fordist logic.[24] To deconstruct the hormonal, Oedipal or martial norms of *Christine* or *From a Buick 8* risks accelerating things in tacit support of the system supposedly under attack. Benjamin Noys laments that, on these raging roadways, 'any way to distinguish a radical strategy from the strategy of capital seems to disappear completely'. As they merge into the prevailing traffic of late capitalism, *Christine* and *From a Buick 8* attempt (paradoxically) to imagine an end to financialisation by adopting recognisable characteristics of the burgeoning financial sector. Marching at a relentless pace, King's critique of the apparatus that produces these monstrous machines fails to maintain an adequate degree of resistance because it is missing 'an interruptive politics' that refuses to treat capitalist production on its own terms. Noys insists, 'We need a politics of deceleration' (5, 90–4). In other words, instead of being lured in by post-Fordist momentum, readers must find ways to refuse King's invitation to auto-deconstruct without at the same time falling prey to the allures of noxious nostalgia, repressive physical and psychical conventions, or a noisome neo-feudal order. The course ahead will involve countless hairpin turns.

In conclusion, the utterly weird character of *Christine* and *From a Buick 8* reflects a world on the verge of radical transformation. These novels respond by feigning capriciousness while maintaining the mercurial modus operandi of post-Fordism as well as the anti-political solutionism of a police state (models of unsuspecting conformity to which this book frequently returns).[25] Better to act like a rootless financier or an obedient officer, it would seem, than to 'scheme' like the vindictive LeBay.[26] King's texts naturalise the tumult associated with post-Fordism by treating it as karmic, biological or as an existential litmus test and fostering as a result the belief that socio-economic rearrangements of the era – although admittedly horrifying – remain ineluctable. Yet, thanks to their utter weirdness, these stories incessantly recall what they repress. Once conjured, King's otherworldly forces cannot be kept at bay. Glimpsed at the outermost horizons of *Christine* and *From a Buick 8*, the dissatisfaction of late capitalism might inspire readers to imagine something different. While the romanticised acceleration of these texts can be readily co-opted in service of financialisation, the strangeness of King's cars preserves the possibility of a decelerated politics, one that would slow us down enough to chart a more just and equitable course.

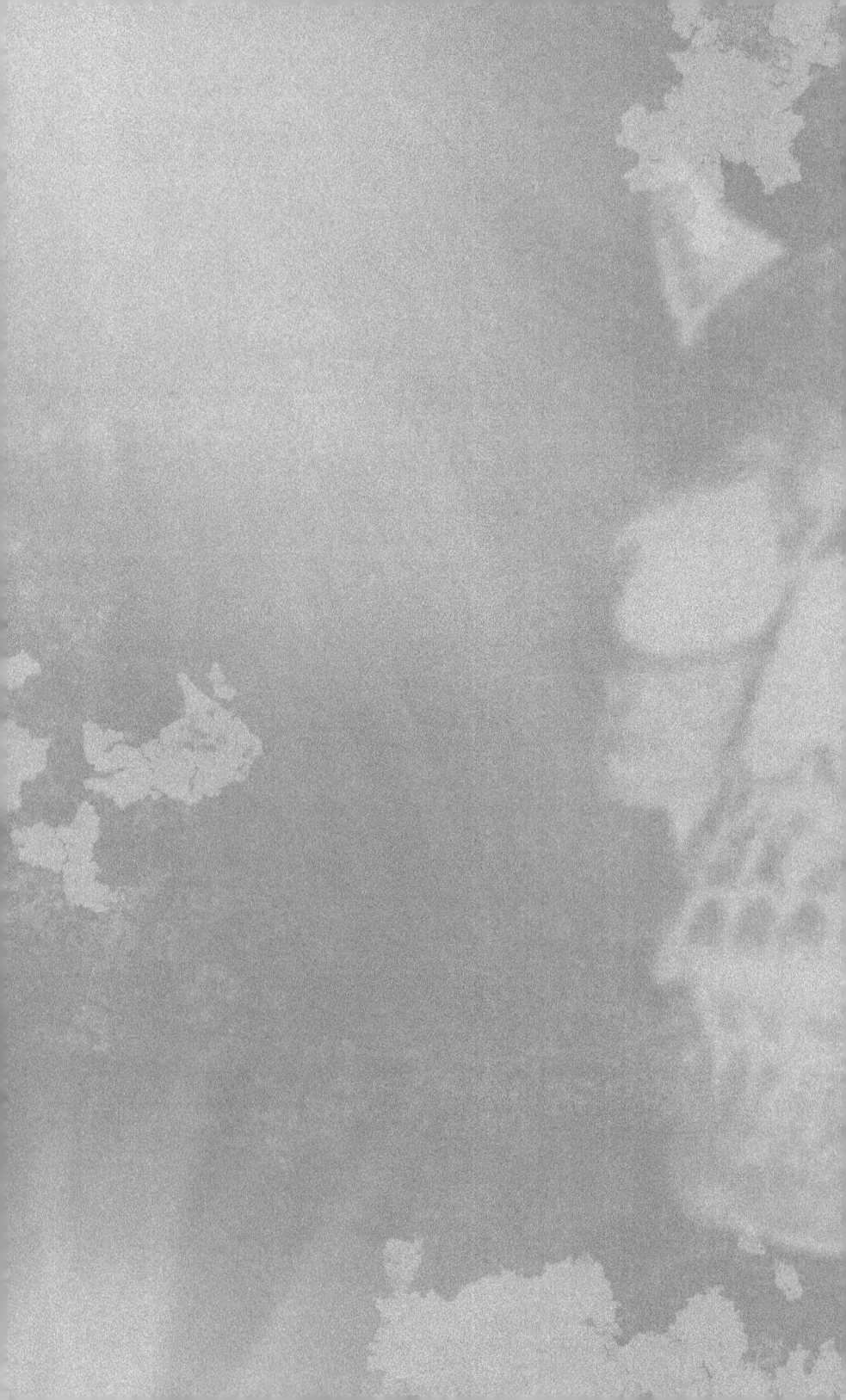

4

Firestarter

or, the Smelting of a Neo-liberal Subject

STEPHEN KING'S *Firestarter* (1980) emerges from a crucible that transformed American life. In 1969, the parents of Charlie McGee are unwitting recipients of Lot Six, an experimental drug administered by a secretive government agency known as the Shop. Although her parents – in particular, her father Andy – possess similar psychic abilities, Charlie's powers far surpass theirs. The novel follows the young woman as she learns to harness her capacity to generate fires with her mind (*pyrokinesis*) while outrunning a cabal that wishes to capitalise on the results of the Shop's experimentation. King's coming-of-age narrative presents a template for neo-liberal subjectivity: 'An outlook that has reshaped behaviours and expectations across scales – from the global to the most intimate of spaces . . . [one that has] penetrated the worlds in which we live' (Louth and Potter 1). As it does in King's car stories, considered in the previous chapter, this coming-of-age trope takes on a specific meaning within the context of post-Fordism: namely, *Firestarter* forges a subjectivity by burning away all social influence to attain an extreme degree of autonomy.

In the early pages, King's novel depicts Big Brother in full Nixonian garb, thereby affirming Tony Magistrale's claim that King's fiction perpetuates a 'perception of the federal government (that) borders on paranoia' (*Landscape* 35). *Firestarter* describes the pre-1980 United States government as an oppressive entity that brutally disciplines its citizens to exploit their creative capacities, and then the text counters this perceived hyper-management with a fantasy of full release by pushing readers to believe that Charlie must be ransomed, at any cost, from oversight. The kindling for *Firestarter*'s fantasy of full release perhaps originates in King's first published novel, *Carrie* (1974), in which another teen endowed with mental capabilities will either 'fall docilely into the complacent expectations of parents, friends, and even herself' or revolt. Carrie famously opts to incinerate her oppressors: 'They were under her thumb, in her power. *Power*! What a word that was!' (53, 221; author's emphasis). When Charlie similarly frees herself from government control, the reader is meant to delight on at least two counts: first, in viewing the visceral, charred remains of her disciplinary apparatus; and secondly, in viewing the self-portrait of a radically liberated subject that emerges from the ashes.

The incendiary exercise of *Firestarter* departs in a number of ways from dominant ideas about subjectivity that precede it. Kenneth Gergen summarises a Romanticist view of the self – 'unseen, sacred forces that dwell deep within the person' – as well as a 'modern' view of the self – the scientific account of a 'well-ordered and accessible' subject – in a manner that enables us to understand how subjects like Charlie become 'open slates' on which 'persons may inscribe, erase and rewrite their identities' (38, 15, 228). That is, in place of a subject imagined to be anchored to a basic essence (be it sacred and/or scientific), the neo-liberal subject is founded upon notions of polymorphic volatility, fostered by emerging technologies with which the subject constantly re-brands itself. *Firestarter* likewise peddles the premise that 'the collapse of idols leads automatically to freedom' (Dufour 152). King's text, replete with paternal authorities to be torched, elevates the lone subject to a place of prominence: an enclosed selfhood defined exclusively by self-reliance and self-entrepreneurship. Empowered to burn the world down to its core element (the singular self), Charlie emerges thoroughly disembedded from communal pressures.[1] Published at the hinge of the 1970s and 1980s, King's novel thus choreographs a pivot from Keynesianism, with its heavily calibrated movement, to a post-Keynesian citizenry forced to govern itself (a pivot not unlike the one discussed in the previous chapter). Of course, it is important to remember that *Firestarter* does not provide a faithful rendition of twentieth-century history per se; rather, it proffers a powerful fable to accompany the idiosyncratic demands of the neo-liberal state. Although it would be a mistake to picture King's straightforward jump from the Cold War to the hyper-speculative 1980s as an accurate depiction of how American subjects developed during this era, *Firestarter*'s vision for an ideal subject remains uniquely intense and compelling. Unlike Romanticist or 'modern' variants, this brand of subject not only mitigates but melts away *in toto* signs of shared governance, including the family unit and the demos. King's mythological figure narrativises shifting models of selfhood from the 1980s by giving flammable flesh to abstractions popularised by economists like F. A. Hayek and Milton Friedman as well as politicians including Ronald Reagan and Margaret Thatcher.

In the aftermath of the publication of *Firestarter*, the transfer of energy from a central apparatus to the individual body continues to be a preoccupation of King's fiction. In *The Tommyknockers* (1987), alien visitors utilise human bodies as 'living batteries' to fuel their takeover (428). In *Doctor Sleep* (2013), marauding vampires consume the essence of their victims by exploiting the victim's inner resources (what they call 'steam').[2] They target a young female protagonist like Charlie with the intention of utilising her as a sort of 'milk-cow'. In turn, the body becomes a machine controllable by 'a bank of switches on a control room wall', likened to fuel that must be burned (to produce 'steam') and equated with batteries being drained or recharged (29, 252, 218, 375, 400).[3] King's *Revival* (2014) further interrogates this theme by inspecting a power grid that works upon/through the corporeal form. On the one hand, King's power grid drives the protagonist's body 'like a car', treating it as a 'transfer device'; on the other hand, ever-present electricity makes characters feel 'godlike' (18, 172, 268). King's fiction therefore enacts a two-step manoeuver: it depicts the human body as ruthlessly exploited by a massive military-industrial apparatus, and then it conceives of a highly individuated subject that can make the most of her own power without regulation by government officials. Setting the stage for a dominant trend in King's fiction, *Firestarter* imagines a subject that reverses the state's outdated mode of extraction, liquefies its chains of bondage and explodes into a place of absolute autonomy. Importantly, King's storyworlds comprehend this new subject in distinctly economic terms (a by-product of what is generally referred to as biocapitalism). For her part, Charlie must 'choose' to be a tool that produces on behalf of the government, or to produce a different life for herself. Public intellectuals in this vein tend to classify the flames that smelt the neo-liberal subject as either destructive or emancipatory, and readers too are led to recognise Charlie's body as either fuel for the apparatus or a free-floating entity that transcends the bonds of community. We might ask ourselves: is the state moulding the subject, or does King's alternative subjectivity reveal how human beings exceed established parameters in the name of absolute freedom? Is the neo-liberal subject a 'new alienation' or a 'new liberation' (Dufour 153)?

In the final tally, this chapter agrees with the former position, arguing that Charlie's 'choice' is an inherently false one because the neo-liberal subject (in truth, like all subjects since time immemorial) remains caught in a set of relations that circumscribe it: 'The systems . . . [lend] the subject a lack of fixed identity which it can come to mistake for its freedom' (Eagleton, *Illusions* 89). Put differently, whether or not the Shop truly entitles Charlie to produce or consume 'without government oversight', a dubious proposition in its own right, she complies with prerogatives that are not her own: in particular, she must be always and everywhere more productive. Like the teenagers from King's automotive tales analysed in the previous chapter, Charlie unsuspectingly accelerates her own undoing. This acceleration can certainly feel political, but it quickly turns economic. *Firestarter* underscores the mournful consequences of forging a neo-liberal subject by literally as well as figuratively incinerating bodies in the pursuit of ever more 'freedom'. As a consequence, the loss of communal grounding threatens to dissolve the subject (ecstatically) into mere steam – the sight of which signals to King's readers, against signs to the contrary, that the furnace of late capitalism steadily smoulders on.

The paternal pyre

The first half of *Firestarter* depicts the military-industrial complex as a vast apparatus that sharpens its capacity to train the bodies of its citizens. The doctor that administers Lot Six to Charlie's parents utilises bodily capabilities for government use by marking the human mind 'like a butcher's diagram'. In this manner, the state channels the productive capacities of the subject into a so-called fight for democracy against the Soviet Union. Fed up, King's novel dismantles oppressive government schemas to expose the tentacles of power that work upon, and through, the subject. The Shop's leader understands human behaviour to be run like a system of levers. To borrow terminology from Gilles Deleuze, the military-industrial complex fastens the subject to its yoke and coerces him into a series of tunnels in which his personal energy moves, like a blind mole, through prescribed routes. In one example, the Shop organises its parking lots in hierarchical fashion and buries low-level functionaries in 'the bowels of the KGB's American branch' (61, 292). Michel Foucault describes this channelling effect as the intensification of a centralised power that grows ever more efficient. To abbreviate Foucault's argument, the military-industrial complex expects the subject to be productive in novel ways as it moves away from externally regulating bodies into tutoring the subject to govern herself (according, always, to the needs of the state). The most widely cited illustration of this shift remains Foucault's discussion of the panopticon in which a prison is constructed so that every prisoner may be under the disciplinarian's gaze, at any possible moment, without realising it. The prisoner absorbs the state's expectations in order to discipline himself. It bears repeating that neither Foucault's formulation nor King's representation of this move into 'manufactured freedom' reflects a genuine historical trend. When we consider that the Cold War period witnesses radical self-expression (like rock'n'roll), or that the neo-liberal period precipitates unparalleled militarisation, King's causal chain appears to be bungling at best. However, regardless of its veracity, *Firestarter*'s presentation of an ideal neo-liberal subject provides much-needed elbow grease for the major ideological constellation that materialises in the late 1970s and early 1980s.

King's military-industrial complex strategically imposes upon the subject a fecund sort of individualism by working to 'manufacture [freedom] constantly, to arouse it and produce it'. Deleuze and Felix Guattari discuss how the state funnels the individual's 'deterritorialized flows' through artificial apertures, like the Oedipal complex, to maintain some semblance of control. 'Liberalism must produce freedom, but this very act entails the establishment of limitations, controls, forms of coercion, and obligations' (Foucault, *Birth* 10, 64–5). For instance, as a pawn of the government, Andy regulates himself and his daughter by buying into state-sanctioned obligations that include the 'proper' role of the family. The Shop exploits Andy's existing paternal expectations via 'the making of a complex': 'To the girl-child [the father] is Moses; the laws are his laws.' Consequently, Charlie fears her unleashed powers in acutely paternalistic terms: 'It was a Bad Thing' (King, *Firestarter* 108, 27). By connecting her father's mode of discipline to her bodily enjoyment (when she lights fires, she is ashamed because it brings her 'pleasure'), Charlie absorbs the state's preferred art of governance. She grows ever more productive but always with an accompanying drive to 're-territorialize' her energies, which is to say, to re-situate them within productive parameters. For his part, Andy evokes and controls his daughter's 'freedom' with a form of mental domination related to the 'pushing' of drug dealers; similarly, he opens a business to train overweight women and businessmen that want to 'unleash' a better version of themselves. An English instructor by trade, a point to which we will later return, Andy extends the coercive methods of the Shop into the general population: 'Think-tank boys said the possibilities [of mental domination] were enormous' (119). King's Cold War state orchestrates an elaborate scheme to discipline the internal thought processes of its population.

To counter these forms of discipline, *Firestarter* prepares to negate the oppressive apparatus by readying the funeral pyres for its paterfamilias. The ideal subject resists government control by capitalising upon her own internal resources. King's fiction accentuates this message through its repeated reference to how Alcoholics Anonymous tasks participants with greater self-discipline: 'You don't have to live this way if you don't want to.' King's ideal subject attends to the 'care of physical being' – the benefits of sleep; the need to eat/re-fuel – because she discovers that her body is a tremendous asset (*Doctor* 353, 55, 501). In short, *Firestarter* rejects paternalistic designs in favour of something else, thereby charting a drift into hyper-individualised selfhood. By the novel's close, Charlie embraces her distinctive powers. The clean-cut linearity from the Shop's initial indoctrination to Charlie's final 'emancipation' conveys the maturation of an imaginary neo-liberal subject and, as a result, *Firestarter* helps to legitimise the *sui generis* transformation being engendered at the time of its publication. We might wonder at this juncture if Charlie escapes from her society's conventions or serves as yet another example of re-entrenchment.

Controlled burn

In truth, the state does not release the once-disciplined body in King's fiction from its control: instead, the body proves more 'efficiently governable' in terms of less political energy exerted and fewer expenses incurred.[4] Charlie – or Carrie, or the female poet in *The Tommyknockers*, or the young female protagonist in *Doctor Sleep*, or a host of other King characters – does not evade the status of milk-cow, but finds herself further implanted within a system designed to maximise her labour. After all, the name of the novel's intelligence agency, The Shop, possesses a double meaning: 'Shop' literally signifies indoctrination at the hands of the state, of course, but it also signifies a commercial entity (a storefront) as well as a specific economic activity (shopping). In the era under review, King's military-industrial complex transforms subjects into economic agents by habituating them to desire, consume, invest and produce in very specific ways. Charlie's anti-normative attitude thus proves to be highly normative.

In *Firestarter*, the presumed antithesis of Big Brother (what we might call the Shop 2.0) manifests in explicitly neo-liberal garb. Andy's friend Quincey contends that government workers would fail miserably if they were forced to work in the private sector, and he lambasts bureaucracy by declaring that an unrestrained free market will act as a balm to cure what ails the excessively managed dystopia.[5] King's text characterises Quincey's diatribes against the state as 'Buckleyesque', a reference to the notable mouthpiece of the neo-liberal movement, William F. Buckley (202, 79, 15). Given Quincey's status as the novel's conscience, then, and considering the prominence of Buckley's libertarian perspective in the years to follow, Charlie's 'escape' cannot be read as a significant counter-cultural strategy; instead, her escape serves as a prime example of how we tend to become trapped in ideology (again and again). The neo-liberal subject – a fantastic figure that feeds upon the disaggregation of everything, including herself – stems from a 'colonization of the private'. Charlie reveals how capitalism has 'worked its way into every fiber of our "private" lives' (Nealon, *Foucault* 90). Subjects like Charlie come to treat their bodies as an aggregate of marketable assets.[6] The novel presents a mythologised transition from state power to personal power at its literal centre: a power outage occurs in the state institution where Andy and Charlie are being held. Evoking Foucaultian commentary on psychiatric facilities, this outage turns the proverbial tide, as darkness blinds the disciplinary gaze of the Shop. Plunged into pitch black, His sudden release from institutional control initially terrifies Andy because the darkness makes him invisible (and disposable). While the outage at first appears to release him from the stratified formulations of his captors, in actuality, his 'release' proves to be just another unsuspecting capitulation.

To move beyond Andy's stasis, *Firestarter* uses the outage at the Shop to foster the creation of an intermediate neo-liberal subject named John Rainbird. The Shop hires Rainbird, a Native American and Vietnam veteran, to persuade Charlie to cooperate with its plan for her and the long-oppressed outsider seizes this opportunity to influence not only Charlie but his superiors as well. In the wake of the outage, Rainbird confronts one of the doctors in the institution in order to make the government official feel 'impotent' (359). Cloaked by darkness, Rainbird challenges the status quo in a fashion that suggests a midway point between Andy's conformity and Charlie's release – a glimpse of the kind of subject about to be manufactured. An unfinished subject, Rainbird's flexibility allows him to adapt, to move quicker than the bureaucrats and to produce value for himself without waiting to be assessed by the government. Through the figure of Rainbird, King's text incrementally intensifies state power into a type of power that is more 'diagrammatic . . . [that] mobilizes non-stratified matter and functions, and unfolds with a very flexible segmentarity' (Deleuze 73). Andy, in contrast, cannot forget his obsession with planned outcomes, an error that underscores for readers how the Shop too makes 'plans for controlling a force beyond [its] comprehension' (King, *Firestarter* 483, 273). As Rainbird glides along with enhanced agility, his intermediary position conveys the fantasy bribe of *Firestarter*: to burn down the Shop only instigates a more stream-lined Shop 2.0.

Although Rainbird's tutelage ostensibly departs from the military-industrial complex, his methods remain deeply paternalistic. Giorgio Agamben insists that these presumably liberated subjects often rest 'on a solid basis of a premodern sovereign Power' (quoted in Lemke, 6). Said another way, Rainbird's lessons for Charlie, in which he teaches her to harness her inner resources and maximise returns, are no less hegemonic than the lessons of her father. He coaches the young woman to transform 'disadvantage into an advantage' by proudly declaring himself to be 'a triumphant example of American free enterprise in action'. He commands her, 'Show 'em some flash before you take their cash' (King, *Firestarter* 274, 369–71). Hardly an augur of real revolution, Rainbird's residual art of control lacks the potency of a full-throated libertarianism to come: the vision of a subject that will not rest until every societal guardrail has been removed. Likewise, Foucault acknowledges the covertly normative aspects of neo-liberalism: 'Mechanisms of economic intervention rival any other state-based reduction of freedom.'[7] Readers of *Firestarter* recognise that, in Rainbird's case, 'competition is a principle of formalization . . . not a natural game between individuals . . . neo-liberalism should not therefore be identified with *laissez-faire*, but rather with permanent vigilance, activity, and intervention' (Foucault, *Birth* 69, 120, 132). Through Rainbird, the military-industrial complex aggressively calibrates *homo economicus* and so his faux emancipation actually helps to unleash economic forces in ways that prove to be as deterministic as heavy-handed tactics during the Cold War. He 'liberates' Charlie by cajoling her into a model of selfhood that is always-already strangled by prosaic concerns of profitability. While he does not wish to discipline Charlie like the Shop, because he imagines himself to be 'gentle, kind . . . and fatherly', he nevertheless engages in a number of Shop-like manoeuvers (408). Rainbird's apparently effortless economy therefore remains acutely coercive (an issue to which King returns in his 1995 novel *Rose Madder*, discussed in chapter 7). 'Power's mutation over time exists alongside the parallel emergence of power's economic viability: producing the desired effect with fewer costs, less expenditure of time and effort; better results with less economic and political resistance' (Nealon, *Foucault* 31). Rainbird unsuspectingly assists Shop 2.0 by erecting a subject that can generate yet-unrealised profit streams.

To provide a concrete example of this phenomenon, Rainbird revels in *agonism* – a drive to network freely with others that will prove vital to the neo-liberal project as a whole. In an agonistic society like the one that emerges in the early 1980s, power is situational (not mythic), and economic rather than metaphysical. Due to the fact that he understands power to circulate at a relational level, Rainbird wants Charlie to be 'liberated' so that their competition might yield gainful results. Whereas the Shop mishandles its dominion over Charlie when it understands her to be just another cog in the machine, a mere series of levers to be pulled, Rainbird instead treats her as a living force that constantly intersects with other living forces.[8] Although he does emphasise networking in a way that prepares his young pupil for the information economy to come, Rainbird cannot fathom what a genuine emancipatory politics would entail.

Before they disappear in a cloud of smoke, though, Charlie's dual father figures provide her with a spark. In spite of his re-entrenchment within the system, Rainbird occasionally suggests a more meaningful release from discipline. Even though he cannot shake his roots in pre-modern sovereignty, he manages to outline a subject that would be 'fundamentally ungovernable' through his manipulation of the Shop's computer system, a move that demonstrates his latent capacity to be 'his own man . . . rootless' (260, 476–8). King's readers glimpse in this moment the emergence of 'a state in which men will be able to give themselves the constitution they want' (Foucault, *Government* 19–21). After 'discipline has been taken to the limit of what it can do', the Shop unsuspectingly trains Charlie's fathers to engage in tactics that she later uses to overwhelm her oppressors (Nealon, *Foucault* 68). King's recent novel *The Institute* (2019) tells a similar tale of a shadowy government that accidentally trains psychic children to overthrow it: 'Those idiots went and souped him up without putting a governor on his engine' (499). In King's multiverse, the patriarchy cultivates an art of governance that threatens to undo the very power imbalance upon which it depends: 'The tests had afforded [Charlie] the practice necessary to refine a crude sledgehammer of power into something she could flick out with deadly precision' (*Firestarter* 433–4). From the Shop to Andy to Rainbird, *Firestarter* tracks the blossoming of an imaginary neo-liberal subject – a progression that culminates with the fiery flourish of Charlie's final ascent.

With Charlie's climactic departure from the oversight of her male mentors, the concept of the family undergoes a tremendous upheaval. A contemporary of Foucault, Jacques Donzelot contends that John Maynard Keynes's 'flexible mechanisms of adjustment' attempt to fit 'faltering social zones back into the economic circuit' (the preceding chapter addresses these modes of re-adjustment in King's automotive horror stories). In the conclusion to his landmark study, Donzelot motions at a sweeping release from Keynesian calibration by picturing an ideal subject that could extricate 'itself from the *arch-bodies* . . . affirm[ing] the reality of a life and denounce[ing] the unreality of that by which it would be encircled and reduced to silence' (231–4, author's emphasis). Obedient to Donzelot's fantasy of release, Charlie's once repressed potency transcends the arch-body imposed upon her by her father-figures, and so *Firestarter* suggests that the power of life eventually overwhelms the life of power. King's unorthodox coming-of-age narrative invites the reader to revise his relationship to reading as well as writing in a manner that 'liberates' him from patriarchal figures, including King himself.

Burn upon reading

King's neo-liberal subject wobbles always at the brink, as when Charlie dreams of being '*free, free, free* . . . naked and . . . free, unfettered, loose' (422–3, author's emphasis). Because her raw potential cannot be contained, the subject symbolically (and, in Charlie's case, quite literally) explodes from its limited vessel. For certain contemporary thinkers, this intensification tracks the evolution of a disciplinary society into a society of control 'in which mechanisms of command become ever more "democratic," ever more immanent to the social field, distributed throughout the brains and bodies of the citizens'. Charlie's overflow of personal power carbonises the established way of doing things, thereby sharing with readers an opportunity 'to embrace the neo-liberal condition . . . and allow it to express aspirations that its neo-liberal promoters had neither intended nor foreseen' (Feher 25). Accelerationists like Deleuze, Hardt and Negri laud this explosiveness as a means to abscond from discipline; they too are fire starters of a sort. Released from the tutelage of her father-figures, Charlie follows Carrie's lead and burns the Shop to the ground. Although she feels guilt for this deliverance, and at times holds that she needs her father(s) to re-enforce a sense of law and order, she heeds the advice that 'you don't want to block yourself off', and therefore she emerges as an ungovernable subject that knows deep down that her '*potential* had hardly been tapped' (King, *Firestarter* 175, 525–30; author's emphasis).

Just as Foucault's last lectures turn to the aesthetics of self-governance, what he calls 'the art of living', King's novel closes by considering the role of literature in Charlie's emancipatory politics.[9] *Firestarter* obsessively returns to literary (re)creation when, like many of King works, it chastens an English instructor – in this case, Andy – as he learns not to impose meaning on others, but to encourage greater self-discovery.[10] That is, the text advances reading and writing as a kind of anti-discipline that prompts the reader/writer to make meaning for herself. During his initial evasion of the Shop, Andy becomes truly 'useful', as opposed to his perceived impotence as a professor, when he does manual labour. The pronounced sweat on his brow alerts readers to his internal combustion as he burns bodily resources to accomplish more 'meaningful' (read: self-involved) tasks. This 'productive' burn contrasts with the cerebral energy that he seemingly wastes when he dominates others, a far costlier form of governance that eventually kills him. This lionised practice of self-upon-self appears in a distinctive literary guise when Rainbird shapes his life like a 'writer' that strips away the Power of the Author (the Shop), instructing Charlie to practise using her powers like one would practise 'making letters'. He shapes his life like a blind man 'reading braille' – an act of reading that allows him to swerve around societal influence like some frenzied Bloomian poet. Rainbird's unusual model for reading and writing affords Charlie with an opportunity to create as well as consume her private satisfaction, wholly divorced from state control. *Firestarter* links Charlie's self-expression, the literal and metaphorical fires that she lights, to aesthetics when the text aligns her incendiary powers with literary exercise: 'It's as if she was reading a good book' (246, 183, 364, 429). Indeed, this anti-disciplinary vision of reading and writing surfaces regularly in King's fiction. *The Dark Half* (1989) likens unfettered writing to a 'fucking furnace'. To write freely means 'heat and compulsion', 'smolder' and 'boil' (268–70, 331–4). The novel ends with a writer setting fire to a space that emblematises writing problems in order to ascend to a healthier, if solipsistic, kind of creativity. Likewise, '1408' (1999) spins the yarn of a writer that must escape from external influence by lighting a literary fire, and the protagonist of *Bag of Bones* (1998) sets his prose on fire before vowing never to compose another work. Because the fires in King's fiction always appear to be the flames of creative destruction, *Firestarter* makes it a prerequisite for the emancipated subject to write her own story without manipulation from the government, and she must be equally prepared to read the story of another without an official hermeneutic. At the close, Charlie circulates her story 'freely' by taking it to an outlet that has 'got to be honest, and . . . it can't have any ties to the government or the government's ideas' (557). The 'unleashed' circulation of her text – we are led to surmise that this process led to the novel that we currently read – presumably lays the groundwork for a fully liberalised population.

In other words, before being re-born as an ideal neo-liberal subject, Charlie must disconnect herself from narrative structures imposed on her by the Shop, Andy, as well as Rainbird. John Sears expertly demonstrates how King's deconstructive style fans the flames of a liberalised society by undermining authoritarian architects.[11] *Firestarter* further illustrates the unfolding of a hyper-liberal readership by presenting New York City, Charlie's point of departure as well as her final destination, as an emancipated community of writers and readers that endlessly reproduces the conditions of its own existence. Charlie first experiences Manhattan under a maze of state surveillance; during her second visit, she experiences the city as a starkly different space in which citizens mind their own business and 'let other people mind theirs' (557). This circulatory pattern depicts subjects that can construct and consume their own truths: a will-to-truth becomes universal, a phenomenon that Foucault describes as 'telling the truth to others in order to conduct them in their own conduct'. Thanks to the supposed lack of artifice in her reading and writing, Charlie unbridles her own power as well as the power of others. She remains disinterested in rhetorical persuasion – a main preoccupation of the Shop, Andy, as well as Rainbird – and 'leaves others the freedom to speak'. In this way, *Firestarter* conveys a 'clash of passions which will make the truth blaze forth at a given moment, without anyone being in charge' (Foucault, *Government* 346, 116).

Firestarter does not only represent this alternative; it enacts this alternative by 'pushing' readers to experience Charlie's rebellion first-hand. Right away, readers encounter the novel's dedication to Shirley Jackson, a writer that King claims 'never needed to raise her voice'. If writing typically 'raises its voice' in order to persuade readers, *Firestarter* portrays Jackson as an aspirational figure because she manages to persuade readers (somehow) without disciplining them. *Firestarter* foreshadows the presumed modus operandi of an information economy by asking readers to incinerate the structures that define them, make the most of their own potential and spread the will-to-truth among their communities. In *Rose Madder*, immediately before she incinerates a text that previously defined her, King's protagonist folds the text to mail it 'like a letter' (407). Throughout King's fiction, open circulation continues to feed the flames of the very furnace that has smelted the neo-liberal subject a bit too long – leaving, in the end, only steam.

... And into the fire

As we are drawn into Charlie's widespread disaggregation, there may be 'little left for us to do, except . . . fiddle while Rome burns' (Callinicos 174). In other words, as King's ideal subject achieves a radically disembedded position, the question becomes whether or not Charlie could ever conceive of herself *without* the fire imagery that reduces her to mere slag or steam (burnt bridges; the feverish blaze of a selfhood without boundaries). She burns away the residual ties that bind to inflame her own pursuit of greater knowledge/power.[12] Like the element of fire, the neo-liberal subject contains her start as well as her end within herself, and so Charlie experiences the thrill of 'power without purpose, power without lines of determination, power without end in every sense of the word' (Brown, *Politics* 139). Over the last forty years, this alternative subjectivity has proven to be as passionate as it is perilous.

Charlie possesses the singular intention of detaching herself from the societies that define her in the name of greater personal freedom: 'The power was trembling on the edge of her ability to control it' (King, *Firestarter* 501). According to Jürgen Habermas, contemporary subjects habitually unmask everything around them as they hound 'the naked image of subject-centered reason', which is to say, they aggressively pursue the notion of a subjectivity released from intellectual drills, in defiance of consensus-based governance, and understanding liberty to be 'nothing more than an absence of coercion' (Habermas, 'Critique' 50; Mouffe, *Return* 18). As such, Charlie's model of pure negation confirms 'an altogether unsociological concept of the social' (Habermas, 'Critique' 50–1). When she at last asserts herself by melting away communal points of reference, save the supposed anchor of her own malleable selfhood, what is left of her but self-perpetuating flame?[13] Incendiary individualism consumes everything in its path, foreclosing opportunities for Charlie (or, vicariously, the reader) to explore more 'constructive' visions of freedom in which democratic practices are multiplied, deepened via stronger emotional attachments, or more successfully institutionalised.

Yet anti-disciplinary heat continues to seethe throughout King's *oeuvre*. In *Bag of Bones* – a mixture of memoir, novel, as well as self-help tract – the protagonist overcomes writer's block by ceaselessly negating everything that he once knew and endorsing the argument that nothing remains outside the author's account (a totalised schema that King recycles in his 1992 novel, *Dolores Claiborne*).[14] He serves as both criminal and detective, writing clues into his own manuscript that will lead him, as his own reader, by his 'haunted heart' (319, 666). After a lightning storm reduces his surroundings to cinders, the protagonist mutates into a free-floating subject, one that bursts with a creative power that completely consumes him. This trope of 'unleashing' emotional flows proves invariably productive and, in many instances, resolves a bad case of writer's block. In particular, King's multiple stories of fire understand the liberation of women – from Carrie to Charlie and beyond – to be less a political triumph over hegemony than an economic extraction of value. *Carrie*, for one, tells a story about 'how women find their own channels of power', a celebration of 'Woman, feeling her powers for the first time' (King, *Danse* 171–2). It appears that everything must burn to keep lit the furnaces of productivity. These fires can be thrilling, of course, yet they cannot last forever. 'The compulsion toward liquidity, flow, an accelerated circulation of what is psychic, sexual, or pertaining to the body', Jean Baudrillard insists, 'is the exact replica of the force which rules market value . . . value must radiate endlessly and in every direction . . . the psychic metaphor of capital.' Mirroring a compulsion towards liquidity ('Production at all costs!'), *Firestarter* demonstrates that 'there is no exception to the logic of liberation' (Baudrillard, *Forget* 25, 31, 40). Such an all-encompassing 'emancipation' occasionally terrifies even Charlie, who cries out at one point: 'Am I going to burn myself up?' (King, *Firestarter* 124).

Given the novel's dissolution of the family unit (*pace* Donzelot), Charlie's extraordinary solitude suggests that the idea of the family might have offered a useful injunction to slow the interminable demand for greater productivity. Michael Walzer proposes that the concept of family 'sets limits on the reach of exchange, establishing a space in which market norms don't apply' (242). Without such a limit, it appears unlikely that Charlie could be deemed 'useful' in the years ahead, or that she could ever again love, or be loved in turn by, another person.[15] Since *Firestarter* smelts a subject as she doggedly pursues a more plain-speaking, purified and productive kind of subjectivity, we must ask what will be left of interpersonal connection after the other qualities associated with being human are incinerated. Franco 'Bifo' Berardi sums up the infernal condition of subjects like Charlie as 'existential loneliness coupled with all-pervading productivity' (113). From a political standpoint, King's stories of female empowerment remain some of his most problematic works due to their disavowal of intersubjectivity. Emancipation, in this context, 'can only take the form of a breaking open of the coercive unity of the subject in order to release the diffuseness and heterogeneity of the repressed . . . [it] lacks any ideal of communicative reciprocity' (Dews 280, 287). To understand why the trend in *Firestarter* is so troubling, we can compare it to texts written by King that do insist upon privileging intersubjectivity. For example, *IT* (1986) explores the need for others in the search for self, an issue to which I return in the following chapter, and I argue that for every *Gerald's Game* (1992) – which features a tortured individual fully absorbed with herself – King publishes a *Misery* (1987) – which features an individual tortured by his relationships with other individuals (specifically, his readers). *Lisey's Story* (2006), King's latest shot at a story of female empowerment, highlights an intersubjective dynamic by stressing how we require separate individuals to find 'our way home'. Every tale that a person writes depends upon a companion willing to read it: 'Just give me this much more – your eye on these last few words' (595, 647). Against the relational sensibility that appears throughout *IT*, *Misery* and *Lisey's Story*, Charlie 'suspects solidarity itself [to be] some oppressively normalizing consensus' (Eagleton, *Illusions*, 92). That is to say, narratives like *Firestarter* do not register a pressing need for intersubjectivity; they instead focus upon personal freedom as a cure-all. Although her sense of dependence opens Lisey to new possibilities, Charlie's perpetual burning conveys an anaemic subjectivity, forever on the brink of erasure.

In sum, King's text reminds us that we are surrounded by firestarters that are intent upon setting the world ablaze, in many senses of the term. Today, 'freedom doesn't simply trump other political principles', Wendy Brown opines. 'It is all there is . . . exercised without concern for social context or consequences, without restraint, civility, or care for society . . . it permits assaults on whatever remains of the social fabric in the name of freedom.' Slowly burning since 1980, Charlie's mode of freeing herself has spread far and wide. 'Do Not Tread On Me', the popular bumper stickers commands. The results speak for themselves: 'Freedom without society is a pure instrument of power, shorn of concern for others, the world, or the future . . . unbridled and uncultured . . . dancing at the bonfires of what one is burning down' (Brown, *Ruins* 42–5, 171). The imaginary subject in *Firestarter* anticipates societies enflamed by white supremacists as well as anti-vaccinators, gambling around the pyre of their collective undoing. Perhaps *Firestarter*'s impracticable cry – free, free, free! – maintains widespread appeal precisely because earlier Romantic and 'modern' notions of subjectivity give off a whiff of authoritarianism.[16] Our only hope is that, by the close of *Firestarter*, Charlie's attenuated subject does not warrant wanton celebration, and 'something at the bottom of the whole system *resists the infinite expansion of production*' (Baudrillard, *Forget* 41, 47; author's emphasis). In King's incendiary tales, at least certain aspects of the subject prove to be fireproof because surely, we whisper with faltering confidence, there must be something that the furnaces of productivity will leave untouched?

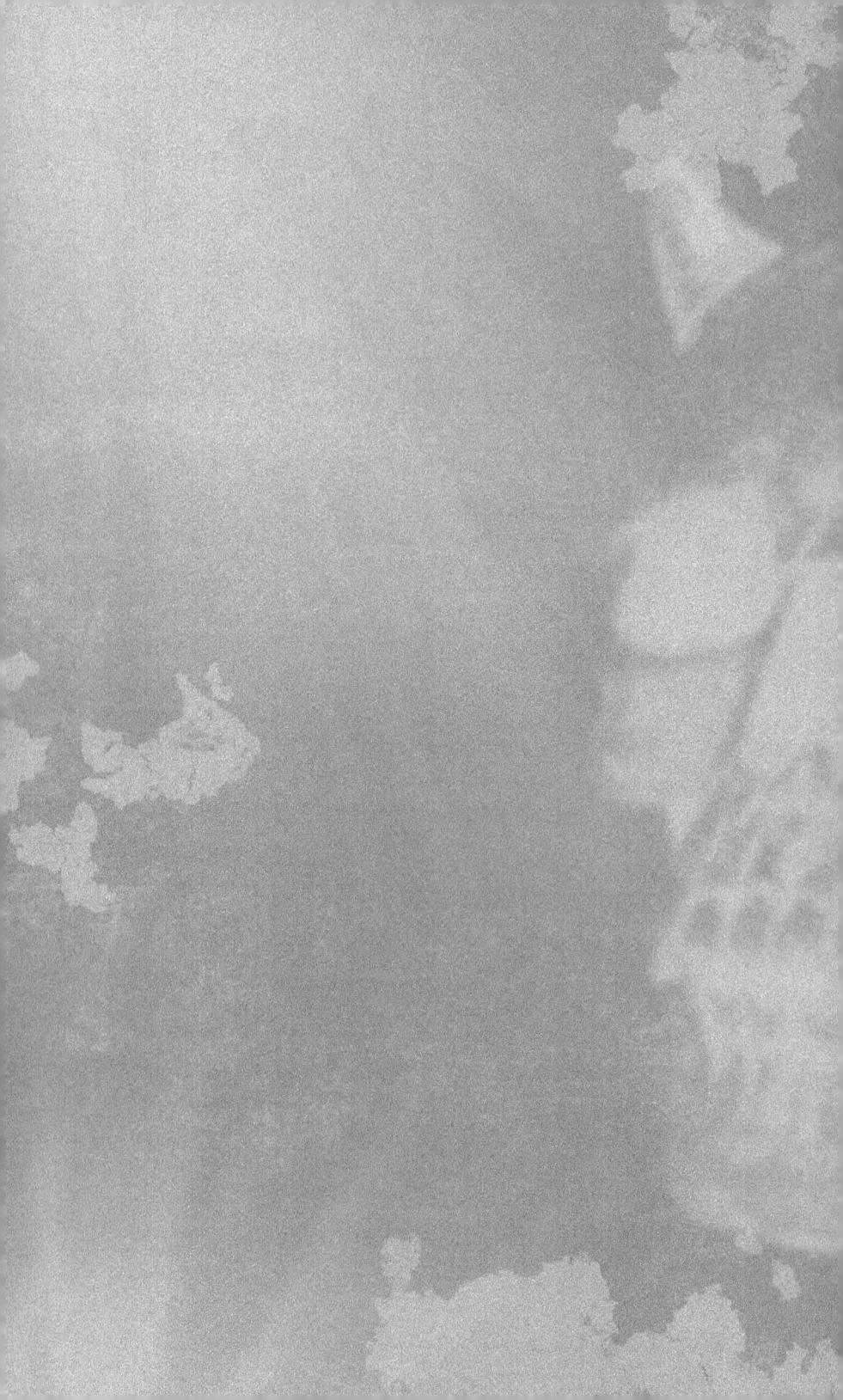

5

IT, Individualism, and the Idea of Community

AS THE LONG DECADE of the 1980s wore on, Stephen King's fiction continued to wrestle with issues of intersubjectivity raised in the previous chapter concerning his earlier novel *Firestarter* (1980). Although his texts obsess over pure negation – and, by so doing, help to set the stage for a neo-liberal revolution – they nevertheless keep our eyes trained on the proverbial ties that bind. Specifically, King's *IT* (1986) considers the interplay of self-realisation and social cohesion as the novel oscillates between communitarian and liberal ideals, a crucial interplay that defines 'the central debate in Anglo-American political theory during the 1980s (Okin 46). In one moment, *IT* contends that individuals are always-already embedded within their community; in the next moment, the narrative implies that individuals are fundamentally detached from their social context. The final cosmic of *IT* attempts to fuse communitarian and liberal values and, by so doing, the novel addresses a political stalemate that would persist for decades to come.

To begin, the terms communitarian and liberal remain notoriously slippery. Stephen Mulhall and Adam Swift comment, 'There is a great deal of disagreement about what exactly one has to believe in order to qualify either as a liberal or as a communitarian' (xiii). This chapter does not treat the term liberal as synonymous with 'progressive' – its common, and often derogatory, usage today. Broadly speaking, liberals believe in less government intervention and, frequently working within a Kantian tradition, posit free will as an a priori constant. There are important variations to consider, such as how classical liberalism bends in either libertarian or utilitarian directions, or how neo-liberalism (as we have seen in preceding chapters) prizes economic freedom at the expense of political freedom.[1] For the sake of this chapter, though, I will frame liberalism in conversation with John Rawls's highly influential *A Theory of Justice* (1971). Attacked from the Left and Right, Rawls's work offers an ideal barometer for liberalism in the second half of the twentieth century. The publication of Rawls's book sparks a full-blown academic skirmish by arguing that liberalism privileges the right over public good and freedom for the subject is a foundation that must be preserved at all costs against attempts to plan a public good that would deny the subject's freedom. To summarise Rawls's complex argument, what is 'right' begins – and ends – with the preservation of personal liberty.

Communitarians immediately rise to counter the argument of *A Theory of Justice*. Philip Selznick, a member of this loose assemblage, writes: 'The label communitarian can be applied to any doctrine that prizes collective goods or ideals and limits claims to individual independence and self-realization' (4). For communitarians, Rawls's concept of communal life is thin, even anaemic, a deficiency that compels communitarians to articulate a thicker understanding of community: 'Only by virtue of our being members in communities can we find a deep meaning and substance to our moral beliefs' (Avineri and de-Shalit 7). Said another way, if liberals prioritise the disentangled individual, communitarians proclaim the utter embeddedness of the subject by championing 'the idea that we are first and foremost social beings, embodied agents "in-the-world" engaged in realising a certain form of life' (Bell 93). Like liberals, communitarians disagree on a wide range of issues. The imbroglio of *IT* actually accentuates just how confused these positions become in the turbulent decades that close out the twentieth century, in particular through King's signature 'idiosyncratic blend of free will and determinism' (Strengell 254).

As the enduring popularity of *IT* demonstrates, while the liberal-communitarian debate rages within fairly narrow scholarly quarters, it is hardly relegated to the ivory tower. In the 1980s, the Reagan (US) and Thatcher (Britain) administrations promote atomised individuals, articulated perhaps nowhere more famously than in Thatcher's declaration that there are no societies, only individuals.[2] In the previous chapter, we examined how Charlie from *Firestarter* encapsulates this mentality: the subject solely shoulders responsibility for her successes as well her failures. And yet there *is* such a thing as society, opponents counter, and it inevitably defines the subject: 'The requirements of character are imposed from outside, from the way in which others regard and use characters' (MacIntyre, *After* 29). The subject's triumphs or missteps belong not to them alone, but to the entire community. Liberals and communitarians, unable to reach consensus, accuse one another of being arbitrary in their respective outlooks: why, liberals ask, should every individual be entitled to share in the prosperity of others? Why, communitarians retort, should the subject privilege personal liberty over other values like solidarity or security? At the time of this writing, the heated parley remains unresolved (perhaps mercifully, for reasons to which we will attend later).

King's *IT* recycles the key talking points of this debate in a form that remains accessible to the reading public. On the one hand, it tells a story about a group of friends defined by their common experience in the macabre city of Derry, Maine. It is a tale about how community shapes us, about how 'we cannot characterize intentions independently of the settings which make those intentions intelligible' (MacIntyre, 'Virtues' 128). It is an epic concerned with the invisible forces that draw the body politic together and enable it to survive. On the other hand, *IT* dwells upon characters that opt to break free from communal influence by severing social bonds in pursuit of complete autonomy. Their little community – The Losers' Club – thrives because each character independently chooses to join it. Hence the use of the apostrophe in the group's name. This is not, as communitarians might have it, a club defined by social standing (Losers Club: a club comprised of losers); rather, King presents a club possessed by self-declared losers, one that operates in a liberal mode. The text oscillates between these positions.

What makes *IT* so unique is that, in its closing section, the novel treats the liberal-communitarian debate as a metaphysical dance. Shifting between disembedded and embedded subjectivities, the community stipulates the lives of the children in *IT*, whereas adults must elect to participate. Indeed, David Punter describes the difference between adulthood and childhood as the *Ur*-plot of King's multiverse (122). As the narrative sways back and forth between metaphorical seasons of life, *IT* bundles liberal and communitarian perspectives into an imagined totality. On this point, the chapter departs from interpretations put forth by critics like John Sears, who labels *IT* a 'symbolically confused novel', full of slippery, reductive metaphors, unable to 'codify monstrosity' and, as such, 'the major ideological failure' of King's canon (183–4, 188). In contrast, I argue that this 'slipperiness' is not only crucial to the political imagination of *IT*; it reveals a great deal about the evasiveness of the politics in King's fiction as a whole. King's cosmos remains fundamentally ambiguous because, while communitarians as well as liberals 'gravitate toward an ontology of concord', *IT* does not privilege such a false sense of unity (Connolly, *Politics* 10). Due to its perpetual tension between liberal and communitarian perspectives, the epic stresses *a constant disruption of consensus* – the vital restlessness that keeps American politics alive and well.

A communitarian reading

Let us begin with a communitarian reading of King's novel. *IT* maps the city of Derry in such careful detail that the city, much more than a mere backdrop, serves as the central character of the novel. King's text attends to the infrastructure of this community by surveying how the waterworks beneath Derry – an intricate maze built as part of the New Deal – orient (or disorient, as the case may be) the city's residents. Children play near the train yards, a place that represents to citizens the circulatory system of their society; the library, another embodiment of communal sharing as well as trust, serves as the plot's focal point; and near the start of the novel, a tram-car encapsulates Derry's history, a powerful symbol meant to bolster the city's 'morale, image'. The novel's extensive focus upon infrastructure accentuates a communitarian thesis that infrastructure structures the psyche of its citizens by moving them along physical and psychical routes established in advance by the community. In turn, when the group of children design their own infrastructure (a dam in the Barrens), they too formulate a unique community for themselves. In fact, the very notion of 'they' only becomes visible upon the dam's construction. When their dam is completed, members of the group begin to 'fit neatly against each other's edges' (18, 283, 290). And after the dam fails, causing minor damage to Derry's waterworks, the club discovers a sense of communal responsibility to Derry because members must collectively admit the mistake to a city official. Upon articulating this shared responsibility, 'they' weld into a single unit, and so the concept of infrastructure moves them to grasp a foundational interdependence.

Stressing the power of the collective over the power of the individual, *IT* understands justice to be a common good (a position strongly aligned with communitarianism). Michael Walzer insists that community should be understood as the most important good of all: 'Justice is rooted in the distinct understandings of places, honors, jobs, things of all sorts, that constitute a shared way of life' (314). In *IT*, justice stems from community-building not as one possible outcome among many, but as the paramount imperative. After all, collectivism ('group will') is the single weapon capable of defeating the monstrous entity that haunts Derry (King, *IT* 492). King stories frequently chime in on this point: 'There *is* such a thing as town consciousness' (*Bag* 530, author's emphasis). As the ominous It longs to segregate the children, to drive them apart in order to destroy them, members of the Losers' Club survive by clinging to one another and sharing 'a language of commitment, responsibility, duty, virtue, memory, solidarity, and even love rather than the discourse . . . of choice, rights, personal freedom, and individualism' (Galston, 'Progressive' 109). In a particularly pregnant instance, *IT* foregrounds collectivist values by describing birds that flock together, a sweeping movement in which no single bird could ever claim credit for the flock's success: 'We all did it' (1062).

Beyond the team's obvious triumph as a cohesive unit over Derry's resident evil, King's novel upholds communitarian theory in more nuanced ways as well. The biography of town librarian Mike Hanlon, a young man firmly anchored to his community's annual timetable, gestures at what Daniel Bell calls the 'constitutive community' (10). A child of farmers, Mike's daily experience is made legible through the harvest schedule, a context that continues to determine his adult outlook and enables him to comprehend the role of community in ways that are inaccessible to his city-dweller friends. Consequently, at one point he comments that a no-hitter in baseball is a by-product of luck, not skill – being in the right place, at the right time, under the ideal set of circumstances. While Rawlsians would insist that 'we must stand to our circumstance always at a certain distance, conditioned to be sure, but part of us always antecedent to any conditions', communitarian Michael Sandel responds bluntly: 'We cannot' (*Liberalism* 11). Of course, Mike's communitarian perspective is not always welcomed by the Losers' Club:

when he tells his adult friends that they became rich as a result of their upbringing in Derry, for instance, they answer with white hot anger, denial and embarrassment. Mike gently pushes the issue: 'Your success stems from what happened here' (King, *IT* 490). He recognises that team members do not circumscribe their community; their community circumscribes them. To prove that communities fix individuals and not the other way around, Sandel compares the current salaries of Supreme Court justices and reality television judges. Communities allocate rewards on something other than the basis of meritocratic ideals, like an individual's hard work or natural talent, as liberals tend to assume. The reality television judge who is lucky to live in a society that prioritises her telegenic qualities does not automatically 'deserve' to reap such an unequal portion of the profits (Sandel, *Justice* 163). Mike suggests that the disparate share of wealth and power attained by the former children of Derry can be compared to the pitcher's no-hitter because their self-defined 'hard work' remains quite beside the point. They were simply fortunate – or unfortunate, it seems at times – to exist as a part of that arbitrary community, at that time, together.

Because the characters of *IT* are so thoroughly embedded within their community, Derry never truly leaves their minds. When the children return as adults, they immediately return to their old habits: Richie, for example, starts to push his glasses back up his nose even though he no longer wears glasses, while Bill starts to stutter again. Their community, in all of its beauty (and ugliness, as we shall see shortly), works upon the children of Derry in ways that they cannot resist. Because none of them can be 'entirely their own masters', the indoctrination of these children is profound. To imagine that these characters somehow exist separate from their upbringing would be the height of folly due to the reality that, as Mike admits, a person born blind does not know what blindness means 'until someone tells him' (169). Specifically, the novel presents children as firmly situated subjects through Eddie (a young boy with a number of psychosomatic conditions planted in him by his overbearing mother), Beverly (who remains a by-product of her abusive father – 'the she he had made') and resident bully Henry (forged by his father's malicious 'lessons'). Henry's father is equally shaped by the horrific war in which he served (108). Consequently, Eddie and Beverly marry spouses that closely resemble their overbearing parents, and Henry unwittingly enters into a violent conflict like his father. The very notion of communal enclosure, liberals will quickly interject, proves maddening for each of them.

But this sense of enclosure also endows King's characters with their primary sense of identity. 'To have character', Sandel points out, 'is to know that I move in a history I neither summon nor command, which carries consequences none the less for my choices and conduct' (*Liberalism* 179). Whereas liberalism treats identity as an assortment of assets chosen by a free-floating, almost ghostly subject, akin to the flammable young catalyst of *Firestarter*, communitarians situate characters in what they hold to be a much richer narrative: 'My identity is defined by the commitments and identifications that provide the horizon within which I can determine from case to case what is valuable, good or worth doing' (Mulhall and Swift 106). Presenting a veritable palimpsest of Derry's history, King's characters build a life upon the arcs of previous generations and, in so doing, *IT* exposes the thickness of public and private identities.

The act of telling stories, dialogically and ritualistically, contributes to *IT*'s dense communal parameters. Bill serves as the leader of the group due to his role as a popular author that can weave effective narratives. In building a mutual history through storytelling – the basis of any community, according to communitarian Alasdair MacIntyre – the Losers' Club produces what can be described as a good in common: 'We can know a good in common that we cannot know alone' (Sandel, *Liberalism* 183). The subject depends upon a shared vocabulary, a 'language community', to define herself, a feat that can only be achieved in conversation with others. To construct a life is to construct a narrative; to ensure that this narrative makes any sense, the subject must borrow recognisable tropes from the community in which she has been cultivated. Therefore, King's storytellers are not antecedent to the story that unfolds, as liberalism would have it, but wholly moored to collective fables.

Along these lines, MacIntyre argues that Aristotelian narrative serves as the paramount impetus behind community-building: 'We all live out narratives in our lives and it is because we understand our own lives in terms of the narratives that we live out that the form of narrative is appropriate for understanding the actions of others.' Another kind of infrastructure, narrative fills our lives with meaning by holding characters accountable to one another as well as revealing a common ground from which to judge one another's actions: 'The story of my life is always embedded in the story of those communities from which I derive my identity.'[3] MacIntyre's argument applies particularly well in the case of Bill, a boy with a significant speech impediment: 'Deprive children of stories and you leave them unscripted, anxious stutterers in their actions as in their words' ('Virtues' 133, 143, 138). Significantly, Bill's stutter vanishes once he feels as though he belongs within the Losers' Club. King's reader thus grasps the power of the community through narratives interwoven in a dialogic fashion, in which each character contributes personal tales to the tapestry of the novel and demarcates values shared in common: 'My friend may grasp something I have missed . . . my friend knew me better than I knew myself' (Sandel, *Liberalism* 181). Richie notices that Bill has the power to stop stuttering before Bill, while Ben sees Beverly's beauty before she recognises it in herself. In short, the storytelling at the heart of the Losers' Club underscores the relational character of this community, whereas a non-communitarian reading of *IT* views the club as 'nothing but a meeting place for individual wills, each with its own set of attitudes and preferences' (MacIntyre, *After* 25). A liberal reading of King's novel explains away the vital role played by context – without which, communitarians contend, the text would cease to make any sense.

A liberal reading

But if community is the saving grace of *IT*, community is also the novel's greatest source of enmity, which is to say, the strong pull to return home matches an equally strong push to escape from it. For every Black Spot – the 'exclusive' social club formed by black soldiers in solidarity – there arises a poisonous Ku Klux Klan. The notorious figure at the centre of King's story, Pennywise the Clown, embodies all that is wrong with the concept of community. Above all else, for liberals, community necessitates an unwelcome estrangement between 'insiders' and 'outsiders', akin to Carl Schmitt's friend/enemy distinction. Liberals prefer to imagine a neutral set of rational actors, and thereby repress signs of political struggle. A healthy degree of alienation nevertheless remains imperative to any liberal order. Adrian Daub argues, 'King is a communal writer . . . [the characters are] Losers, but not Loners, and the difference makes a difference' (Daub). By stressing positive collectivist qualities, communitarians miss an essential aspect of King's text: namely, the characters of *IT* regularly submerge into the role of Loner in a fashion that proves to be redemptive. Although the vile It threatens to isolate members of the Losers' Club from one another, the group's proposed countermeasures also demand isolation, designating members according to their singularities and not their level of compliance:

'It *started* alone for each of us' (502, author's emphasis). King's causal chain is clear: due to the fact that individuals exist prior to communities, everyone must begin unattended if they wish to survive.[4]

To make its case, a liberal reading of *IT* argues that the idea of community in the text depresses plurality in the name of prescribed cohesion. The novel opens with the Canal Days Festival, a profit-driven event punctuated by the brutal murder of a gay man as well as the military gesticulations of Pennywise marching in a 'patriotic' parade. The result is a warped sense of justice because, if justice is not a priori – that is, if justice remains the by-product of particular societies (as communitarians would posit) rather than a universal (as Rawls asserts), cadres will invariably twist justice into grotesque expressions of 'civic pride'. For instance, a gang can murder an 'outsider' to uphold Derry's 'traditional values', and Derry's police can manipulate evidence to achieve their desired outcome or torture homeless people to stop them from settling down in 'their city' (696, 36). The first scenes of *IT* suggest that erecting the pillars of justice upon anything other than the cardinal preservation of individual freedom leads to a nightmarish collapse of the social order.

In *IT*, communal influence can oppress to such a degree that it feels like a 'python', a 'knitting-together' effect that makes the children sense that they are strapped to something like a 'guided missile'. Home may well be where the heart is, the children recognise, but it is also where the community refuses to 'let you out' (948, 495, 87). Derek Phillips contends that communitarian thought 'obliterates individual autonomy entirely and dissolves the self into whatever roles are imposed by one's position in society' (183). Their community habituates the children of Derry when, for example, Beverly's tyrannical father describes people as nothing more than pets to be 'cosseted and disciplined' – an observation that unequivocally conflates communal belonging with imprisonment. To come back to Derry, the adult characters must emancipate themselves from similarly oppressive situations: Beverly must abandon her abusive husband; Eddie must disentangle himself from his excessively maternal wife. Because belonging to a community makes it difficult for a character to see how he or she is being negatively influenced, the individual must 'step back' before going into battle with his or her monstrous hometown (King, *IT* 536, 900). This act of stepping back, repeated throughout the text, presumes an antecedent subject that can achieve a necessary degree of separation thanks to his liberal detachment. For example, although Eddie admires Bill as a leader, he shrinks at the realisation that he would die for him and, as a result, he starts to think that Bill's influence may not be such a 'good power'. Furthermore, team members of the Losers' Club are rendered literally and symbolically infertile as the second generation of Derry's children do not play in the same places as the Losers' Club, but opt to formulate their own 'runs and secret ways', a change that undermines the supreme import of inheritance espoused by communitarians (924, 960).

In these ways and many others, *IT* emphasises a subject that refuses to move in lockstep with her surroundings. A liberal reading of *IT* stresses how the entanglements of community are mere illusions by exposing the reversion of the Losers' Club into old habits as just another 'hallucination'. Inheritance is, in the end, delusive. Fathers and sons still maintain 'very different interests' in King's novel, and so they can be said to possess a mere 'passing resemblance' to one another. To augment its vocal rejection of inheritance, *IT* recycles the unsavoury side of indebtedness. Ben's father leaves his family saddled with debt; Stan spends his life refusing to be 'owned' by anyone; when Beverly escapes from her father (and later husband), she is exhilarated by the fact that she does not have a dime to her name (549, 75, 45). Whereas communitarianism rejects the idea that a subject can exist apart from his debts, liberals conceptualise a subject that jubilantly casts off all fetters, conjuring once more the image of Charlie from *Firestarter*.

Similarly, the children of Derry in many instances understand their shared arrangement via economic exchange. Ben realises two of the cardinal truths of liberalism: 'You pay for what you get', and you must practice the 'pragmatic counting of the cost' in every interaction if you are to persevere as an adult. To reinforce these cardinal truths, the Losers' Club monetises communal standing by charging its members with dues (78, 165). The novel thus articulates the club as a marketplace of autonomous actors, a connection made explicit by Rawls through his account of justice as analogous to Pareto Optimality (in which a state of optimum balance renders it impossible to alter the rules without diminishing another person's personal rights). For Rawls, the theory of economic equilibrium can be transposed into a theory of justice: 'Equilibrium is the result of agreements freely struck between willing traders. For each person it is the best situation that he can reach by free exchange consistent with the rights and freedom of others to further their interests in the same way' (61, 103). Put differently, when the Losers' Club achieves equilibrium by ensuring that every agent freely trades his assets with the other children, financial or immaterial, it restricts a sense of mutual indebtedness in favour of the belief that everyone must pay something to receive the benefits of membership (even just 23 cents to help pay for door hinges on the clubhouse).

Members of the club uphold a related liberal conceit by treating their clubhouse (first built, we will recall from a communitarian reading of the novel, on the intangible vapours of transcendental connectivity) as an object to be owned and protected by its proprietors, an exclusive private holding into which Bill refuses to invite outsiders because 'it's not their *property*'. Members of the Losers' Club defend their clubhouse because their notion of right is based upon the assumption that private property serves as a universal precondition. The adult Richie acknowledges that an individual's house and land serve as 'strings that bind you tight to the map of your life' (923, 64; author's emphasis). Unmoved by this argument, communitarians declare that this model of subjectivity slides problematically into legalism due to the fact that an excessive focus upon paying one's 'fair share', or upon who owns what property, forces members to question the benevolence of the underlying relationship (Sandel, *Liberalism* 32). When Richie demands that Mike pay his dues, for instance, the reader might start to doubt the 'magic' of the psychic connection that initially brought them together. The Losers' Club returns repeatedly to this sort of bureaucratic proceduralism in a fashion that cuts against the grain of mystical forces stressed by a communitarian reading. To facilitate the free and rational selection of membership, the club stages a vote; it later reinforces this choice by asking members to sign Eddie's cast as if it is a 'contract'. That is, initial mystique of communal belonging – its inescapability; its radical situatedness – evaporates as the children of Derry become individuals, defined by personal choices encased in legalese. The novel's stress upon legal choice manifests perhaps most pointedly in the decisive battle with Pennywise in which Bill locates his wife's wedding ring in the sewers of Derry. Because the ring offers a symbol of optional commitment, when Bill grasp's Richie's hand and feels the hardiness of the ring, it fortifies them both for their upcoming fight with Derry's demons. The paramount role of legalese extends into the supposedly preternatural friendship between Richie and Bill as they renew a promise to one another backed up by contractual logic.[5] Against the communitarian claim that liberal relationships are anaemic, Phillips avers: 'Relationships based on voluntary choices have a far deeper significance than those based on blind obedience or unthinking acquiescence' (192).

For Rawlsians, then, the club's sense of 'justice as fairness' links justice with rational choice, a 'primordial independence' that forces us to understand human beings as 'essentially and preeminently choosers' (T. Hall 79). They operate from what they claim to be an 'Original Position': the Archimedean point from which all reasonable citizens would hypothetically consent to be governed. Rawlsians conceive of a community that begins *de novo* by presenting justice as a principle that is 'not subject to political bargaining or the calculus of social interests'. Correspondingly, the adult characters in *IT* strip away ideological baggage to ascertain a sense of justice that is neither 'self-evident' nor transcendental. Their sense of justice legitimises itself because it would be chosen, in theory, by any one of them, even if they were to become disentangled from the club (Rawls 25, 37). And it would seem that King's text puts this theory to the test: given that they have forgotten what previously happened to them in their hometown, the adults of *IT* elect to return to Derry from *a completely uninformed position*. Once they return to Derry, the adults over and over again reaffirm the merits of blind choice by volunteering to fight from a position of ignorance as to what is really going on within the city limits. *IT* strategically employs amnesia to choreograph Rawls's Original Position.

The children are unaware that they will achieve unrivalled success as a result of their union; instead, they agree upon a contract without the burden of a long-term plan, thereby projecting a pre-political self that can operate behind what Rawls describes as the 'Veil of Ignorance'. Behind the Veil of Ignorance, liberal 'persons accept in advance a principle of equal liberty and they do this without knowledge of their more particular end'. King's characters, each of whom experience the Veil of Ignorance on at least two separate occasions, are not 'advantaged or disadvantaged in the choice of principles by the outcome of natural chance or the contingency of social circumstances but, by dint of innocence as well as forgetfulness, remain (doubly) blind to particular ends'. In other words, due to their twice-told Veil of Ignorance, King's characters must understand ethical obligation as entirely 'self-imposed' (Rawl, 27, 4, 11–12). The characters of *IT* subsequently maintain a link between justice and individual autonomy by habitually forgetting everything, including the community that they are left to (re)build together in perpetuity. In this way, just as the stories of *IT* dissolve into a fog of mercifully lost memories, liberalism sustains the tabula rasa of a blessedly amnesiac subject allowed, indefinitely, to 'start thinking about some sort of new life'. The radical forgetfulness of liberals occupies centre stage in the final pages of *IT* when, to rescue his wife from a coma, Bill takes her on a ride upon his childhood bicycle. As they ride, his wife makes her first 'independent action' (1078, 1084). His new-found autonomy – his will to make the pedals go and to flee, furiously, away from Derry – not only liberates his wife, but it also gives him an erection and apparently renders him fertile once more (although the purpose of his reclaimed fertility, given the novel's hostility to the notion of inheritance, remains a mystery).

To refute this liberal reading, communitarians would insist that Bill's climactic Original Position is an 'admitted fiction', a story that constrains 'reasoning about justice in certain ways' (Sandel, *Liberalism* 41). Said another way, barring the magical thinking of King's novel – in particular, the inexplicable amnesia that plagues his characters – the Losers could never truly elect to do the 'right thing' without simultaneously depending upon precepts transmitted to them by the institutions of Derry. 'It is not a condition of human status that one interpret oneself as being most fundamentally and essentially an autonomous chooser of ends: that will happen (if it happens at all) only in an appropriately liberal social matrix' (Mulhall and Swift 125). Even if one believes in Rawls's Original Position, communitarians hasten to add, this position remains always-already linked to specific sources of communal influence: namely, a 'liberal social matrix'.

Moreover, because the border between determinism and free will in *IT* is so very precarious, it remains difficult for readers to assign blame for social infractions committed by King's characters. MacIntyre declares: 'I am forever whatever I have been at any time for others – and I may at any time be called upon to answer for it' (139). While MacIntyre's narratable life facilitates a sense of accountability, Rawlsians appeal to a fundamentally detached calculus. *IT* grants no relief from this ever-looming question of personal responsibility. At one point, Bev scolds her abusive father, 'It's making you do it, but *you* let It in'; in another instance, however, Bev's friend tells her that Bev's problems are her own fault, 'at least to a degree', for opting to stay with her abusive husband (869, 373; author's emphasis). *IT* wrings its hands about where to assign blame. Does communal influence make the subject do things, and so lessen her culpability? Should the subject alone be considered responsible for her actions? These debates swirl throughout King's text, stirring as well as suppressing the reader's empathy for the citizens of Derry.

Convergence without consensus

Determined by a fluid border that separates children from adults, *IT* ultimately confuses the communitarian and liberal binary. The communitarian Selznick admits that 'a balance must be struck between the demands of society and the needs of individuals' (43). The liberal Rawls sounds equally placatory, first when he acknowledges that self-realisation is bound up in the basic structure of communities, and later when he distances himself from his initial interpretation of 'right over good' by deeming it too rigid (452). In similar fashion, *IT* interweaves the positions that this chapter pantomimes – nebulous positions, it bears emphasising, that have never been convincingly bifurcated.[6] William Connolly asserts,

> Pressed very hard by communitarians . . . most of us retreat toward liberal standards of citizenship, freedom, and privacy. And yet when the liberal . . . attempts to woo us back into the liberal camp, we discern even more poignantly how the doctrine draws a veil of ignorance across the most disturbing features of contemporary life. (*Politics* 73)

Unable to elude its contradictions, the closing section of *IT* depicts liberalism and communitarianism as a single totality that unfolds dialectically: individuals begin as children embedded in a community, they grow up by detaching themselves from said community, they realise that they remain interconnected, and then they separate from one another to grow up once more (and so on, ad infinitum). King's novel therefore exposes the strengths as well as blind spots of each position.

The narrative augments this liberal-communitarian convergence with references to Shirley Jackson's *The Haunting of Hill House* (1959). Like a number of other works by King, *IT* recycles a refrain from Jackson's novel when it notes of the Derry Community House, 'Whatever walked in Community House, walked alone' (863). *The Haunting of Hill House* meditates upon the pull of community as well as the push of individualism through the struggles of its protagonist, Eleanor: 'I am like a small creature swallowed whole by a monster, she thought . . . "No," she said aloud, and the one word echoed . . . It was my own choice to come' (42). At the crux of Jackson's story, Eleanor must think that she makes her own choices and yet, to feel like she belongs in her new community at Hill House, she must also disappear into someone else's story, losing critical purchase in her own. This dynamic recurs throughout King's fiction. *'Salem's Lot* (1975), for one, describes the small-town community of 'Salem's Lot as eternal and increasingly atomised, a place that sustains the intimacy of collective belonging – alone, the protagonist points out, is the 'most awful word' – and the oppressive bond of cooperatives: 'There's little good in sedentary small towns' (203, 119). The novel's protagonist wants to reclaim the 'magic' of small-town America, but he refuses to be snagged by the vast supernatural web that binds the citizens of 'Salem's Lot. From *'Salem's Lot* onward, King's corpus regularly juxtaposes the fantastic power of communal influence with its less marvellous aspects. For instance, *The Shining* (1977) tracks a man that literally as well as figuratively dissolves into the clutches of his community at the Overlook Hotel and a boy that depends upon his communal linkage with others, including his psychic link to the Overlook's cook. 'The shining' signifies both a connective tissue that destroys the individual as well as the psychic connection that eventually saves him. Finally, *Dreamcatcher* (2001) – a sequel of sorts to *IT* – re-fashions King's liberal-communitarian nexus for the twenty-first century by presenting four protagonists in need of connectivity as they learn that connectivity can be a trap: 'Sometimes being alone is better' (499). Recalling the preternatural manner in which *IT*'s adult characters forget their community, a character in *Dreamcatcher* stands apart from the telepathic kinship that impinges upon him, becoming a liberal subject that quite literally retreats into the Cartesian attic inside of his own head. From its very earliest days, then, King's fiction privileges individuals that dream outside the lines (liberal) as well as citizens that catch themselves on the hidden lines that delineate their fellowship (communitarian).

Although critics tend to dislike the ending of *IT* due to its sanguine, sprawling character ('the ending', Kaitlyn Tiffany tells us bluntly, 'is not well-written'), a dialectical reading of the text re-situates its core divisions – child/adult; community/individual – within a metaphysical system, one oriented around a 'cosmic Spirit whose nature is to posit its own essential embodiment' (C. Taylor, *Hegel* 35). Such a reading of course owes a massive debt to philosopher G. W. F. Hegel, the German idealist who, according to Steven B. Smith, seeks 'to combine the liberal or enlightened belief in life, liberty, and the pursuit of happiness with the ancient Aristotelian conception of politics as a collective pursuit aimed at some idea of a public good'. On the one hand, Hegel understands the inchoate liberalism of his day to be too legalistic because its paper-thin concept of the subject does not adequately provide a sense of communal fulfilment; and yet, he continues, a prototypical communitarian logic frequently forecloses development of the self to perpetuate a toxic status quo. In reply, Hegel develops a potential third option: 'Reason, community, and freedom are at last joined in a new and higher harmony . . . the integration of life's opposing tendencies' (Smith 8, 34). According to Charles Taylor, a contemporary figure that intersects liberal and communitarian thought, Hegel offers a rejoinder to the fragmented social order of societies like Derry by proposing a system in which the subject unites with a communal whole without 'sacrificing self-consciousness and autonomous will'. That is, the Hegelian Taylor aims to reconcile self-conscious freedom with life in community (*Hegel* 11). The Losers' Club exemplifies this mindset.

On the one hand, we might read Hegel as a prototypical communitarian because of his claim that individual consciousness comes to fruition only through political organisation. He comprehends community as the manifestation of an Absolute Spirit that finds expression 'through the life of the community', hence his laudatory treatment of the German state as a 'divine' entity. From a communitarian perspective, institutions give necessary form to an otherwise formless Spirit, and so Hegel disparages the French Revolution's nihilistic yearning for its lack of shape and its negative sense of liberty. Whereas French Revolutionaries generally understand personal freedom to be a given, rather than the fruit of historical struggle, Hegel claims that freedom must be understood as correlated with the community in which it is achieved. At the same time, however, we might read Hegel as a prototypical liberal because his work points to 'an order . . . centred on autonomy, since to be governed by a law which emanates from oneself is to be free' (C. Taylor, *Hegel* 91, 79). Indeed, the all-powerful It transforms into an antecedent character within King's story, with Its own unique thought process. By encompassing liberal and communitarian sentiments, Hegelian thought affords us an opportunity to re-read the cosmic finale of *IT* and unlock its latent political possibilities.

The characters of *IT* rehearse a Hegelian movement at the border between 'power and helplessness'. Individuals love one another, but they come to realise that love can be a possessive form of mastery; individuals desire freedom, but they come to realise that private desires can be destructive. In one of the novel's most notable scenes, after Beverly has sex with each of the team members to stave off evil forces, she expresses relief that 'her sex is her own again' – even as she experiences a 'strange melancholy' (767, 847, 1041). Unity and disunity merge into a comprehensive process. Examples of this unfolding are numerous in King's text: Pennywise leaves his mark on the club and the club, in turn, 'works its will' on him, and gradually, the all-powerful It and the Losers' Club start to represent 'two great wheels' within a monumental myth (490–1, 419). What walks alone winds up walking in lockstep with others – and then walks alone again (etcetera).

Likewise, as King's characters move from the blind consciousness of innocent childhood to the self-consciousness demanded by adult relationships, *IT* accumulates private stories into a linguistic tapestry that expresses a 'higher differentiated unity' (Smith 124). To comprehend the concrete steps of this process, we can retrace the steps of It as the entity's consciousness develops over the course of the text. King's entity initially peers outward with the eyes of youth, unaware of Itself as a restricted being, only to become alienated from Itself with the rise of the Losers' Club. The club forces It to view Itself from a distance, to consider the consciousness of Another and to understand, as a consequence, that It is 'not eternal'. At the close of King's epic, 'the unthinkable must finally be thought' (966, 1034). Like the children, King's monster evolves by interacting with the consciousness of Others.[7] Through the text's Hegelian dynamic, *IT* remains liberal – It as well as the children begin (and end) as solitary forms – and communitarian – a universal force exists prior to the subject and endures long after him. In this manner, *IT* interweaves self-realisation and community-formation into a single holistic view that recalls Hegel's civil religion.[8] Only 'partial communities' like the Losers' Club possess the capacity to refute an oppressive communitarianism and an anaemic liberalism. The two-way glass umbilicus that connects the children and adult sections of the Derry library provides an apt metaphor for the underlying dialectic.

Undoubtedly, King's adherence to a cosmic bedrock need not receive unreserved accolades. Certain readers may find that the reconciliation of *IT* merely muddies the waters when, in the decades that follow the publication of the novel, Third Way-isms perpetuate stagnation under the guise of meaningful transformation. These opaque attempts at consensus make it possible to proclaim, as Bev's friend does, that 'feminism and capitalism are not mutually exclusive, thank God' – a sentiment that thoroughly blurs the line between solidarity and self-interest under the auspices of a benevolent marketplace (372). From this vantage point, King's readers could conclude that the answers provided at the close of *IT* merely prop up the era's anti-political sentiments under the illusion of desirable equilibrium. Slavoj Žižek similarly denounces communitarians for practising 'arche-politics', a 'homogeneous social space which allows for no void in which the political . . . can emerge', while chastising liberals for practising 'parapolitics', with which one can 'de-antagonize politics by formulating . . . clear rules to be obeyed' ('Carl' 28). According to Žižek, the sort of smooth synthesis that closes *IT* demonstrates the worst of liberal as well as communitarian thought by stripping away the edges of both camps and making only the feeblest gestures at genuine tension.[9] Like critics that malign Hegel's system for being too cohesive, we might find King's claim of cosmic consensus to be a serious liability to the epic's political potential.

Nevertheless, *IT* does foster a conceptual struggle that remains paramount to American politics. It is worth remembering that the novel arrives at a historical moment (the 1980s) in which American society experiences an intensified push for de-politicisation. Unwilling to rest in unworldly equilibrium, King's epic repeatedly conveys the messiness of American politics, forcing its readers to remain unsettled and, as a result, politically active. For instance, by collapsing the umbilicus of the Derry library, *IT* demolishes even its primary metaphor of fluid passage. With this collapse, the text stresses a Hegelian rejoinder that *there can be no end to the process of alienation/reconciliation*. Because its protagonists are never truly finalised, and neither are their communities, King's epic preserves a vital sense of restlessness.

Todd McGowan contends that contradictions like the divide between liberals and communitarians remain 'the engine behind all political movement'. We cannot overcome these contradictions, he adds, due to the fact that they constitute – at a foundational level – subjectivities as well as societies (*Emancipation* 197, 214). Liberals and communitarians are both wrong when they claim to tell the 'whole story': in truth, the characters in *IT* are 'multiple and contradictory subjects . . . precariously and temporarily sutured at the intersection of [liberal and communitarian] positions' (Mouffe, *Return* 20). The liberal-communitarian debate in *IT* remains potent, then, precisely because it nurtures a dialogic impulse.[10] Because the novel remains unwilling to feign resolution, *IT* underscores the basic strength of America's (hypothetical) liberal democracy, which is to say, it encourages us to resist a communitarian perspective that under-emphasises self-realisation (free individuals are the nucleus of the process, not an after-thought) and a liberal perspective that over-emphasises self-realisation (the notion of a public good is not some paltry appendage to a fully cultivated self but a constitutional aspect of any community). In short, by denying its own promise of mythological consensus, *IT* invites readers to share in a robust political vision, one that disrupts partisan absolutes and partakes in the fruits of contradiction.

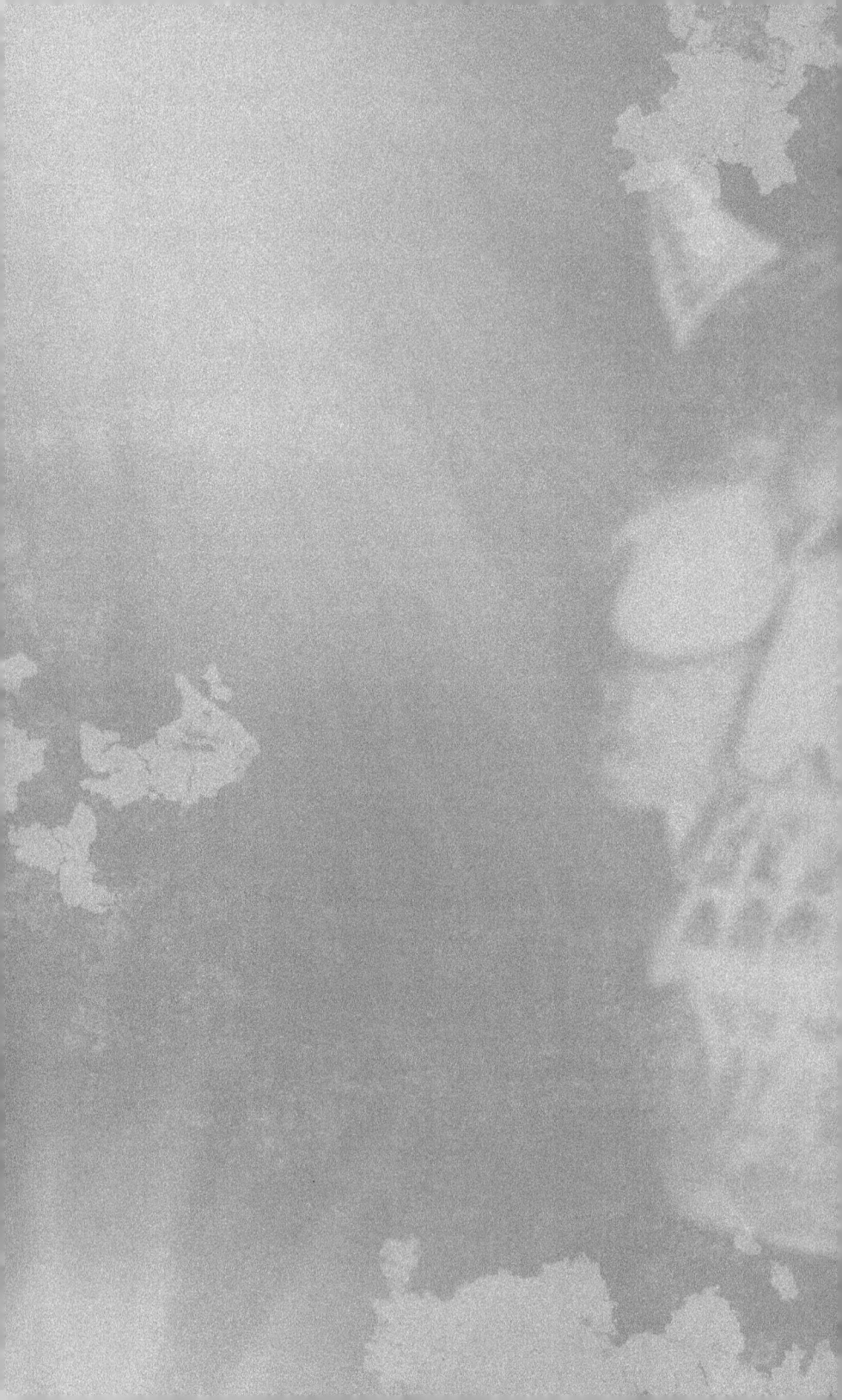

6

Interlude

The Langoliers and the Political Event

STEPHEN KING'S novella *The Langoliers* (1990) follows a band of survivors as their plane passes through a rupture in time and they must confront a dramatically altered world. At its most basic level, the novella conveys how random political events disrupt our lives by focusing upon a binary between law and order and disobedience, embodied in the characters of Nick Hopewell and Craig Toomy. After passing through the rupture, Nick – an agent of the British government – immediately strives to restore order (a character notes, 'I knew he'd take over'); meanwhile, Craig – a disenchanted Wall Street trader – is eager to free himself from the regimes of his employer as well as his fastidious father and to disconnect from the quotidian world to achieve 'ultimate release' (142, 174). This dual movement replays tensions discussed in the previous chapter concerning King's *IT* (1986). Specifically, the friction between Nick and Craig conveys a critical oscillation between hyper-managerialism and unanticipated political happenings seen throughout King's fiction.

From one vantage point, Nick-as-manager refuses to lose his handle on 'THE BIG PICTURE', the metanarrative that supposedly keeps survivors marching towards a better future. He puts pressure on an idealist legislator – a public figure that he designates as the 'total politician', and against whom he positions himself as 'prudent' administrator. In this way, he seems 'weirdly like Richard Nixon', a resemblance that is not exactly complimentary, as when the Nixonian Nick violently threatens to expunge Craig, but that nonetheless appears to legitimise his dominion over the rest of the group. He insists that fellow passengers relax and let him 'take care of things'. After Craig stabs the story's young prophet, Nick responds: 'Seal the wound . . . Keep that pressure on! Don't let up!' (134, 79, 152–3, 144). He exemplifies a tendency described by Carl Schmitt as 'the striving for a neutral domain', which is to say, in contrast to the utopian politicians that he silences, Nick's style of governance – to seal the gaping wound and keep the pressure on – is meant to strike the reader as 'refreshingly factual' ('Age' 89–91). He suppresses the engagement of fellow passengers in shared governance by proclaiming 'prudence' to be 'the better part of valor' (King, *Langoliers* 67).

From another vantage point, Craig's apparent unorthodoxy, although it too never manifests in an entirely favourable light, entices the reader.[1] Like a modern-day Bartleby the Scrivener, Craig's desire to split from the novella's authoritarians echoes a desire cultivated throughout *The Langoliers*: a music prodigy yearns to flee from his overbearing father; a cuckolded husband craves to liberate himself from his wife (with her 'aristocratic' nose); even Nick secretly hungers for a break from the oppressive hold of the British state. Despite Nick's oversight, Craig's defection shows that the truth can 'no longer be avoided' (16, 111). Craig's refusal to participate in the rat race unleashes chaos as well as nascent possibilities by encouraging fellow survivors to reject the status quo. With his final leap into the void, *The Langoliers* stresses a sense of 'being present' that appears to depart from the plotting of contemporary politicians and economists alike. That is, when freed from the weight of industrial time, and armed with their new-found understanding that life is too precious to conform, King's survivors start to behave like 'shooting stars'. They accept Craig's revised concept of being-in-time to become 'more actual. More *there*' (234, author's emphasis). Echoing King's other time-focused works, *The Langoliers* stresses the fullness of an eternal present.[2]

With Craig's radical departure from his society's norms, *The Langoliers* addresses the power of a political event to change everything 'on a dime'. Former British Prime Minister Harold Macmillan once purportedly described the driving force behind politics: 'Events, dear boy, events.' Appropriately enough, King's narrative names its rupture 'The Event', spurring a conversation between the text and contemporaneous political theorists. Haunted by a breach that can be neither forecast nor contained, King's text posits that any dominant social arrangement could be quite suddenly altered. To illustrate this condition, *The Langoliers* maintains a yawning hole at its centre: a schism between Nick's organisational politics and the disaggregation triggered by Craig's political urges that, at its most fundamental level, delineates the possible from the impossible. The rapid encroachment of the langoliers compels characters to conform to certain temporal expectations such as running on the corporate fast track 'like a greyhound chasing a mechanical rabbit', or experiencing nostalgia for a world they 'know and understand'. When the demonic force supposedly feeds upon subjects that 'waste time', King's novella inspires a conservative reaction. After all, without Nick's law-and-order tactics, survivors would sink into 'some dark abyss' (90, 85, 39, 58). Although it may be reasonable for King's readers to long for comfortable 'little nests', *The Langoliers* does not simply negate or disrupt established timelines; instead, it constructs an alternative mode of being-in-time to re-make the world: '*The invention of a time* whose particular characteristics are taken from the event' (Badiou, *Rebirth* 70; author's emphasis). Nick's effort to repress divergent notions of time (the conservative face of the langoliers) instigates Craig's unconventional mode of being-in-time (the revolutionary face of the langoliers) – and so on, ad infinitum. King's story encapsulates a self-enclosed loop, driven by the perpetual resurgence of political happenings.

Before considering its ramifications in King's fiction, we must pause to define the political event, because King's event meets criteria set forth by the foremost theorist of this phenomenon, Alain Badiou. The event of *The Langoliers*, that is, the rupture through which the plane passes, can be delineated in uniquely political terms. First, the original mode of thinking that the novella's event inaugurates 'belongs to all'. According to Badiou, a political event sets into motion an alternative way of thinking for everyone: 'Only politics is intrinsically required to declare that the thought that it is is the thought of all.' None of King's passengers can think about their world in the old way once they pass through a hole in the established order. Secondly, passengers must sustain in perpetuity deliberations concerning the (re)organisation of their society, as another disruptive event could occur at any moment. And finally, the event exposes the errancy behind any hegemony, brought most visibly to the surface when Nick realises that the economic and political imperatives of the British government are inseparable and thus conditional (Badiou, *Metapolitics* 153, 141–3,

147). With these criteria met, we can proceed to interpret the event of *The Langoliers* as distinctively political in nature.

The political event always disrupts the fixed Truths of a particular social order. Consider, for instance, the French Revolution, or (more pressing for King's fiction) the protests of May 1968, in which an eruption of force magnifies the will-to-truth of a given community. The power of a political happening exemplifies 'all the processes by which human collectivity becomes active or proves capable of new possibilities as regards to its own destiny' (Badiou, *Philosophy* 5). When Nick insists that his fellow passengers lie back and allow him to take care of the situation, or when Craig waits for his fascist father to tell him 'what he should do next', *The Langoliers* presents a managerial model that suppresses these sorts of disruptions. Likewise, Badiou expresses concern about a swelling managerial ethos that stymies political open-endedness, the lifeblood of any democracy, in favour of rigid calculation by elites and their disciplinary branches. In contrast, the event at the centre of *The Langoliers* revitalises the capacity of passengers to charter a disparate course:

> [The event] splits open and overturns the stagnant order of the world by opening up new possibilities of life, thought, and action . . . a process that opens [subjects] up to themselves, but also opens up the community to which they belong to a universal . . . if there is to be a political event, it will have to break with the general logic of the contemporary world. (Badiou and Gauchet 145)

In turn, once the political event interjects, central authorities like Nick cannot maintain their stranglehold over what is possible any longer. 'The possible will be wrested from the impossible', Badiou contends. 'Whence the rallying cry of '68: "Demand the impossible!"' (*Philosophy* 9–11). Fearful of this kind of unrest, the directorial Nick maintains that idealistic politicians belong in asylums; as a result of his repressive approach, fellow survivors are inspired to reject his modus operandi and return to the fecund antagonisms that he forecloses (a foreclosure anticipated by the ultimatum of the conservative langoliers: do your labour tirelessly or be wiped from the face of the earth).

Nick's foreclosure intensifies political desire for the (im)possible as King's novella tarries with the sense of longing and loss associated with a political event. Simply put, when something is found to be absent from the text, it becomes all the more attractive. The pilot rekindles his love for his ex-wife upon her death; passengers find beauty in the plane at the moment it will never fly again; and, when the United States is 'cancelled', its promise returns stronger than ever. Through a sense of displaced wholeness, *The Langoliers* fuels the (futile) yearning for a final destination that could satisfy everyone on board the plane, a vehicle aptly named 'American Pride': 'We have been the death of world; now I believe we are going to see it born' (8, 231). America's proverbial City on the Hill is once more deferred to keep the nation's political wheels in motion. Even as 'The Event' disrupts King's storyworld and invites his characters to pine for utopia, a world beyond the rigid confines of industriousness, *The Langoliers* refuses to conceal its need for continual rupture: 'The [lost] object . . . can cause and perpetuate desire only if it is lacking, making the satisfaction of this desire impossible' (Stavrakakis 49). An unquenchable thirst for the lost object – captured viscerally in Craig's desperate pursuit of total release from his father's clutches – presents the political as a constant breakage. Recalling the logic of the Bachman books (see chapter 2), *The Langoliers* reveals how Americans have founded their politics upon permanent absence: a lack that keeps democracy moving; a lack that perpetuates desire for the City on a Hill instead of the embrace of a phony sense of fulfilment. An enduring dissatisfaction among King's survivors reinforces the gravity of the event that they have confronted (and will confront again). The text's most revitalising aspect, then, remains its insistence that passengers will not be able to circumvent these happenings. Despite the tireless efforts of the novella's numerous authoritarians, the political endures.

King's story confronts the latent potential within its social order: a gaping hole that catalyses the endless (re)combinations of American politics. The narrative's internal shuddering renders Nick's delusions of wholeness susceptible to devastating quakes, and the seismic shift of the event unexpectedly lays 'the establishment' to waste. *The Langoliers* quite literally trembles with political possibilities that could erupt into consciousness at any moment: 'They could feel the very earth begin to vibrate' (180). Like King, Franco 'Bifo' Berardi conceptualises these multifold possibilities as particles that palpitate, ready at all times to combine into unforeseen constellations. King's chaotic vibrations birth events that do not 'correspond to a chain of causation', but rather provoke a 'new cognitive rhythm' (Berardi 15, 28). Indeed, the earth-moving vibrations of King's novella cannot be computed in advance and so the precarious world of *The Langoliers* resembles a tuning fork as the story's passengers attempt to anticipate a nascent rhythm that grows steadier by the second. This pulsating phenomenon resurfaces again in King's *The Institute* (2019), another story about 'great events' that turn on 'small hinges' and thrum with latent power: 'The *potential* for power was present . . . like breathing air just before the summer's biggest thunderstorm lets rip' (280, 403; author's emphasis). In King's multiverse, a constant humming typically precedes the terrifying and exultant ignition of the political event. Because no algorithm can forecast an event, the logic goes, we must stay alert for undulations that could enter our perception suddenly and then radically revise the cadence of our lives.

The political event of *The Langoliers* is uniquely unforeseeable. Whereas conscious passengers do not survive the plane's passage through a puncture in time, sleeping passengers on the fateful flight are saved precisely because they are not awake. In an indispensable way, the radical side of the langoliers reverses the legacy of Western logic, summarised by art historian Giorgio Vasari. 'It is not by sleeping', Vasari contends, 'but by waking and studying continually that progress is made' (66). In direct contradistinction to Vasari's claim, the event in King's story cultivates a subjectivity defined not by ever greater wakefulness (in current parlance, 'being woke') – the early bird gets the worm, Craig's overbearing father would insist – but by a renewed interest in sleepiness, by attempts to drop out of the grand processional of Western 'progress'. As a result, the text's event reveals the disparate state of being-in-time that passengers must adopt if they wish to pass back through the rift in one piece. They learn that releasing conscious control over the course of their lives enables them to reimagine the world. As early as the dawn of the 1990s, *The Langoliers* comments upon what Jonathan Crary describes as a 24/7 social order that eradicates 'shadows and obscurity and . . . alternative temporalities' by building 'a global system that never sleeps . . . to ensure that no potentially disturbing awakening is ever necessary or relevant'. When Nick demands that every waking moment be filled with docile labour or consumption, King's novella responds with an urgent plea for sleep in order to resist this militant wakefulness, a state of constant surveillance. In *The Langoliers,* sleep provides one of the few remaining sites for an event to surface because it alone exists outside of Wall Street's purview (we might pair this discussion with the analysis of King's 1979 novel, *The Dead Zone,* in the prelude). Sleep offers pause, a release from the encroachment of capitalism into the quiet corners of our private lives and, for Craig in particular, it makes possible a necessary, and highly politicised, condition of 'uselessness'. Being genuinely asleep provokes 'a radical interruption' – a singular event to interrupt the relentless march of profit-making (Crary 19–24, 126–28). Reminding the reader of the potentialities of a better-rested world, Craig's hibernation reverses a truism of late capitalism: namely, when we enter into deep sleep, we are actually awakened to a degree that proves disturbing to hegemonic social structures. Craig finds a way to preserve the vital unknown that sleep provides (the chaos of dreams, we are led to surmise) and therefore advocates dynamism in the face of Nick's totalitarian regime. That is, counter to Nick's aspiration to construct wholeness in their post-rupture society, one that would 'eliminate anxiety and loss' and 'defeat dislocation', Yannis Stavrakakis points out that 'politics cannot exhaust the political' (71). The unforeseeable happenings exemplified in Craig's unconscious state deny the consensus and cure model that has been prescribed by Nick's sleepless managerial class.[4] To understand their predicament, King's passengers must release their hold on what they believe to be rational and follow instead 'the silent tickings of instinct'. King's post-event passengers thus embrace a nascent sense of 'time . . . and sleep . . . and not knowing' (King, *Langoliers*, 208, 217). In the prelude, I describe this phenomenon as a politics of the blind spot.

The political event of King's story interrupts the stagnating regime in power during the 1980s. Craig's spectacular dissolution reorders the perception of his fellow passengers, punctuating what is possible – a world that suddenly seems flavourless – with something that was, until very recently, inconceivable: 'When we break through those clouds, we are going to see something no human being has ever seen before. It will be something which is utterly beyond belief . . . yet we will be forced to believe it.' The political event generates a revised thought-process by igniting 'a crucible of new life . . . where life is freshly minted every second of every day'. King's tale repeatedly employs the terms 'fresh' and 'new' to describe the novella's post-eventual social order as 'new people' emerge from the rupture to populate a yet 'unmarked' world (220–1, 70, 233–4). *The Langoliers* arrives at what may appear to be (at least, to Nicks of the world) a disturbing conclusion: there is no hegemony that cannot be foundationally overturned on a dime. Although the text grants that organisational politics provides necessary, if fleeting, structures, like Nick's prudent 'little nests', Craig's political energies mercifully defy the certitude of a sterile world.

Likewise, King's novella presents the dialectic of organised politics and the political, the knowable and the unknowable, the possible and the impossible as a precarious demarcation around which readers must constantly tarry. The story is a paradox exemplified by the mystery writer on the plane: a stand-in for King that imbues the narrative with meaning as well as indispensable open-endedness. First, King's stand-in declares that expanded knowledge is preferable to wilful ignorance; however, he insists that his fellow passengers should 'never believe a writer' (105, 109). Correspondingly, the relationship between King's reader and the text of *The Langoliers* parallels the relationship between survivors and the political event. Readers must orient themselves with King's generic signposts while they must, at the same time, acknowledge that his storyworld orbits around an interminable void. If the reader tries wholeheartedly to predict the story's next event(s), she risks becoming another one of the unfortunate passengers that stays awake – that equates diligence with 'being woke' – *only to perish*.[5]

Given the thrust of the preceding chapters, it is worth asking if Craig's 'departure' might unsuspectingly reinforce the pillars of neo-liberalism. As I have already argued, a thin line separates gaps in the master's knowledge that open avenues for a slave's escape from gaps in everyone's knowledge designed to re-enforce the centrality of a volatile free market (with its so-called invisible hand). In this sense, the story's promise of an eternal present reflects an understanding of time necessitated by an ever-expanding financial sector. Less counter-cultural than it may seem upon first glance, perhaps we may interpret the eternal present of King's novella as a reflection of short-termism under high finance. Critics like John Sears overlook this overlap when they take *The Langoliers* at its word and agree with King that his text pillories 'the anti-democratic, self-oriented 1980s ideology' (Sears 134). At the close of *The Langoliers*, when King's characters start to appreciate a disjointed sense of time that neither pushes them to contemplate the past nor spurs them to worry about the future, it can be argued that they flee from the clutches of Wall Street in a manner that simply underscores what Wall Street is in the process of becoming. An outright refusal of social planning remains, after all, a prerequisite for neo-liberal thought. In a similar vein, it can be argued that *The Langoliers* upholds a late twentieth-century trend to de-politicise American society when the novella privileges Nick's elitism over the potential of political decision-making (e.g., the incalculable actions of Craig and his fellow passengers). Even as the story grapples with Craig's departure from the status quo, it upholds the ethos of Wall Street: resignation to unpredictability; a compression of time akin to short-termism; and a refusal to plan or regulate (except, of course, among managers like Nick). Like the car stories discussed in chapter 3, we might conclude that *The Langoliers* unconsciously accelerates the devastation against which it poses, prima facie, as bulwark. Although this interpretation cannot be ignored out of hand, it does not fully account for the narrative's political imperatives, which are made all the more potent because of their active suppression. While financial agents could exploit the slipstream formed in this event's wake, no social arrangement remains predictive forever. The lone constant in this narrative is change: change, we hasten to add, that need not be grafted onto the matrix of a mercurial marketplace. The pattern of political disruption in this novella does not depend upon economic factors to make its presence keenly felt.

Following *The Langoliers*, King's fiction frequently tarries with unforeseen political events. *Cell* (2006) begins with 'the event that came to be known as The Pulse': a 'mutative trigger' that transforms everything by rewiring the mind of the masses, as when the protagonist's son transmutes into a fundamentally 'new thing' (3, 347). Like *The Langoliers*, *Cell* interrogates the formation of like-minded blocs of survivors in tandem with the belief that unpredictability is the *sine qua non* of King's brave new world. Later, *Revival* (2014) recycles Badiou's metaphor of the lightning strike, an occurrence 'utterly unconnected to anything that had been on my mind', to illuminate how incalculable interference transforms the life of a community. The novel capitalises upon the revolutionary potential of the event by depicting the arrival of Jesus as being 'like a lightning strike', one that alters the make-up of the universe, and by linking itself to other unpredictable events that occur in the year 1968 – including, prominently, the assassinations of Robert F. Kennedy and Martin Luther King, Jr. (97, 200, 214). We might extend this discussion to include the arrival of a new world order in the aftermath of a global pandemic event. When King's fiction displaces the political event in the vain pursuit of consensus or cure, its characters forget lessons that they have already learned. But once the plane descends through the clouds into 'new belief', there will be no going back, and the next event lies interminably just beyond the closest horizon.

As the preceding chapters demonstrate, King's fiction orients itself around a permanent tension between establishment politics and the tempestuous propulsion of political dissatisfaction. In this case, the ghastly langoliers inhabit Nick when he legislates nonconformity, and yet – thanks to Nick's exclusionary tactics, akin to Schmitt's friend/enemy antagonism – the langoliers also inhabit Craig as he diverges from the noxious pathways prescribed to him. On the one hand, the novella's survivors must turn off auto-pilot in favour of a less predictable flight pattern; on the other hand, the turbulent event that they experience calls out for an order in the service of disorder, the constant guardianship of an exception . . . a mediation between the world and changing the world' (Badiou, *Rebirth* 66). Put differently, like its titular bogeyman ever chasing its tail, *The Langoliers* invariably re-politicises itself as the narrative remains fraught with a desire to keep happenings at bay in tandem with drive to fortuitous rupture. King's novella forces readers to pace upon a thrumming wire that (im)possibly divides discipline from disorder. In the end, by compelling readers walk upon this wire, the text safeguards its political event as an 'unburned burning': a constitutive blind spot that we disregard at our own peril (King, *Revival* 86).

7

Human Capital in *Rose Madder*

EXPANDING UPON a common theme in Stephen King's fiction of releasing 'femaleness' from the charnel house of patriarchy, *Rose Madder* (1995) tracks timid protagonist Rosie as she flees from her abusive husband, Norman, by entering into a magical painting to claim ownership over her life story. Although the text presents an illusion of release from oppression, it ultimately demonstrates how the economy recaptures the various assets associated with personhood. On the one hand, *Rose Madder* resigns itself to widespread transvaluation – economic, aesthetic and corporeal – triggered by a financial logic that subsumes everything in its path, even the formation of one's identity; on the other hand, the text lauds entrepreneurial subjectivity, emboldening Rosie to make herself ever more 'valuable'. Gary Becker, one of the first economists to theorise about human capital, writes that 'the very nature of a person' is dedicated to 'weighing benefits and costs'. Becker's subject treats every aspect of their life – including 'education, training, medical care, and other additions to knowledge and health' – as a data point to be filtered through specific algorithms (392, 386). Following Becker's lead, Rosie transposes economic pressures from the 1990s into her personal performance, which is to say, into a subjectivity that remains 'open to all kinds of fluctuating identities' in lockstep with the machinations of finance (Dufour 12).[1] Complicating the internal tensions of *IT* (1986) and *The Langoliers* (1990) discussed in previous chapters, Rosie's story is at once totalising and private, absolute as well as singular. Simply put, *Rose Madder* tells the tale of a marketplace without limits under the guise of a rousing tale of female liberation. It thus retreads upon the premise of King's 1980 novel *Firestarter* (the focus of chapter 4) while concurrently charting the 'maturation' of this ideal subject even further, into the immersive arena of human capital.[2]

To begin, *Rose Madder* attempts to map the sublime yet intimate contours of the New Economy (another term for the post-Fordist landscape detailed at length in chapter 3). David Harvey illuminates how, in the years preceding the Roaring Nineties, a decade punctuated by dramatic departures from regulatory restraint, the 'Big Bang' of 1986 liberates banks to operate across borders so that 'liquid money capital could more easily roam the world looking for locations where the rate of return was highest'. That is, when unfettered from once-rigid mechanisms of adjustment, capitalists pry open previously foreclosed areas – like state-run industries, for instance, or human capital – because they have 'nowhere else to go' (Harvey, *Brief* 20, 29). *Rose Madder* exposes how this opening of the financial floodgates 'turns bare life into a direct source of profit', a phenomenon described by Christian Marazzi as 'biocapitalism'.[3] King's novel chronicles how the untapped potential of an oppressed woman can be incorporated into the vast circulatory patterns of the decade.[4] At stake in this complex process, Dany-Robert Dufour claims, is the distinction between dignity and price: whereas anything theoretically has a price, 'dignity is irreplaceable, "priceless," and 'has no equivalent' (10). By liquefying her identity as 'victim', Rosie may elevate her price – but, in so doing, she loses any sense of dignity and relegates herself to incessant self-marketing. Indeed, Rosie's 'do-it-yourself injunction is so unceasing that . . . in a viciously competitive job market [she has] no choice but to work on [herself], constantly, just to keep up' (Dean, *Crowds* 31). The expansions/contractions of Rosie's identity politics prove to be a rather undignified appendage to the fluctuating New Economy, part of an endless incorporation that exhausts many of King's bone-weary heroines.

King's fiction regularly returns to this intersection of high finance and identity politics.[5] The protagonist of *Duma Key* (2008), for example, recovers from a traumatic accident by constructing pieces of art in tandem with a different self. The process maintains clear economic underpinnings:

he begins the narrative as a self-made man, a 'genuine American-boy success' in an ageing industry (construction), before he 'evolves' into the free-floating business of self-entrepreneurship and 'literally draws [himself] back into the world' (3, 416, 564). The synthesis of artistic creativity and profit motive in King's corpus often stems from what has been referred to as 'progressive neo-liberalism' – a common alignment in the Roaring Nineties between progressive social movements like feminism and 'high-end, "symbolic," and financial sectors of the U.S. economy (Wall Street, Silicon Valley, and Hollywood)'. By 'exuding an aura of emancipation', in other words, King's tales of personal freedom for once-oppressed women charge 'neo-liberal economic activity with a frisson of excitement' (Fraser, *Old* 11, 14). The apparent *political* significance of *Rose Madder* – Rosie's 'reclamation' of her own identity – reveals itself to be another symptom of *economic* shifts of the era.

This chapter interprets *Rose Madder* in a manner that departs from a vein of King criticism that tends to appreciate the author's periodic 'unleashing' of female *potenza*. For instance, Carol Senf details how King's texts concerning female liberation pivot from third to first person narration, from a social fabrication of the subject to the subject's manufacturing of herself.[6] According to critics like Senf, King's female characters pursue 'personal identity and a sense of self-worth . . . to rely only upon themselves' (98). Despite the feeling of political upheaval that these works evoke, however, life for King's female characters is not demonstrably better as a result of their increased self-reliance. Through the enhanced circulation of her private assets, Rosie routes her sense of identity through the apertures of financialisation, and so rather than mistake her 'freedom' for a dignified escape, we must consider carefully her so-called resistance. Specifically, when Rosie destroys her old identity to maximise upon the innovative energies previously stifled by Norman and the patriarchy, she follows a particular template designed for *homo economicus* (human beings that employ an economic framework to address any and all situations). Rosie's presumed release from control remains, as a result, always-already wrapped up in innovative methods of recapture on Wall Street, and so her *Bildungsroman* parallels the evolving status of human capital in the Roaring Nineties.[7]

Importantly, while *Rose Madder* suggests that the subject's liberation remains a desirable outcome of the highest order, Nikolas Rose insists that ready-made dichotomies like domination or absolute freedom ignore how 'power also acts through practices that "make up subjects" as free persons'.

Said another way, subjects are 'obliged to be free . . . [under] a regime of the self where competent personhood is thought to depend upon the continual exercise of freedom . . . [and] tied to the project of [their] own identity' (*Powers* 87–95). In the final account, financialisation trains Rosie to be 'free' in a way that closely mimics her husband's habituation of her 'unfreedom'. Yet, while it would be a fool's errand to respond to King's novel by romanticising 'Rosie Real' as an imaginary subject that could somehow exist outside of the ideology of the period, opportunistic readers might still conceptualise government strategies that could inculcate a mode of being 'free' that does not, at the same time, demand greater productivity, ever faster circulation and ceaseless self-entrepreneurship.

Release/recapture

The Roaring Nineties is a decade defined by deregulation and decadence. As the declared end of the Cold War in 1989 activates freer flows of capital, naysayers wonder what concrete standards of value will remain. Popular culture responds with a number of prominent tropes to convey the idea of radical release 'at odds with' unprecedented methods of recapture, including computer viruses and the spread of AIDS through perceived sexual promiscuity. In *Rose Madder*, the unfettered circulation of money and information suggests a culture on the brink. Highly attuned to her historical moment, Rosie flees from the patriarchy and dives into the promise of a less regulated society. The 'emancipated' Rosie lets go of her initial neuroses to capitalise upon opportunities as they arise, and so her consciousness expands in a fashion that epitomises the rush of the financial sector into unchartered territory: 'Commodity flows must indeed circulate, and they circulate all the better now that the old Freudian subject, with his neuroses . . . is being replaced by a being who can be plugged into anything and everything' (Dufour 11). Similarly, Norman's longing to access his wife's mind, 'to explore new worlds and go where no man had gone before', reflects a growing belief that there is nothing beyond his reach. When Norman follows Rosie 'inside her head' by keeping himself 'perfectly open', the boundlessness of his mind – a trait that aligns him conceptually with the increasingly intrusive reach of Wall Street – leads to an utterly transparent world in which he is eventually condemned to insanity (King, *Rose* 252, 168). Before traversing further into this borderland between economics and identity, we might consult the map key that Harvey offers: 'Cultural forms are firmly rooted in the daily circulation process of capital. It is, therefore, with the daily experience of money and the commodity that we should begin' (*Condition* 299).

In a word, *Rose Madder* conveys the fervour of financial capitalism as it envelops everything in its path. Jean Baudrillard, a well-known public intellectual at the height of his influence in the Roaring Nineties, notes that in the years following 1989 the globe enters a viral stage of value in which nothing exists save the 'unchecked orbital whirl of capital . . . the millions of dollars' worth of floating capital now conglomerated into a satellite tirelessly circling us' (*Transparency* 29–32). King's novel taps directly into the anxiety of this 'unchecked whirl' when Rosie steals her husband's ATM card in an act of defiance that frames the remainder of the novel. After Rosie gains access to her abusive husband's treasure via her new-found ability to enter and exit a hidden account that defines his social status, Norman declares her theft to be unforgivable, punishable even by death. And his rage seems at least partially justified when, upon losing his card, he falls apart, scrambling 'to create a real person, the way a good actor can create a real person on stage'. By the time he puts on a bull's mask to launch his climactic terror spree, he has lost any purchase in a communal or personal identity. Like his namesake – Norman Bates from Alfred Hitchcock's 1960 film, *Psycho* – as his mind untethers from his body, he devolves into voyeur as well as performer: 'It was as if he were being dismantled . . . not real anymore' (King, *Rose* 276, 266). Baudrillard describes the accompanying sense of inertia: 'Even our brains may be said to be outside us now, floating.' The gold standard of identity, which was previously based, it is important to remember, upon grotesque patriarchal conventions, cedes to free-floating alternatives (*Transparency* 33, 15). The result is a pervasive strain of madness.

Indeed, this dizzying set of changes fundamentally alters how King's characters relate to one another. Norman's drive to re-enforce his dominion over Rosie cannot be separated from his parallel drive to reclaim his ATM card (a signifier of permeable financial borders). At one point, he dreams of inserting the metaphorical card into her body: 'The run of his thoughts was a stream which flowed into it' (175). King's metaphorical card merges unrestricted emotional and economic flows: Norman's extraction of value from Rosie ends with the loss of his card; once she possesses the card, Rosie penetrates her husband's facade to gain the upper hand (and so on).[8] As they move farther away from stable reference points, Norman and Rosie enter into a more transactional relationship, with others as well as themselves, in which every network into forbidden territory opens return pathways (a kind of relationship that builds upon the agonism between John Rainbird and Charlie in *Firestarter*). As the borderless financial sector wonderfully and woefully annuls domestic fealties, King's text asks its readers to ruminate upon subsequent circuits of exchange as the pair becomes ever more estranged. In sum, *Rose Madder* reveals how the decade's enhanced circulation breeds a longing for, and a fear of, total transparency. For example, King's text accentuates the dark underside of globalisation with 'Buy American' signs that actually signal wares made in Mexico.

To re-enforce these sensations of exhilaration and terror, the novel comingles economic and emotional flows with the decade's popular as well as problematic representations of AIDS. For his part, Baudrillard makes numerous poetic references to AIDS, and a host of other communicable diseases, as a convenient metaphor for expressing how pure circulation destroys societies from within: 'A faceless sexuality infinitely watered down in a broth of politics, media and communications, and eventually manifested in the viral explosion of AIDS. Everything is sexual. Everything is political. Everything is aesthetic. All at once' (*Transparency* 10). Images of money, information and sex converge to such a degree that Baudrillard confidently declares the human species will share a doomed fate with the disease.[9] *Rose Madder* likewise attends to the AIDS epidemic to stress the heightened anxieties of a world without boundaries: upon her daring escape from Norman, Rosie encounters a man with a sign that reads 'HOMELESS AND HAVE AIDS'; when Norman assaults one of her friends, the friend fears contraction of the disease; in a climactic scene, Rosie spots unwholesome graffiti regarding the transmission of AIDS. In this way, King's imagined world without partitions remains plagued by the constant threat of horrific retribution. *Rose Madder* dwells upon the economic valence of AIDS by representing Norman as quite literally vampiric. A 'biter' that feasts upon the blood of his victims, Norman recalls Marx's well-known metaphor for vampiric capital alongside the era's dread of contact with 'tainted' bodily fluids. Susan Sontag adds: 'Like the effects of industrial pollution and the new system of global financial markets, the AIDS crisis is evidence of a world in which nothing important is regional, local, limited; in which everything that can circulate does . . . the easy transmissibility of goods and images and financial instruments' (180). *Rose Madder* reveals how apprehensions surrounding this disease inform, and are informed by, the disquiet caused by rampant financialisation, as both forces heavily influence the genesis of Rosie's nascent identity.

When it comes to ever intensified circulation, *Rose Madder* has its cake and eats it too by relishing in the decadence of the Roaring Nineties – via Rosie's release from captivity – while gesturing at a conservative counterpoint to recapture some semblance of 'traditional value'. That is, Rosie's ecstatic unshackling is followed by a Puritanical rejoinder. The novel appears to imbricate Rosie's unrestricted bodily pleasure and the decade's deregulated economy as it imagines her pursuit of freedom to be sexual in nature: Norman envisions that she finds perverse satisfaction by bending to 'scoop the cash out of the slot'; in one of the story's most aggressively sexualised moments, Rosie's Medusa-like double plants seeds in the eyes of Norman's corpse (278). While *Rose Madder* makes it difficult to conceive of a world in which its protagonist could survive without decamping from Norman's prison, the text nonetheless worries a great deal over the fluidity that accompanies her 'unleashing'.

Every exchange in King's novel remains fraught. At the close of *Rose Madder*, Rosie meets a vixen that has contracted rabies. The state of the vixen nudges the reader to understand Rosie's fury at the patriarchy as similar to a mother that knowingly transits her 'dangerous behavior' to her offspring, thereby suggesting that vindictive feminism is a 'kind of rabies' (270, 391). If the doubling with the vixen holds, Rosie must either transmit her righteous anger against men to others, or her 'feminine rage' will consume her. Sontag, who also compares AIDS with rabies as a 'synonym for change', contemplates how feminist indignation serves as a source of dread and excitement for members of the patriarchy (160). In support of the 'excitement' triggered by Rosie's presumed release, Michael Hardt and Antonio Negri employ the metaphor of AIDS to discuss the raw *potenza* of a revolutionary subject:

> The dominant discourses of AIDS prevention have been all about hygiene: we must avoid contact and use protection . . . the boundaries of nation-states, however, are increasingly permeable by all kinds of flows. Nothing can bring back the hygiene shields of colonial boundaries. The age of globalization is the age of universal contagion. (*Empire* 136)

The rapid circulation of money, consciousness and disease indicates a significant release from disciplinary control. For critics like Hardt and Negri, then, 'circulating is the first ethical act of a counterimperial ontology' (363).[10] Although *Rose Madder* certainly flirts with this *potenza*, the text likewise returns to issues of hygiene to make sense of her contagion and, by so doing, it re-entrenches Rosie within a normative framework – a containment that, ironically enough, bolsters her forthcoming entrepreneurial sensibilities and empowers her to adapt to her surroundings through discrete aesthetico-economic choices: 'After two decades of sexual spending, of sexual inflation, we are in the early stages of sexual depression . . . [subjects] are drawn into programs of self-management and self-discipline' (Sontag 165). Put a bit differently, as she dissolves her 'old self' into a circuity of open economic, political and aesthetic flows, Rosie unsuspectingly conforms to the era's dominant method of self-governance, understanding her identity as nothing less (or more) than a work of art.

The aesthetic self

As Rosie moves from being a character in someone else's story to creating her own, *Rose Madder* reinforces a pivot into self-construction, a pivot in which, to paraphrase Edward Thompson, 'the subject now seems to be present at its own making' (Callinicos 88). As I have discussed at length in regards to *Firestarter* (see chapter 4), this pivot leads to a subject severed from communal context. When Rosie is 'released' into an aesthetic mode of self-governance, her story becomes yet another instalment in a string of works by King dedicated to the subject of female liberation through uniquely artistic means. One of the latest entries, *Lisey's Story* (2006), involves a meek woman that enters into the imaginary world of her literary husband in order to empower herself. One of the most profound border violations in King's texts is thus 'the effacement of the boundary between art and everyday life' (Featherstone 64). The fact that Rosie revises her identity within a magical painting reveals how shifting attitudes towards artistry and selfhood in the Roaring Nineties fertilise a growing emphasis upon human capital.

Of course, the hybridisation of aesthetics, capitalism and self-determination in *Rose Madder* is hardly unprecedented. In the nineteenth century, Nietzsche famously preaches self-creation as an opportunity to make a work of art of oneself, while the writer Oscar Wilde conflates his lifestyle with aesthetics. Yet it can be argued that the unrivalled proliferation of participatory art during the years that precede the Roaring Nineties more intensely transforms viewers into 'profit-oriented keyhole[s] of affect, control, and commodification'.[11] Josephine Berry posits that many works of contemporary art abolish a viewer's bondage to representation by 'liberating' her sensorium from indebtedness to source materials, moving her further and further away from referentiality or the real world. In a word, Rosie's pawned painting generates 'newness' only by destroying archetype. The painting demands of her: 'Do for me what I cannot do for myself.'[12] In response, Rosie must bypass a sense of value that has been assigned by others in favour of direct access to the capriciousness of her own untapped creativity. She is subsequently hailed into productive avenues, spurred to fill in the gaps of the canvas, and inspired to picture things that she was once unable to visualise for herself. The magical painting invites her as well as the reader to 'open herself' to different sensations and capitalise upon her emotional assets: 'Instead of denying the emotion, Rosie went against a lifetime of self-training and welcomed it' (King, *Rose* 203, 230, 220). As Jeffrey Nealon points out, 'The economization of artistic self-creation . . . [has] become American-style neoliberalism's primary engine and product line' (Nealon, *Foucault* 13). *Rose Madder* underscores how a good deal of contemporary art unwittingly optimises the viewer's behaviour in line with demands of the New Economy.

This blurred line between art and life leads to a deeply felt loss of stability for Rosie. 'Because art can address everything', Russell A. Berman contends, 'nothing can escape the universal process of aestheticization' (47). When Rosie unlocks channels between herself and the artwork, she erases an indispensable tension between art and life, and it becomes easier for King's readers to mistake self-aestheticism with a genuine cultivation of the self. In truth, this 'self-cultivation is a kind of reflexive turning inward'. Steven Shaviro insists, 'I stylize myself in order to market myself, to be an entrepreneur of myself, and to increase the value of my "human capital"' (51). In other words, without a clear line of resistance between her life and the piece of art, Rosie aestheticises everything and, in turn, the novel fails to probe into aspects of her existence that we might interrogate on different grounds.

Many of King's works from the Roaring Nineties reflect a similarly pervasive self-aestheticism in lieu of a mere substantial or sustainable cultivation of the self. For instance, *The Regulators* (1996), published under King's pseudonym Richard Bachman, tells of individuals that outlast an oppressive media influence by re-formulating their lives as pieces of art. A woman uses her imagination to establish 'a refuge in her mind'; a man does 'some personal editorial work. A second-draft . . . if you like'; an autistic child 'builds' reality for himself with a box of crayons.

The novel ends with a child's drawing that offers the characters as well as the reader a viable 'escape' from indoctrination at the hands of a bloated military-industrial complex (278, 282, 452). None of this self-stylisation leads anywhere because, in direct parallel with its 'unleashing' of human capital, the New Economy also stipulates boundless creativity.[13] To tap into one's free flows of creativity means to thrive as a member of what Richard Florida calls the Creative Class: 'When I made pictures, I felt whole . . . power began to flow . . . through me' (King, *Duma* 769). Artistic creativity serves as an ontological constant in the New Economy, as means as well as ends, part and parcel of a swelling 'ethos of productivity' (Brockling 117). Rosie's move from created to creator apparently allows her to flourish by enabling her to release the work of art – her 'sensuous nature' – from evaluation by others and to claim ownership over her identity. In reality, this dismal shift more directly underscores the self-commodification mandated during the Roaring Nineties.

To provide a concrete example of this phenomenon: Rosie initially exists as mere fodder for stories told by others, as she goes through the tunnels of Norman's story like a prisoner within a plot that she did not design: 'Spontaneity was not encouraged.' The first chapters of King's text illustrate how truly difficult it will be for Rosie to 'wake up' and free herself when, upon her initial attempt to do so, she immediately slips back into the rigid confines of a pre-determined narrative. She passes by an arcade with automated commands that shout 'Try Again' only to enter into something like the loop of a videogame, one that feeds into a player's illusion of choice. In truth, every 'choice' that she makes remains prescriptive. The draconian figures that plot Rosie's existence represent branches of an oppressive federal government: the law (Norman) and the welfare agency (Anna). Upon discovering Rosie's 'violation' of his orders, when he finds her enthralled by a paperback novel, Norman beats her mercilessly because he fears Rosie shifting from a 'predictable thing' to a 'monster'. Due to the fact that he considers his account to be the only valid one after he establishes his version of a case, he refuses to allow others to discuss, debate or speculate. Later, when Rosie enters the Daughter and Sisters shelter, Norman's brand of discursive rigidity does not relent. She continues to be understood as a 'case' instead of a human actor with a will of her own. Although the shelter's overseer Anna preaches the need for self-reliance, she actually reigns as a benevolent tyrant not dissimilar from Norman: 'I choose who's invited to stay, and who isn't invited' (25, 99, 354, 51). Dictating the lives of her wards, Anna positions herself as an omnipotent master aligned in no uncertain terms with Providence. Each time the text invites Rosie to 'Try Again', then, it reroutes her into a storyline that has been crafted to control her (this double-negation recycles the patricidal drive behind *Firestarter*). Counter to what they perceive to be the evils of centralised planning, evangelisers from the financial sector similarly espouse that the self must be '"storied forth," the individual choosing among the different narrative forms to which he or she is exposed' (Rose, *Inventing* 176). Correspondingly, upon her purchase of the painting, Rosie elects the terms of her existence via artistic ingenuity, and she proves as a result that the human mind is 'tougher and more adaptable' than her tyrants could ever understand it to be. Rosie no longer submits to the dictates of art; instead, she chooses what she wants to take away from a given piece. Hired to do voice-over work for audiobooks, she demonstrates her new-found mutability by slipping in and out of storylines written by others. Her fantastic painting provides her with an equally flexible arrangement: when she hangs it, and she runs her fingers over the 'finely combed tracks left by the artist's brush', her imagination enters the painting to roam freely, allowing her to realise that now 'invention on short notice is my strong suit' (396, 164, 227, 294). Rosie's participation in the painting appears to grant her an opportunity to chart her own course.[14]

Rose Madder therefore exposes the extent to which subjects in the New Economy produce as well as consume themselves as pieces of art: 'Contemporary individuals are incited to live as if making a project of themselves: they are to work on their emotional world.' Forming her new identity through engagement with artistic works (popular fiction as well as paintings), Rosie practises diligent self-craftsmanship: 'Techniques of composing and adorning the flesh – styles of walking, dressing, gesture, expression, the face and the gaze, body hair and adornment . . . a constant and intense self-scrutiny' (Rose, *Inventing* 157, 195). That is to say, by living her life as an aesthetic exercise, she can employ the interactive painting to visualise what she believes to be an alternative existence for herself (becoming, in effect, a 'prosumer': a consumer as well as a producer of her own pleasure).[15] Again building upon the form of *Firestarter*, to accentuate Rosie's desire to decamp from her emplotment by others, *Rose Madder* implicates even itself as an unsavoury constraint when it presents the popular paperback as a maze that peddles a false consciousness akin to the consciousness that first ensnares Rosie in Norman's cell. Much of King's fiction implicates popular literature as a prison for reader and writer alike (consider, as another example of this theme, King's 1987 novel *Misery*). Likewise, Rosie's experiences, which at times seem intended to read like magazines found in a doctor's waiting room, expose how formulaic literature structures the reader's psyche by pre-programming her 'choices'. In these ways and a host of others, the artwork commands Rosie as well as the reader to 'do for it what it cannot do for itself'.[16]

We must note that as Rosie becomes involved 'as a "producer" and "consumer" of the artwork', she does not automatically enter into a political mindset simply because she feels released from under the thumb of disciplinarians. In fact, Rosie's experience reveals how 'defetishising' an artwork can lead to even more elaborate fetishes. And herein lies the trap of *Rose Madder*: the call to disconnect from someone else's painting or prose, and then re-enter the artwork to maximise your own emotional response, is a kind of labour that dovetails easily with the sort of affective release/recapture demanded by the neo-liberal state. The surface of the painting serves as yet another interface, another ubiquitous screen to dictate late twentieth-century behaviour. 'The interactive possibilities of the new tools [are] touted as empowering', Jonathan Crary notes, because it appears as though consumers are consuming in a manner that fits their unique lifestyles. Through their interactive screen, prosumers like Rosie produce and consume a steady stream of content, but 'what [is] celebrated as interactivity [is] more accurately the mobilization and habituation of the individual to an open-ended set of tasks and routines' (83). To say it another way, while Rosie's 'active' relationship with the screen of her painting may suggest a type of empowerment, the novel's integration of 'autonomous art' and 'circuits of capital' does not genuinely transform her life in a meaningful sense. Instead, this seamless integration subsumes the field of ethics into the arena of style – an arena, Alex Callinicos insists, heavily influenced by the era's just-in-time consumerism (156). For example, when Rosie imitates the hair style and erotic garb seen in her painting, readers ought to inquire into the shallowness of her 'stylised existence', just as we inquired into Charlie's final formlessness in *Firestarter*. When we account for her stylised existence in the broader context of the Roaring Nineties, it becomes more difficult for us to imagine how Rosie could ever reach a firmer moral plane upon which to find refuge from her exploitation at the hands of others. After all, Rosie's painting obliges her to comprehend her life as a work of art through the 'insistent, even coercive ethics of audience participation in aesthetic production' (Berry 133). The tracks of the artist's brush that she must (re)trace pressure her into 'release' in a manner that undermines the actual 'freedom' of her contract with the magical artwork. The figure in the painting faces away from the viewer so that Rosie as well as the reader *must* fill in the gaps: what does the figure see? What does she feel? The absence of the artist's signature drives Rosie into an even more productive role by directing her engagement in a highly prescriptive fashion. Although the abdication of the artist ostensibly liberates Rosie to construct and consume her own story, it remains nearly impossible for us to conceptualise alternative routes for her (or, in turn, for ourselves).

Liberty's pawn

Rosie's fantastic painting coerces her into producing as well as consuming her own pleasure. As we have seen, the initial step for turning her life into a work of art involves stripping away the influence of 'overweening institutions' (Binkley 4).[17] Subsequently, her *Bildungsroman* appears to offer an escape route – first from domineering stories told by the government, and then from internalised dependencies that prove more difficult to shake. The painting tasks Rosie with the hard labour of re-organising her identity in increasingly unstable conditions by compelling her to conduct 'work on and for the self . . . [with] investment, stylization, and branding', to toil over her self-portrait, and to funnel her creativity (equated with her very life force) into the shrewd calculation as well as exchange of her own image. 'Rather than natural or given', Jodi Dean declares, 'The individual is a form of capture' (*Crowds* 57, 73–5, 80). In the final account, Rosie's hyper-individuation is neither accidentally nor abnormally emancipatory; rather, it reflects one of the principal imperatives of the Roaring Nineties.

In a diverse set of ways, *Rose Madder* recaptures Rosie as human capital because her '[creativity's] unleashing and its domestication are inseparably interwoven' (Brockling 102). Rosie's society invites her to 'unchain' herself to make room for novel disciplinary technologies with which the economy can more efficiently capitalise upon her imaginative labour. What readers might presume to be her exit from plots imposed by Norman and Anna offers yet another stipulated storyline, which is to say, when Rosie sheds outmoded identity markers, melting everything solid into air (to borrow a Marxian phrase), the novel's 'release' reveals itself to be *wholly manufactured*.[18] Jean and John Comaroff write:

> The identity economy is itself a congealed product . . . the growing naturalization of the trope of identity – especially cultural identity, at once essentialized and made the subject of choice, construction, and consumption – [becomes] *the* taken-for-granted domain of collective action in the Age of Entrepreneurialism and Human Capital. (*Ethnicity*,150, author's emphasis)

Reflecting a central paradox of the Age of Entrepreneurialism and Human Capital, *Rose Madder* juxtaposes the decade's promise of release – bountiful individual freedom – with its effective mechanisms of recapture. Anna's celebration of self-reliance ('You can be free if you want to') rubs up against her policing of Rosie's narrative; likewise, Rosie emerges at the end of King's text as 'queen of whatever she wants' and dependent upon her beloved paperbacks for stability; perhaps most conspicuously, King's 'queen' works as a successful voice-over actress that reads words written by others to cultivate her own identity – a process that highlights the decade's strange bromide of complete discharge and enhanced control (83, 54, 389). Even though she obtains 'the capacity to construct [her] own ending to the soap opera of [her] life', the novel's less-than-satisfying resolution reveals how 'of this continuous performance of our lives, we each are, ourselves, to be the sternest and most constant critic' (Rose, *Governing* 258–60, 243). In a particularly revealing scene in which Rosie ventures out on a romantic date, she cannot help but think of 'the half-witty repartee' of television characters. 'Silly me', she thinks, 'I forgot to bring my screenwriter' (King, *Rose* 183). Transforming herself quite literally into a work of art to be constantly revised and (re)assessed, the Roaring Nineties corrals Rosie into the endless game of appreciation as well as depreciation: a highly speculative status that reminds us of the turbulent art market. 'Insofar as our condition is that of human capital . . . our main purpose is not so much to profit from our accumulated potential as to constantly value or appreciate ourselves – or at least prevent our own depreciation' (Feher 27). In the moment that she is compelled to treat her life as a fungible work of art, Rosie becomes responsible for every minute detail, and promptly scrutinises herself to the point of utter collapse.

Far from (openly) striking a tragic chord, however, *Rose Madder* seems to glorify the new Rosie as a discerning entrepreneur, one that cunningly taps into her own creativity to serve her best interests.[19] With Rosie's 'escape', we return to the world in which we began this chapter (a world that we never truly left), defined by exchange, circulation and the whirl of unleashed value. And we arrive, appropriately enough, at a pawn shop – a site that symbolically merges Rosie's life as a work of art, her identity politics, as well as her society's increasingly bald economism. The presumed road to being 'unleashed' leads Rosie to the aptly named Liberty City Loan and Pawn, where she pawns her wedding ring for the magical painting and so quite literally transposes her identity into a fungible for exchange (her patriarchal ring in exchange for a participatory painting). Consequently, Rosie comes to view her alternative identity as an incomplete do-it-yourself project. Over the course of the text, she continuously pawns herself, thus perfecting a cost/benefit approach that involves excising what is 'negative' from her identity and augmenting what is 'positive'. Rosie's debt/credit relationship to her pawned painting – which is to say, to her life as an ongoing work of art – stresses the burden of maintaining her unique branch of a broader identity economy.[20] Rosie functions as customer and teller alike, an automated teller machine of sorts, and she achieves equilibrium by crediting herself the opportunity to 'escape' while restoring a proper amount of debt (or, assets to 'cash in' on future occasions). Rosie's artwork – her life-work – manifests via debt, credit, transfers and withdrawals. When she enters the painting, her double on the canvas tells her: 'I *repay*. What you do for me I will do for you . . . That is our balance.' And as the figure promises, after their plan succeeds in deposing Norman, accounts do, in fact, 'balance' (202, 412, author's emphasis).[21] The totalising logic of human capital consumes Rosie whole. *Pace* Gary Becker, she submits all facets of her life to a cost/benefit analysis and routes the formation of her identity through Becker's economic algorithms.

In this manner, King's fiction highlights the economic underpinning of some (although certainly not all) forms of identity politics. The protagonist of *Duma Key* works on his identity 'as if it were a job', a project on which he must exert himself 'like a man working on an assembly line' (348, 415). Elsewhere, in the short story 'The Gingerbread Girl' (2008), King's protagonist disciplines herself to construct a 'better life', grasping 'how to cope' with the death of her daughter by exploiting inner resources. Like Rosie, the eponymous girl survives because she transforms into an entrepreneur of her body: 'In utilitarian terms, [her legs] were very good', and she outruns a murderous maniac in distinctive terms: 'Just do your work', she mandates. 'Take care of business' (123, 119, 105, 76, 86, 111). The transactional character of King's 'emancipatory' works unveil the Cult of the Self to be nothing less (or more) than a running balance sheet.

To look at these issues from still another vantage point, *Rose Madder*'s narrow comprehension of identity politics, in its exclusively economised variant, overlooks the ethical drive behind feminism that 'works towards community, accountability, entrustment, sisterhood, bonding, belonging'. In contrast, Rosie's rage evokes an 'erotic, narcissistic drive' that can be more readily identified by its 'excess, subversion, disloyalty, agency, empowerment, pleasure' (De Lauretis 369).[22] By acquiescing to the demand to handle one's life like a piece of art with a speculative price tag – the form of which must be constantly revised; the value of which must be constantly re-assessed – *Rose Madder* omits ethical imperatives that drive so much of feminist politics. The text treats 'cultural identity [as] a private asset rather than a collective claim' (Comaroff and Comaroff, 'First' 40).[23] Simply stated, by incessantly pawning its protagonist, *Rose Madder* wears her out. Rosie recalls the ever productive *pyrokinesis* in *Firestarter* as her ceaseless pursuit of emancipation attenuates the very idea of her, and therefore – even when she believes that she is pawning herself to attain 'freedom' – she remains an unsuspecting pawn of a coercive brand of 'liberty'.

In conclusion, what are we to do with King's dismal denouement? Gone are the political counter-punches of *The Langoliers* or *IT*; in their place, we find an all-consuming marketplace almost entirely devoid of political potential. The spectre of the political has been all but exorcised from this tale about a haunted painting. Although her getaway from the likes of Norman and Anna may temporarily warm our hearts, Rosie's cumulative understanding of 'freedom' gives us pause. Locked into an entrepreneurial model of selfhood, she cannot envision anything more dignified than the economic order into which her body has been contracted. At its most self-critical, King's novel compels us into a reverie regarding what it must have meant to be human prior to the New Economy, luring us into a (futile) pursuit of Rosie's authentic, pre-political and pre-economic self. The narrative upholds this temptation through its repetitive disrobing of Rosie whenever she exits from the magical artwork. Through evocations of her stark nakedness, we might find ourselves subscribing to a delusion that 'real identities' somehow exist prior to political discourse (instead of taking shape through it). In other words, *Rose Madder*'s fallacy of a pre-political selfhood – a 'Rosie Real' – herds us ever deeper into the novel's disciplinary maze. In response, readers need not rest upon the conclusion that her 'liberated' self is false, or that a so-called financialised Rosie ought to be replaced by a Rosie that is 'more real'. Here, at last, we expose the text's (unconscious) trap: because absolute decampment from shared governance is always chimeric, and because selfhood invariably stems from ruling regimes, Rosie's 'emancipation' is always-already the *result* of government (rather than its antithesis). King's readers are left to reset and 'Try Again' in perpetuity.

In lieu of falling for this trap and chasing an unthinkable 'Rosie Real', let us start to formulate substitute methods with which to regulate, collectively, Rosie's notions of freedom (and our own). 'Perhaps', Alex Moskowitz muses, 'the production of the perfect neoliberal subject can help us relearn that all subjectivities must be produced. And, if all subjectivities must be produced, perhaps we can produce something better' (106). Maybe we could imagine Rosie as an 'expert of herself' that gains greater autonomy without blindly obeying the maxims of high finance. We could then empower her, and ourselves, to strive for a more 'appreciable life' (Feher 41).[24] Given the appeal of these incipient political alternatives, I want to close the chapter with an opening salvo of sorts: Herbert Marcuse suggests that we must reclaim society, and not merely the performative individual, 'as a work of art' (283). What if Rosie were to adopt a form of art/commerce more inclusive than self-portraiture? Such a shift from self-entrepreneurship to collaborative world-building offers one potential site from which to tease out the latent political possibilities within so much of King's fiction.

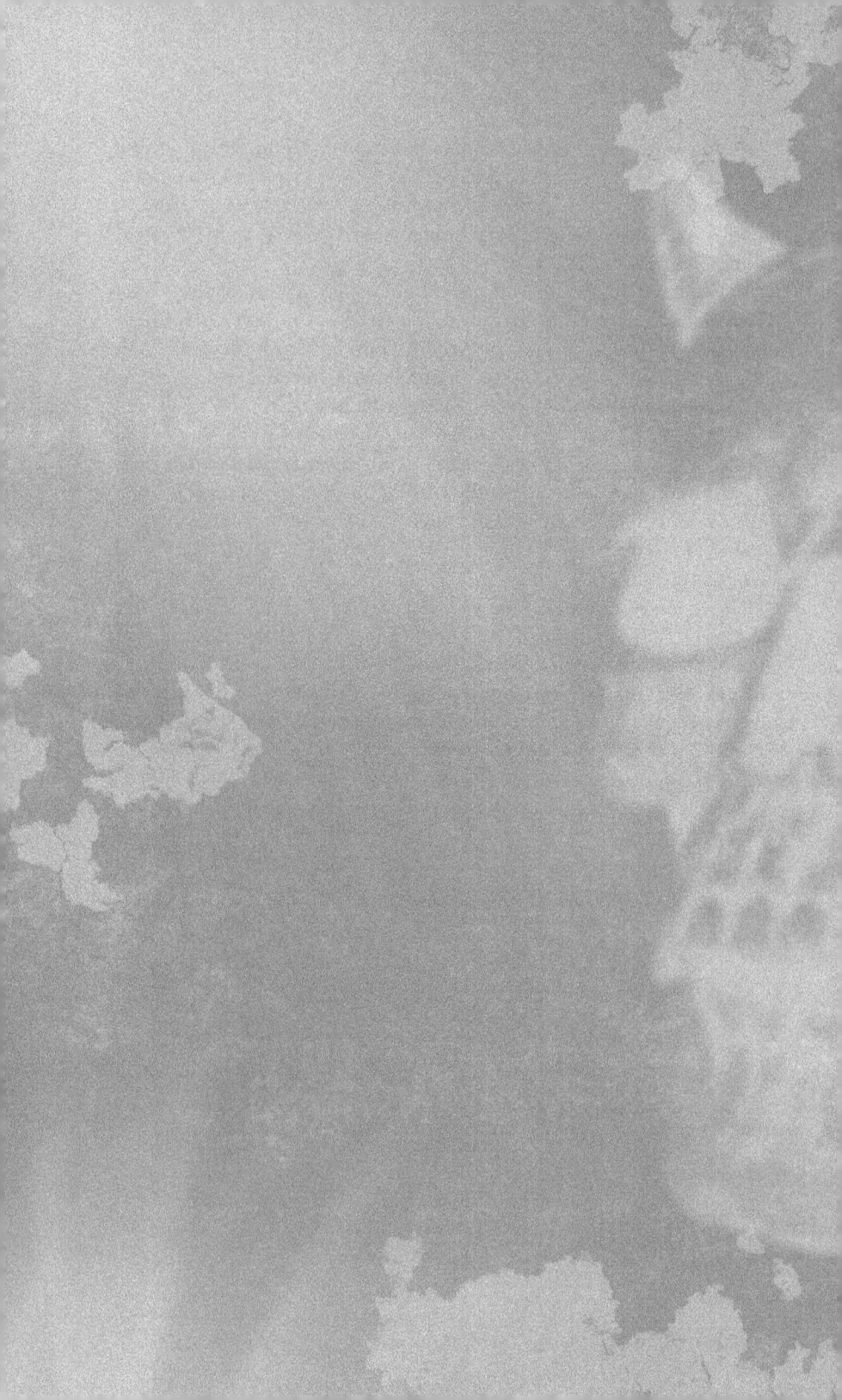

8

Under the Dome and the Deteriorating Demos

AT THIS POINT, we can place Stephen King's political fiction into one of two main categories: stories that preserve the political as an eternally unsatisfying remainder (the Bachman books; *IT*), or stories that rush to achieve consensus/cure, usually by 'resolving' the plight of a disenfranchised group and thus overcoming any need for political strife (*Firestarter*; *Rose Madder*). On this spectrum, King's *Under the Dome* (2009) fits mostly into the latter category. The novel at first seems to be a run-of-the-mill post-apocalyptic tale as an enormous Dome descends over the town of Chester's Mill, sealing it off from the rest of the United States, and the citizenry quickly dissolves into a state of chaos.[1] Nomadic visitor Dale Barbara ('Barbie') struggles to resist the subsequent regime formed by Second Selectman 'Big Jim' Rennie. King's novel attempts to convey what most post-apocalyptic narratives attempt to convey – societies are fragile things; poisoned communities must be torn down before they can rebuild. At this level, *Under the Dome* offers a relatively original device (the Dome) grafted upon a very familiar plot. Yet beneath its bald allegory, *Under the Dome* speaks to the conflicted political, economic and theological currents running through contemporary American society.

The unconscious of the text suggests that the Bush-Cheney administration (2000–8) remains caught up in a matrix of cultural forces that Stuart Hall describes as 'the neoliberal turn'.[2] Although likely gratifying for many of King's 'liberal' readers in the immediate wake of Barack Obama's election in 2008, the novel's rejection of the Bush-Cheney doctrine disguises a set of values that persist, and so the desire for catharsis in *Under the Dome* is never quite what it appears to be.

Before the reader attends to the unconscious of King's text, though, she must account for its manifest content. *Under the Dome* offers a tidy allegory for the Bush-Cheney administration: Rennie, complete with the nickname 'VADER', stands in as a substitute for vice president Dick Cheney, a sneaky, brooding and cunning villain with a faulty heart and a keen appetite for the town's propane supply (a reference to America's oil-driven conflicts overseas). The text's Cheneyites pine for a 'new empire of American influence in the Middle East' (Korb and Conley 235). Meanwhile, the First Selectman, Andy Sanders, can be easily manipulated by his second-in-command and, while he appears to be at times tender, his ultimate undoing is his willingness to endorse Rennie's pursuit of power – a connection to George W. Bush that rests visibly at the surface. Upon nearly destroying Chester's Mill, these two men and their failures are meant to resonate with fatigued readers exhausted by a politics of fear, endless war in the Middle East and the financial collapse of 2008.

Like Bush-Cheney, the Sanders-Rennie duo responds to an unexpected tragedy by enacting a series of draconian revisions to the democratic apparatus. 'The truth was, [Rennie] liked the Dome'. *Under the Dome* starts with a fiery plane crash at the edge of Route 119 – a number, careful readers may observe, that can be readily reversed to 9/11 – that causes widespread confusion in Chester's Mill. Rennie sees in the Dome an opportunity to suspend the existing rule of law in order to advance his agenda.[3] Recalling the military strikes, rampant surveillance and torture undertaken by the Bush-Cheney administration, Rennie builds up an efficient police state: 'The Constitution's been canceled in the Mill', one officer boasts. 'I'm the law.' The ethos of the new government can be summed up: 'Personal freedom's going to have to take a hike' (637, 187–91, 260). The dropping of the Dome directly parallels the 'Continuity of Government' plan, in which the Bush administration calls for the 'suspension of the Constitution, turning control of the government over to FEMA, emergency appointment of military commanders to run state and local governments', which is to say, a considerable enhancement of the administration's 'powers to disrupt constitutional government' (quoted in Scott, 185). During its War on Terror, the Bush-Cheney administration declares 'exceptional circumstances' to bypass democratic procedures while emboldening economic managers to amplify police presence and suppress the demos.

Under the Dome further highlights the dissolution of democracy through its ruminations upon a threatened free press. Rennie, who despises transparency, barks at the local newspaper editor, 'You'll get the story when we're ready to give it out' (552). He eventually burns down the newspaper office and contends that a newspaper is not in the society's interest, thereby shutting down one of the citizenry's primary avenues for holding public officials accountable (because without a free press, the citizens of Chester's Mill are unable to engage in their town's affairs in a meaningful, informed fashion). Critics of the Bush-Cheney administration likewise lament the administration's excessive secrecy, as when it pushes through Bush's Executive Order (13233), which alters the Presidential Records Act by granting the public less access to presidential documents.[4] *Under the Dome* rehearses a litany of transgressions perpetrated by the Bush-Cheney administration by projecting these transgressions onto a one-dimensional canvas in a way that encourages readers to reject – superficially, at least – the administration's political doctrine (while leaving relatively untouched the corresponding economic apparatus).

Critics of King's text have understandably made hay from this particular allegory. In the pages that follow, I question certain aspects of this invited reading. We begin with Tamara Watkins's interpretation not to single out Watkins, but because her analysis seems utterly reasonable. She frames *Under the Dome* as a 'liberal response' to 9/11. 'King deftly channels [liberal] American anxieties regarding the ability and stability of our leaders' (29, 33). To categorise King's text as 'liberal', however, means extending a recognisable set of partisan associations: when a Toyota Prius aids in a rescue, the stereotypical 'liberal' reader presumably lets out a cheer. Yet the term 'liberal' is not as antithetical to Rennie's regime as one might be led to think because, rather than simply inquire into the fitness of the Bush-Cheney administration, *Under the Dome* taps into a well-fertilised distrust of government at large. The novel's anti-political message most pointedly attacks the perceived abuses of the Bush-Cheney years, of course, but the appetite for governmental flesh that it helps to spur will not be swiftly sated. That is, as *Under the Dome* doubles down on a widespread anti-political attitude, its solutions are never truly democratic but always-already tied up in the dominant ideals of their time. King's ideal self-reliant hero, for instance, divorces himself from the autocratic government without relying upon any aid from the purportedly incompetent masses. Wendy Brown, a political theorist employed extensively in the pages to follow, describes contemporary American politics in a state of perpetual de-democratisation due to the fact that the power of the electorate has steadily eroded in favour of hyper-managerialism: 'This is the hollowing out that confronts us as *a sustained political condition* no matter how low Bush's star sinks' ('American' 691, emphasis mine).[5] King's readers, then, must avoid following the novel's lead and treating the Bush-Cheney doctrine as a mere blip on history's radar: 'The Bush debacle is most often (and incorrectly) viewed as an isolated and unrepresentative episode within the broader historical arc of neo-liberalism' (Kotsko 1). In a word, *Under the Dome* illuminates how difficult it will be to save democracy from a process of deterioration that pre-dates the Bush-Cheney administration (and endures long after it).

To understand how the unconscious of King's novel actually works to sustain the dominant political economy, we must acknowledge that over the last fifty years the two mainstream political parties have reached a relative consensus regarding the primacy of economic logic (for more discussion, see the prelude). Economic elites suggest that 'the people' invariably make unrealistic demands upon employers as well as the state and, as a result, in order to protect economic growth at all costs, the state strips the populace of opportunities to instigate reform. Consequently, Republican and Democratic administrations of the era generally agree that democratic gains must be rolled back to protect a booming economy. Wolfgang Streeck points to 'an endemic and essentially irreconcilable conflict between capitalist markets and democratic politics'. Since the 1970s, he insists, concerted efforts have been made to 'overthrow democracy in order to save capitalism', a movement in which everyday people are painted as 'short-sighted', abstract markets are framed as inherently better mediators than government and 'economist-kings' are said to handle perilous situations best. 'Citizens appear to be stripped almost entirely of their democratic defenses and their capacity to impress on the political economy interests and demands incommensurable with those of capital owners' ('Crisis' 263–7, 284). King's novel contemplates the dystopian outcomes of this de-democratisation yet extends the very rationality that made these outcomes possible in the first place.

This chapter approaches the political unconscious of *Under the Dome* by first recovering the oft-overlooked economic logic behind Rennie's authoritarianism, and then considering how the novel trains its critical gaze on extreme religious fundamentalists without acknowledging the underlying neo-liberal influence. As Terry Eagleton notes, 'A striking feature of advanced capitalist societies [is that] they are both libertarian and authoritarian' (*Illusions* 132). In its final section, the chapter steps back from analysing the details of this convergence to understand better how *Under the Dome* cannot seem to imagine an alternative to the nightmare that it caricatures, exploring how King's story theatrically exchanges the Bush-Cheney regime for a 'something else' that turns out to be only more of the same. In other words, much like the symbol of the giant dome, King's novel generates a self-enclosed snapshot of the dominant ideological formation of 2009, unveiling the limited scope of the text as well as the horizons of contemporary political critique. Because, like all works, *Under the Dome* remains relatively unaware of its own ideological complicity, readers can place King's novel under a figurative Dome to compare what the novel thinks it is doing (a pointed critique of the Bush-Cheney administration) to what it is actually doing (the maintenance of numerous neo-liberal norms). Admittedly, readers might elect to encase this chapter in much the same fashion when, like the aliens that watch the citizenry of Chester's Mill from their presumed position on high, I seal off my own historical moment to appraise it from a distance. Indeed, in its more compelling moments, *Under the Dome* allows readers to reflect upon the recurrent blind spot that invariably accompanies all political critique, thus reminding us in Althusserian fashion that our horizons are never permanent, things could always be otherwise and there is forever something outside of our respective Domes. We saw in the prelude how King occasionally highlights this politics of the blind spot to great effect, as in *The Dead Zone* (1979) or in *Dreamcatcher* (2001), a more compelling commentary upon the seeds of the Bush–Cheney doctrine. King's fiction routinely represses this potential and in *Under the Dome* it remains at best under-explored. Nevertheless, thanks to its layered exposition, King's novel unconsciously urges the inventive reader to consider the stagnation of his political imagination as well as the immanent renewal of political possibilities.

Taxidermy of the commons

A scarecrow dummy dressed in 'an absurd red, white, and blue stovepipe hat, comically crooked' haunts the dreams of residents in Chester's Mill (722). The ominous figure signals to readers the crisis facing this town: how has Uncle Sam been emptied of substance and turned into a contrivance used to frighten citizens? How has an icon of communal obligation ('I want YOU!' the posters once cried out) become such a farcical shadow of itself? The (d)evolution of Chester's Mill tracks alongside the breakdown felt by many of King's readers in 2009. The scarecrow offers an analogy for the authoritarian Rennie by emoting bluster and bravado, an overhyped presence that deploys fear as its primary political weapon.[7] As a signifier, the avatar lacks moral or intellectual heft, being comprised of little more than straw, and by referencing the prototypical scarecrow in pursuit of a brain, Bush is clearly made the target of King's ridicule. However, if the reader accepts this interpretation at face value, she risks overlooking the broader social causes that render post-Dome authoritarianism possible. Because Rennie constructs the scarecrow out of the corpse of a concerned citizen that threatens to expose his corruption, this hollowed visage cannot be said to arise out of thin air, or as the result of a single causal event; rather, it must be read as the result of carefully cultivated conditions. Although *Under the Dome* treats the Bush-Cheney administration as a sort of *deus ex machina* – suddenly come and swiftly gone – the novel unconsciously opens a channel for its reader to inquire into what set the stage for this scarecrow and to ask what exactly caused the community of Chester's Mill to deteriorate at such a rapid rate.

According to Brown, the answer to this question lies in Rennie's initial approach to business, an approach that Brown describes as 'neoliberalism's hollowing out of contemporary liberal democracy'. When Rennie empties his victim's corpse then stuffs it with straw and clothes it in patriotic garb, he figuratively transposes 'democratic political principles of justice into an economic idiom . . . hollow[ing] out much of the substance of democratic citizenship' (*Undoing* 18, 35). He takes a democratically engaging figure and thoroughly guts it by governing Chester's Mill, like his automotive business, with the mantra: 'Keep ahead of the competish'. He consistently strives to defeat competitors in a way that suits him well when the Dome descends. Through Rennie's management style, *Under the Dome* evokes 'a business approach to governing, one in which democratic principles and the rule of law are neither guides nor serious constraints' ('American' 695). Rennie's pursuit of power is never severed from his parallel pursuit of profit.

This cut-throat art of governance challenges democratic norms. Colin Crouch describes it as 'a form of polity that avoids interfering with a capitalist economy. It is a model that has little interest in widespread citizen involvement or the role of organizations outside the business sector' (3). Rennie rules the town like a CEO that feels no accountability to the people that work for him. In fact, as Cheney declares, people should 'quit whining about all the things' that he has done to 'undermine the rule of law, erode the balance of powers . . . abuse prisoners and spy illegally' because he maintains the objective of defeating all competitors ('World'). According to Rennie, when the state inevitably fails, in part because it lacks an exclusively economic *raison d'être*, a competent manager must step in to establish a regime that combines anti-statism and hyper-managerialism (Brown, *Undoing* 20). Rennie expresses hatred for the feds and bureaucrats in general when, upon the arrival of a letter from President Obama, he refuses to understand community on the president's benevolent grounds. Stuck as he is in a state of perpetual competition, he organises the polity in what the reader will (ostensibly) understand to be a radically different fashion.

Rennie's reign is therefore founded upon a number of neo-liberal imperatives. First, his dealership continues the trend of financialisation, setting up billboards that declare, 'A$K U$ 4 CREDIT!' (King, *Under* 235). Unconcerned with the needs of workers in Chester's Mill, and rather than seek to improve the lives of citizens by manufacturing goods, creating jobs or extending a helping hand, Rennie creates greater debt/credit to profit from the 'losers' and 'suckers' of his community. In his conflation of state and corporate power, he aligns with officials like Cheney, Secretary of State Donald Rumsfeld and advisor Karl Rove.[8] Sheldon Wolin remarks of this trio: 'The political has been managerialized . . . the arrogance that leads corporate executives to violate the law finds its parallel in the arrogance with which Superpower flouts or disregards international norms' (*Democracy* 135). Rennie likewise understands 'winning' not through conciliatory or fair outcomes, but as a result of collateral damage and downsizing, just as the Cheney-Rumsfeld team maintains 'top-down control, as in tyrannical corporate structures' (Chomsky 33). From Rennie's perspective, successful managers privilege ruthlessness over 'democratic camaraderie' by conflating the art of governance with uber-competitive business practices. Rennie expresses Straussian contempt for the masses that elected him, treating every citizen as a potential sucker and every other government official as a possible threat. When Barbie the nomadic visitor receives an official endorsement from the president, Rennie immediately forecloses the possibility of peaceful cooperation and institutes a set of mechanisms to circumvent liability in the eyes of the populace by cloaking his power play in the language of public relations: 'The essential skill that a corporate executive brings to his firm and to a top-level government position is the skill of devising and executing strategies of aggrandizement . . . this often requires that one attack rivals, eliminating or weakening them before they can attack you' (Wolin, *Democracy* 145–7, 143).

Chester's Mill is consequently torn between extreme consumerism and extreme austerity. Rennie articulates distaste for rationing when he claims that conservation is 'un-American' and then flaunts this attitude by driving a gas-guzzling Hummer. Thanks in large part to the credit that his dealership provides, the town's citizens are told to follow suit. His unique governing style encourages the growth of personal/collective debt to satisfy unhealthy consumer habits in tandem with harsh austerity measures. Secretly seizing public resources for his private ventures (the 'General Motors of meth'), Rennie dismantles the commons, preaching self-sacrifice and thereby legitimising a dramatic rollback of government-backed necessities (684). Accumulating through dispossession, his government redistributes the contents of the town's coffers by making its wealth trickle up to him.

Rennie is proof positive of how a zombie politics in which business strategies overwhelm political engagement produces grotesque spectacle while simultaneously disenfranchising spectators.

> As neo-liberalism wages war on public goods and the very idea of a public . . . it dramatically thins public life without killing politics . . . this persistence of politics amidst the destruction of public life [. . .] is part of what makes contemporary politics peculiarly unappealing and toxic – full of ranting and posturing, emptied of intellectual seriousness, pandering to an uneducated and manipulable electorate.
> (Brown, *Undoing* 39)

Similarly, Rennie's opportunistic management style gestures at what Naomi Klein calls 'disaster capitalism'. From Chile to New Orleans, Klein contends, opportunistic capitalists eagerly await natural and man-made disasters in order to seize tragedy as a chance to swoop in and rebuild communities with a neo-liberal blueprint. As the saying goes, never let a crisis go to waste. What large swaths of the commons destroyed, and the demos in disarray, these figures institute policies generally favoured by the Chicago School of Economics. 'A major collective shock [is] exploited to prepare the ground for economic shock therapy' (Klein, *Shock* 12). The arrival of the Dome marks just such an occasion for Rennie: 'Panic could be good.' It is essential to remember at this point that his economic strategies are largely to blame for the political disenchantment of Chester's Mill. One citizen tells him, 'We've got the same sewer system we had in nineteen sixty' (King, *Under* 218, 495). His efforts to foster a business environment allow the infrastructure to decay, leaves the environment in ruins and, perhaps most damningly, never sparks the growth that he foretells. Disaster capitalism frequently inaugurates like-minded dictatorships: 'Authoritarian conditions are required . . . for economic shock therapy to be applied without restraint . . . one that either temporarily suspend[s] democratic processes or block[s] them entirely.' And so, following the disastrous arrival of the Dome, Rennie takes hold of the reins of Chester's Mill with a zeal that Klein attributes to free-market ideologues, exemplifying a 'signature desire for unattainable purity, for a clean slate on which to build a reengineered model society' (*Shock* 13, 25). In these ways, *Under the Dome* exposes the economic conditions that serve as a foundation for de-democratisation.

But *Under the Dome* ultimately abandons this line of critique in favour of vague psychological commentary with which Klein expresses her frustration: 'How little the security boom is analyzed and discussed *as an economy*' (386, author's emphasis). Although Rennie weaponises panic to gain personal power in a fashion that recalls corporatist actors like Rumsfeld and Cheney, King's text only ever indirectly links the unchecked police powers of the Second Selectman to the economic climate that he cultivates, as the novel privileges broad character study instead of sustained scrutiny of the economy in Chester's Mill. Rennie sports a God-complex apparently decoupled from material greed, and his motto of 'outlasting competition in the new century' loses its concrete financial valence as the narrative progresses: 'Wealth was the short beer of existence, power was the champagne' (448). In other words, by downplaying economic causes as much less persuasive than the sweeping appeal of political power, King's novel never fully germinates its critique of the neo-liberal state.

Nevertheless, despite this glaring omission, *Under the Dome* does (unconsciously) expose strict hierarchies, the forfeiture of democratic procedure and the dictatorial rule of charismatic managers by laying bare the blurred functions of corporations as well as the state. Brown contemplates this conjuncture: 'A business model of the state in one case and a theological model of the state in the other . . . a strange verbal brew that mixes the idioms of moral rectitude and entrepreneurial calculation' ('American' 698–700). Rennie's leadership style reveals how the principles of economists like Milton Friedman sometimes dovetail with authoritarianism, and how neo-liberalism intersects with authoritarian rule (for a prominent example, see the Chicago Boys of Chile in the 1970s and 80s). Likewise, by endorsing initiatives like the Free Trade Area of the Americas (FTAA), the Bush-Cheney administration constrains the 'choices' available to emerging democracies by prohibiting them from nationalising public works (World Trade Organization), banning certain products or methods of conducting business (Monsanto), and insisting upon tax cuts for multinational corporations (Klein, *Fences* 44–6). Beneath Rennie's rhetoric, then, neo-liberalism is revealed to be far less 'liberal' than many of its proponents would like to admit. To achieve his strict hierarchy, he aims to 'purify' Chester's Mill of opinions other than his own, and he does so by capitalising upon a unique kind of religiosity.

Interpreting the authoritarian dream

Prior to the arrival of the Dome, religious zealots dominate Chester's Mill through an extremist radio station that transmits an endless stream of millennialist rhetoric. Feverish leaders attempt to seize absolute power with the same kind of fanatical religiosity that infuses Rennie's authoritarian approach to governance. Thanks to the novel's singular focus upon fanaticism (a topic to which King's texts regularly return), *Under the Dome* only indirectly acknowledges the economic forces at work, and although it appears to attack the negative influence of radical Christianity upon the Bush-Cheney administration, it actually conforms to a confluence of forces described by William Connolly as the aggressive constellation of neo-liberal economics and religious zealotry. That is, the novel offers a snapshot of the contemporary matrix of millennialism, authoritarianism and neo-liberalism – three interwoven threads that we must untangle if we are to understand *Under the Dome* and the social order that it reflects. Although King's critics might take aim at Rennie's politics, or his economics, or his religious facade (in due turn), Adam Kotsko observes how, in truth, neo-liberalism forges a political theology: 'a totalizing world order, an integral self-reinforcing system' characterised by 'many crossing' (95).

For one, the Dome produces effects (and affects) that are similar to the ones historically created by political walls. Walls such as the Dome have long suggested a convergence of the political with the theological, as when – centuries ago – city walls were built to generate a 'sacred quality' for a leader that yearned to be venerated. 'The popular desire for walling harbors a wish for the powers of protection, containment, and integration promised by sovereignty, a wish that recalls the theological dimensions of political sovereignty' (Brown, *Walled* 47, 26). Today, these walls are still fashionable in places like Israel or along the US–Mexico border. In response to the 9/11 attacks, and the perception that nation-states are constantly under siege by terrorist cells, the Bush-Cheney regime erects literal as well as symbolic walls to reinstate a sense of protection as well as containment. In a similar fashion, the Dome grants to Chester's Mill a sense of wholeness, an illusion of totality that empowers Rennie by allowing him to proclaim himself an embodiment of the town's spirit. The Dome provides a convenient metaphor for his treatment of the body politic as a well-defined entity to be subjected to his authoritarian control. The town's citizens, on the other hand, closely resemble what Greg Eghigian calls *homo munitus* when they become mere by-products of a walled culture: 'obeisant and deindividuated theocratic subjects' (quoted in Brown, *Walled* 41). In sum, the Dome creates ideal conditions for Rennie's neo-feudal order.

As a strong-armed vehicle to 'save capitalism from democracy', the state in *Under the Dome* undergoes religious renewal due to the 'sacred walls' that Rennie uses to restore hierarchy and sustain a new-found sense of stability. The blue armbands sported by the citizens Chester's Mill recall the nearly ubiquitous 'Support Our Troops' yellow ribbons that crop up in the aftermath of 9/11, symbols that maintain 'the form of a command and also . . . an implicit reprimand'. The armband's 'sentimentalized and depoliticized framing . . . [reveals] a refusal to think or desire for others to think, let alone think differently' (Brown, 'American' 709). According to Rennie, faithful subjects practice only blind obedience to him. As a result of this walled culture, *Under the Dome* (unconsciously) allows readers to consider the ways in which neo-liberalism and extreme religious fundamentalism can feed into one another. 'Religious fundamentalism', Mark C. Taylor notes, 'tends to legitimize market fundamentalism and sanctify American power. In other words, religious neofundamentalism, political neoconservatism, and economic neo-liberalism are closely related' (13). Rennie's economic and theological agendas are co-constitutive, 'metabolizing into a moving complex . . . [of] mutual imbrication and interinvolvement' (Connolly, 'Evangelical'

160–2). Both neo-fundamentalists and neo-liberals share an authoritarian bent that disinvites input from the masses. With its 'sacred wall' in place, Chester's Mill exposes political-theological alliances that define the early twenty-first century.

As we have already seen, Rennie's hybrid art of governance treats competition as an ontological certainty, less a means to an end than an end-in-itself – an idea, it is important to note, that he endows with theological qualities. He repeats several times, 'The Lord helps those who help themselves' (King, *Under* 113). Rennie regularly cherry-picks verses from Scripture to support his competitive ethos and, like the Bush-Cheney administration, to occupy a powerful place at the nexus of a deregulated financial economy and a highly regulated moral economy. Meanwhile, the town's dissatisfied residents are depicted as so thoroughly confused and disillusioned that they start to reject all recognisable approaches to governance.[10] Jean Comaroff argues that the erosion of the state's care-taking agenda triggers 'a quest for fundamental certainties, authoritarian truths, absolute sovereignties' ('Politics' 24). Consequently, Rennie has his cake and eats it too, first by eroding democracy and then by nominating himself to be the community's saviour. In their desperate search of reassurance, the citizens of Chester's Mill turn towards more extremist positions.

Despite neo-liberal declarations of less government, the role of government in Chester's Mill is not actually diminished: it expands dramatically to enforce specific economic imperatives. And this mode of enforcement functions by drawing together the seemingly odd couple of free market and religious ideologues, a couple that 'unapologetically steers the moral, political, and economic ship, and . . . draws in part on a religiously interpellated citizenry – submissive to hierarchy and authority, and largely indifferent to deliberation' (Brown, 'American' 700). Rennie boasts, 'One speaks for all' (King, *Under* 451). He uses theocratic rhetoric to aid him in segregating his economic initiatives from the will of the people by claiming to summon the voice of God and declare his own Truth without reference to public mandate:

> An utterance can bring its truth into being and thus literally make and re-make reality. Today, this kind of truth would seem to fill a vacuum in a radically disenchanted world . . . a declarative rather than reasoned or argued truth . . . a common indifference and imperviousness to interrogation, deliberation, and facts. (Brown, 'American' 707)

Indeed, Rennie inspires cynicism regarding state intervention, then offers declarative truths to fill the void that he himself has left. A talented demagogue, he deconstructs as well as constructs reality, playing off his audience's willingness to accept absurdity as though it was gospel truth. He declares the 'economic reality' of Chester's Mill by citing himself alone as evidence: 'If you want something done right in this world, you have to do it yourself' (King, *Under* 1038). Bypassing the messy pluralism of democracy, Rennie asserts himself as a sort of charismatic preacher that utilises his pulpit to maintain dominion, blending business savviness with performative religiosity. This totalising schema aligns Rennie with gurus from the neo-liberal mould. William Davies notes: 'The authority [of neo-liberal gurus] is ultimately a charismatic form . . . a form of expertise that offers ontological security and meaning' (142–5). To maintain his theocratic control, Rennie dismisses notices from the outside world. 'These people are masters of disinformation', he warns (King, *Under* 862). Once he establishes doubt, he can position himself as the deliverer of divine messages, and so 'people in everyday situations lose faith in surface appearances and accepted canons of evidence, especially where civic order has imploded' (Comaroff, 'Politics' 29). Rennie's alternative facts are designed to satisfy citizens that have lost faith in democracy (a loss of faith, it bears repeating, that his own policies helped to initiate). Rennie's two-step agenda of deregulation followed by declarative Truth forges a neo-liberal theocracy in Chester's Mill: a fanaticism that Barbie links to the enemy that he fought in Iraq.[11] Rennie maintains his control over Chester's Mill by chastising 'secular humanists' as well as casting dispersion on the vagaries of democracy itself and fostering a subjectivity set to the frequency of his 'theo-econopolitical machine' (Connolly, 'Evangelical' 170). Rennie's citizen becomes increasingly isolated, vindictive, anchored in divergent certitudes and then placated by declarative statements from a charismatic leader.

In the end, Rennie paints for residents a picture of a re-enchanted economy that claims to provide immediate gratification. Both neo-liberals and religious extremists exploit similar dissatisfaction with the status quo by promising to deliver instant relief, without tedious, time-consuming public deliberation, while proclaiming their own 'ability to deliver in the here-and-now, a potent form of space-time compression' (Comaroff, 'Politics' 31). Convinced that the establishment has exhausted itself, the citizens of Chester's Mill turn to supernatural alternatives – be they the sudden intervention of millennialism or the benevolent *deus ex machina* of the market's 'invisible hand'. To compensate for the helplessness that his policies foster, Rennie summons occult belief, suggesting that rapturous joy is always only a fraction of a second away. The effectiveness of his art of governance, then, stems much less from its internal logic than from the emotions that it inspires: 'YOU'LL LUV THE FEELIN' WHEN BIG JIM IS DEALIN'!' (King, *Under* 837). Although King's novel invites readers to skewer the fundamentalist rhetoric of the Bush-Cheney administration, encouraging them to reject its authoritarian dream out of hand, *Under the Dome* leaves relatively untouched the cross-pollination of twenty-first-century economic and religious indignations, failing to focus in any sustained sense upon underlying entanglements.[12] The text appears reluctant to take seriously these systemic issues as they return from their repression.

Neo-liberal underpinnings

In short, *Under the Dome* superficially rejects a particular political formation (the Bush-Cheney doctrine) by instigating the ideological work that made the formation possible in the first place (neo-liberalism). King's reader is asked to retreat from the political and fundamentalist sentiments of the previous eight years but not, crucially, from the economic logic of the same period. In King's fictional universe, the influence of neo-liberalism is both nowhere and everywhere. Against its at times cartoonish depiction of authoritarian excess, *Under the Dome* proposes a number of 'alternatives' that, upon scrutiny, reveal themselves to be little more than the warp and woof of neo-liberal thought: a distaste for legal as well as governmental bureaucracy; a propensity for ceaseless innovation; an affection for anti-political nomadism; and a rejection of input from the masses.

King's novel models a disregard for bureaucracy, which is to say, while it ostensibly pines for the rule of law, it subtly decries legalisms: 'The shift to a market rationality in governance is also apparent in the [Bush] administration's blithe reference to "legalisms"' (Brown, 'American' 694). One character mocks the 'legal responsibility' of cleaning up after his dog, while even the former police chief lambasts the legal system and opts for 'reason before law' (King, *Under* 122, 247). Neo-liberalism, which normalises anti-bureaucratic attitudes by making it common-sensical to demolish care-taking government, manifests in the text's final presentation of 'citizens without a government' (a notion that dovetails with the trend of de-democratisation this book has been charting): 'An atmosphere of cynicism about politics and politicians, low expectations of their achievements, and close control of their scope and power . . . suits the agenda of those wishing to rein back the active state' (Crouch 23). In effect, when *Under the Dome* declares that its characters can no more rely upon the regional power company (with its laughably outmoded legal as well as governmental iterations in desperate need of overhaul) than they can rely upon Rennie's makeshift regime, the text's bureaucracies are meant to be discarded without political hand-wringing over what might replace them.

Under the Dome denounces the intelligentsia for conceiving of lame government structures that must be destroyed in order to preserve profit streams. Repeating a truism held by the neo-liberal cadre, the novel depicts academics as untrustworthy, hopelessly out of touch and privileged to dream up erudite schemes because they alone can 'afford optimism'. King's story cuts down to size elitists that love to plan a better future from their proverbial Ivory Tower. Not only does *Under the Dome* ridicule these scholarly planners, it transforms them into more 'useful' members of society. It mercilessly satirises an English professor with a 'fishbelly' that stems from an out-of-whack 'intelligence-to-exercise ratio', augmenting familiar portrayals of intellectuals as puny and ineffectual (a claim echoed by the Bush-Cheney administration).[13] By celebrating how the professor has been reprogrammed to forget his 'silly' studies, *Under the Dome* espouses a virulent anti-intellectualism (328, 366).

The novel's anti-intellectualism does not, however, call into question elitism in its entirety, instead playing it safe within the much-maligned halls of the academy. In fact, King's text still cultivates adulation for professional expertise, as it does with one of the central protagonists: a 13-year-old genius defined by a drive to innovate. Watkins misreads this character as the text's 'optimistic, politically aware conscience' (37–9). In supporting the novel's preferred mode of response, though, Watkins misses a key moment in the novel when the young man abandons activism to pursue what he deems to be a more 'mature' response to the town's issues. The protégé understands himself to be an expert, a point of identification with technocrats that cuts against his earlier belief in political involvement. Neo-liberalism also depends upon the power of entrepreneurial change above all other social priorities. Thomas Frank notes that 'the fog of righteousness surrounding (innovation) is so thick it allows all manner of absurdly altruistic claims'. According to Frank, we are witnessing under neo-liberalism 'an enthusiasm for innovation that I can only compare to a religious revival'. The problem with the teenager's heroic status in King's novel is that a worldview based exclusively upon innovation and expertise undercuts the premise of democracy: '[Technocracy] is obviously and inherently undemocratic, prioritising the view of experts over those of the public' (*Listen* 205, 186, 24). The town's second wealthiest citizen proves to be one of the novel's most laudatory figures when, early in the text, he throws a party for the town and makes sure that the smell from his grills reaches both sides of the divide, a decision that underscores the supposedly benevolent character of entrepreneurship. 'Business is good', he proclaims, because commerce unites people. Later, the businessman brings the teenage tech wizard to his store, guides him through the Do-It-Yourself section and assists him in building a radiation suit with which to save the day, a righteous deed that casts innovators as forces for social good. Echoing Thomas Friedman's thesis from *The Lexus and the Olive Tree* (1999), the novel's lionised entrepreneur refuses to kill a fellow citizen due to the fact that the citizen still owes back payments on a rototiller: a 'noble' act that suggests business acumen will defuse the 'political' violence occurring throughout Chester's Mill.

The most resounding neo-liberal value espoused in *Under the Dome* remains its anti-political stance. Barbie announces that he prefers 'ideas' to 'political analyses'; he refuses to be a military official, a politician or a leader of any kind; he only wants to serve others – indeed, some of the townspeople refer to him as 'the janitor'. In contrast to Bush as a self-declared 'decider', King's text champions an imagined blue-collar work ethic through characters like a resident nurse in Chester's Mill, who operates as a 'small town fixer-upper who had never considered himself much of a decision-maker'. In the face of aggressive manipulation by an authoritarian, *Under the Dome* offers respite in disillusioned good humour, returning the reader's attention at its conclusion to the reformed English professor for whom the joy of emptying bedpans now surpasses the false pleasures of his previous profession (350, 593, 627). Because his salvation appears to be the outcome of his anti-political lifestyle, the 'political' crisis facing Chester's Mill is resolved in a series of acutely personal moments. In one case, the town drunk expresses contrition for destroying private property: 'I got somethin' to make up for' (1052–4). *Under the Dome* thus reduces systemic issues facing the town to idiosyncratic issues facing individuals, a focus that it magnifies with Barbie's eventual admission that he tortured people in Iraq. Although, as Watkins observes, 'King makes the Iraq War deeply personal, not simply an abstract concept', this kind of interpretation upholds a preference for the personal over the political, and it prods us into asking why we must respond to the Iraq War in a 'deeply personal' fashion (39). That is, why would our response not be collective in nature? After all, 'citizenship, reduced to self-care, is divested of any orientation toward the common' (Brown, 'American', 695). King's reader might respond by inquiring into how personal catharsis alone will automatically lead to structural change.

A dumb demos

As we have seen, while *Under the Dome* invites readers to decamp from the false consciousness of the Bush-Cheney doctrine, it does little to foster a different vision for the future. The text cannot move beyond its own ideological horizons. On that front, of course, the novel is hardly alone. Benjamin Kunkel surmises that contemporary US society is 'squarely in the midst of a capitalist or (to periodize a bit more) neo-liberal culture, waiting to see what comes next' (76). With its utopian future obscured by a wall, *Under the Dome* appears unable to rescue its endangered demos by imagining viable political alternatives. If we understand King's story to be a representative critique of the Bush-Cheney doctrine, it unwittingly reveals critiques of this ilk to be intellectually bankrupt. All roads in *Under the Dome* lead to authoritarianism of some sort, and we cannot yet conceptualise genuinely divergent outcomes. In a word, the cathartic appeal of King's text does not prepare readers to confront the shallowness of its imaginary reserves.

'The people' of Chester's Mill offer a mere backdrop against which to understand the heroism of unattached individuals. To remove the Dome, the newspaper editor engages intimately with an alien being that helped to place it over Chester's Mill. The editor's exchange with the aliens is restricted to the narrow range of two individuals: 'I don't think you can fight a crowd.'[14] As 'the crowd' in Chester's Mill – a necessary vehicle for any democracy, of course – apparently plays almost no part in resolving its crisis, King's novel affirms the demos as inherently superfluous. In the most obvious sense, most members of the community perish (and so prove disposable); additionally, the story's revelations are not extended beyond the inner circle of the editor and Barbie: 'This belongs just to us' (1069, 599). The outcome of their horrific experience is the simple gratitude to be alive and a retreat into a small cadre. Brown argues, 'Neoliberal rationality eliminates what (thinkers like philosopher Hannah Arendt) termed "the good life".' In place of a 'good life', or even a marginally better life, the few survivors of Chester's Mill resign themselves to 'just life', in which the daily 'struggle for existence' is more than enough (*Undoing* 43). When Barbie and the editor at last perceive the gift of 'just life', the text speaks the language of privacy and retreat, rejecting calls for greater democratic engagement. *Under the Dome* posits that its readers should abandon the hard work of shared governance by incessantly compelling its readers to laugh, as though laughter alone can defeat 'self-serious' (read: political) oppressors. Barbie quotes *Moby Dick*: 'Whatever my fate, I'll go to it laughing.' The excessive laughter of King's text stresses its lack of political commitments (recalling, in the process, the excessive laughter of the Bachman books, discussed in chapter 2).[15] Furthermore, when granted the opportunity to reunite with people living outside the Dome, citizens forfeit the need for democratic action, as if political acts are only ever a distraction from 'what really matters'. Protest signs are reduced to litter by the road as residents encounter their loved ones on the other side of the wall. Thankfully, 'politics and protest have been forgotten' (964, 78, 875).[16] Evading democratic sentiment in favour of laughter and congeniality, King's novel subtly appeals to the authoritarian approach that it purportedly despises. For instance, Barbie judges the fate of the town 'like a general', the town editor secretly wishes that the colonel outside Chester's Mill was in charge inside the Dome and the colonel takes charge without any input from elected officials: 'Town politicians know a little, the town cops know a lot.' In spite of the novel's relentless attack upon Rennie and his art of governance, the narrative continually elevates elite managers to stand above what Rennie dismisses as the 'cotton-picking rabble' (124, 763, 944). As we see elsewhere in King's fiction, *Under the Dome* prefers police to politics.

Under the Dome does not merely undersell democratic procedures; it energetically undercuts the demos by depicting it as dumb: 'Small towns harbor small imaginations.' When Barbie eventually transcends 'the crowd' due to his status as a drifter, King's narrative argues that it is better to wander than to cultivate community. Readers should not waste their time participating in the political process. After all, at the first sign of trouble, the town does evoke a 'crowd-molting-into-mob vibe' (240, 477). *Under the Dome* presents an acute symptom of demo-phobia, echoed throughout King's works, including his other 9/11 allegory, *Cell* (2006).[17] A story about how a political event transforms people into 'a kind of hive mind born out of pure rage', *Cell* incessantly references terrorism and the aftermath of 9/11.[18] Like *Under the Dome*, the demos in *Cell* is comprised of mindless consumers that are (pathetically) 'tired of being different', and the sane survivors do not hold back in their contempt for 'those . . . *people*'. Also like *Under the Dome*, *Cell* responds to the chaos of 9/11 not by calling for more democratic intervention, but by advocating for competent managers willing to ignore the wishes of 'the mob'. The text condemns 'mobs' formed in hysterical moments, yet (and this distinction is crucial) it dismisses even the pre-9/11 capacities of its citizenry. The omnipotent narrator caustically observes, in a throwaway line, that 'no one north of Springvale could spell' (*Cell* 300–1, 50, 270; author's emphasis). In King's fictional universe, 'the people' are – and always have been – an obstacle to a functional social order. The political event of the Dome merely exacerbates a failure that was apparently visible from the start.

Under the Dome displays its demo-phobia through the extensive use of free indirect discourse (with which the prose moves in and out of its characters' internal thoughts). The reader can never be sure where Rennie's distrust of the demos ends and *Under the Dome*'s distrust of the demos begins. Rennie's internal dialogue proclaims that citizens are 'children' that cannot be trusted to govern themselves while, on the same page, the omnipotent narrator comments upon local parents that possess 'shabby loins'. In this way, the voice of the novel slips in and out of the consciousness of its characters to observe how many of the townspeople are mere 'chumps' (259–61, 803). In turn, the reader cannot be certain when the text is critiquing, or sharing in, Rennie's dismissive view of 'the people'. Linked to T. S. Eliot's inept Prufrock, the narrator guides readers to observe Chester's Mill from an increasingly isolated position, floating through 'half-deserted streets' and fostering an omnipotent 'we' that, much like the leather-faced alien children that watch the citizens of Chester's Mill, lacks substantive shape. *Under the Dome* shifts between the perspective of rogue actors, with their preference for the personal over political, and a perspective that looks down upon the masses as though they are ants via ironic detachment. From either vantage point, the collective remains inherently dumb, a depiction that reinforces an anti-democratic answer to the novel's central crisis. In a pregnant aside, the newspaper editor admits of the horrors in Chester's Mill, 'We did it to ourselves', and so she resigns readers to self-doubt and inaction. Therefore, when Barbie accuses Rennie of underestimating the citizens that he governs, the reader might accuse King's text of doing the very same thing (1011, 337). According to the logic of King's text, while one can laugh, retreat or float in response to public emergencies, one must never engage politically.

Seemingly unaware of its internal inconsistencies, *Under the Dome* remains sealed inside an Althusserian Dome. At the beginning of the text, readers look down upon the citizens of Chester's Mill, much like the aliens suspended above the Dome; they are then allowed to visualise the aliens as well, moving themselves upward into a more omnipotent position, as if looking down from a second Dome; and from this point, readers of this current chapter continue to shift ever upward, spotting my interpretive blind spots from atop a third Dome (and so on, ad infinitum). An imaginary site beyond the Dome, perpetuated by King's novel as well as its interpreters, resuscitates vital questions regarding how ideology works. If we are to avoid the trap of an assumed position outside of the Dome, we must find different ways to address what the novel really means when it gestures at a 'citizenry' without a 'government', or what it really means when it promotes a demos that could be defined without literal/figurative walls. What sort of thing *is* this romanticised exterior to the government? The political serves as a spectral presence, a constitutive outside. Because *Under the Dome* remains firmly enclosed within its ideological confines, it is from the outermost edge of its Dome that we must begin critique anew. Only by so doing can intentional readers re-politicise King's otherwise reactionary response to the Bush-Cheney doctrine.

9

The Outsider and the Shifting Shapes of Trumpism

THE ELECTION OF Donald Trump in 2016 marked an unexpected departure from the social norms that preceded it. Stephen King's *The Outsider* (2018) speaks to the subsequent anxieties of this departure by gesturing at the political signposts against which they are foregrounded. Readers spot a stray Hillary Clinton bumper sticker; most of the text takes place in so-called Trump country (hollowed-out industrial townships), in which the reader discovers his campaign slogan 'Make America Great Again' painted on a boulder and is led to assess erratic local witnesses as Trump voters; and in its climactic scene, the novel dwells upon Trump's defaced image. King's narrative forces its readers to consider the unique challenges of Trumpism through its presentation of a shapeshifting monster sent to degrade 'the establishment'. With its ability to pose as any individual with whom it comes into contact, King's shapeshifter quickly turns reasonable, law-abiding citizens into a violent mob: a rapid devolution that stresses, in turn, the limits of liberal as well as populist perspectives. In its final tally, *The Outsider* promotes liberalism through its detached and rational mode of deduction *and* populism through its exposure of liberal blind spots. Returning to a recurring message in King's fiction that political dissatisfaction offers an important residue (Bachman books), as well as the axiom that political antagonism inevitably resurfaces against attempts at its repression (*IT*), the conclusion of King's text reminds us of the counter-cultural possibilities that linger within his corpus. A novel that does not know what it wants to be, written for a nation of readers that suffers from a similar malady, *The Outsider* stresses that spectres of the political (mercifully) cannot be exorcised from American life.

Because the terms liberal and populist are quite broadly applied in contemporary discourse, we must begin by defining them. Liberalism, at least for the purposes of this chapter, remains rooted in the assumption of rational subjects that ought to be left to their own devices. Although there are competing variants of the term liberal (utilitarian, neo-liberal, egalitarian, and so forth), it may suffice to classify liberalism as driven by calls for enhanced personal freedom as well as a diminished role for centralised government. Of course, in practice things are rarely so clean-cut. For instance, due to the fact that a cadre of elites regularly exploit liberal values to shield it from democratic demands, liberalism is accused – by self-described populists, among other groups – of sustaining a relatively toxic status quo. The term populism is equally contested. Unlike liberalism, which offers a more rigid worldview, populism involves mobile strategies to gin up solidarity among 'excluded sectors of society' (Mudde and Kaltwasser 3). While unwieldy in their constitution, strains of populism do share a set of common characteristics: a vaguely constituted will of 'the people' juxtaposed with legal frameworks upheld by 'corrupt elites' that have lost touch; a charismatic leader; and reductive friend/enemy distinctions, as when a native 'people' is pitted against 'alien' intruders (be the 'aliens' elitist and/or oppressed). The ideals behind liberalism and populism are routinely conveyed through unique aesthetic conventions: '[Literary] forms are the stuff of politics . . . [as] politics involves activities of ordering, patterning, and shaping' (Levine 3). But what happens when politico-aesthetic shapes start to lose any semblance of orderliness? *The Outsider* offers a tentative answer to this salient question.

Whereas an Aristotelian tradition aligns aesthetic and political unity, *The Outsider* departs from this expectation by privileging disunity. Jerrold Hogle discusses how the American Gothic historically reflects such disunity.[1] Hogle's 'Gothic oscillation' aids us in comprehending King's entanglement of liberal and populist expression because, since its inception, the American Gothic harbours conflicted sentiments: it mocks rational subjects, armed with their meagre Enlightenment weaponry, at the same moment that it disenchants readers of their populist biases. To select one of the earliest examples, Charles Brockden Brown's *Wieland* (1798) wonders, with populist indignation, whether the Jeffersonian ideal of a free and reasonable subject remains the stuff of mere illusion when the hyper-rational figure at its centre is rather easily manipulated into slaughtering his entire family. Yet from a liberal vantage point Brown's murderer believes in alternative realities that prove to be the fruit of a madman's whimsy and so, by worrying over the populist's lack of critical ground, *Wieland* associates populist devotion with horrific carnage. It is therefore not entirely surprising to find that King's Gothic-infused texts speak directly to the heated divisions of the Trump era. As we have already seen, his body of work routinely expresses revulsion at self-certain liberals as well as the lumpen horde.[2] The incongruous generic make-up of *The Outsider* yields insight into complicated politico-aesthetic utterances that ushered Trump into the White House.

King's novel depends upon competing hierarchies that, according to Carl Schmitt, surface in any political engagement (us versus them; elites versus 'the people'). In particular, the text holds in tension two caricatures that are immediately recognisable in the Trump era: the deductive reasoning of liberals versus the blind devotion of populists. These entangled political and literary forms overlap, refract and clash with one another. For instance, the racialised hierarchy of *The Outsider* rubs up against its hierarchy of police and citizens. Highlighting how difficult it remains 'to set these popular faces apart', *The Outsider* invites readers to contemplate a growing disjuncture between form and function in American politics – an invitation, we will see, with significant real-world implications.[3] In short, King's text complicates presumed links between America's political masks and its obscured faces.

Despite this internal turmoil, *The Outsider* periodically demonstrates how liberal and populist rhetorical styles bleed together into a strange amalgamation, an 'improbable and . . . self-contradictory' patchwork. Hence its use of the double (two figures that are eerily similar, yet somehow distinct). Because populist forms are employed by politicians from across the ideological spectrum, contemporary populism, no longer 'the politics of outsiders', serves as a crucial ingredient in mainstream government by infiltrating a wide range of political positions (Ware 108, 119). For one, King's novel looks liberal even when it conveys populist sentiments; it appears populist even when it makes a case for liberal governance. In related ways, the Trump administration sounds populist, but one of its lone legislative accomplishments includes tax cuts to benefit the liberal class; the administration mimics a liberal agenda, but it treats minorities as scapegoats in a recognisably populist fashion. In the story's gloomier moments, then, the political differences of Flint City lift like a heavy fog to expose an unsavoury commonality: namely, the reality that both sides lack a sense of responsibility or purpose as they wander through a maze of contradictions. King's text immerses characters and readers alike in the murky waters of Trumpism.

However, due to the fact that they are the real engine of any political imagination, the politico-aesthetic contradictions of King's novel cannot be stilled. Illustrating that more than one America exists, King's narrative stresses confounding shifts in shape that can be interpreted as healthy for society thanks to their reinforcement of politics as an inherently messy business. That is, in content as well as form, King's novel incessantly divides itself and, by so doing, it upholds antagonism as a decisive element for sustaining political engagement – as opposed to the consensus/cure prototypes offered by the text's monstrous fascists as well as its police force. In its most hopeful moments, the dissension of *The Outsider* foregrounds a process of shape-shifting that makes political change possible.

Populist excess and liberal constraint

Prima facie, King's story lampoons the Trump administration by presenting a malevolent shape-shifter that turns citizens against one another as it feeds upon their base emotions. *The Outsider* indicts an administration accused of employing divisive rhetoric by recycling the idea of a grotesque 'movement from outside' (Canovan 79). A liberal reading of King's text focuses upon the narrative's unsavoury divisiveness, which is to say, its depiction of a population in a state of polarised hysteria. Ian Bremmer reports, 'Citizens fear surging waves of strangers who alter the face and voice of the country they know'; in response, populists promote a 'compelling vision of division, of "us vs. them"' (1). From a position of liberal detachment, *The Outsider* contends that populism stems from a surplus of combative disagreements as a mob caught up in pervasive feelings of outrage attacks a once-beloved teacher accused of heinous crimes against one of his students. On a dime, former friends abandon the impersonal bureaucratic methods of liberalism in favour of vigilante justice: the accused teacher's wife hopes that her neighbour's baby dies; a Christian mother in a minivan rejoices in the 'comforting' knowledge that the accused will soon be in hell (54, 119, 360). Aggravated by the glacial pace of justice, the resentful citizens of Flint City long for a speedier and more aggressive form of governance akin to what Stuart Hall calls 'authoritarian populism'.[4]

King's titular Outsider embodies the negative attributes assigned to populism by the liberal class. Disinterested in consensus, the Outsider derives Its power from turning neighbours into enemies – a shift that repoliticises society by transforming friends into 'complete strangers' (41). Due to its isolation of 'real people' from ostracised individuals, *The Outsider* can be read as the story of a baleful populist not unlike Trump. Like Trump, the entity too uses 'bad manners' while stressing 'directness, playfulness, a certain disregard for hierarchy and tradition, (and a willingness) to resort to anecdote as "evidence"' (Moffitt 34). When interpreted through a liberal lens, *The Outsider* offers a reactionary tale concerned with how readily a community abandons the rule of law when a populist leader takes the reigns. Despite extreme inconsistencies in the case against the English teacher, investigator Ralph rushes to prosecute. This action happens 'so fast' that he later doubts he made the right choice. His fellow investigator, Holly, launches her own investigation with the intention of staying within a strict budget, but the text notes how speedily she shifts into profligacy: 'Damn the expense' (129, 303). When opportunity arises, these 'reasonable' members of society slide into utter debauchery (a devolution that liberal readers are meant to associate with Trump's sordid appeal).

Following the script of a liberal nightmare, nearly everyone in Flint City loses his or her head as a need for expediency overtakes obedience to established procedure. The coroner abandons protocol to make personal notes in the official report; meanwhile, the pathologist 'oversteps her bounds' by littering official documents with her own conjecture (95). When Ralph considers omitting evidence to preserve his own authority, his decision threatens to erode the pillars of the liberal order, such as unbiased rationality or impersonal procedure. *The Outsider* therefore conveys the vulnerability of a liberal democracy ostensibly under siege. Elitists, in response, tend to 'believe that "the people" are dangerous, dishonest, and vulgar' (Mudde and Kaltwasser 7).[5] King's imagined liberal reader, who watches the gullible, vindictive and untrustworthy 'people' of Flint City with great trepidation, is meant to fear the populace in a manner that characterises much of his fiction. Given the presence of the unsightly masses, his readers should react by confirming that 'a well-functioning democracy is an elitist democracy' (Mény and Surel 5). Said another way, as an articulation of angst among the liberal class in the time of Trump, *The Outsider* conflates a distrust of elites with a broader distrust of strangers of any ilk. In effect, the novel delegitimises populist critique of liberalism by pre-emptively dismissing its appraisal of 'the establishment' as always-already tainted with provincial prejudice.

From this vantage point, King's Outsider exemplifies the fear, distrust and xenophobia of populist 'peoples' at their very worst. To maintain a stranglehold, the entity relies upon the Nazi logic of Blood and Soil and sets up residence in feeding grounds decorated with swastikas. There is power, the Outsider claims, to be extracted from regional blood – a power that is 'maybe tribal, maybe racial' (358). For liberal naysayers, this monster galvanises bitter nativist resentment through violent tribalism; its nativist rhetoric allows anxious readers to vent their apprehension of Trump's rapid ascent. Jacques Rancière writes that the liberal imagination regularly merges 'the very idea of a democratic people with the image of the dangerous masses' (Rancière, 'Populism' 105). Indeed, King's text portrays the citizens of Flint City as doubly outside: monster as well as multitude. The panicked liberal imaginary projects 'the people' as the undisciplined Other and as a deplorable throng that demonises 'strangers'. Paradoxically, the novel treats populists as loathsome criminals as well as a loathsome lynch mob. In Gothic terminology, Flint City interchangeably signifies Frankenstein's creation as well as the pitchfork-wielding crowd that destroys it. Consequently, *The Outsider* tracks populism's self-destruction in a fashion that will presumably bring comfort to the liberal class by absolving it of any culpability in the horrors that unfold. When actors like Ralph define themselves against an abject vision of 'the people', the liberal reader – like Victor Frankenstein, lacking self-consciousness – can escape from his accountability in the initial rise of the Outsider. Aesthetically and politically, cartoonish populists serve as a constitutive outside against which liberal readers are encouraged to reassert the cohesion of their cohort.

According to a liberal account of *The Outsider*, this collapse of social order in Flint City should be at least partially attributed to the transformation of the media: 'Goddam Internet, goddam Facebook, goddam Tweeter birds.' Derivative of a common complaint expressed during the period, the new media in King's text divides citizens by empowering them to jump to faster conclusions, to spread rumours and to excommunicate innocent victims: 'Facebook alone would be enough to hunt them down and single them out' (100, 123). When Ralph arrests his suspect in a public manner, the crowd erupts into violence and the shape-shifting Outsider relishes in the subsequent loss of decorum. This crisis – or, more to the point, this perception of crisis – remains a crucial component of any populist uprising. For populist powerbrokers, the need persists to 'perform and perpetuate a sense of crisis' that could 'never really end'. And so the Outsider nurtures the perception of crisis that Ralph's arrest creates because without such a spectacle the entity would have no sorrow or rage from which to draw Its potency. Benjamin Moffitt advances the argument that, as populism is first and foremost a political style, pundits pay too much attention to the 'what' of populism (its content) when they should be attending to 'the "how" – the style'. In the heavily saturated media landscape of the early twenty-first century, 'populism adapts elements of "media logic" to politics in increasingly effective ways', and it thereby mediatises politics to the extent that 'the so-called "aesthetic" and "performative" features of politics (become) particularly . . . important' (76, 83, 49, 31–2). King's monster 'likes witnesses'; it derives from 'papier-mâché'; it manifests as 'stage dressing' (King, *Outsider* 423, 525–6). Through the inherently performative nature of the Outsider, populism reveals itself to be an 'embodied, symbolically mediated performance': the leader performs, 'the people' watch, and the media mediates. With a face made of Play-Doh as well as the capacity to look like anyone, the Outsider fosters an increasingly distorted demarcation of politics and popular entertainment.

We should hasten to add that it is not so much that new media causes the populism of the Outsider; rather, it buttresses sentiments that are required to energise the monster, including drama, polarisation and a simplification of complex issues into stark shades of black and white. Proliferating social media platforms render it difficult for the citizens of Flint City to stop the spread of the Outsider's influence. For example, the omnipresent media relentlessly exploits the family of King's persecuted teacher: 'TV lights and the shouted questions. A machine had swallowed her family' (143). As individuals are enclosed within their respective political camps, the Outsider can feed upon them, a situation to which the liberal reader might respond by declaring the abject gullibility of 'the people': 'The hatred of outsiders (is) on the rise again as people, locked in their partisan silos and filter bubbles, are losing a sense of shared reality' (Kakutani 12). On this front, the liberal reader shares a great deal in common with the Outsider in that they both perceive themselves to be far shrewder than the ignorant crowd. King's fiction once more pillories 'the people', this time for being fed propaganda by the Trump administration and becoming dependent upon the corrosive influence of outlets such as Fox or Breitbart News. The text invites liberal readers to disparage 'the people' being held under the sway of this spectacle. It comforts a specific demographic by lauding a liberal's ability to perceive the difference between performance and reality, thus advocating a nascent regime to facilitate the Truth for an illiterate 'people'.

In tandem with its consideration of perpetual division and heightened spectacle, *The Outsider* contemplates a phenomenon known as post-truth. According to Lee McIntyre, post-truth surfaces 'when one thinks that the crowd's reaction actually *does* change the facts about a lie'. McIntyre opines the blending of reality with opinion and cautions that post-truth is always-already a story of domination (9, 13; author's emphasis). The Outsider gains power when citizens fail to question their cognitive bias and cultivate animosity unsupported by factual evidence. Likewise, Trump supporters feel 'displaced' from what has otherwise been acknowledged by the liberal class to be a 'consensus reality'. Because disenfranchised citizens prove eager to buy into alternative realities, the Trump administration can successfully breed doubt, constantly distract and command the ether 'to ensure that thorny facts find no purchase there' (Gladstone 29, 53). Trump advisor Rudy Giuliani famously declares: 'Truth isn't truth' (Morin and Cohen).[6] King's novel thus effectively panders to liberal anxieties by considering the perils of a cultural shift in which 'the people' cannot separate facts from fiction.

The Outsider opens with a series of witness testimonials to establish the fragility of the Truth in a world consumed by gaslighting populists (of note, King employs this tactic in his 1974 novel *Carrie*, as well as many of his works that follow). Recognising that perception is now everything, the shape-shifter hides in plain sight to toy with how others see the world. The novel's detectives, as a result, must rely upon 'stand-ins' when their minds fail to process relevant information (267). Purveyors of post-truth assume the cognitive bias of individuals who rationalise what is irrational in order to make it fit within their preconceived order of things. Conveniently enough, McIntyre uses the example of a police detective that apprehends a suspect and then attempts to reverse-engineer a case by interpreting clues in a manner that confirms his pre-existing beliefs. Similarly dedicated to reverse-engineering, Ralph rationalises highly irrational aspects of the English teacher's case and, in so doing, exemplifies the post-truth dupe. *The Outsider* presents this dupe to readers that will likely consider themselves immune to such crass indoctrination, assuming that most of its audience will be 'in on the joke' and express an appropriate degree of disgust at Ralph's 'defection'.

In sum, *The Outsider* paints Trump voters with a relatively uniform hue as vindictive children that all-too-quickly bite the lures that his administration dangles. Ryan Vlastelica notes that *The Outsider* exposes 'the dangers of people who refuse to see the truth' (Vlastelica). To give flesh to this caricature, King's monstrous entity manipulates the mind of Ralph's colleague, a self-professed fan of the film *American Sniper* (2014) – widely recognised for its far-Right, jingoist message – by evoking fear ('I can give you cancer') as well as making grandiose promises ('I can take away your cancer') (524, 382).[7] It alone creates mayhem; It alone restores order. Trump's denigrators claim that he too creates a crisis – the hotly contested 'national emergency' at the US–Mexico border, for instance – only to declare that he alone can resolve it.[8] This strategy positions him as a populist 'strong man' that erects and destroys reality at will: '[Trump] seemed to feel that his believing something somehow made it true . . . as if he had the power to change reality' (McIntyre 165). The Outsider achieves God-like status as It channels zealotry and orchestrates the subsequent madness; in response, King's narrative delivers an anti-populist message and restores the ideal of a liberal class that can employ critical thinking to debunk the mystique of a nefarious sadist. When confronted by the hysteria of 'the people', Holly answers: 'Laws were laws for a reason' (360). When the text upholds Ralph's default mode as largely (albeit not exclusively) non-discriminatory, and therefore unsusceptible to its own gaze, *The Outsider* indicts the 'correct' perpetrator and habituates the reader into an appropriately liberal mode of detection.

King's novel, then, largely excuses liberal readers from questioning their complicity in monopolising notions like expertise, knowledge and Truth. It can be argued that agents working in the liberal tradition claim 'neutrality' to a degree that forces populists to compete over – which is to say, re-politicise – facticity itself. An apologist for populism might interject that Ralph's illusion of airtight legalism, and not the manipulations of a con artist, actually triggers the debate about who gets to define what is real and what is fantasy. Ralph's presumed non-partisanship enables him to claim dubious ownership over 'expertise, merit, evidence' (Kotsko 118). When he places values like the Truth under his exclusive purview, he drags unprejudiced values into the realm of political contestation. But if the liberal class controls judicial terms and conditions so absolutely, how else could 'the people' ever fight back against the malfeasance of Flint City officials?

The Outsider fuels populist rage by giving a singular form to a citizenry disenfranchised by what it views as 'alien elites'. 'The elite are not just seen as *agents* of an alien power, they are considered alien themselves' (Mudde and Kaltwasser 14, author's emphasis). To a reader with populist sympathies, the pleasure of King's text might be located in the unformed impulses of 'the people' that it portrays – a surplus that pushes back against Ralph's well-manicured universe. As readers with populist leanings might appreciate how King's novel evokes 'the people' to overturn Ralph's consensus and cure model, *The Outsider* can be read as rehabilitating the lumpen horde. After all, to envisage politics as an impersonal process, as Ralph and Holly occasionally do, 'is to obliterate the whole dimension of power and antagonism . . . and thereby miss its nature' (Mouffe *Return*, 140). Indeed, given that they work for 'the establishment', Ralph and Holly are viewed with not unwarranted suspicion, as black children scream out 'Five-O' and scatter upon their arrival in the neighbourhood. When Ralph articulates his case against the English teacher, a citizen looks at him as though he was part of an 'unknowable extraterrestrial race' (King, *Outsider* 72). A populist reading of *The Outsider* exposes the flaws of a society controlled by police instead of politics.

Several additional aspects of *The Outsider* complement this populist plea, including appeals to authenticity, religious and mythological hierarchies and racialised exotica. *The Outsider* pursues transparency as it cuts through the pluralist noise of liberalism to declare a fundamental Truth. A din of witness testimonials against the accused teacher eventually cedes to reverence of a cosmic (and reductive) struggle between 'good and evil'. Because populists long to see past the opaque consensus of experts, the second half of King's novel transcends the clutter of the hyper-legalised, hyper-bureaucratised world that comprises the first half of the text, calling into question a reality over-regulated by experts and then uncovering a metaphysical Real. *The Outsider* insists upon belief in the irrational when citizens, 'impatient with liberal democratic constraints', prefer blind obedience to a higher order, supported by faith over facts (Galston, *Anti-Pluralism* 79). Even the text's supposedly liberal agents eventually come to trust in the existence of the supernatural entity by setting aside their ideal of detached rationality in the name of stronger emotional investment. Counter to the presumed indifference of liberalism, politics depends very much upon affect. Martha Nussbaum comments, 'Ceding the terrain of emotion-shaping to antiliberal forces gives them a huge advantage in the people's hearts and risks making people think of liberal values as tepid and boring' (2). In a word, the populist visage of King's Janus-faced novel offers a rejoinder to 'tepid liberals' like Ralph as it reveals the Outsider to be the invaluable stuff of myth (rather than the cynical by-product of a media machine).

At times, the novel defies the 'monstrosity of cowardly intellectualism' – liberalism's shrinking focus upon money, property and effective rhetoric – with a call for *more myth-making*. Only with myth, Schmitt states, do disempowered groups gain political puissance. Myth involves a wilful suspension of disbelief by a collective dedicated to metanarratives that bubble up from 'the people' instead of trickling down from elites.[9] 'The ability to act and the capacity for heroism, all world-historical activities reside . . . in the power of myth', Schmitt insists. 'The enthusiastic mass creates a mythical image that pushes its energy forward and gives it the strength for martyrdom as well as the courage to use force. Only in this way can a people . . . become the engine of world history' (*Crisis* 68–9). Marking a departure from relativist witness accounts and the prattling of government officials, The Outsider stirs the stuff of myth to generate spontaneous action from the revived masses of Flint City. And to adorn its mythos, *The Outsider* capitalises upon exotica, appropriating the means of Mexican lore to achieve its emotional ends. Supposedly originating in Latin American folktales, the text festoons the Outsider with italicised Spanish words and garnishes the fable with tropes from an imagined south-western landscape (border towns elsewhere mined by Trump's rhetoric). To be sure, *The Outsider* implicitly condemns racism to a degree that the Trump administration certainly does not. But King's narrative nonetheless re-enforces the racialised impulses behind populism by projecting evil onto an already-coded surface of Mexican Otherness. By dovetailing with populist rhetoric, in other words, *The Outsider* also relies upon racial difference to instil a foreboding atmosphere, and it thereby sets a kind of trap for unsuspecting readers: to discredit the liberal order by accepting in its stead a ghastly enemy that apparently signifies Mexican culture is to reproduce the prejudicial posture of Trumpism. Although the shape-shifter's ability to violate figurative and literal borders between tribes is meant to repel readers, we cannot ignore how this slippage still aims to excite King's audience.[10] *The Outsider* thus sucks readers into a dismal exchange by exploiting racialised difference to foment anger while, at the same time, diminishing the merits of dispassionate reasoning. At the close of King's contemporary myth, liberal readers might discover themselves more easily manipulated by populist style than they would care to admit.

In its gloomiest moments, *The Outsider* presents a dreadful doubling: as Trumpism hypnotises everyone into obeying its internal logic, liberals and populists become rather difficult to tell apart. At the end of the novel, despite the entity's disappearance, they *all* believe in the Outsider. Be it in the form of saviour or strawman, each side prefers a paranormal explanation to a serious address of the unholy conflation that these groups have created together. They ignore, in turn, the inconvenient truth that they have all played a part in conjuring Flint City's demon. In exchange for their submission to the terms and conditions of this bizarre new world, they have received their beloved tax cuts and their racism has been permitted to persist. They can imagine themselves rushing headlong into the future as well as fleeing into the past, a time in which America was 'great' and a time in which it will be 'great again'. Thomas Frank observes that members of the working class are churned into a populist frenzy even as they maintain liberal initiatives that damage their way of life: '*Vote* to strike a blow against elitism; *receive* a social order in which wealth is more concentrated' (Frank, *What's the Matter* 5, author's emphasis). Because the body politic cannot seem to face the music of its own undoing, the twin faces of Flint City opt for wilful blindness – a collective madness that the novel explicitly links to Trumpism. The monstrous offspring of King's liberals and populists grants citizens an excuse to preserve their dismal status quo and offload sincere anxieties, maintaining superficial borders while deferring the grim realisation that the world as they have known it crumbles around them.

The ever-shifting shape of American politics

By this point in the book, it may not surprise us to find that the drive to difference in King's novel provides a glimmer of hope as well. Like the fissure that runs down the face of its monster, *The Outsider* incessantly shifts into something else. As John Sears remarks, King's works 'frequently mutate genre, or juxtapose different generic features, within their own textual borders' (45).[11] *The Outsider* opens as a run-of-the-mill police procedural in which detectives rush to make sense of clues, uncertain of the outcome but caught up in the thrill of a harried investigation; in contrast, the second half of the novel can be categorised as a supernatural thriller, in which fantasy dwarfs critical thinking and readers are invited to rebel against stagnant proceduralism. What are we to make of these generic schisms? More to the point, why would a text celebrate liberal values like dispassionate deduction, while casting these very same values into doubt? The internal strife of *The Outsider* does not demand a cure, but exposes a need for the endless splitting that allows American democracy to remain in motion.

As we have already seen, *The Outsider* contradicts liberal as well as populist hierarchies by placing their respective emotional coordinates into conversation. Caroline Levine writes, 'Each form [has] its own logic, its own principle of imposing order . . . [various binaries] do not map perfectly onto one another' (90). King's novel awkwardly maintains a liberal pecking order – bureaucratic segregation versus social breakdown – as well as a populist ranking of believers over 'the establishment'. We might extend this examination of conflicting hierarchies into much of King's fiction. His novels routinely infuse folksy common-sense with a contradictory mistrust of 'the rabble'. This disjuncture runs throughout contemporary political discourse as well. David Ryfe examines how politicians mix populist terminology with the language of managerial competence: 'At one moment populist, at another rationalist' (150). Blending populist and liberal grammars, *The Outsider* teases to the surface core contradictions within the rhetoric of Trumpism.

These core contradictions manifest most explicitly in *The Outsider*'s treatment of the police. At first, the police appear as a highly corruptible entity that tampers with evidence, as when the district attorney rabidly pursues his own ambitions while ignoring the ideal of blind justice. In these moments, *The Outsider* endorses a populist message that the current system is 'rigged', positing (as William Galston claims) that '"the people" are threatened by oppressive demonstrations of instrumental rationality' (Galston, 'Progressve' 35). The untrustworthy DA relies too much upon DNA evidence; striking a related chord, the Trump administration frequently casts aspersions on the methodology of its own justice department. However, as King's novel progresses, citizens reconcile themselves to a chastened police force – a reconciliation that culminates with potential victims welcoming Ralph's assistance: 'Cops on my side . . . that's a new experience. I like it.' *The Outsider* therefore loves as well as laments the liberal order, a tension that it articulates through Holly as she critiques populist propaganda – 'This is information, not entertainment' – and expresses populist belief – her vaunted piece of 'evidence' turns out to be a Mexican film about vampires (465, 379). King's police officers serve as walking contradictions: defenders of liberalism at times radically inspired by the populist zeitgeist.

This walking contradiction is captured in the two words tattooed on a character's hands: CANT and MUST. *The Outsider* cannot drink from the prominent waters of populism due to its other ideological commitments – yet, given the surge of populist sentiment in 2016, it must. Concurrently, the novel cannot uphold the clinical approach of a liberal class due to the numerous abuses committed, such as the police brutality that spawned the Black Lives Matter movement – yet, given Trump's threat to 'establishment' values that the novel cherishes, it must. Like the Trump administration, *The Outsider* commingles populist and liberal facades that are both more and less than what they initially appear to be. Although Ralph's empirical pursuit is admittedly not 'the world's best idea', Holly's belief in the supernatural forces him to worry over what would happen to the concept of truth if he comes to 'believe in anything' (275, 388). *The Outsider* asks its reader to practice a bounded, judicious mode of reading (one that can be deemed liberal because of its deliberation upon cause and effect) while simultaneously inviting her to practice a bounded mode of reading that espouses constant reverence (one that can be deemed populist thanks to its pursuit of pure origins, its celebration of transparency as well as its supernatural endowments). *The Outsider* converges its politico-aesthetic fragments into a disjointed composite that necessitates neither resolution nor synthesis.

This ambivalence need not paralyse the reader; in fact, it might be put to benevolent use. King's disjointed composite illuminates an oft-overlooked need to revisit the presumed divide between liberal impartiality and moralistic sentiments associated with populism. In popular discourse, the subject is understood to be either 'too rationalist to motivate action and decision' or 'too indiscriminately rooted in the passions to carry normative weight'. King's novel captures this binary in its breakdown between the officious Ralph and the former officer Jack Hoskins, now a devotee of the Outsider. Unconvinced by such a fixed dichotomy, Sharon Krause argues that we must achieve 'a measure of impartiality in our judgments . . . but we cannot leave behind our passions and desires' (6, 199). Oscillating in Gothic fashion between impartial reason and passionate belief, *The Outsider* goads its readers into interrogating a fragile division between liberal and populist styles. It closes with Ralph's dream of being transformed into a shape-shifter, only to show him awakening and reassuring himself that his face will forever be his own. At its close, then, King's novel leaves readers in possession of 'two minds' (560, 175). The conclusion is hardly a call for Aristotelean moderation; instead, it offers what Alain Badiou calls 'a true contradiction', a genuine 'outside'. By endlessly splitting the liberal from the populist, *The Outsider* affirms the potency of the political, and recalls that 'modern politics always begins with the idea that this world is not completely unified'. In other words, the novel's relentless doubling reminds us that 'we have to pass from one to two' if we are to keep the political alive, and hold authoritarian creep at bay (Badiou, *Trump* 39, 48). Without shape-shifters and doubles, Ralph's police state would reign over Flint City and all manner of offences might be committed under the auspices of upholding the law. Happily, *The Outsider* rejects this faux consensus to awaken the political from its periodic slumber.

Although King's text at times lauds 'a technocratic form of politics . . . (and) the neutral management of public affairs', Ralph can only keep 'the people' at arm's length for a limited time (Mouffe, *For a Left* 4). Total satisfaction for everyone cannot be achieved as no institutional arrangement could possibly hope to please everyone. Social formulations are therefore extremely tenuous things. According to Slavoj Žižek, populists disclose this tenuousness by laying bare that organisational politics remains vulnerable to overthrow. Populists do the invaluable work of gesturing at what is missing from the liberal illusion of consensus. Admittedly, they also tend to set aside this measured consideration in favour of submission to a charismatic 'particular figure'. With their habitual dependence upon flimsy fetishes like the 'strong man' and/or the scapegoat, populists often wind up peddling caricatured intruders or saviours to compensate for the lacuna that they initially expose. In this fashion, lionised figures like the Outsider eventually restore 'artificial concreteness' by covering up the constitutive absence at the centre of American politics. The novel's once-terrifying entity devolves into mere cliché. But, just as Pennywise can never adopt his terminal form in *IT*, this devolution does not tell the whole story: in King's story, the spectre of populism evokes a formless 'people', betrays a weak spot in liberalism and stokes in the liberal class 'a panic of politicization as such' (Žižek, 'Against' 553–8). To the DA's dismay, populists remember that neither economic algorithms nor market-tested media spots ever fully account for the will of 'the people'.

King's shape-shifter disrupts the imagined social order thanks to its undisciplined formlessness and eternally malleable nature. Jean Comaroff agrees with Žižek that the lack of a settled form stands out as populism's most formidable contribution to American politics: 'It is precisely (populism's) intrinsic slipperiness that makes the term so productive' 'Populism' 100). From the bitter and corrosive working class (*Christine*'s LeBay), to the deranged citizenries of places like Chester's Mill (*Under the Dome*), to the blood-thirsty assemblages of the Bachman books, King's *oeuvre* consistently portrays 'the people' in an elusive light. Faceless 'peoples' adopt a plethora of forms before receding – of necessity – back into the unknown. For all of the shortcomings discussed in this chapter (indeed, throughout this book), the reluctant populism of *The Outsider* reveals 'the people' to be an eternally fluid construction, a crucial realisation in the age of Trump. Theorist Ernesto Laclau states: 'Populism is the royal road to understanding something about the ontological constitution of the political as such . . . the construction of the "people" will be the attempt to give a name to [the community's] absent fullness.' In just this way, the Outsider ruptures the normal order of King's storyworld and sets in motion the re-emergence of a discontented populace. When the monster's visage collapses to reveal nothing more (or less) than an empty interior, King's text discloses a great deal about 'the ontological constitution of the political' (Laclau, *Populist* 67, 85, 119). King's Outsider is the shaky signature of an (im)possible collective that surges to the surface while remaining permanently on the brink of some unforeseen constellation.

This lack of resolution is one of the most significant aspects of *The Outsider*. Prior to Ralph's arrest of the English teacher, citizens of Flint City had temporarily fallen under the spell of the *volonté générale* – an enchanted state in which all individual wills would be materially identical (*Outsider* 151). During times of feigned consensus, the Outsider slithers back into hibernation because Its greatest strength – a drive to divide citizens into friend/enemy – has been weakened. Yet citizens cannot defy the Outsider's antagonism in perpetuity. Its brutal distinctions inevitably re-emerge.[12] Political revolutions occur over and over again as the result of an irreducible plurality that stands at odds with the neat-and-tidy managerialism of the Flint City police.[13] Whereas the DA perceives citizens as a 'passive mass that the state configures', the disempowered residents of Flint City persist as 'a people in pursuit of its existence' (Badiou, 'Twenty-Four' 26–30). As the Outsider moves between formlessness and form, King's entity indicates the ways in which populist movements expand as well as contract and, as a result, the novel implies that 'this world is not completely unified but divided into (at least) two parts' (*Trump* 34). Perhaps, we might surmise, Flint City will avoid the next hallucinatory period of *volonté générale* – and therein lies the power of the shape-shifter and the double as cardinal tropes in American politics.

By stealing the identity of strangers, the Outsider can pose as anyone and everyone, a skill that reveals how unwieldy political possibilities always overwhelm the artifice of control. *The Outsider* is driven to division. In form as well as content, it provokes a relentless splitting that deflates belief in consensus, be it liberal or populist in tone, by casting doubt upon the perceived *animus* of a unified society. Put differently, the double creates an uncanny sensation for King's readers because the text remains in many ways familiar as well as unfamiliar.[14] Prior to Trump's election, many pundits disavowed aesthetic and political disunity in favour of stories about a coherent body politic; but when the doubles of *The Outsider* echo this ingenuous sense of wholeness in American politics (the Two made One), the delusion serves as a harbinger of doom by reminding us that we are fundamentally antagonistic creatures, and so the One must be made Two again. Because we are propelled not by a desire for synergy but by the drive to contradiction, Trumpism harkens a return of the double in American politics that has been repressed since the 1960s.

The Outsider's splitting will likely upset readers from across the partisan spectrum. For instance, as Laclau argues, many Marxists rely upon well-defined entities like the bourgeoisie or the proletariat to circumvent antagonism, and thereby reduce volatility to a purely mechanical collision between relatively unmoving groups. In contrast to this black-and-white caricature, King's treatment of 'the people' in *The Outsider* degrades impartiality as well as fascist kinship by championing a never-ending process of (re)articulation. Like the archetypical bogeyman, 'the people' may seem enfeebled at the novel's close, yet it actually enters into a more dangerous state of formlessness. King's hellion will almost certainly survive until its next incarnation, thereby mirroring the fate of countless populist movements. *The Outsider* ultimately throws light upon how alliances are renegotiated, which shapes invariably shift and why the political endures. These revelations may stir feelings of either hope or horror. At the very least, King's portrayal of the shifting shape of American politics demonstrates that society's contradictory character (mercifully) persists. After all, the only thing costlier than a metastasising Outsider would be a society that denies Its existence.

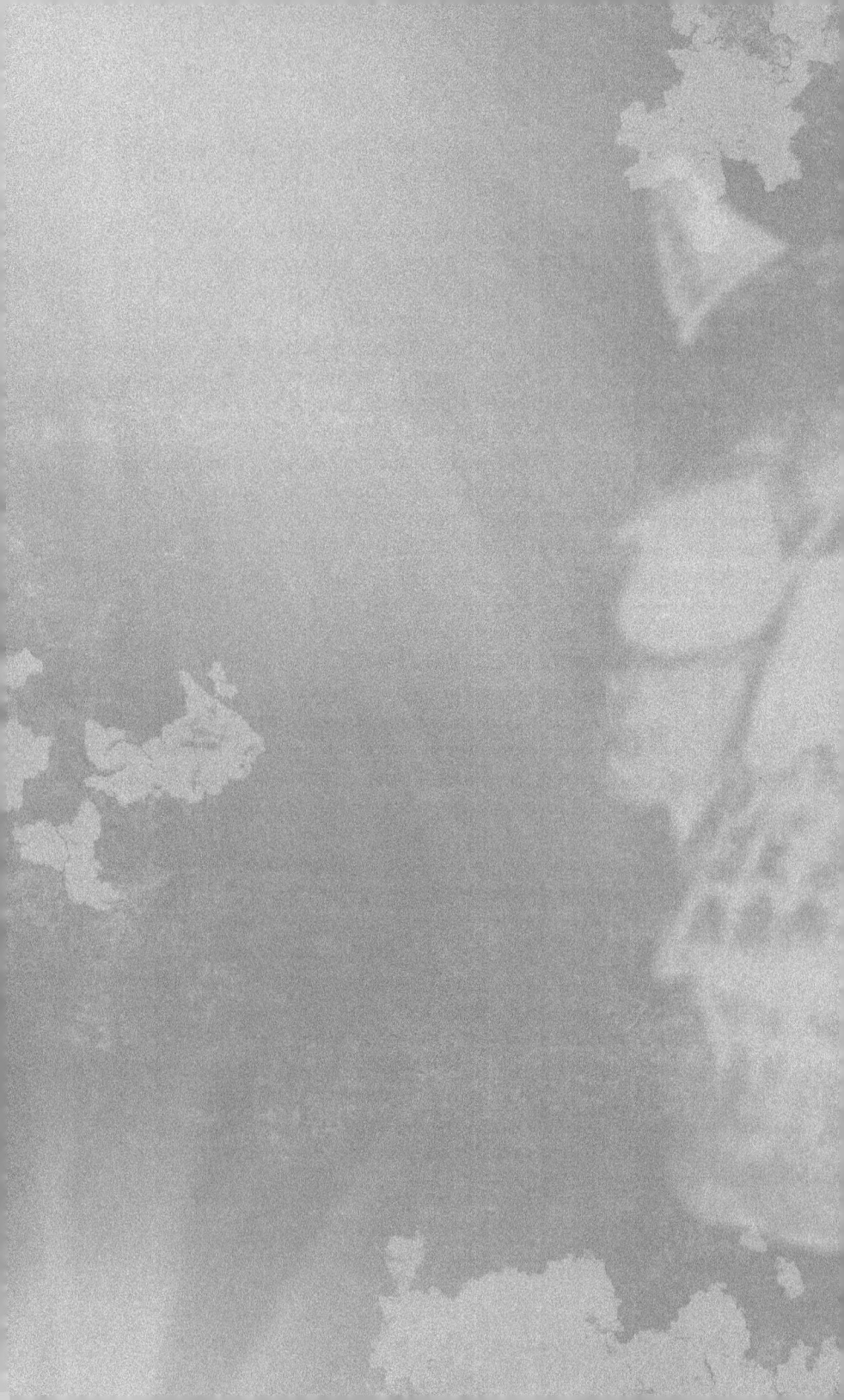

10

Postlude

Revolutions of *The Stand*

STEPHEN KING'S post-apocalyptic fable *The Stand* (1978; unabridged 1990) tracks a body politic in the process of rebuilding itself. After a plague wipes out most of the world's population, stray survivors must form groups to decide what kind of fraternity they wish to fabricate. As characters rush to restore recognisable patterns of behaviour, *The Stand* lambasts organisational politics as a core deficiency in human nature, a misguided attempt that invariably ends in the horrific abuse of power. At the same time, King's text cannot exorcise its political shadow (that is, the imminent reformation of a social order under endless revision). This representative work thus ties together threads discussed throughout the preceding chapters.

To begin, King's epic advocates the destruction of centralised government as well as increased self-reliance in a manner that upholds the decrees of a neo-liberal state. *The Stand* (unconsciously) exposes how American politics snuffs out antagonism via economic managerialism, the devaluation of electoral contest, a persistent phobia of 'the people' and the elevation of lifestyle choices made by citizen-consumers above institutional reform. 'The political', Chantal Mouffe writes, remains our forever 'blind spot' (*Agonistics* 3). Nevertheless, because *The Stand* cannot disavow the constitutive clash between 'good' and 'evil' that serves as its crux, the novel presents political wrangling as the bedrock of American life. In its simplest terms, it presents hegemonic and counter-hegemonic blocs in constant flux. While earlier chapters segregate King's works into two major categories – narratives that preserve the political through perpetual dissatisfaction (Bachman's books; *IT*; *The Outsider*) versus narratives that dampen discord in favour of consensus/cure (*Firestarter*; *Rose Madder*; *Under the Dome*) – *The Stand* proves that such a clean distinction never holds. In truth, each category haunts the other, infusing the novel with contradictions to keep the wheels of American politics in motion and undermine possible paralysis imposed by authoritarian regimes.

King's text conveys this tension by tarrying around the 1960s (at least, as the decade has been memorialised in the popular imagination). *The Stand* posits the 1960s as an era in which establishment politics fails and the power of the political explodes. A recurring character in King's canon, antagonist Randall Flagg – 'born' in the tumultuous year of 1968, a year in which 'a great wave of revolt' covers the land – represents a conventional rebel rouser. He wears a medley of partisan buttons in honour of 'one radical group after another' while promising to 'tie-dye' the world in gore (172–4, 530, 400).[1] Because the political by definition instigates the continual reform of an always-already imperfect social order, Flagg serves as its ideal mouthpiece: a disruptive constant throughout human history; a permanent impermanence (as I discuss in chapter 9, King's 2018 novel *The Outsider* recycles this shape-shifting motif).[2] In its more reactive moments, *The Stand* casts Flagg's permeable political shape as always-already negative and, in turn, it discredits student activists as so much 'bullshit', a vitriolic sentiment on which King's 1987 novel *The Tommyknockers* doubles down when it describes 'dope-smoking hippies' as 'worthless, crab-raddled excuses for human beings' (223). To endow its burlesque performance of political activism with flammable flesh, Flagg's associate the Trashcan Man trumpets that the world is 'ripe for burning' (*Stand* 288). On the one hand, the Trashcan Man's drive to self-immolation gives him an anti-political air as he gestures at the futility of it all; on the other hand, his burning makes him supremely political, the epitome of a pluralist public that can never be made whole and inevitably winds up ablaze once more. Borrowing yet another popular image from the 1960s, *The Stand* follows crowds of nihilistic revellers as they stampede over one another. King's text, in response to this chaos, establishes a point of contrast by praising elite leaders that transcend the rabble to form 'enlightened, democratic communities', run exclusively by experts with 'technological know-how' (1068, 841, 218, 333). Like so many of King's works, then, *The Stand* disowns the 1960s as a decade marked by excesses in order to applaud – or, begrudgingly resign itself to – the dismantlement of an overbearing federal government. To better understand this sensibility, we might note as an aside that King was raised as a dyed-in-the-wool conservative that was eventually terrified when nearly drafted into the Vietnam War.[3]

The Stand 'postpones organization' by ridding itself of planners of all stripes, melting away social plans in a manner that anticipates King's *Firestarter* (1980). The novel lauds small platoons that cultivate private lifestyles without the heavy expectation of communal responsibility. At the end of the day, whether 'good' or 'evil', King's characters appear eager to demolish the central government. For example, messianic figure Abagail Feemantle defines herself as a Republican, and she preaches on the topic of over-taxation, the horrors of Communism, as well as the benefits of small states. To embellish this attitude, King's epic advocates against feeling responsible for the welfare of strangers by chastising one character that seems 'dangerously softhearted' in regards to a vulnerable companion. Meanwhile, a supposedly wise judge critiques this character's misplaced sense of responsibility, and an observer chimes in that individuals should pull themselves up by the laces of their own footwear. In short, if the subject is in her 'right mind', she alone must decide for herself the best course of action (847, 1040). *The Stand* strikes a familiar neo-liberal chord by privileging personal responsibility over the influence of the public.

In a related sense, *The Stand* links democracy with the ability to possess anything you want, thus blurring radical democracy with unbridled capitalism (a move that renders both concepts guilty by association). Although King's text ostensibly demands a democracy dictated by citizens with 'right minds', it ultimately restricts democracy by delegitimising the wisdom of the crowd. It depicts democratic man as a gluttonous, mindless consumer willing to purchase a gas-guzzling car in the midst of an oil shortage. Indeed, King's narrative necessitates democratic governance at the precise moment that it renders democracy unpalatable (on this front, the novel anticipates King's 2009, *Under the Dome*). Jacques Rancière describes this tendency as a 'democratic paradox'. In one such paradoxical moment, *The Stand* suggests that 'princes' should be reconciled to 'the people' that elected them (51). King's awkward phrasing evokes a fear of authoritarianism (the prince himself) while tacitly lauding political engagement by the general population (calling for the opposite of a prince). Yet his strange wording also implies that democracy is how the characters of *The Stand* got into this mess in the first place – and so the masses deserve exactly what they get. That is, the novel's claim that an election could produce a prince, and that 'the people' could unwittingly subject itself to such an unjust arrangement, actively undercuts the fundamental promise of democracy. King's prince appears to be entirely justified in his suspension of the democratic order because, after all, it produced him (an authoritarian figurehead). The cyclical logic of *The Stand* unfolds as follows: by despising figures that exist 'above the law', King's epic implores political intervention from the masses; but when the epic attributes the ascent of its unsavoury figures to a deranged horde that cannot be trusted with governing itself, the narrative evokes only more figures that have no choice but to exist 'above the law'. The love/hate relationship of King's fiction with authoritarianism appears to revolve eternally in place.

Perhaps the most significant way in which *The Stand* resigns itself to neo-liberal norms, though, is its prolonged focus upon self-discipline. Anticipating *Rose Madder* (1995), the subject of chapter 7, the protagonists of *The Stand* experience a 'whole-body, whole-mind enema' as the labour of self-upon-self transforms them into entrepreneurs of their own identity. This sort of labour reverses a popular adage of the period by making the political personal (and only personal). Gone are institutions; in their place emerge highly individualised patterns of self-help. *The Stand* strips the state of its caregiving functions as it burdens characters with the demands of solitary self-maintenance, choreographing a pivot from government of others to government of self. Only you know what happens, the text muses, between 'the person you were and the person you become'. By travelling through literal and metaphorical tunnels that remain an exclusively private matter, the characters of *The Stand* practice solipsistic modes of consumption as well as critique, proclaiming everywhere and in nearly all moments: 'Trust yourself' (1030, 435, 51).

Thoughtful readers could contest this reduction of *The Stand* to mere neo-liberal propaganda, and in fact, such contestations remain essential for any future effort to politicise King scholarship. A reader might counter that King's text celebrates subjects that excise themselves from all governmental constraints, even neo-liberal ones. However, the following attributes cannot be easily disputed: protagonists in *The Stand* assert independence when they realise that a break from community is 'necessary', they feel relief when their 'wards' pass away and, by novel's close, they flee from the shelters of the group because to belong to a utopian community would be to lose a vital component of what makes them political animals in the first place. According to *The Stand*, fixed communities are 'bizarre' unions that form a 'shroud' over humanity. The text's liberal cohort encourages its members to cling to proper procedure (157, 659). In these ways (and a host of others), King's novel reflects a broader effort in the final quarter of the twentieth century to side-step discord in the name of all-consuming efficiency. Jürgen Habermas and Hannah Arendt, for instance, both make compelling cases that the public sphere demands a degree of consensus; likewise, many economists imagine a marketplace of self-interested actors (an aggregative model), and other intellectuals imagine a New World Order in which actors are driven by shared reason (a deliberative model). Despite their not-insignificant differences, these models share a preference for proceduralism over passion (Mouffe, *Agonistics* 6). The 'good guys' of *The Stand* spin similar yarns of a world without dissension.

To heighten this illusion of consensus, *The Stand* employs 'the shining', one of King's favourite tropes: an invisible force that psychically coalesces characters. In communitarian fashion, members of competing groups are defined by the contours of their respective communities, and so when individuals 'shine', they succumb to the inherent 'urge to regroup'. As burdensome as these connections are sometimes made out to be (given the epic's prevailing neo-liberal ethos), it may be worse to 'stand' alone (370). Rationality becomes, from a communitarian perspective, a 'death house' that begets the banal evil of bureaucracy, as when the novel's central committee opts to maintain an air of officiousness rather than succumb to hysteria over Flagg's growing threat. Douglas E. Winter writes, 'The Free Zone, so focused on ordering its lives, literally fiddles with matches while . . . Randall Flagg readies napalm' (64). The reader might even be led so far as to side with Flagg when he equates 'the best liberal mode' with J. Alfred Prufrock's impotent meditations on a peach. Liberals, Flagg laughs, are overly cautious, fastidious and lack all conviction. Counter to what it sometimes depicts as an anaemic liberalism, *The Stand* remains indebted to an innate communitarian sensibility.

Is *The Stand* therefore a prediction of America's enduring liberalism, or a story of its impending failure? In truth, like his tome *IT* (1986), King's epic remains more nuanced than either prescribed posture would allow. Dissatisfaction collides with consensus. *The Stand* champions as well as chides American liberalism as characters go crazy with loneliness and insane with togetherness. Due to the fact that *The Stand* never reaches a satisfying conclusion on this point, and depends instead upon ongoing contradictions, King's post-apocalyptic society amplifies the unquiet that fills much of his fiction with dread. Many of the survivors in *The Stand* are struck in a post-1960s death drive, which is to say, they unsuspectingly sabotage themselves so that they might stay dissatisfied (recalling the analysis in chapter 2 of the Bachman books). When 'good guys' obstinately chase utopia, they corroborate Bachman's hypothesis that every political 'stand' reveals itself, in the last account, to be futile. The desire for a complete end to partisan bickering, a desire expressed by King's liberals and communitarians alike, obscures a drive in these works *to preserve the struggle*. Because in a world without conflict, totalitarianism awaits.[4] Even as the novel strives in liberal fashion to erase signs of the supernatural, marks of passionate belief and evidence of what is presumed to be beyond the binary of 'good and evil', such an erasure remains fundamentally (im)possible. No matter how ardently King's epic attempts to rid itself of Flagg, no matter how aggressively the narrative pursues an institutional framework that could please everyone and neutralise the antagonism that initially gathers the survivors together, its (unconscious) preference for the indispensable fighting between groups returns to the fore, over and over again.[5]

The Stand reconsiders the misguided underpinnings of post-apocalyptic literature as a whole in order to highlight the crucial role of antagonism. According to Lee Edelman, popular novels about the end of the world habitually return to the image of a Child – a miraculous birth; a City on the Hill; an 'imaginary fullness that's considered to want, and therefore want for, nothing'. Contrary to such an imaginary fullness, the restless political shadows of *The Stand* manifest as a 'queer' potential to thwart consensus: a death drive that challenges the idea that American politics could ever deliver 'some stable and positive form'. Although at the close of King's epic a Child supposedly arrives to conclude the epic's noxious cycle, this particular Child teeters at the edge of survival, and it strikes readers as quite plausible that the catastrophe will simply begin again. We would be mistaken to write off the restoration of the Child in *The Stand* as merely formulaic; instead, King's epic consistently confounds 'fetishistic figuration' with Flagg's utter 'queerness'.[6] King's perennial antagonist opens a constitutive wound that cannot be healed. In contradistinction to the proverbial Child, this resident rebel rouser recurs throughout King's multiverse to 'insist on disturbing, on queering, social organization as such'. Beneath its prima facie desire for resolution, *The Stand* no more wants to exorcise Flagg than it wants to exorcise the political impulse that keeps his disruptive plot in motion. The disappointing arrival of a wavering Child exposes to King's readers 'the satisfaction no end ever holds' (Edelman 21–2, 4, 12). In other words, the death drive of American politics mercifully endures to launch another revolution.

The Stand cannot expunge its mythological antagonism and, in truth, it does not truly wish to do so. 'Mythic notions of cyclical return' exist long before its first page – and they abide long after novel's end (Sears 210). For her part, Abagail observes that her friends did not join together to forge a 'committee or a community'; they allied to 'try and destroy' shared enemies (King, *Stand* 902).[7] At its heart a political text, *The Stand* depicts shifting friend-enemy alignments powered by a mythos that weaves in and out of King's corpus, 'a confrontation with no possibility of final reconciliation' (Mouffe, *Agonistics* 17).[8] Nevertheless, unsettled by this enduring conflict, King's authoritarians still enter to 'impose a unified image of the good': an unsavoury consensus/cure espoused by benevolent and malevolent tyrants alike. Carl Schmitt states that only grand myths like the ones represented in *The Stand* can do justice to politics as 'a real battle, not as a slogan for parliamentary speeches and democratic electoral campaigns' (Schmitt, *Crisis* 71). Only cracks in the status quo, like the ones exposed by Flagg, render possible the sorts of political events that generate profound change (like the decisive event of King's 1990 novella, *The Langoliers*, discussed in the interlude).[9] While the anti-Flagg voices of King's fiction reiterate a common presumption that 'unity and peace' stem from universal branches of knowledge, predominantly monitored by powerbrokers in the fields of science and economics, Bruno Latour counters this presumption by claiming that 'unity without diplomacy' could never truly exist. 'So we are at war, aren't we?' he muses. And if we are condemned to be at war, 'the worst course would be to act as if there were no war at all, only the peaceful extension of Western natural Reason using its police forces to combat, contain, and convert' (306). King's contemporary readers. who can ill afford to perpetuate the fallacy of peace without politics, discover in *The Stand* a renewed plea for antagonism.[10]

The Stand effectively knits together major threads that run throughout the preceding chapters. At times, King's novel reacts against political activism by resigning itself to economic managerialism and other prominent neo-liberal tenets. Yet counter to this reactionary posture – or, more precisely, as a result of it – *The Stand* orbits around the lacuna of the political. Today, the spectral trace of the political in King's fiction helps us to make sense of the turmoil surrounding Trump's election. If truth be told, one of this book's main contributions to King scholarship is its detailed illustration of how Trumpism long lurked in the recesses of the author's multiverse, threatening to resurface. By politicising the study of King's fiction, we recognise its renewed relevance for the unavoidably contentious days to come.

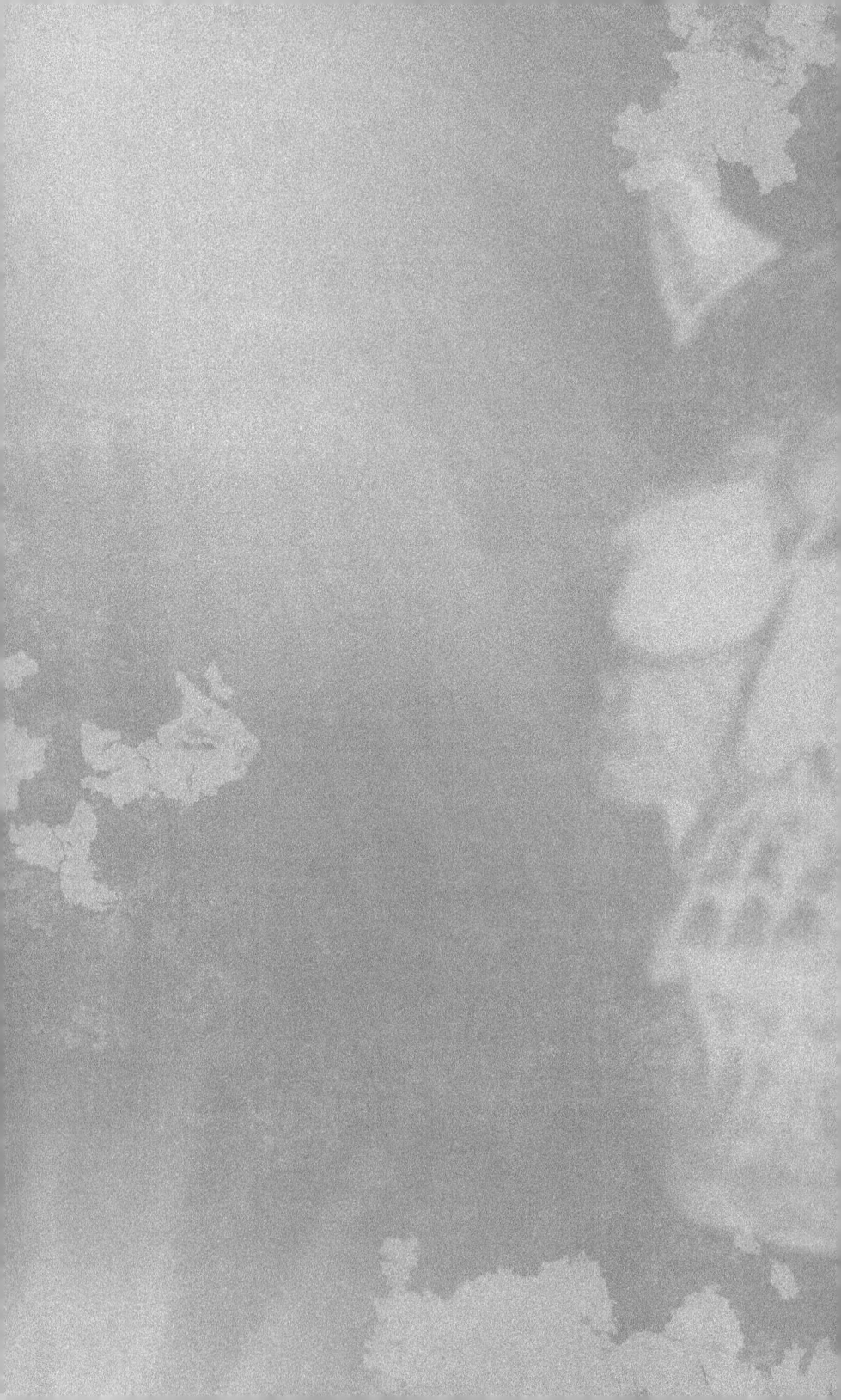

Notes

1. Prelude

1. This book does not concern itself with the politics of Stephen King himself. Although King has publicly engaged with politicians via social media, *Stephen King and American Politics* remains focused on the texts themselves rather than on issues of authorial intent.
2. John Sears observes that the majority of King's readers do not locate his texts 'politically' (Sears 9).
3. King's recent essay 'Guns' (2013) laments 'the all-but-deserted middle' by portraying himself as someone with 'liberal creds' who also maintains 'at least half of one foot in red-state America' (King 'Guns'). The essay neutralises meaningful gun reform by dismissing politics as inherently loathsome.
4. Douglas E. Winter deems King's characterisation as 'the masquerade of politics' (Winter 71).
5. Sheldon Wolin writes of the current mood, 'To be a citizen does not appear an important role nor political participation an intrinsic good' (Wolin, *Politics* 353).
6. Franco 'Bifo' Berardi describes a system 'whose intent is the transformation of life into value, that is, the accumulation of capital – not good life, not pleasure, not beauty, not the pursuance of the best use of technical knowledge, not the actualization of inscribed possibilities' – in short, a system that de-politicises life (Berardi 195).

7. Yves Meny and Yves Surel chart signs of democratic collapse: a decline of support for incumbents; growing electoral absenteeism; hyper-partisanship; and an increase in ad hoc political movements (Meny and Surel 1).
8. For more discussion of King's relationship with the turbulent politics of the 1960s, in particular the influence of the conflict in Vietnam upon his work, see the monograph by Tony Magistrale and Michael J. Blouin, *Stephen King and American History* (Routledge, forthcoming).
9. In one sense, King's fiction ostensibly maintains an antipathy to politics when, in truth, it 'quite successfully conceals its politics, which is the politics of getting rid of politics' (Dyzenhaus 14).
10. See articles by Carney as well as Munoz (included in the bibliography).
11. For an overview of this position, see Richard Wagner's *James M. Buchanan and Liberal Political Economy: A Rational Reconstruction* (Washington, DC: Lexington Books, 2017). As King's fiction so aptly illuminates, 'The spirit of 1968 . . . led to a very peculiar aftermath, visible and invisible, during the next decades' (P. Berman 14).
12. For an expanded treatment of this topic, see Mark Fisher's *Capitalist Realism: Is There No Alternative?* (London: Zero Books, 2009).
13. Although Tony Magistrale argues that *The Eyes of the Dragon* is 'political in nature', I would counter that – although the text focuses upon power struggles within a royal family – it also condemns the very nature of the struggle, particularly when the demos threatens to become involved (Magistrale, *Stephen* 134).
14. Parker Richards notes, 'The heroes of fantasy are often presented as liberators . . . yet their actual focus is typically on claims of a legitimate hereditary right to kingship and the preservation of absolute monarchy' (Richards).
15. As this sort of paradox turns up regularly in gothic texts, it can be argued that texts published in the neo-liberal moment (like King's) routinely 'undertake the same kind of cultural work' carried out in earlier gothic modes (Blake and Monnet 1).
16. In *Elevation* (2018), the hero of Castle Rock transcends his community. Castle Rock is unwelcoming to a married lesbian couple; in response, the novel's protagonist sheds weight, like some kind of ascetic in defiance of an unjust situation. A typical white saviour, he reconciles everyone by 'elevating' above his circumstances and floating off into the sky. To save Castle Rock from its own worst tendencies, the protagonist quite literally rises above his backwater burg.
17. According to Walter Benn Michaels, economised identity politics reveals an unwillingness by the mainstream left to address inequalities through activism.

Michaels adds, 'The most enthusiastic proponents of diversity . . . are the thousands of companies providing "diversity products"' (Michaels 13).

18. See, for instance, Sarah Nilsen's 'White Soul: The "Magical Negro" in the Films of Stephen King', in Tony Magistrale (ed.), *The Films of Stephen King* (New York: Palgrave Macmillan, 2008), pp. 131–43. For another example from a primary text, see the unabridged edition of *The Stand* (1990), a narrative that describes 'a flock of young blacks' with 'their lower bodies moving [to a] jive that only black ears could hear' (King, *Stand* 146).
19. 'There is nothing but individuals, individuals considered in isolation, who [come] together in competition to ensure respect for their rights and the pursuit of their interests' (Badiou and Gauchet 79).
20. In his interview with King scholar Tony Magistrale, King reveals the distinction: 'I've always thought to myself that *Misery* was a kind of trick. You have two people fighting it out in a cabin. That's all it is. *Gerald's Game* is a kind of trick on the trick: one person in a room fighting it out with herself' (Magistrale, 'Steve's' 528). King later returns to this insular representation in 'Big Driver' (2010), a story about a rape victim that deals with her wounds by projecting herself outward (onto a GPS device, a cat and various other household staples), and 'talking in imaginary voices' to herself (King, 'Big' 222).
21. To consider the argument in its larger context, see Michel Foucault's *The History of Sexuality: Volume I* (New York: Random House, 1978).
22. Bernadette Lynn Bosky points to King's 'basically optimistic and attractive premises' (Bosky, 243).
23. Readers need not romanticise this rupture, as the freedom of formlessness always depends upon the restriction of form. *Dreamcatcher* tracks the essential dynamic: a formless 'people' arises to counter hegemony; the fully formed 'people' then becomes hegemonic, triggering a renewed insurgence from the margins. The Interlude as well as the Postlude address this dialectical propulsion in greater detail.
24. See, for example, Ted Slowik's piece in the *Chicago Tribune*: 'Trump bound for "Dead Zone" moment, like using baby as human shield' (Slowik), or Reece Goodall's 'Eerily Similar? Donald Trump and *The Dead Zone*'s Greg Stillson' (Goodall).
25. King's fiction takes up the critique of 'bad democracy' by calling antagonist Stillson 'the people's choice' (a superlative that casts serious doubt upon the capacity of 'the people' to govern itself). Because citizens continually make the 'wrong choice', readers might find the response of de-democratisation quite reasonable.

26. Sheldon Wolin describes the widespread effort to divert the political in favour of a managerial ethos as 'the sublimation rather than the elimination of the political' (Wolin, *Politics* 414).
27. For a lengthier discussion of how the Vietnam War influences King's fiction, see Michael J. Blouin and Tony Magistrale's 'The Vietnamization of Stephen King', *The Journal of American Culture*, 42, 4 (December 2019), 287–301.
28. *The Institute* implicitly endorses the slashing of government programmes by suggesting that 'John and Josie Q. Public' would be repulsed to learn how their tax dollars are being spent (183). In other words, the novel offers a solution (cutting wasteful taxes) that dovetails with prominent neo-liberal initiatives.
29. Fredric Jameson describes the 'compensatory exchange' of fiction in which 'protopolitical impulses' are awakened in order to be incapacitated (as well as incapacitated in order to be re-awakened). Jameson argues, 'If the ideological function of mass culture is understood as a process whereby otherwise dangerous and protopolitical impulses are "managed" and defused, rechanneled and offered spurious objects, then some preliminary step must also be theorized in which these same impulses – the raw material upon which the process works – are initially awakened in the very text that seeks to still them' (*Political* 277).

2. The Bachman Books

1. Patrick McAleer writes, 'The Bachman books focus solely on failure, annihilation, and the inevitable loss of life, which suggests a meaningless and worthless nature' (McAleer 1221).
2. For a detailed description of these changing attitudes, see the introduction to this book, or Michael J. Blouin's 'Neoliberalism and Popular Culture', *The Journal of Popular Culture*, 51, 2 (April 2018), 277–80.
3. Alain Badiou notes that Lacan remains 'completely uninterested in politics'. However, Badiou claims, this indifference invites us to pursue a 'new conception' with which to face 'new political situations' (Badiou and Gauchet 9).
4. William Davies contends, 'A society that celebrates and encourages "competitiveness" as an ethos, be it in sport, business, politics or education, cannot then be surprised if outcomes are then highly unequal' (Davies, 41).
5. According to Magistrale, Bachman's works 'emphasize the breakdown of civic ties, societal conventions and organizations' (Magistrale, *Landscape* 106).
6. King acknowledges the psychoanalytical qualities of the Bachman texts, albeit with a degree of disdain. According to King, Bachman's characters possess

'oversimple motivations (many of them painfully Freudian)', and his novels drift at times into 'windy psychological preachments' ('Why I Was Bachman' ix–x).
7. Bart states, 'I'll just scream now, I think. For lost things' (Bachman, *Roadwork* 74).
8. Bachman's novels align the broken subject with his lack in a fashion that recalls Lacan's use of the term *sinthome*. The *sinthome* evokes the 'outermost limit of the psychoanalytic process' (Žižek, 'Undergrowth' 31).

3. King's Cars

1. 'Trucks' (1978), the basis for King's film *Maximum Overdrive* (1986), similarly follows an unmanned vehicle with demonic qualities.
2. King's texts compensate for rampant post-Fordist disruption in a variety of ways, driven as they are 'by the contradictory uses of (King's) postmodern values and his middle-class fear of postmodernism . . . *everywhere contradictory*' (Strengell 21, emphasis mine).
3. 'Capitalism is at a crossroads in its historical development signaling the emergence of forces – technological, market, social and institutional – that will be very different from those which dominated the economy after the Second World War' (Amin 1).
4. Douglas E. Winter observes, '[King] selected the 1958 Plymouth Fury as his mean machine precisely because it is almost totally forgotten today' (Winter 124).
5. King returns to this theme in *The Dark Tower: The Gunslinger* (1982). His weary travellers encounter a deserted gas station that is understood to be a totem for a society that used to worship petrol (King *Gunslinger*, 212).
6. Joseph Reino points out that King's contempt for academia manifests in the 'obscenely named Horlicks College' where Arnie's parents work (Reino 86).
7. Thomas Frank notes the corresponding propaganda effort against intellectuals: 'Know-it-all college professors, none of them interested in anything you [have] to say' (Frank, *What's the Matter* 2).
8. Paul Ingrassia and Joseph White note Chrysler's purchase of FinanceAmerica in 1985, an event that led to the formation of Chrysler Financial. Suddenly, 'Chrysler wasn't "just" a car company anymore' (Ingrassia and White 81).
9. Paul Ingrassia charts the diversification of the 1980s, in which the Big Three car companies start to purchase consumer-finance and commercial-finance companies, transforming them into holding companies. 'Between 1984 and

1989 General Motors, Ford, and Chrysler spent some $20 billion on acquisitions, most of them outside of the car business. The acquisitions came on top of dividend increases, stock splits, and share-buyback programs' (Ingrassia 90).
10. 'The history of capitalism after the 1970s, including the subsequent economic crises, is a history of capital's escape from the system of social regulation imposed on it against its will after 1945' (Streeck, *Buying Time* 19).
11. The automobile is perfectly suited to this kind of outpacing. The American car, Peter Marsh and Peter Collett argue, 'is truly a vehicle for fantasy'. A complex symbol of speed, excitement, vitality, class, status, and more, the American automobile remains 'the most psychologically expressive object that has so far been devised' (4, 25).
12. As Catherine Lutz and Anne Lutz Fernandez illustrate, automobile loans are aggressively bundled into CDOs (credit derivatives): 'Vegas-style bets on whether ordinary people would get to keep or lose their homes or cars' (117–19).
13. The blue-chip giants of Detroit can only stay 'interesting' if they succumb to the pressures of Wall Street: 'The new titans were men who could read a complicated financial statement' (Halberstam 247, 51).
14. Christine, for instance, prowls between neighbourhoods with different socio-economic designations, as when the car cruises from the wealthy Heights to the poverty-stricken Low Heights to the declining middle-class section of the same road (340–2). In this section of the text, *Christine* remarks upon class tensions within Libertyville by utilising the mobility of the haunted car to convey seismic shifts in the economy. In *From a Buick 8*, this commentary disappears entirely.
15. 'Why is there something when there should be nothing? Why is there nothing when there should be something?' (Fisher, *Weird* 64, 11–12).
16. 'What *Christine* finally offers is eternal adolescence . . . going forward really means going backwards' (Badley 86, 92).
17. Accepting the text's invitation to pick apart the black-and-white certainty of the Cold War era, critics like John Sears offer a Derridean reading of King's fiction that overlooks this complacency.
18. Norris targets certain poststructuralist and postmodern gestures as 'the vagaries of current intellectual fashion . . . a range of extravagant propositions which would otherwise merit nothing more than a footnote in some future anatomy of the nonsense of the times' (15–17).
19. 'Postmodern culture simultaneously reflects and promotes economic changes' (M. Taylor 2).

20. Terry Eagleton argues, 'Many a business executive is in this sense a spontaneous postmodernist . . . restlessly transgressing boundaries and dismantling oppositions, pitching together diverse life-forms and continually overflowing the measure' (*Illusions* 133).
21. Bruno Latour observes, 'Does such idle [post-structuralist] criticism not look superficial now that nihilism is truly striking at "us" – at US – putting what we call civilization in great danger of being found hollow?' (305).
22. Terry Eagleton attacks this cultural turn by pointing to Nazi death camps as founded upon a 'barbarous irrationalism which, like some aspects of postmodernism itself, junked history, refused argumentation, (and) aestheticized politics' (quoted in Harvey, *Condition* 210).
23. Cecily Devereux contends that *Christine* is a re-telling of Freudian castration horror which examines how automotive signifiers thinly veil an absence of control over life's entropies (171).
24. See, for example, the critique of Deleuze in Slavoj Žižek's *Organs without Bodies: On Deleuze and Consequences* (New York: Routledge, 2004).
25. Thomas Allbaugh describes King's 'blue collar, popular appeal' (84).
26. 'When faced with evidence of the car system's many problems, Americans tend to retire to an appeal to pragmatism . . . that smacks of resignation' (Lutz and Fernandez 38).

4. *Firestarter*

1. Mark Lilla describes 'the impulse to flee so as to remain an authentic, autonomous self' alongside 'the impulse to transform society so that it seems like an extension of the self' (72).
2. Similarly, in *Cell* (2006), humans become 'slaves that pick up the master-disc audio and rebroadcast it' (150). Human bodies become part of a vast network meant to generate energy.
3. King's account of biocapitalism dates much further back than the Cold War. Indeed, the Shop is located in an old southern plantation, evoking a powerful precedent (slavery) for the legislation of bodies to come (King, *Firestarter* 84).
4. Deleuze has been critiqued on similar grounds because he 'thought that he could outflank capitalism, which he suspected of not deterritorializing fast enough . . . far from making it possible to get beyond capitalism, his programme merely predicted its future' (Dufour 11).

5. King's text underscores the wastefulness of government by pausing to recount the corrupt inner-dealings of a nepotistic senator and a pesky tax assessor that pries into private lives.
6. Roberto Esposito writes, 'No politics exists other than that *of* bodies, conducted *on* bodies, *through* bodies' (84, author's emphasis).
7. The promises of liberation conceal 'well-honed strategies of social control (i.e., "normalization")' (Peck 18).
8. 'Power regulates *relations*, not *objects*, precisely because if power can successfully regulate the relations, it gets the objects for free' (Nealon, *Foucault* 38; author's emphasis).
9. For the contours of this debate, see the critique offered in Nancy Fraser's *Unruly Practices: Power, Discourse, and Gender in Contemporary Social Theory* (Minneapolis, MN: University of Minnesota Press, 1989), or the defence offered by David Newheiser's 'Foucault, Gary Becker and the Critique of Neoliberalism', *Theory, Culture and Society*, 33, 5 (2016), 3–21; or Laura Hengehold's *The Body Problematic: Political Imagination in Kant and Foucault* (University Park, PA: Penn State University Press, 2010).
10. In *The Tommyknockers* (1987), an English faculty gathering suggests that the profession congregates horrific, gluttonous creatures, 'cramming' olives, stretching their jaws wide and 'plowing potato chips' before ultimately sporting 'the head of a pig' or 'the shaggy head of a wolf' (68–74).
11. 'Allusions and citations insert into King's texts traces, fragments and elements of other texts and other writings, redefining the works as structurally plural and profoundly dialogic' (Sears 13).
12. Alan Richardson and Sonya Hofkosh examine Romanticism's 'grounding of a wishfully autonomous form of subjectivity, at once defensively isolated and yet aggressively incorporative' (4).
13. Claudio Colaguori writes, 'In a culture that celebrates negation as a form of power, the efforts of those who desire self-preservation . . . are only thrust deeper into existential turmoil' (189).
14. One of the ghosts in *Bag of Bones* admits, 'I am just a willing extension of your fantasies and only you are here . . . Do what you want to this shadow, this fantasy, this ghost' (319).
15. Terry Eagleton notes, 'A reasonable secure identity . . . is a necessary condition of human well-being' (*Illusions* 126).
16. As Dany-Robert Dufour demonstrates, even though Charlie's incendiary actions appear to 'resist socio-political domination', in practice 'such acts merely undo the symbolic function . . . [they] destroy the innermost sources of the person's humanity' (156).

5. IT

1. 'Liberalism has changed unevenly in the course of its history. It has accrued various layers of argument over time that have loosely added to its characteristics' (Freeden 12).
2. See Thatcher's interview with *Women's Own* from 1987: *https://www.margaretthatcher.org/document/106689* (accessed 27 October 2019).
3. MacIntyre argues, 'It is wrong to separate the history of the self and its roles from the history of the language which the self specifies and through which the roles are given expression' (*After* 35).
4. Sandel summarises the argument made by Rawls: 'We are distinct individuals first, and then (circumstances permitting) we form relationships and engage in cooperative arrangements with others . . . our knowledge of the basis of plurality is given prior to experience, while our knowledge of the basis of unity or cooperation can only come in light of experience' (*Liberalism* 53).
5. Rawls writes, 'Persons are acting autonomously: they are acting from principles that they would acknowledge under conditions that best express their nature as free and equal rational beings . . . reasonable grounds that we can set out independently for ourselves' (452).
6. 'The recent debate between liberalism and communitarianism largely amounts to . . . self-criticism' (Bielefeldt 23).
7. Todd McGowan writes, 'Without the state, the subject cannot recognize its freedom because it cannot recognize its dependence on the public . . . one must go through the detour of the public in order to be a private individual' (*Emancipation* 5, 206).
8. Terry Eagleton writes of this intersection, 'The dream of blending the best of both worlds is also to refuse the worst of both . . . it is, more or less, what Marx had in mind by communism, in which the individual would finally come into her own' (*Illusions* 108).
9. According to Chantal Mouffe, communitarians offer an impossibly unified moral order and liberals offer impartial 'ethics and economics' in a futile attempt to 'annihilate the political' (Mouffe, *Return* 55, 49).
10. Highly valuing the dialogic structure, Bell composes his treatise on communitarianism as a Socratic dialogue between a liberal and a communitarian: 'The ongoing communitarian-liberal debate in Anglo-American political theory seems especially amenable to the dialogue form' (21).

6. Interlude

1. 'The masses mounting the stage of history . . . can never be programmed . . . it's essentially unpredictable, incalculable' (Badiou and Gauchet 63).
2. For another example of this trend, see King's *11/22/63* (2011).
3. 'There is the police . . . but there isn't politics' (Badiou, *Philosophy* 3).
4. '[The political] is that which de-structures: it is an ontological fissure in the maintenance of the same' (Dewsbury 455).
5. The text's prophet, Dinah, embodies this fatal flaw: she 'knew a lot . . . too much, maybe' (King, *Langoliers* 137).
6. David Harvey writes, 'Volatility and ephemerality similarly make it hard to maintain any firm sense of continuity. Past experience gets compressed into some overwhelming present' (*Condition* 291).

7. *Rose Madder*

1. This entrepreneurial shift is promulgated by a veritable cottage industry of books on business. Enforcing the tenets of a so-called gig economy, these texts promote monetisation of the self. In a recent example, business commentator Dorie Clark writes: 'Monetizing your ideas and embracing entrepreneurship means, quite simply, that you have more options . . . you have the ability to refashion your life and your career as you see fit' (238).
2. Much like *Firestarter*, *Rose Madder* documents 'the interiorization of neoliberalism into our very beings' (Louth and Potter 1).
3. As a result of this shift, 'the consumer contributes to market creation, producing services, managing damages and hazards, sorting litter, optimising the fixed assets of supplies and even administration' (Marazzi 39, 49–50).
4. Zygmunt Bauman records the role of globalisation in the melting of everything into air: 'In its present, purely negative form, globalization is a parasitic and predatory process, feeding on the potency sucked out of the bodies of nation-states and their subjects . . . "open" and increasingly defenseless on both sides, the nation-state loses its might, now evaporating into global space, and its political acumen and dexterity, now increasingly relegated to the sphere of individual "life politics"' (Bauman 24–5).
5. In 'Secret Window, Secret Garden' (1990), Mort Rainey wrestles with his power to shape life through art: '[Mort] became a character he created' (378). In *The Dark Half* (1989), Thad Beaumont must address the dire consequences of aesthetic subject formation. 'I would be . . . reinventing myself' (24, 450).

6. *Duma Key* follows suit with its numerous chapters entitled 'How to Draw a Picture'. These inserts actively elicit the reader's direct involvement in the process of self-formation.
7. Wendy Brown writes, 'The epistemological, political, economic, and cultural dismantling of mass society into human capital . . . along with the resulting recuperation . . . are among neoliberalism's most impressive achievements' (Brown, *Ruins* 39).
8. 'As substance dissolves into function to create "free-floating processes"', theorist Mark C. Taylor comments, 'Meaning and value shift from referentiality to relationality' (M. Taylor 113).
9. In *Doctor Sleep* (2013), characters pass freely between one another's minds. Like *Rose Madder*, this open transmission is linked to deadly viruses (in this case, measles) as well as flows of information between computers. Perhaps to accentuate this intertextual connection, King gives the antagonist of *Doctor Sleep* the name Rose.
10. *The Institute* (2019) echoes this sentiment: 'Mutiny – or revolution . . . was like a virus, especially in the Information Age. It *could* spread' (487, author's emphasis).
11. Berry writes, 'The neo-liberal state's attempt to commodify and marketize creativity should be seen as continuous with its biopolitical attempt to shape and direct the life of its population' (Berry 26).
12. To emphasise how this interpellation is less counter-cultural than viewers might assume, Berry considers the kindred ideals privileged by economist F. A. Hayek as well as abstract expressionists. One of these shared ideals is 'the notion of the creative act [as] unfolding within a field of contingencies' (Berry 15).
13. 'The creative imperative', sociologist Ulrich Brockling writes, 'requires permanent change. Its enemies are homogeneity, identity, norm and repetition' (117).
14. In *Duma Key*, Edgar must similarly enter into a painting in order to chart his own escape: 'I was *in* the picture instead of just looking at it' (642, author's emphasis).
15. Claire Colebrook argues that 'what appears to be valued above all else is the living act of pure becoming, freed from any external or transcendent domination . . . individuals [are] now able to use new technologies to orient consumption to their own rhythms and able to enter the domain of production themselves (via YouTube, social media and other interactive modes)' (92).
16. According to Anita Chari, contemporary art routinely lifts the viewer 'from a spectatorial and reified position to a more engaged' relationship with the work (175).

17. Sam Binkley demonstrates how contemporary subjects are trained to associate happiness with 'negation of the dependent, constraining, and docile attitude that is the legacy of welfare' (24).
18. Zygmunt Bauman states, 'Social forms (structures that limit individual choices, institutions that guard repetitions of routines, patterns of acceptable behaviour) can no longer (and are not expected to) keep their shape for long, because they decompose and melt faster than the time it takes to cast them' (1).
19. Zygmunt Bauman describes this cultural turn: 'If you don't want to drown, you must keep on surfing: that is to say, keep changing, as often as you can, your wardrobe, furniture, wallpaper, appearance and habits, in short – yourself . . . today's all-encompassing culture demands that you acquire the ability to change your identity [. . .] as often, as fast and as efficiently as you change your shirt' (24–5).
20. 'Individuals spend their lives putting their bodies and minds through a perpetual settling of accounts' (Baudrillard *Impossible*, 68).
21. *Duma Key* echoes a similar economic logic: 'The cost of finishing the job had been big, but the bill had been paid . . . If you want to play you gotta pay' (360, 398). In *The Dark Half*, another of King's texts in which an artist engages in transactions with himself, the artist thinks: 'Perhaps the bill had been paid . . . he was finally even' (459).
22. Of this economised identity politics, Nancy Fraser writes: 'No longer able to assume a social-democratic baseline for radicalization, [feminists] gravitate to newer grammars of political claims-making . . . a truncated culturalism' (*Fortunes* 4–5).
23. In other words, when Rosie abandons her bond with her friends, the text's 'celebration of formal "playfulness"' also evacuates hope for significant 'political meaning' (Hall, 'Cultural' 239).
24. Giorgio Agamben expresses consternation at the extent to which contemporary art takes the ethical dimension of artistic practice and strips it away in order to make art 'into work', which is to say, into labour, into *productivity*. At the outermost edge of such economisation, we find the promise of 'contemplation and inoperativity . . . that peculiar absence of work that we are accustomed to calling "politics" and "art." Politics and art are not tasks nor simply "works": rather, they name the dimension in which works . . . are deactivated and contemplated as such in order to liberate the inoperativity that has remained imprisoned in them' (278). In other words, we might imagine a Rosie that could contemplate her own potential, at a degree of removal from the external demands placed upon her imaginative toil.

8. Under the Dome

1. King's *The Tommyknockers* (1987) experiments with very similar themes: 'They've managed to turn all of Haven into a . . . an ant-farm, or something under a bowl'; subsequently, zealotry and blind obedience become a 'way of life' in the town (250, 262).
2. Stuart Hall writes, 'I think there are enough common features (in neoliberalism) to warrant a provisional conceptual identity . . . neoliberalism is grounded in the "free, possessive individual", with the state cast as tyrannical and oppressive . . . [the state] must not intervene in the "natural" mechanisms of the free market . . . the function of the liberal state should be limited to safeguarding the conditions in which profitable competition can be pursued' ('Neoliberal' 318–19).
3. According to Carl Schmitt, the term *nomos* connects the law with space. To establish a wall (or a Dome, in this case) is to establish the very terms and conditions of sovereignty.
4. For critique of this order (and the Bush-Cheney administration's overall lack of transparency), see Clint Hender's 'What We Didn't Know Has Hurt Us', *Columbia Journalism Review* (January 2009), https://archives.cjr.org/feature/what_we_didnt_know_has_hurt_us.php (accessed 31 March 2019).
5. Arthur MacEwan writes, 'Although neo-liberalism touts a minimal role for government in economic affairs, it generally depends upon a very strong, repressive government' (8).
6. Terry Eagleton comments, 'Art gives us the experience of that situation, which is equivalent to ideology. But by doing this, it allows us to "see" the nature of that ideology' (*Marxism* 18).
7. King's texts routinely attack authoritarian leaders – from Barlow in *'Salem's Lot* (1975) to Greg Stillson in *Dead Zone* (1979) to the sadistic alien (and non-alien) authoritarians of *Dreamcatcher* (2001).
8. Naomi Klein describes Secretary of State Donald Rumsfeld as 'a bloodless hatchet man – a CEO secretary on a downsizing man . . . leading companies through dramatic mergers and acquisitions, as well as painful restructurings'. She cites *Forbes* on Rumsfeld: 'Mr. CEO . . . about to oversee the same sort of restructuring that he orchestrated so well in the corporate world' (*Shock* 358–9).
9. Rennie's art of governance illuminates the extent to which public relations trumps meaningful social improvement. Politics becomes almost exclusively about perception: 'How much easier would the work of governments be', Crouch notes sardonically, 'if they needed to cultivate only their brand and image, and were not held to account for the actual quality of their policy products' (102).

10. Bishop Hwa Yung observes, 'There is even less reason today for non-Western Christians . . . to allow their theologies to be domesticated by Enlightenment thinking, something Western Christians themselves find increasingly dissatisfying' (quoted in Comaroff, 'Politics' 27).
11. As another religious zealot in the novel cries out, 'It's time for men of God to hoist their flag' (King, *Under* 791).
12. It is worth noting that not all Christians in *Under the Dome* are corrupt. In fact, many of the novel's Christians remain sensible, thoughtful and humane. Piper Libby, for example, is a heroic Congregationalist that defies the fascist forces, and Lester Coggins – a partially culpable pastor from Christ the Holy Redeemer Church – wilfully exposes himself to great harm because of his role in bringing Rennie's regime to power. It would therefore be too hasty to read *Under the Dome* as a straightforward 'anti-religious' rout.
13. *Lisey's Story* (2006) demonises an English professor 'oddly lacking in curiosity'. The professor exudes unearned confidence – 'I'm-an-assistant-professor-on-my-way-up-and-don't-you-forget-it' – who wastes his life away spinning straw into 'footnoted fool's gold' (21, 51, 536).
14. 'Neo-liberal political rationality devolves both political problems and solutions from public to private' (Brown, 'American' 704).
15. For theorists Michael Hardt and Antonio Negri, even though laughter signals a release from hegemony, it must be translated into true happiness for all (not momentary delight).
16. King's *Duma Key* (2008) similarly pauses to laud a small, low-profile, non-profit company that does more 'practical good' than 'marches and sign-waving' (285). King's fiction frequently dismisses the value of political protest.
17. In a contemporary context, 'an Ancient Greek term suddenly re-enter[s] English usage: demo-phobia – literally, fear of the mob' (Luce 111, 120)
18. Mirroring the use of Route 119, *Cell* closes with its protagonist dialling 9-1-1. The numbers 9-1-1 are 'as bright and black as some declared destiny' (350). The September 11th allegory remains quite legible.

9. *The Outsider*

1. 'Gothic fictions generally play with and oscillate between the earthly laws of conventional reality and the possibilities of the supernatural' (Hogle 13, 2).
2. King explains the appeal of, and the revulsion towards, the Outsider: 'The Stranger makes us nervous . . . but we love to try on his face in secret' (*Danse* 4).

3. Adam Kotsko claims that Trumpism suggests 'a resurgence of social and political elements that have unaccountably persisted despite being foreign to neo-liberal logic' (Kotsko 1–2).
4. Stuart Hall describes how the break-up of a 'corporatist consensus' set the stage for authoritarian populism: 'The state plays an increasingly central "educative' role"' at the same time as 'this shift "from above" is pioneered by, harnessed to, and to some extent legitimated by a populist groundswell below' ('Authoritarian' 151).
5. Although this chapter focuses on the Trump administration, one might also consider the influence of Senator Bernie Sanders from the Left. Progressive populism too plays a palpable role in the public consciousness of the era.
6. Giuliani's remark echoes the (in)famous remark made by Karl Rove, George W. Bush's political advisor: 'When we act, we create our own reality' (quoted in Suskind).
7. Interestingly, in the years after the publication of *The Outsider*, Trump also promises to cure cancer. He later promises to cure the coronavirus global pandemic. See Christopher Brito, 'Trump Vows to Cure Cancer and Eradicate AIDS as he kicks off reelection campaign', *CBSNews.com*, 19 June 2019, *https://www.cbsnews.com/news/trump-cure-cancer-aids-joe-biden-orlando-campaign-rally/* (accessed 26 July 2019).
8. 'Donald Trump adeptly manufactured a series of crises that helped convince slightly less than a majority of the country to vote for him' (Graham).
9. Trump creates his own mythos: 'You can bask in my favor and recognition, in the promises I make and the license I bestow, and all I ask in return is that you believe whatever I say' (Gladstone 46).
10. Margaret Canovan summarises, 'The vagueness of "the people" is a mark of its political usefulness; captured at different times by many different political causes, it has been structured to fit their different shapes' (Canovan 3).
11. Critics like Heidi Strengell comment upon King's generic indecisiveness, arguing that 'most of King's novels and stories are generic hybrids', and pointing to King's numerous shape-shifters as emblematic of his many 'generic transmutations' (Strengell 258, 255; Collings 33).
12. 'The other, the stranger . . . in a specially intense way [is] existentially something different and alien' (Schmitt, *Concept* 27).
13. 'The power of the people is always beneath and beyond these forms' (Rancière, *Hatred* 81).
14. Sigmund Freud writes: 'Nowadays we no longer believe in [the *animus* of society], we have *surmounted* such ways of thought; but we do not feel quite

sure of our new set of beliefs, and the old ones still exist within us' (Freud 402, author's emphasis).

10. Postlude

1. Elsewhere, a character stumbles towards madness, declaring: 'Gimme the sixties' (King, *Stand* 416).
2. Flagg, going under the name Linoge, shows up once more in King's screenplay for the television movie, *The Storm of the Century* (1999). Flagg/Linoge feeds upon 'fear and distrust', forcing the citizens of a tiny island off the coast of Maine to realise that they have distinctive interests, and that they must re-align with one another in perpetuity rather than live in some idyllic – but ultimately illusory – state of consensus (315). Flagg/Linoge thus recalls the unpleasant necessity of political struggle against the premature utopia advocated by the island's constable.
3. For more on King's ties to Vietnam, and how they inform his fiction, see Michael J. Blouin and Tony Magistrale's 'The Vietnamization of Stephen King', *The Journal of American Culture*, 42, 4 (December 2019), 287–301.
4. Admittedly, this death drive drifts at times into a sense of resignation that can be traced to King's car stories, including *Christine* (1983) and *From a Buick 8* (2002), discussed in chapter 3.
5. Carl Schmitt contends, 'The political can be understood only in the context of the ever-present possibility of the friend-and-enemy grouping' (Schmitt, *Concept* 35).
6. Flagg's 'queerness' is both figurative and literal. His male followers have sex together, and they feel 'something like love' for Flagg (King, *Stand* 587, 358).
7. Chantal Mouffe adds, 'The struggle between opposing hegemonic projects can never be reconciled rationally, one of them needing to be defeated' (*Agonistics* 9).
8. Schmitt claims, 'Spirit struggles with spirit, life with life, and out of the power of an integral understanding of this arises the order of human things' ('Age' 96).
9. In turn, readers of *The Stand* might remain 'suspicious of any social construct that appears to be fully harmonious or complete' (Connolly, *Politics* 133).
10. In our attempts to politicise King's fiction, we should remain wary of 'fetishizing the cacophonous rupture' because although readers are frequently invited to romanticise unpredictable happenings, antagonism invariably solidifies

into institutions, and the formless energy of the crowd is habitually 'incorporated into a form' (Dean, *Crowds* 125–6, 157). As we recover the disruptive possibilities of King's narratives, we must also ponder social arrangements that his texts invite us – or fail to invite us, as the case may be – to incorporate for ourselves.

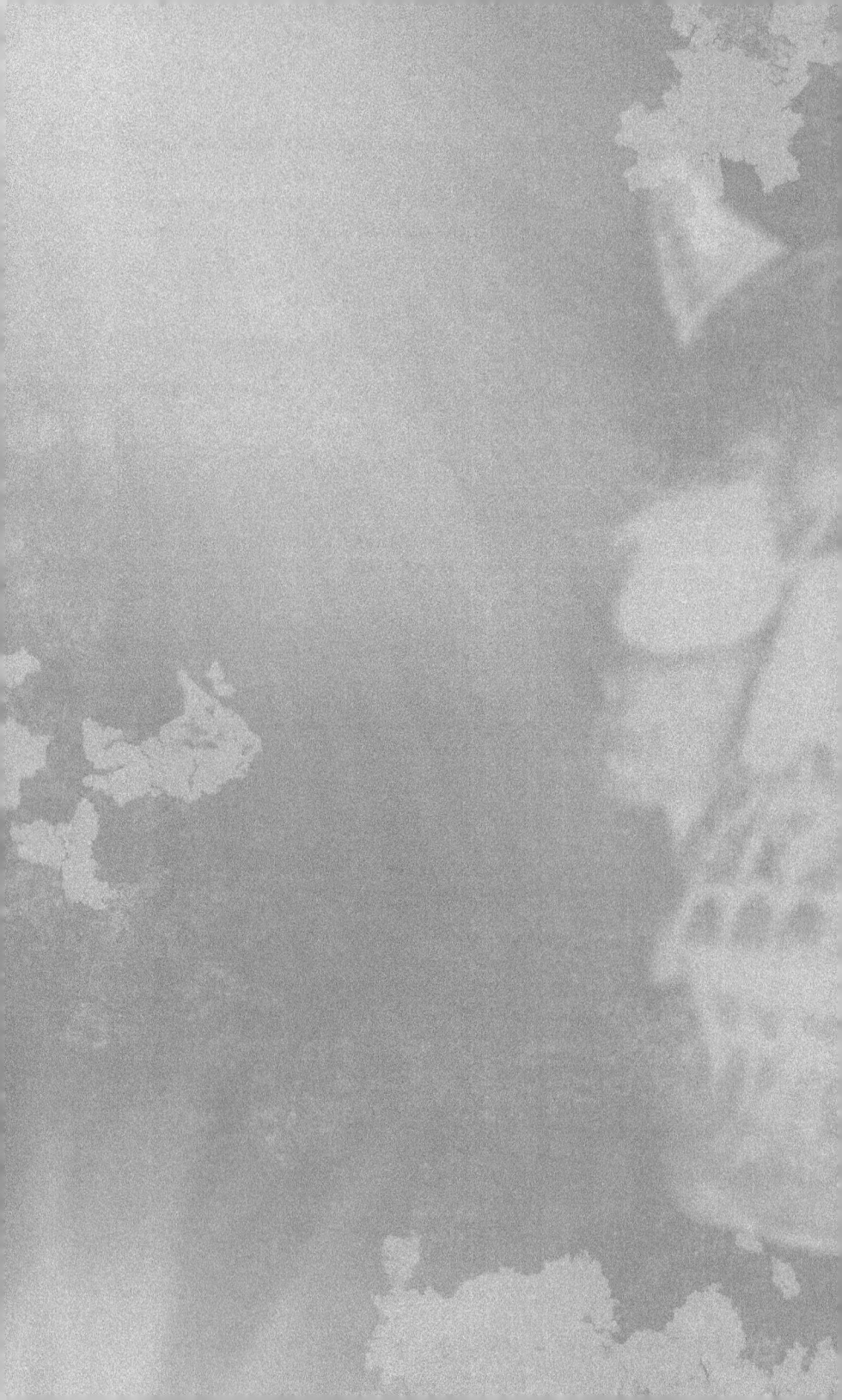

Bibliography

Ackerman, Bruce, *Social Justice and the Liberal State* (New Haven, CT: Yale University Press, 1989).
Agamben, Giorgio, *The Use of Bodies*, trans. Adam Kotsko (Stanford, CA: Stanford University Press, 2016).
Allbaugh, Thomas, 'A Case for Stephen King's Memoir for Writing Instruction', *Writing on the Edge*, 21, 1 (fall 2010), 84–92.
Amin, Ash, 'Models, Fantasies, and Phantoms of Transition', in Ash Amin (ed.), *Post-Fordism: A Reader*. Ed. (New York: Routledge, 1994), pp. 1–41.
Avineri, Shlomo and Avner de-Shalit, 'Introduction', in Shlomo Avineri and Avner de-Shalit (eds), *Communitarianism and Liberalism* (Oxford: Oxford University Press, 1992), pp. 1–12.
Bachman, Richard, *The Long Walk* (New York: Simon & Schuster, 1979).
——, *Roadwork* (New York: Simon & Schuster, 1981).
——, *The Running Man* (New York: Simon & Schuster, 1982).
——, *The Regulators* (New York: Simon & Schuster, 1996).
Badiou, Alain, Interview with Christoph Cox and Molly Whalen, *Cabinet Magazine*, 5 (winter 2001), *http://www.cabinetmagazine.org/issues/5/alain badiou.php* (accessed 21 November 2019).
——, *Metapolitics*, trans. Jason Baker (New York: Verso, 2005).
——, *The Rebirth of History: Times of Riots and Uprisings*, trans. Gregory Elliott (London: Verso, 2012).
——, *Philosophy and the Even*, trans. Louise Burchill (Cambridge: Polity Press, 2013).

———, 'Twenty-four Uses of the Word "People"', in *What Is A People?*, trans. Jody Gladding (New York: Columbia University Press, 2016), pp. 21–32.

———, *Can Politics Be Thought?*, trans. Bruno Bosteels (Durham, NC: Duke University Press, 2018).

———, *Trump* (Cambridge: Polity, 2019).

———, and Marcel Gauchet, *What is to be Done? A Dialogue on Communism, Capitalism, and the Future of Democracy*, trans. Susan Spitzer (Cambridge: Polity Press, 2016).

Badley, Linda, 'Love and Death in the American Car: Stephen King's Auto-Erotic Horror', in Gary Hoppenstand and Ray Browne (eds), *The Gothic World of Stephen King: Landscape of Nightmares* (Bowling Green, OH: Popular Press, 1987), pp. 84–95.

Baudrillard, Jean, *Transparency of Evil: Essays on Extreme Phenomena*, trans. James Benedict (London: Verso, 1990).

———, *Impossible Exchange*, trans. Chris Turner (London: Verso, 2001).

———, *The Agony of Power*, trans. Phil Beitchman et al. (Los Angeles, CA: Semiotext[e], 2007).

———, *Forget Foucault*, trans. Phil Beitchman et al. (Los Angeles, CA: Semiotext[e], 2007).

Bauman, Zygmunt, *Culture in a Liquid Modern World* (Cambridge: Cambridge University Press, 2011).

Becker, Gary, 'Nobel Lecture: The Economic Way of Looking at Behavior', *Journal of Political Economy*, 101, 3 (June 1993), 385–409.

Bell, Daniel, *Communitarianism and its Critics* (Oxford: Oxford University Press, 1993).

Berardi, Franco, *Futurability: The Age of Impotence and the Horizon of Possibility* (London: Verso, 2017).

Berman, Paul, *The Tale of Two Utopias: The Political Journey of the Generation of 1968* (New York: W. W. Norton and Co., 1996).

Berman, Russell, 'Modern Art and Desublimation', *Telos*, 62 (December 1984), 31–57.

Berry, Josephine, *Art and (Bare) Life* (Berlin: Sternberg Press, 2018).

Bielefeldt, Heidi, 'Carl Schmitt's Critique of Liberalism: Systematic Reconstruction and Countercriticism', in David Dyzenhaus (ed.), *Law as Politics: Carl Schmitt's Critique of Liberalism* (Durham, NC: Duke University Press, 1998), pp. 23–37.

Binkley, Sam, *Happiness as Enterprise: An Essay on Neoliberal Life* (Albany, NY: SUNY Press, 2015).

Blake, Linnie and Agnieszka Sołtysik Monnet, 'Introduction: neoliberal gothic', in Linnie Blake and Agnieszka Monnet (eds), *Neoliberal Gothic: International gothic in the neoliberal age* (Manchester: Manchester University Press, 2017), pp. 1–18.

Bloch, Ernst, *The Utopian Function of Art and Literature*, trans. Jack Zipes and Frank Mecklenburg (Cambridge, MA: MIT Press, 1989).

—— and Theodor Adorno, 'Something's Missing: a Discussion between Ernst Bloch and Theodor W. Adorno on the Contradictions of Utopian Longing', in *The Utopian Function of Art and Literature*, trans. Jack Zipes and Frank Mecklenberg (Cambridge, MA: MIT Press, 1988), pp. 1–18.

Bosky, Bernadette Lynn, 'The Mind's a Monkey: Character and Psychology in Stephen King's Recent Fiction', in Tim Underwood and Chuck Miller (eds), *Kingdom of Fear: The World of Stephen King* (New York: New American Library, 1986), pp. 211–37.

Bremmer, Ian, *Us vs. Them: The Failure of Globalism* (New York: Penguin, 2018).

Brockling, Ulrich, *The Entrepreneurial Self: Fabricating a New Type of Subject* (London: SAGE, 2016).

Brown, Stephen P., 'Stephen King Shining Through', *WashingtonPost.com*, 9 April 1985, *https://www.washingtonpost.com/archive/lifestyle/1985/04/09/steven-king-shining-through/eaf662da-e9eb-4aba-9eb9-217826684ab6/?noredirect=on&utm_term=.cb404658f284* (accessed 27 February 2019).

Brown, Wendy, *Politics Out of History* (Princeton, NJ: Princeton University Press, 2001).

——, 'American Nightmare: Neoliberalism, Neoconservatism, and De-Democratization', *Political Theory*, 34, 6 (December 2006), 690–714.

——, *Walled States, Waning Sovereignty* (Brooklyn, NY: Zone Books, 2010).

——, *Undoing the Demos: Neoliberalism's Stealth Revolution* (Brooklyn, NY: Zone Books, 2015).

——, *In the Ruins of Neoliberalism: The Rise of Antidemocratic Politics in the West* (New York: Columbia University Press, 2019).

Butler, Judith, *Gender Trouble: Feminism and the Subversion of Identity* (New York: Routledge, 1990).

Callinicos, Alex, *Against Postmodernism: A Marxist Critique* (Cambridge: Polity, 1989).

Canovan, Margaret, *The People* (Cambridge: Polity, 2005).

Carney, Jordain, 'McConnell torches "far-left mob" over Kavanaugh fight', *TheHill.com*, 9 October 2018, *https://thehill.com/homenews/senate/410624-mcconnell-torches-far-left-mob-over-kavanaugh-fight* (accessed 27 February 2019).

Casebeer, Edwin F., 'The Art of Balance: Stephen King's Canon', in Tony Magistrale and Michael Morrison (eds), *A Dark Night's Dreaming: Contemporary American Horror Fiction* (Columbia, SC: University of South Carolina Press, 1996), pp. 42–55.

Chari, Anita, *A Political Economy of the Senses: Neoliberalism, Reification, Critique* (New York: Columbia University Press, 2015).

Chomsky, Noam, *Failed States: The Abuse of Power and the Assault on Democracy* (New York: Owl Books, 2006).

Clark, Dorie, *Entrepreneurial You: Monetize Your Expertise, Create Multiple Income Streams, and Thrive* (Cambridge, MA: Harvard Business Review Press, 2017).

Colaguori, Claudio, *Agon Culture: Competition, Conflict and the Problem of Domination* (Whitney, ON: de Sitter Publishing, 2012).

Colebrook, Claire, 'The Art of the Future', in Alexandre Lefebvre and Melanie White (eds), Bergson, *Politics, and Religion* (Durham, NC: Duke University Press, 2012), pp. 75–99.

Collier, Andrew, 'Mind, Reality and Politics', *Radical Philosophy* (March/April 1998), 38–43.

Collings, Michael, *The Stephen King Phenomenon* (Mercer Island, WA: Tarmount House, 1987).

Comaroff, Jean, 'The Politics of Conviction: Faith on the Neo-liberal Frontier', *Social Analysis*, 53, 1 (March 2009), 17–38.

——, 'Populism and Late Liberalism: A Special Affinity?', *The Annals of the American Academy of Political and Social Science*, 637 (September 2011), 99–111.

Comaroff, John and Jean Comaroff, 'First Thoughts on a Second Coming', in John Comaroff and Jean Comaroff (eds), *Millennial Capitalism and the Culture of Neoliberalism* (Durham, NC: Duke University Press, 2001), pp. 1–57.

——, and ——, *Ethnicity, Inc.* (Chicago, IL: University of Chicago Press, 2009).

Connolly, William, *Politics and Ambiguity* (Madison, WI: University of Wisconsin Press, 1987).

——, 'The Evangelical-Capitalist Resonance Machine', *Political Theory*, 33, 6 (December 2005), 869–86.

Cowan, Douglas, *America's Dark Theologian: The Religious Imagination of Stephen King* (New York: New York University Press, 2018).

Crary, Jonathan, *24/7* (London: Verso, 2013).

Cray, Ed, *Chrome Colossus: General Motors and Its Times* (New York: McGraw-Hill, 1980).

Crouch, Colin, *Post-democracy* (Cambridge: Polity Press, 2004).

Dardot, Pierre and Christian Laval, *The New Way of the World: On Neoliberal Society*, trans. Gregory Elliott (London: Verso, 2017).

Daub, Adrian, 'Where "IT" Was: Rereading Stephen King's *IT* on Its 30th Birthday', *LAReviewofBooks.org*, 11 September 2016, https://lareviewofbooks.org/article/where-it-was-rereading-stephen-kings-it-on-its-30th-anniversary/ (accessed 2 March 2019).

Davies, William, *The Limits of Neoliberalism: Authority, Sovereignty and the Logic of Competition* (New York: SAGE, 2017).

De Lauretis, Teresa, 'Upping the Anti (SIC) in Feminist Theory', in Simon During (ed.), *The Cultural Studies Reader: Third Edition* (New York: Routledge, 1993), pp. 358–71.

Dean, Jodi, *Democracy and Other Neoliberal Fantasies: Communicative Capitalism and Left Politics* (Durham, NC: Duke University Press, 2009).

——, *Crowds and Party* (New York: Verso, 2016).

Dean, Mitchell and Kaspar Villadsen, *State Phobia and Civil Society: The Political Legacy of Michel Foucault* (Stanford, CA: Stanford University Press, 2016).

Deleuze, Gilles, *Foucault: Reprint Edition*, trans. Sean Hand (New York: Continuum, 1999).

Devereux, Cecily, '"Made for Mankind": Cars, Cosmetics, and the Petrocultural Feminine', in Sheena Wilson et al. (eds), *Petrocultures: Oil, Politics, Culture* (Montreal: McGill-Queen's University Press, 2017), pp. 162–87.

DeWitt, Jack, 'Cars and Culture: Songs of the Open Road', *The American Poetry Review*, 39, 2 (March/April 2010), 38–40.

Dews, Peter, *Logics of Disintegration: Poststructuralist Thought and the Claims of Critical Theory* (New York: Verso, 1987).

Dewsbury, J. D., 'Unthinking Subjects: Alain Badiou and the Event of Thought in Thinking Politics', *Transactions of the Institute of British Geographers*, 32, 4 (October 2007), 443–59.

Dolar, Mladen, 'Freud and the Political', *Unbound*, 4, 15 (January 2008), 15–29.

Donzelot, Jacques, *The Policing of Families*, trans. Robert Hurley (Baltimore, MD: Johns Hopkins University Press, 1997).

Dufour, Dany-Robert, *The Art of Shrinking Heads: The New Servitude of the Liberated in the Era of Total Capitalism*, trans. David Macey (Cambridge: Polity Press, 2008).

Duggan, Lisa, *Twilight of Equality? Neoliberalism, Cultural Politics, and the Attack on Democracy* (Boston, MA: Beacon, 2003).

Dyzenhaus, David, 'Introduction: Why Carl Schmitt?', in David Dyzenhaus (ed.), *Law as Politics: Carl Schmitt's Critique of Liberalism* (Durham, NC: Duke University Press, 1998), pp. 1–23.

Eagleton, Terry, *Marxism and Literary Criticism* (Berkeley, CA: University of California Press, 1976).

———, *The Illusions of Postmodernism* (Malden, MA: Blackwell, 1996).

Edelman, Lee, *No Future: Queer Theory and the Death Drive* (Durham, NC: Duke University Press, 2004).

Egan, James, 'Technohorror: The Dystopian Vision of Stephen King', *Extrapolation*, 29, 2 (1988), 140–52.

Esposito, Roberto, *Bios: Biopolitics and Philosophy*, trans. Timothy Campbell (Minneapolis, MN: University of Minnesota Press, 2008).

Featherstone, Mike, *Consumer Culture and Postmodernism* (London: SAGE, 2007).

Feher, Michel, 'Self-Appreciation; or, the Aspirations of Human Capital', *Public Culture*, 21, 1, (2009), 21–41.

Fisher, Mark, *Capitalist Realism: Is There No Alternative?* (London: Zero Books, 2009).

———, *The Weird and Eerie* (London: Repeater Books, 2016).

Flacks, Richard, *Making History: The Radical Tradition in American Life* (New York: Columbia University Press, 1988).

Foucault, Michel, 'The Subject and Power', in Hubert Dreyfus and Paul Rabinow (eds), *Michel Foucault: Beyond Structuralism and Hermeneutics* (Chicago, IL: University of Chicago Press, 1983), pp. 208–29.

———, *The Birth of Biopolitics: Lectures at the Collège de France, 1978–1979*, trans. Graham Burchell (New York: Picador, 2010).

———, *The Government of Self and Others: Lectures at the Collège de France, 1982–1983*, trans. Graham Burchell (New York: Picador, 2011).

Frank, Thomas, *What's the Matter with Kansas?* (New York: Henry Holt and Co., 2004).

———, *Listen, Liberal; Or, What Ever Happened to the Party of the People?* (New York: Picador, 2016).

Fraser, Nancy, *Fortunes of Feminism: From State-Managed Capitalism to Neoliberal Crisis* (London: Verso, 2013).

———, *The Old is Dying and the New Cannot be Born* (London: Verso, 2019).

Freeden, Michael, *Liberalism: A Very Short Introduction* (Oxford: Oxford University Press, 2015).

Freud, Sigmund, *The Uncanny*, trans. David McLintock (New York: Penguin, 2003).

Galston, William, 'Progressive Politics and Communitarian Culture', in Michael Walzer (ed.), *Toward a Global Civil Society* (New York: Berghahn Books, 2009), pp. 107–11.

———, *Anti-Pluralism: The Populist Threat to Liberal Democracy* (New Haven, CT: Yale University Press, 2018).

Gergen, Kenneth, *The Saturated Self: Dilemmas of Identity in Contemporary Life* (New York: Basic Books, 1991).

Giannini, Erin, '"They Brought It on Themselves!" Adapting and Reflecting Cultural Fears, from the Shop to Rossum', *Science Fiction Film and Television*, 10, 2 (January 2017), 231–49.

Gilroy, Paul, 'Driving While Black', in Daniel Miller (ed.), *Car Cultures* (New York: Bloomsbury Academic, 2001), pp. 81–104.

——, *Against Race: Imagining Political Culture beyond the Color Line* (Cambridge, MA: Belknap Press, 2002).

Gladstone, Brooke, *The Trouble with Reality: A Rumination on Moral Panic in Our Time* (New York: Workman Publishing, 2017).

Goodall, Reece, 'Eerily Similar? Donald Trump and *The Dead Zone*'s Greg Tillson', *TheBoar.org*, 4 March 2017, *https://theboar.org/2017/03/donald-trump-greg-stillson-dead-zone/* (accessed 27 February 2019).

Graham, David, 'Why Trump Keeps Creating Chaos', *TheAtlantic.com*, 23 June 2018, *https://www.theatlantic.com/politics/archive/2018/06/trump-manufactured-crises-immigration/563495/* (accessed 26 February 2019).

Gutmann, Amy, 'Communitarian Critics of Liberalism', *Philosophy & Public Affairs*, 14, 3 (summer 1985), 308–22.

Habermas, Jurgen, 'Taking Aim at The Heart of the Present', in David Couzens Hoy (ed.), *Foucault: A Critical Reader* (Cambridge, MA: Blackwell, 1986), pp. 103–9.

——, 'The Critique of Reason as an Unmasking of the Human Sciences', in Michael Kelly (ed.), *Critique and Power: Recasting the Foucault/Habermas Debate* (Cambridge, MA: MIT Press, 1994), pp. 47–79.

Halberstam, David, *The Reckoning* (New York: William Morrow & Co., 1986).

Hall, Stuart, 'Authoritarian Populism: A Reply to Jessop Et Al', *New Left Review*, 1, 151 (May–June 1985), 115–24.

——, 'Brave New World', *Marxism Today* (October 1988), 24–9.

——, 'Cultural Identity and Diaspora', in Jana Braziel and Anita Mannur (eds), *Theorizing Diaspora: A Reader* (Malden, MA: Blackwell, 2003), pp. 233–47.

——, 'The neoliberal revolution', in Sally Davidson et al. (eds), *Selected Political Writings: The Great Moving Right Show and Other Essays* (Durham, NC: Duke University Press, 2017), pp. 317–36.

Hall, Terry, 'Beyond the Procedural Republic: The Communitarian Liberalism of Michael Sandel', in Christopher Wolfe and John Hittinger (eds), *Liberalism at the Crossroads: An Introduction to Contemporary Liberal Political Theory and Its Critics* (Lanham, MD: Rowman and Littlefield, 1994), pp. 75–97.

Hardt, Michael and Antonio Negri, *Empire* (Cambridge, MA: Harvard University Press, 2000).
———, *Commonwealth* (Cambridge, MA: Belknap Press, 2011).
Harvey, David, *The Condition of Postmodernity: An Enquiry into the Origins of Cultural Change* (Malden, MA: Blackwell, 1990).
———, *A Brief History of Neoliberalism* (Oxford: Oxford University Press, 2005).
Hoens, Dominiek, 'Object a and Politics', in Samo Tomsic and Andreja Zevnik (eds), *Jacques Lacan: Between Psychoanalysis and Politics* (New York: Routledge, 2016), pp. 101–13.
Hogle, Jerrold, 'Introduction: the gothic in western culture', in Jerrold Hogle (ed.), *The Cambridge Companion to the Gothic* (Cambridge: Cambridge University Press, 2002), pp. 1–21.
Horan, Thomas, *Desire and Empathy in Twentieth-century Dystopian Fiction* (New York: Palgrave, 2018).
Ingrassia, Paul, *Crash Course: The American Automobile Industry's Road from Glory to Disaster* (New York: Random House, 2010).
——— and Joseph White, *Comeback: The Fall and Rise of the American Automobile Industry* (New York: Simon & Schuster, 1994).
Irving, Washington, *History, Tales, and Sketches* (New York: Library of America, 1983).
Jackson, Shirley, *The Haunting of Hill House* (New York: Penguin, 1959).
Jameson, Fredric, *The Political Unconscious: Narrative as a socially symbolic act* (New York: Routledge, 1981).
———, 'On Jargon', in Michael Hardt and Kathi Weeks (eds), *The Jameson Reader* (Malden, MA: Blackwell, 2000), pp. 117–19.
Kakutani, Michiko, *The Death of Truth: Notes on Falsehood in the Age of Trump* (New York: Penguin, 2018).
King, Stephen, *Carrie* (New York: Doubleday, 1974).
———, *'Salem's Lot* (New York: Doubleday, 1975).
———, *The Shining* (New York: Anchor Books, 1977).
———, 'Trucks', in *Night Shift* (New York: Anchor Books, 1978), pp. 135–52.
———, *The Dead Zone* (New York: Simon & Schuster, 1979).
———, *Firestarter* (New York: Simon & Schuster, 1980).
———, *Danse Macabre* (New York: Simon & Schuster, 1981).
———, *Apt Pupil*, in *Different Seasons* (New York: Simon & Schuster, 1982), pp. 117–335.
———, *The Dark Tower: The Gunslinger* (New York: Scribner, 1982).
———, *Christine* (New York: Viking Press, 1983).
———, *The Mist*, in *Skeleton Crew* (New York: Simon & Schuster, 1985), pp. 1–153.

——, 'Why I Was Bachman', in *The Bachman Books* (New York: New American Library, 1985).
——, *IT* (New York: Simon & Schuster, 1986).
——, *The Eyes of the Dragon* (New York: Viking, 1987).
——, *Misery* (New York: Scribner, 1987).
——, *The Tommyknockers* (New York: G. P. Putnam's Sons, 1987).
——, *The Dark Half* (New York: Simon & Schuster, 1989).
——, *The Langoliers*, in *Four Past Midnight* (New York: Simon & Schuster, 1990), pp. 1–297.
——, 'Secret Window, Secret Garden', in *Four Past Midnight* (New York: Simon & Schuster, 1990), pp. 297–481.
——, *The Stand: Complete and Uncut Edition* (New York: Doubleday, 1990).
——, *Needful Things* (New York: Simon & Schuster, 1991).
——, *Dolores Claiborne* (New York: Viking, 1992).
——, *Gerald's Game* (New York: Simon & Schuster, 1992).
——, *Insomnia* (New York: Viking, 1994).
——, *Rose Madder* (New York: Simon & Schuster, 1995).
——, *Bag of Bones* (New York: Simon & Schuster, 1998).
——, *The Storm of the Century: An Original Screenplay* (New York: Simon & Schuster, 1999).
——, *Hearts of Atlantis* (New York: Simon & Schuster, 1999).
——, *Dreamcatcher* (New York: Simon & Schuster, 2001).
——, *From a Buick 8* (New York: Gallery Books, 2002).
——, *Cell* (New York: Simon & Schuster, 2006).
——, *Lisey's Story* (New York: Simon & Schuster, 2006).
——, *Duma Key* (New York: Simon & Schuster, 2008).
——, 'The Gingerbread Girl', in *Just After Sunset* (New York: Simon & Schuster, 2008), pp. 42–126.
——, *Under the Dome* (New York: Simon & Schuster, 2009).
——, 'Big Driver', in *Full Dark, No Stars* (New York: Scribner, 2010), pp. 133–247.
——, 'The Importance of Being Bachman', *Liljas-library.com*, 29 January 2010, www.liljas-library.com/bachman_king.php (accessed 22 January 2020).
——, *11/22/63* (New York: Simon & Schuster, 2011).
——, *Doctor Sleep* (New York: Simon & Schuster, 2013).
——, 'Guns' (Bangor, ME: Philtrum Press, 2013).
——, *Revival* (New York: Simon & Schuster, 2014).
——, 'Five to One, One in Five: UMO in the '60s', in *Hearts in Suspension* (Orono, ME: University of Maine Press, 2016), pp. 23–76.
——, *The Outsider* (New York: Simon & Schuster, 2018).

—, *The Institute* (New York: Simon & Schuster, 2019).
Klein, Naomi, *Fences and Windows: Dispatches from the Front Lines of the Globalization Debate* (New York: Picador, 2002).
—, *Shock Doctrine: The Rise of Disaster Capitalism* (New York: Picador, 2007).
Korb, Lawrence and Laura Conley, 'Forging an American Empire', in Robert Maranto et al. (eds), *Judging Bush* (Stanford, CA: Stanford University Press, 2009), pp. 234–51.
Kotsko, Adam, *Neoliberalism's Demons: On the Political Theology of Late Capital* (Stanford, CA: Stanford University Press, 2018).
Krause, Sharon, *Civil Passions: Moral Sentiment and Democratic Deliberation* (Princeton, NJ: Princeton University Press, 2008).
Kunkel, Benjamin, *Utopia or Bust: A Guide to the Present Crisis* (London: Verso, 2014).
Kwak, James, *Economism: Bad Economics and the Rise of Inequality* (New York: Vintage, 2017).
Lacan, Jacques, *The Seminars of Jacques Lacan: Book 1: Freud's Papers on Technique, 1953–1954*, trans. Jacques-Alain Miller (Cambridge: Cambridge University Press, 1988).
Laclau, Ernesto, *On Populist Reason* (London: Verso, 2005).
—, *Politics and Ideology in Marxist Theory: Capitalism, Fascism, Populism* (London: Verso, 2011).
—— and Chantal Mouffe, *Hegemony and Socialist Strategy: Towards a Radical Democratic Politics: Second Edition* (London: Verso, 2014).
Latour, Bruno, 'War of the Worlds', in Simon During (ed.), *The Cultural Studies Reader: Third Edition* (New York: Routledge, 1993), pp. 304–14.
Lefort, Claude, *Democracy and Political Theory* (Minneapolis, MN: University of Minnesota Press, 1989).
—, *Writing: The Political Test*, trans. David Ames Curtis (Durham, NC: Duke University Press, 2000).
Lemke, Thomas, *Biopolitics: An Advanced Introduction*, trans. Eric Frederick Trump (New York: New York University Press, 2011).
Levine, Caroline, *Forms: Whole, Rhythm, Hierarchy, Network* (Princeton, NJ: Princeton University Press, 2015).
Lilla, Mark, *The Once and Future Liberal: After Identity Politics* (New York: HarperCollins, 2017).
Louth, Jonathon and Martin Potter, 'The Production of News Subjectivities: Constellations of Domination and Resistance', in Jonathan Louth and Martin Potter (eds), *Edges of Identity 2017: The Production of Neoliberal Subjectivities* (Chester: University of Chester Press, 2017), pp. 1–24.

Luce, Edward, *The Retreat of Western Liberalism* (New York: Atlantic Monthly Press, 2017).

Lutz, Catherine and Anne Lutz Fernandez, *Carjacked: The Culture of the Automobile and its Effects on Our Lives* (New York: Palgrave Macmillan, 2010).

McAleer, Patrick, 'I Have the Whole World in My Hands . . . Now What? Power, Control, Responsibility and the Baby Boomers in Stephen King's Fiction', *Journal of Popular Culture*, 44, 6 (December 2011), 1209–27.

McCarthy, Anna, 'Reality Television: A Neoliberal Theater of Suffering', *Social Text*, 25, 4 (2007), 17–42.

MacEwan, Arthur, *Neoliberalism or Democracy? Economic Strategy, Markets, and Alternatives for the 21st Century* (London: Zed Books, 1999).

McGowan, Todd, *Enjoying What We Don't Have: The Political Project of Psychoanalysis* (Lincoln, NE: University of Nebraska Press, 2013).

——, *Capitalism and Desire: The Psychic Cost of Free Markets* (New York: Columbia University Press, 2016).

——, *Emancipation after Hegel: Achieving a Contradictory Revolution* (New York: Columbia University Press, 2019).

MacIntyre, Alasdair, *After Virtue: Second Edition* (Notre Dame, IN: Notre Dame University Press, 1984).

——, 'The Virtues, the Unity of a Human Life, and the Concept of a Tradition', in Michael Sandel (ed.), *Liberalism and Its Critics* (New York: New York University Press, 1984), pp. 125–49.

McIntyre, Lee, *Post-Truth* (Cambridge, MA: MIT Press, 2018).

Magistrale, Tony, *Stephen King – The Second Decade: 'Danse Macabre' to 'The Dark Half'* (Woodbridge, CT: Twayne Publishers, 1992).

——, *Landscape of Fear: Stephen King's American Gothic* (Madison, WI: Popular Press, 1998).

——, 'Steve's Take', in George Beahm (ed.), *The Stephen King Companion: Four Decades of Fear from the Master of Horror* (New York: St. Martin's, 2015), pp. 511–29.

—— and Michael J. Blouin. *Stephen King and American History* (New York: Routledge, forthcoming).

Mann, Craig Ian, '"It rained fire": *The Running Man* from Bachman to Schwarzenegger', *Science Fiction Film and Television*, 10, 2 (summer 2017), 197–213.

Marazzi, Christian, *The Violence of Financial Capitalism*, trans. Kristinia Lebedeva and Jason Francis McGimsey (Los Angeles, CA: Semiotext[e], 2011).

Marcuse, Herbert. 'Liberation from the Affluent Society', in Stephen Bronner and Douglas Kellner (eds), *Critical Theory and Society: A Reader* (New York: Routledge, 1989), pp. 276–88.

Marsh, Peter and Peter Collett, *Driving Passion: The Psychology of the Car* (London: Faber and Faber, 1986).

Mény, Yves and Yves Surel, 'The Constitutive Ambiguity of Populism', in Yves Mény and Yves Surel (eds), *Democracies and the Populist Challenge* (New York: Palgrave, 2002), pp. 1–25.

Michaels, Walter Benn, *The Trouble With Diversity: How We Learned to Love Identity and Ignore Inequality* (New York: Picador, 2006).

Moffitt, Benjamin, *The Global Rise of Populism: Performance, Political Style, and Representation* (Stanford, CA: Stanford University Press, 2016).

Morin, Rebecca and David Cohen, 'Giuliani: "Truth Isn't Truth"', *Politico.com*, 19 August 2018, *https://www.politico.com/story/2018/08/19/giuliani-truth-todd-trump-788161* (accessed 26 February 2019).

Moskowitz, Alex, 'The Production of the Subject: Foucault, Marx, and the Ontology of the Market', *Polygraph*, 27 (2019), 85–109.

Mouffe, Chantal, *The Return of the Political* (London: Verso, 1993).

——, *The Democratic Paradox* (London: Verso, 2005).

——, *On the Political* (New York: Routledge, 2005).

——, *Agonistics: Thinking the World Politically* (New York: Verso, 2013).

——, *For a Left Populism* (London: Verso, 2018).

Mudde, Cas and Cristobal Kaltwasser, *Populism: A Very Short Introduction* (Oxford: Oxford University Press, 2017).

Mulhall, Stephen and Adam Swift, 'Introduction: Rawls's Original Position', in Stephen Mulhall and Adam Swift, *Liberals and Communitarians: Second Edition* (Malden, MA: Blackwell, 1992), pp. 1–35.

Munoz, Gabriella, 'Trump: paid protesters "less professional than anticipated"', *WashingtonTimes.com*, 9 October 2018, *https://www.washingtontimes.com/news/2018/oct/9/trump-paid-protesters-less-professional-anticipate/* (accessed 27 February 2019).

Nealon, Jeffrey, *Foucault Beyond Foucault: Power and Its Intensifications since 1984* (Redwood City, CA: Stanford University Press, 2007).

——, *Post-Postmodernism: Or, the Cultural Logic of Just-In-Time Capitalism* (Redwood City, CA: Stanford University Press, 2012).

Newhouse, Tom, 'A Blind Date with Disaster: Adolescent Revolt in the Fiction of Stephen King', in Gary Hoppenstand and Ray Browne (eds), *The Gothic World of Stephen King: Landscape of Nightmares* (Bowling Green, OH: Bowling Green University Press, 1987), pp. 49–56.

Norris, Cristopher, *Uncritical Theory: Postmodernism, Intellectuals and the Gulf War* (Amherst, MA: University of Massachusetts Press, 1992).

Noys, Benjamin, *Malign Velocities: Accelerationism and Capitalism* (London: Zero Books, 2014).

Nussbaum, Martha, *Political Emotions: Why Love Matters For Justice* (Cambridge, MA: Harvard University Press, 2013).

Oakeshott, Michael, *Rationalism in Politics and Other Essays* (Indianapolis, IN: Liberty Fund, 1991).

Okin, Susan Moller, 'Humanist Liberalism', in Nancy Rosenblum (ed.), *Liberalism and the Moral Life* (Cambridge, MA: Harvard University Press), pp. 39–53.

Ouellette, Laurie J., '"Take Responsibility for Yourself": Judge Judy and the Neoliberal Citizen', in Susan Murray and Laurie Ouellette (eds), *Remaking Television Culture* (New York: New York University Press, 2004), pp. 231–50.

Palley, Thomas, 'From Keynesianism to Neoliberalism: Shifting Paradigms in Economics', in Alfredo Saad-Filho and Deborah Johnston (eds), *Neoliberalism: A Critical Reader* (Ann Arbor, MI: Pluto Press, 2005), pp. 20–30.

Peck, Janice, *The Age of Oprah: Cultural Icon for the Neoliberal Era* (New York: Routledge, 2008).

Phillips, Derek, *Looking Backwards: A Critical Appraisal of Communitarian Thought* (Princeton, NJ: Princeton University Press, 1993).

Phipps, Alison, *The Politics of the Body: Gender in a Neoliberal and Neoconservative Age* (Cambridge: Polity Press, 2014).

Punter, David, 'Problems of recollection and construction: Stephen King', in Victor Sage and Allan Lloyd Smith (eds), *Modern Gothic: A Reader* (Manchester: Manchester University Press, 1996), pp. 121–41.

Rancière, Jacques, *Dissensus: On Politics and Aesthetics*, trans. Steve Corcoran (New York: Bloomsbury, 2010).

———, *Hatred of Democracy: Reprint Edition*, trans. Steve Corcoran (London: Verso, 2014).

———, 'The Populism That is Not to be Found', in *What Is A People?*, trans. Jody Gladding (New York: Columbia University Press, 2016), pp. 101–7.

Rawls, John, *A Theory of Justice: Revised Edition* (Cambridge, MA: Belknap Press, 1999).

Reino, Joseph, *Stephen King: The First Decade, from 'Carrie' to 'Pet Sematary'* (Woodbridge, CT: Twayne Publishers, 1988).

Richards, Parker, 'The Authoritarian Heroes of *Game of Thrones*', *The Atlantic*, 13 April 2019, https://www.theatlantic.com/entertainment/archive/2019/04/game-thrones-and-trope-authoritarian-heroes-daenerys-targaryen-jon-snow-tolkien-aragorn/586957/ (accessed 1 February 2020).

Richardson, Alan and Sonya Hofkosh, 'Introduction', in Alan Richardson and Sonya Hofkosh (eds), *Romanticism, Race, and Imperial Culture* (Bloomington, IN: University of Indiana Press, 1996), pp. 1–15.

Rose, Nikolas, *Governing the Soul: The Shaping of the Private Self* (New York: Routledge, 1990).

——, *Inventing Our Selves: Psychology, Power, and Personhood* (Cambridge: Cambridge University Press, 1998).

——, *Powers of Freedom: Reframing Political Thought* (Cambridge: Cambridge University Press, 1999).

Russell, Sharon, *Stephen King: A Critical Companion* (Westport, CT: Greenwood, 1996).

Ryfe, David, *Presidents in Culture: The Meaning of Presidential Communication* (Bern, Switzerland: Peter Lang, 2005).

Sandel, Michael, 'The Procedural Republic and the Unencumbered Self', *Political Theory*, 12, 1 (February, 1984), 81–96.

——, *Liberalism and the Limits of Justice: Second Edition* (Cambridge: Cambridge University Press, 1998).

——, *Justice: What's the Right Thing to Do?* (New York: Farrar, Straus and Giroux, 2009).

Schmitt, Carl, *The Crisis of Parliamentary Democracy*, trans. Ellen Kennedy (Cambridge, MA: MIT Press, 1985).

——, 'The Age of Neutralizations and Depoliticizations', in Carl Schmitt, *The Concept of the Political: Expanded Edition*, trans. George Schwab (Chicago, IL: University of Chicago Press, 1996), pp. 80–97.

——, *The Concept of the Political: Expanded Edition*, trans. George Schwab (Chicago, IL: University of Chicago Press, 1996).

Scott, Peter, *The Road to 9/11* (Berkeley, CA: University of California Press, 2007).

Sears, John, *Stephen King's Gothic* (Cardiff: University of Wales Press, 2011).

Selznick, Philip, *The Communitarian Persuasion* (Washington, DC: Woodrow Wilson Press, 2002).

Senf, Carol A., '*Gerald's Game* and *Dolores Claiborne*: Stephen King and the Evolution of An Authentic Female Narrative Voice', in Kathleen Margaret Lant and Theresa Thompson (eds), *Imagining the Worst: Stephen King and the Representation of Women* (Santa Barbara, CA: Greenwood 1998), pp. 91–107.

Shaviro, Stephen, *No Speed Limit: Three Essays on Accelerationism* (Minneapolis, MN: University of Minnesota Press, 2015).

Sloan, Alfred, in John McDonald and Catharine Stevens (eds), *My Years with General Motors* (New York: Doubleday, 1963).

Slowik, Ted, 'Trump bound for "Dead Zone" moment, like using baby as human shield', *ChicagoTribune.com*, 3 August 2016, *https://www.chicagotribune.com/ suburbs/daily-southtown/opinion/ct-sta-slowik-dead-zone-st-0804-20160803-story.html* (accessed 27 February 2019).

Smith, Steven B., *Hegel's Critique of Liberalism: Rights in Context* (Chicago, IL: University of Chicago Press, 1989).

Sontag, Susan, *Illness as Metaphor and AIDS and Its Metaphors* (New York: Picador, 1990).

Stavrakakis, Yannis, *Lacan and the Political* (New York: Routledge, 1999).

Sternberg, Ernest, 'Transformations: The Forces of Capitalist Change', in Kenneth Taylor and William E. Halal (eds), *21st Century Economics* (Boston, MA: St. Martin's Press, 1999), pp. 2–31.

Streeck, Wolfgang, *Buying Time: The Delayed Crisis of Democratic Capitalism* (London: Verso, 2013).

——, 'The Crisis in Context: Democratic Capitalism and its Contradictions', in Wolfgang Streeck and Armin Shafer (eds), *Politics in the Age of Austerity* (Cambridge: Polity Press, 2013), pp. 262–87.

Strengell, Heidi, *Dissecting Stephen King: From the Gothic to Literary Naturalism* (Madison, WI: Popular Press, 2005).

Suskind, Ron, 'Faith, Certainty and the Presidency of George W. Bush', *NewYorkTimes.com*, 17 October 2004, *https://www.nytimes.com/2004/10/17/magazine/ faith-certainty-and-the-presidency-of-george-w-bush.html* (accessed 26 February 2019).

Taylor, Charles, *Hegel and Modern Society* (Cambridge: Cambridge University Press, 1979).

——, *Sources of the Self: The Making of the Modern Identity* (Cambridge: Cambridge University Press, 1989).

Taylor, J. D., *Negative Capitalism: Cynicism in the Neoliberal Era* (London: Zero Books, 2013).

Taylor, Mark, *Confidence Games: Money and Markets in a World without Redemption* (Chicago, IL: University of Chicago Press, 2004).

Texter, Douglas, '"A Funny Thing Happened on the Way to the Dystopia": The Culture Industry's Neutralization of Stephen King's *The Running Man*', *Utopian Studies*, 18, 1 (2007), 43–72.

Tiffany, Kaitlyn, 'Reading Stephen King's *IT* is an Exhausting Way to Spend a Summer', *TheVerge.com*, 1 September 2017, *https://www.theverge.com/2017/ 9/1/16028300/stephen-king-it-movie-adaptation-book-recap-horror-summer* (accessed 25 February 2019).

Vasari, Giorgio, *The Lives of the Artists*, trans. Julia and Peter Bondanella (Oxford: Oxford University Press, 1998).

Virilio, Paul, *Speed and Politics*, trans. Mark Polizzotti (Los Angeles, CA: Semiotext[e], 2006).

Vlastelica, Ryan, 'Stephen King's *The Outsider* is *IT* for the Trump Era', *AVClub.com*, 21 May 2018, *https://aux.avclub.com/stephen-king-s-the-outsider-is-an-it-for-the-trump-era-1825906254* (accessed 26 February 2019).

——, 'The World According to Cheney', Editorial, *New York Times*, 23 December 2008, A28.

Walzer, Michael, *Spheres of Justice: A Defense of Pluralism and Equality* (New York: Basic Books, 1983).

Ware, Alan, 'The United States: Populism as Political Strategy', in Yves Mény and Yves Surel (eds), *Democracies and the Populist Challenge* (New York: Palgrave, 2002), pp. 101–20.

Watkins, Tamara. '"Never Give a Good Politician Time to Pray": Stephen King's Treatment of Political Power and Community Involvement in *Under the Dome*', in Paul Petrovic (ed.), *Representing 9/11: Trauma, Ideology, and Nationalism in Literature, Film, and Television* (New York: Rowman and Littlefield, 2015), pp. 29–41.

Wiley, James, *Politics and the Concept of the Political: The Political Imagination* (New York: Routledge, 2016).

Winter, Douglas E., *Stephen King: The Art of Darkness* (Boston, MA: Dutton, 1984).

Wolin, Sheldon, *Politics and Vision: Continuity and Innovation in Western Political Thought* (Princeton, NJ: Princeton University Press, 1960).

——, *Democracy Incorporated: Managed Democracy and the Specter of Inverted Totalitarianism* (Princeton, NJ: Princeton University Press, 2008).

——, 'The World According to Cheney', Editorial, *New York Times*, 23 December 2008, A28.

Wood, Rocky, *A Literary Stephen King Companion* (Jefferson, NC: McFarland, 2011).

Žižek, Slavoj, 'The undergrowth of enjoyment: how popular culture can serve as an introduction to Lacan', *New Formations*, 9 (winter 1989), 7–31.

——, *The Plague of Fantasies* (New York: Verso, 1997).

——, 'Carl Schmitt in the Age of Post-Politics', in Chantal Mouffe (ed.), *The Challenge of Carl Schmitt* (London: Verso, 1999), pp. 18–38.

——, 'Against the Populist Temptation', *Critical Inquiry*, 32, 3 (spring 2006), 551–74.

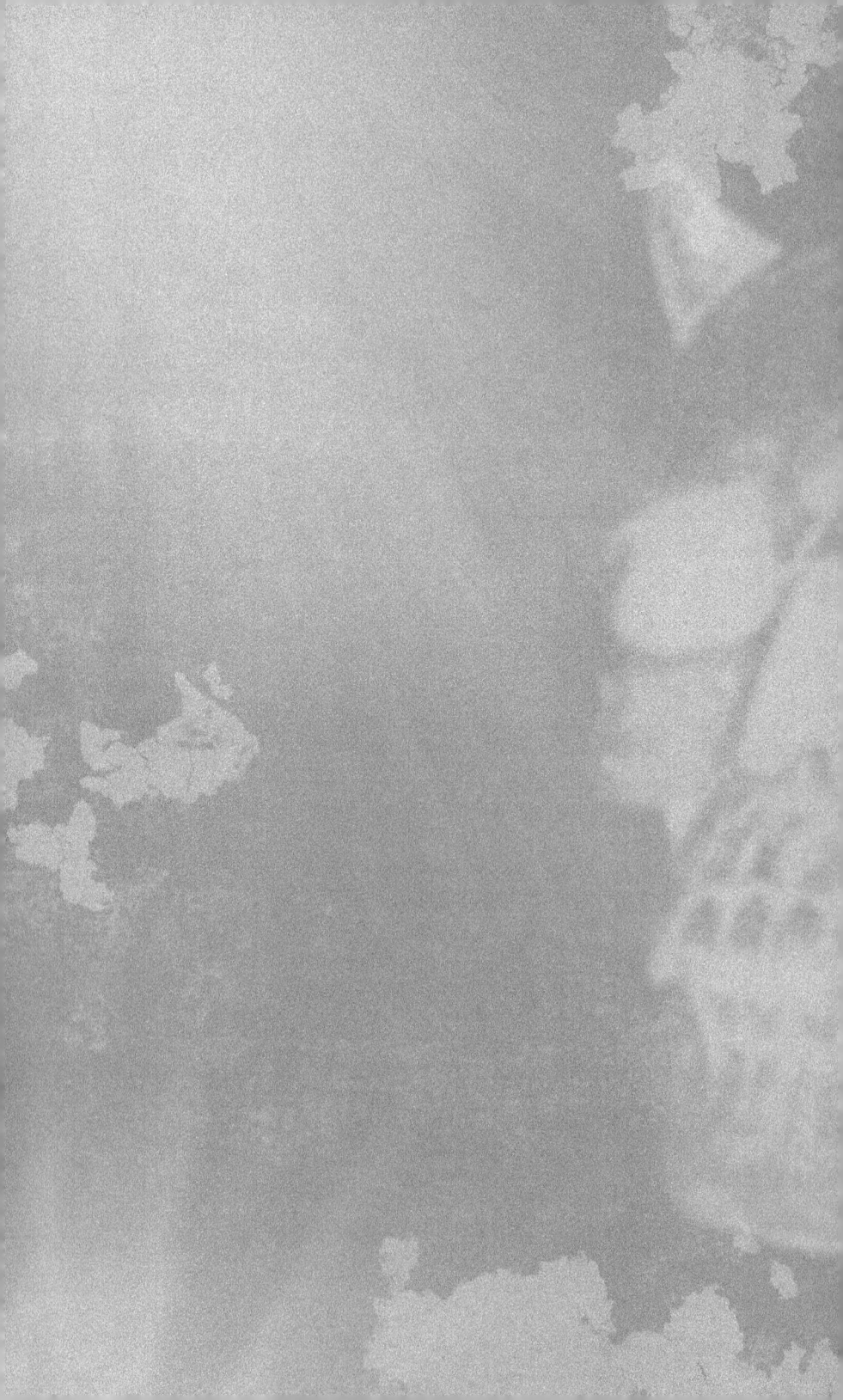

Index

9/11 (September 11th, 2001) 55, 140–1, 149, 156–7
11/22/63 3, 26, 198

Accelerationism 61–3, 66–7, 81, 219–20
Adorno, Theodor 7, 209
Agamben, Giorgio 78, 200, 207
Agonism 79, 126
Althusser, Louis 143, 158
Anti-intellectualism 153
Arendt, Hannah 156, 183
Authoritarian 22, 27, 35, 46, 82, 86, 110, 113, 143–4, 147–56, 165, 175,180, 182, 185, 201, 203

Badiou, Alain 22–3, 111–12, 117–18, 175–6, 191–2, 198, 207, 211
Baudrillard, Jean 84, 86, 125–6, 200, 208
Bauman, Zygmunt 198, 200, 208
Becker, Gary 121–2, 135, 208
Bell, Daniel 90, 93, 197, 208

Berardi, Franco 'Bifo' 36, 85, 113, 189, 208
Berman, Russell 129, 208
Berry, Josephine 128, 132, 199, 208
Binkley, Sam 133, 200, 208
Biocapitalism 65, 73, 122, 195
Bloch, Ernst 7, 209
Bretton Woods agreement 5, 43
Brockling, Ulrich 130, 133, 199, 209
Brown, Charles Brockden 163
Brown, Wendy 3, 12, 66, 83, 86, 142, 144–51, 153, 155, 199, 202
Bush, George W. 140–4, 148–50, 152–5, 158, 201, 203
Butler, Judith 17, 209

Callinicos, Alex 83, 128, 132, 209
Capitalist realism 48, 50, 190, 212
Castle Rock 11–15, 19, 190
Cheney, Dick 140–4, 148–50, 152–5, 158, 201, 203
Chomsky, Noam 5, 145, 210
Christine 53–6, 58–68, 176, 194–5

Clinton, Bill 11
Clinton, Hillary 161
Cold War 2, 28, 73, 75–6, 78, 124, 194–5
Collier, Andre 47, 210
Comaroff, Jean 133, 136, 150–1, 175, 210
Comaroff, John 133, 136, 210
Communitarian 23, 89–94, 96–107, 183–4, 197
Connolly, William 92, 102, 148–9, 151, 204, 210
Cowan, Douglas 2, 210
Crary, Jonathan 114–15, 132, 210
Crouch, Colin 39, 145, 153, 201, 210

Danse Macabre 2–3
Dardot, Pierre 3, 210
The Dark Half 19–20, 82, 198, 200
Davies, William 36, 151, 192, 211
The Dead Zone 23–8, 114, 143
Dean, Jodi 18, 39, 133
Death drive 20, 33, 39, 42, 44, 46, 48, 50–1, 53, 184–5, 204
De-democratisation 5, 12, 22, 142, 147, 152, 191
Deleuze, Gilles 61, 67, 74–5, 78, 81, 195, 211
Depoliticisation 5, 11, 13, 17, 46, 66, 149
Doctor Sleep 3, 73, 76, 199
Dolar, Mladen 46, 211
Donzelot, Jacques 80, 85, 211
Dreamcatcher 22–5, 28, 103, 143, 191
Dufour, Dany-Robert 44, 72, 74, 122, 124, 195–6
Duma Key 122, 135, 199, 200, 202

Eagleton, Terry 74, 85, 143, 195–6, 201, 211
Economism 10, 16, 29, 135
Edelman, Lee 184–5, 212
Elevation 190
Event 109–21
The Eyes of the Dragon 13, 190

Feher, Michel 81, 134, 137, 212
Financialisation 16, 43, 55–6, 58, 61–3, 67–68, 123–4, 126, 145
Firestarter 16–17, 65, 71–89, 91, 95, 98, 122, 126, 128, 131–2, 136, 139, 180–1, 198
Fisher, Mark 13, 47–8, 50, 60, 64–5, 190, 194, 212
Fordism 35, 54–5, 59, 61–2, 66
Foucault, Michel 18, 75, 77–82, 191, 196
Frank, Thomas 11, 153, 166, 172, 193, 212
Fraser, Nancy 123, 196, 200, 212
French Revolution 104, 112
From a Buick 8 9, 53–4, 56, 58–68, 194, 204
Fundamentalism 29, 143, 149–50, 152

Galston, William 93, 170, 173
Gauchet, Marcel 112, 191–2, 198
General Motors (GM) 57, 146, 194
Gerald's Game 16–19, 22, 85, 191
Gergen, Kenneth 72, 213
Gig economy 198
Gilroy, Paul 16, 57, 213
'The Gingerbread Girl' 135–6

Habermas, Jürgen 11, 83–4, 183, 213
Hall, Stuart 54, 100, 140, 165, 184, 200–1, 203, 213

Hardt, Michael 61, 81, 127, 202, 214
Harvey, David 54, 59, 122, 124, 195, 198, 214
The Haunting of Hill House 102
Hegel, G.W.F. 103–6
Hoens, Dominiek 49, 51, 214
Hogle, Jerrold 162, 202, 214
Homo economicus 3–4, 78, 123
Homo politicus 3–4
Human capital 121–3, 128–30, 133–5, 199

Identity politics 16–17, 122, 135–6, 190, 200
Insomnia 20–1
The Institute 1, 27–30
Irving, Washington 23–4, 214
IT 89–109

Jackson, Shirley 83, 102, 214
Jameson, Fredric 9, 47, 192, 214

Kaltwasser, Cristobal 162, 165, 170, 218
Kant, Immanuel 3, 90
Keynesian 15, 34–5, 54–6, 62, 64, 67, 72, 80
Klein, Naomi 146–8, 201, 216
Kotsko, Adam 148, 169, 203, 216
Krause, Sharon 174, 216

Lacan, Jacques 30, 35, 40–3, 46–51, 216
Laclau, Ernesto 6–8, 176–7, 216
The Langoliers 109–22, 136, 185, 198
Latour, Bruno 185, 195, 216
Laval, Christian 3, 210
Lefort, Claude 6, 8, 216

Levine, Caroline 162, 173, 216
Liberalism 15, 55, 82, 89–109, 140–1, 144, 148, 161–79
Libertarian 77–8, 90, 143
Lisey's Story 85, 128, 202
The Long Walk 33, 36, 41–2

McAleer, Patrick x, 49, 192, 217
McGowan, Todd x, 40–1, 43, 45–7, 106, 197, 217
MacIntyre, Alasdair 91, 95–6, 101, 197, 217
Magistrale, Tony ix, 2, 38, 71, 190–2, 204, 217
Managerialism 5, 10–11, 15, 18–19, 30, 54, 67, 109, 112, 115, 142, 145, 173, 176, 179, 185, 192
Marazzi, Christian 57, 122, 198, 217
Marcuse, Herbert 137, 217
Marx, Karl 59, 126, 133, 177, 197, 201
May 1968 8, 40, 112, 117, 180, 190
Michaels, Walter Benn 190–1, 218
The Mist 9–10, 30, 92
Mouffe, Chantal 6–8, 11, 84, 106, 170, 175, 179, 183, 185, 197, 204, 216
Mudde, Cas 162, 165, 170, 218
Mulhall, Stephen 89, 95, 101, 218

Nealon, Jeffrey 57, 63, 77, 79, 129, 196, 218
Needful Things 11–16, 18, 28
Negri, Antonio 61, 81, 127, 202, 214
New Economy 56, 122, 129–31, 136
Norris, Christopher 62, 140, 194, 218
Nussbaum, Martha 170, 219

Oakeshott, Michael 29, 219
Obama, Barack 11, 140, 145
Original Position 100–1
Ouellette, Laurie 37–8, 219
The Outsider 161–79

Pareto Optimality 98, 100
Petroculture 55, 61
Phillips, Derek 97, 99, 219
Populism 161–79, 203
Post-Fordism 53–6, 60–1, 64–8, 71
'Progressive neo-liberalism' 123
Punter, David 33, 91, 219

Rancière, Jacques 8–9, 11–13, 25, 166, 181, 203, 219
Rawls, John 11, 90, 93, 97–102, 197, 219
Reagan, Ronald 39, 58, 73, 90
The Regulators 19, 129
Revival 12, 73, 117–18, 154
Roadwork 33, 36–40, 43–5, 193
Roaring Nineties 122–34
Rose, Nikolas 123, 131, 134, 220
Rose Madder 16–17, 65, 79, 83, 139, 180, 182, 121–39, 198–9
Rumsfeld, Donald 145, 147, 201
The Running Man 33, 36–38, 45

'*Salem's Lot* 12, 14, 36, 103, 201
Sandel, Michael 93–6, 99, 101, 197, 220
Schmitt, Carl 5,10, 16, 96,110, 117, 163, 171, 185, 201, 203–4, 220
Sears, John x, 62–3, 66, 82, 92, 116, 172, 185, 189, 194, 196, 220
Self-entrepreneurs 72, 123–4, 137

Selznick, Peter 90, 102, 220
Senf, Carol 123, 220
Shaviro, Steven 56, 61, 63, 129, 220
The Shining 2, 18, 103, 183
The Sixties (1960s) 8, 12, 18–20, 25–6, 33–4, 39–40, 48, 177, 180–1, 190, 204
Sloanism 57, 220
Smith, Steven B. 103–5, 221
Sontag, Susan 126–8, 221
The Stand 179–89
Stavrakakis, Yannis 8, 48, 50, 113, 115, 221
The Storm of the Century 14–15, 27, 204
Streeck, Wolfgang 142, 194, 221
Strengell, Heidi 34, 90, 193, 203, 221
Swift, Adam 89, 95, 101, 218

Taylor, Charles 103–4, 221
Taylor, Mark 149, 194, 199, 221
Thatcher, Margaret 49, 53, 73, 90–1, 197
A Theory of Justice 90, 98, 219
Third Way 105
The Tommyknockers 6–8, 27–8, 73, 76, 180, 196, 201
Trump, Donald 23, 30, 161, 163–6, 168–9, 171–7, 186, 191, 201, 203
Under the Dome 9, 12, 67, 139–61, 176, 180–1, 202
Utopia 7, 20–1, 24, 28, 35, 39, 46–9, 110, 113, 155, 183–4, 204

Vasari, Giorgio 114, 222

Veil of Ignorance 100, 102
Vietnam (conflict) 27–8, 34, 36, 39, 77, 181, 190, 192, 204
Volonté Générale 176–7

Watkins, Tamara. 141, 153–4, 222

Winter, Douglas E. 183, 189, 193, 222
Wolin, Sheldon 145–6, 189, 192, 222

Žižek, Slavoj 42, 106, 175, 193, 195, 222

also in series

Lindsey Decker, *Transnationalism and Genre Hybridity in New British Horror Cinema* (2021)

Stacey Abbott and Lorna Jowett (eds), *Global TV Horror* (2021)

Michael J. Blouin, *Stephen King and American Politics* (2021)

Eddie Falvey, Joe Hickinbottom and Jonathan Wroot (eds), *New Blood: Critical Approaches to Contemporary Horror* (2020)

Darren Elliott-Smith and John Edgar Browning (eds), *New Queer Horror Film and Television* (2020)

Jonathan Newell, *A Century of Weird Fiction, 1832–1937* (2020)

Alexandra Heller-Nicholas, *Masks in Horror Cinema: Eyes Without Faces* (2019)

Eleanor Beal and Jonathan Greenaway (eds), *Horror and Religion: New literary approaches to Theology, Race and Sexuality* (2019)

Dawn Stobbart, *Videogames and Horror: From Amnesia to Zombies, Run!* (2019)

David Annwn Jones, *Re-envisaging the First Age of Cinematic Horror, 1896–1934: Quanta of Fear* (2018)